PENGUIN BOOKS

Tempting Fate

Tempting Fate

JANE GREEN

PENGUIN BOOKS

PENGUIN BOOKS

Published by the Penguin Group
Penguin Books Ltd, 80 Strand, London WC2R ORL, England
Penguin Group (USA) Inc., 375 Hudson Street, New York, New York 10014, USA
Penguin Group (Canada), 90 Eglinton Avenue East, Suite 700, Toronto, Ontario, Canada M4P 2Y3
(a division of Pearson Penguin Canada Inc.)
Penguin Ireland, 25 St Stephen's Green, Dublin 2, Ireland (a division of Penguin Books Ltd)
Penguin Group (Australia), 707 Collins Street, Melbourne, Victoria 3008, Australia
(a division of Pearson Australia Group Pty Ltd)
Penguin Books India Pvt Ltd, 11 Community Centre,
Panchsheel Park, New Delhi – 110 017, India
Penguin Group (NZ), 67 Apollo Drive, Rosedale, Auckland 0632, New Zealand
(a division of Pearson New Zealand Ltd)
Penguin Books (South Africa) (Pty) Ltd, Block D, Rosebank Office Park,
181 Jan Smuts Avenue, Parktown North, Gauteng 2193, South Africa

Penguin Books Ltd, Registered Offices: 80 Strand, London WC2R ORL, England

www.penguin.com

First published 2013
001

Copyright © Jane Green, 2013
All rights reserved

The moral right of the author has been asserted

Set in 12.5/14.75pt Garamond MT Std
Typeset by Jouve (UK), Milton Keynes
Printed in Great Britain by Clays Ltd, St Ives plc

PAPERBACK ISBN: 978-0-718-15758-6
TRADE PAPERBACK ISBN: 978-0-718-15760-9
OM PAPERBACK ISBN: 978-0-718-17828-4

www.greenpenguin.co.uk

Penguin Books is committed to a sustainable
future for our business, our readers and our planet.
This book is made from Forest Stewardship
Council™ certified paper.

PART ONE

Chapter One

It's just a night out with girlfriends, not the Academy Awards, thinks Gabby, frowning at her wardrobe as she endlessly pushes hangers back and forth, hoping something compelling, something worthy will suddenly appear and jump out at her: the perfect shirt, the perfect dress. It shouldn't matter, this being a girls' night out, but of course it matters far more than on a night out with Elliott. Tonight Gabby is dressing for the other women.

She has heard that on these girls' nights out it is not unusual for men to gather round the girls, not seeing – or, rather, ignoring – the wedding rings they all have on their fingers; ignoring the wedding rings so often on their own. But Gabby doesn't care about these men, she simply wants to fit in. She wants to at least look like she has made an effort. She wants to show that she too can scrub up into something of a glamour puss, that she deserves her place at the bar, just like the rest of this particular group of friends.

She settles on black trousers all the better to hide her thighs with, and knee-high boots, the only pair in her wardrobe that have any heel. These boots are almost twenty years old, old enough for them to have gone completely out of fashion and then revolve full circle to be not dissimilar to all the boots she passes in the store windows in town.

She bought them when it seemed important to look good, before life, children, motherhood got in the way, before it was easier to slip her feet into furry Merrells and be done with it.

In their thirties, all her friends wore the same dull uniforms, but suddenly, in their forties, these same women are breaking free of their self-imposed cocoons, eschewing the dull blanket of grinding motherhood and emerging in a flurry of bright chiffons and silks. And now that their children no longer needed baby-sitters they are tripping out on girls' nights out in impossibly high heels, their hair silky and blown-out, wanting to be *seen*.

Gabby does not have bright chiffons and silks, *would* not have bright chiffons and silks because that is not her style, but she does find a black floaty blouse that no one needs to know was bought for $15.95 in Marshalls. As long as you don't look too closely, you might think it is silk organza rather than the eminently more practical polyester.

There. A shake of her hair, a brush of mascara, a slick of gloss. She looks good, she thinks, without look-ing as if she is trying too hard. Unlike some of the others, in their plunging necklines and glittery jewellery,

Gabby looks as if she is out to have fun with the girls, men be damned.

Gabby orders a second Martini, knowing she won't be able to leave any time soon, wishing she had turned down the invitation to go out and was now tucked up cosily in bed watching a movie.

When Ella invited her to a girls' dinner, Gabby had looked forward to a group of women enjoying themselves at a large table in the corner of the Grey Goose, but when she and Claire had arrived the women had already established themselves at the bar, where they were lapping up the attentions of a swarm of eager older Lotharios, flicking their hair back as they gave the men flirtatious smiles, punctuating every sentence with loud, and to Gabby's ears, slightly forced, laughter.

The energy these women are giving off, their overt flirting, is making Gabby uncomfortable. Used to seeing them with their husbands, or occasionally during the day by themselves, meeting for walks along the beach or for lunch, she is amazed by this transformation. It is discomfiting to see these women, who she had assumed were just like herself, turn into the seductive, provocative creatures who are here tonight. Married to Elliott for eighteen years, Gabby no longer has the desire nor the inclination to flirt. Even if she did, she's pretty sure she's forgotten how to do it.

Although, she thinks, examining herself in the mirror

lining the back wall of the bar, it would be nice if someone, anyone, looked at her these days. Lately she has been
feeling more and more invisible. Last week, when she was
in New York, she noticed that as she walked up Park
Avenue during what was clearly lunch hour, all the men
she passed glanced over at the two younger women flank-
ing her. She didn't blame them particularly, especially as
the women were wearing miniskirts and high-heeled
boots, but surely one would catch her eye, look her up
and down. Even an old one. Someone. Anyone.

The grey hairs she had, only a handful, were subse-
quently banished earlier this week with a chestnut-
brown dye, and she has made an uncharacteristic effort
tonight, but it is nothing compared to the effort her friends
have made. It is because I am English, she often thinks. I
may have lived here for years and years, but I simply can't
pull off high-maintenance. It's just not me. Look at Ella,
with her bouncy curls, her chiffon blouse that displays
more than a hint of cleavage, her high-heeled sandals
bouncing prettily at the end of a tanned leg.

Look at the tanned older man – attractive, if you like
a touch of lechery – now whispering in her ear as she
laughs, her body tilted towards him, her eyes looking
up at him through thick lashes.

What are all these women *doing*? Why are they behaving like this? I know these women, know their families;
my children go to school with their children. How have
I not seen this side of them before, and what does it say
about them? About me?

'Is this as much of a scene as I think it is?' murmurs a voice next to her. Gabby turns, finding herself facing a young man. He gestures at her friends with a shake of his head. 'I feel like I'm in a cattle market.'

'I know,' Gabby says with a polite smile. 'I haven't been here before. It's pretty . . . intense.'

'That it is. And not my scene. I'm Matt.' He offers his hand and Gabby shakes it, noting his rolled-up blue sleeves, his strong arms, and remembering for a split second how it felt to have the bloom of youth, for he must be in his late twenties. At forty-three she is almost – almost – old enough to be his mother, and it is this that causes her to relax, to smile as she introduces herself.

'I'm Gabby.' She settles onto her stool, relieved to have someone to talk to, someone who has no ulterior motive, who has not come here to pick up women. Even if he had, he would definitely not be interested in her.

She looks at him curiously. He is, by any definition, gorgeous. Blond hair, blue eyes. He has a twinkle and a kindness in his eyes that, if she was twenty years younger and single, she would find utterly disarming.

'So why are you here, Matt? Particularly if it's not your scene.'

'Good question.' He smiles, showing straight white teeth, and raises his glass to toast her. 'I'm here on business. One night only. I'm staying across the street, but I thought I'd grab a drink here before I check in.'

7

'Business?'

'I have a social media website.'

'Like Facebook?'

He laughs. 'I wish. Maybe one day.'

'Would I know it?'

'I don't know,' he says, naming a website that Gabby knows well, that everyone knows well.

'That's you?' She looks at him again, reassessingly, because she has read about this company, knows it was started by two young men, the heirs apparent to the Facebook throne. She was mistaken in thinking he was just some kid. He is an accomplished businessman. She recalls articles about him, how they built the company – and she is impressed. And excited.

'You're huge!'

He cocks an eyebrow and Gabby blushes and starts to laugh. 'Sorry. I mean, I know exactly who you are. I've read about you.'

'It's such a weird thing, that I have this strange kind of celebrity that isn't. No one would have any idea who I am, but as soon as I mention the company, everyone knows.'

'At least you're able to sit anonymously at bars. And I bet you have an amazing house.' She peers at him with a teasing smile.

He snorts with laughter. 'It's true. I do have an amazing house.'

'Isn't it in LA?'

'Better. Malibu.'

8

'Oh God,' she groans. 'Do you step outside your living room onto a beach?'

He grins as Gabby prods him for a description of the kind of house she has always dreamed about.

They keep talking, Matt telling her about some of the more glamorous parties he's been to and providing her with celebrity gossip that is better than that in any issue of *People* magazine. Gabby hangs on his every word, and as everyone and everything in the room drops away she notices nothing other than the fun she is having.

'. . . and it was Lil Wayne,' he says, finishing a story. 'Sorry. You probably don't –'

'Don't know who Lil Wayne is?' Gabby scowls. 'Believe it or not, despite being a middle-aged mom, I know exactly who –'

She stops, mid-sentence, as Matt lays a hand on her arm.

'You're hardly middle-aged,' he says, frowning. 'You're, what? In your thirties?'

Gabby looks down at his hand on her arm, noting how beautiful it is, how smooth and strong. Briefly wondering why he has not removed it, she looks back up at him with a burst of laughter, enjoying herself.

'Right,' she says. 'Ten years ago, perhaps. I'm forty-three, and yes, that definitely classifies me as middle-aged.'

Matt shakes his head in genuine bemusement. 'I swear I'm not just saying this, but you really don't look it. I thought you were around thirty-four.'

'I think I may love you,' Gabby says happily. 'Although your point of reference probably stops at thirty-five. At your age you can't imagine there *is* anyone older.'

'Bullshit! And I'm not that young. There's hardly anything between us.'

'Let me guess.' Her eyes run over his face, taking in the smoothness of his skin, the sharp definition of his cheeks and jaw, the lack of lines. She thinks of Elliott: his hair now more grey than brown, the deep lines around his eyes when he smiles, his physique, once so toned, now soft and cuddly, comfortable.

Everything about Matt shouts youth. His jeans, his scuffed-up brown boots. His tucked-in blue shirt that gives hints of intensive working-out rather than the outline of a paunch, like she is used to seeing in Elliott, and in most of the men she knows.

'I think you're twenty-seven,' she says.

'I knew you thought I was younger. For your information, I'm thirty-three. See, we're not so far apart.'

'You may think that now, but wait until you're forty-three and you look back at how much you changed over those ten years.'

He gazes at her over his glass. 'How have *you* changed over ten years?'

'Seriously?'

He nods, calling the bartender over and ordering another Martini for her, giving her pause to think.

For the truth is that not much has changed in the last

ten years. Ten years ago she was married to Elliott, as she is now, only with smaller children. They lived in a different neighbourhood. She drove an old Cherokee. Her life was pre-school and playdates, coffees with women she hardly sees any more. She had fewer lines, less grey hair, was fifteen pounds lighter.

If she thinks back to the years before that, though, to eighteen or twenty years ago, she knows that a lot has changed. Back then she cared about dressing up and going out. Twenty years ago she made an effort, wanting to be popular, pretty, invited to people's houses for dinner. She and Elliott would go camping, up in Vermont. They hiked, and skied. Now it is all she can do to make herself go for a walk.

What has happened since those days? When did life become so . . . she won't use the word 'dull', chooses instead to use 'pots and pans'? How did she and Elliott drift so seamlessly into middle age, and where did all that energy go?

She can't tell all that to this stranger and decides instead to share the positives.

'I am more comfortable in my skin. Turning forty was a turning point. I stopped needing to prove myself to anyone. I probably ought to make more of an effort,' she says, gesturing to her friends, all of whom now make more of an effort, and are currently at the other end of the bar with a new group of men. 'But I love that it doesn't matter to me any more.'

'I think you look great,' Matt says evenly. There is

not a hint of flirtation in his voice, and yet, as he says it, he holds her gaze until she looks away, feeling something inside her give a slight jolt.

Don't be ridiculous, she tells herself. There is no way in hell this lovely young boy is flirting with me. I have no idea what just happened; I only know that whatever it was is in my imagination.

Gabby covers her embarrassment with a forced bark of laughter. 'My friends over there?' she says, nodding towards them. '*They* look great.'

He glances over before turning back to Gabby with a dismissive shake of his head. 'No. To me they all look overdone. Too much make-up, too much hair, too much flounce. I prefer my women natural. Like you.' There it is. That gaze again.

Grateful for the low lighting, Gabby blushes as she says thank you, jumping as the phone in her back pocket starts to vibrate. She pulls it out to see Elliott's name on the screen.

'It's my husband,' she says, hopping off the stool. 'I'll be right back.'

Threading through the crowds, she breathes a sigh of relief. Even if she was imagining it, she has not led him on. She told him she is married. That should put him off, if, indeed, there is anything to put off. Which there couldn't possibly be.

'Hi, honey!' She sits down on a low stone wall outside, aware suddenly that she is not as sober as she had thought. 'Are you having fun?'

'Not as much fun as it sounds like you're having!' Elliott laughs, and Gabby starts. What does he mean? How does he know she's been talking to Matt? But it's only talking. How does he know?

'What do you mean?' she says slowly, attempting to sound as sober as possible, knowing Elliott will know.

'First of all it was noisy as hell when you picked up; secondly, I know you're having a girls' night out tonight; and thirdly, you're drunk, and don't try to deny it because I always know. I can hear it in your voice.'

Gabby laughs. 'You're right. I'm stopping now.'

'What are you drinking?'

'Martinis.'

'Aha! Just remember that Martinis are like a woman's breasts: one is too few, three is too many.'

'I'm on two and done.'

'Who's driving?'

'Ella. How's the camping? How are the girls?'

'They're having the best time. They've gone swimming in the lake with Sasha and Jolie, and they're dying to get to the smores later. This was a great idea, even though we miss you.'

'I miss you too,' Gabby says, out of habit, although she hasn't thought about Elliott for much more than a second since he left early this morning.

'And you were right to suggest I do this with Tim. Not that you and I wouldn't have a great time, but I know you feel a bit done with sleeping bags and tents.'

Gabby laughs again. 'Damn right. What time are you home tomorrow?'

'Not until mid-afternoon, I think. You go and have fun with the girls. I love you.'

'I love you too.'

Gabby walks back inside, seeing Matt through the crowds, her empty stool next to him. As she moves towards the bar he turns and watches her, smiling, and she feels another jolt.

Don't be pathetic, she thinks. Don't think this is something other than a nice guy who's bored and lonely, eager to have a friendly face to talk to. Not that I wouldn't be enormously flattered if he was flirting, but look at me! Look at him, now look at me again. Even if he is flirting, which he isn't, there would be no point. I'm happily married to the loveliest man in the world. But if he is flirting, even though he's not, it would be nice to feel attractive again. It would be nice to feel that I still have it, even if it's only for three more minutes.

'Gabby?' Her arm is grabbed, and she spins to find herself face to face with Claire. 'Who is that adorable guy at the bar? I can't believe you've been flirting with someone all evening! We haven't seen you at all!'

'I'm not flirting,' Gabby says, certain that she is not. 'I don't flirt. I don't know how to flirt any more. I'm just having a really interesting conversation with a sweet young guy.'

'He's not sweet.' Claire glances at him. 'He's a stone-cold fox!'

'Right.' Gabby nods. 'And he's twelve.'

Claire squints as she looks across the room. 'He's not twelve. He's at least twenty-five. Old enough to know what he's doing . . .'

'Claire!' Gabby reprimands. 'For a start, he's ten years younger than me, and secondly, hello? I'm married. Remember?'

'We're all married,' Claire replies, and she winks. 'Doesn't mean we can't have a little fun.'

Gabby doesn't ask her what she means by 'fun'. She shakes her head with a laugh as if Claire's suggestion is ridiculous, then moves towards the bar, where Matt is waiting with a big smile.

On the way there, Gabby is aware that she is holding herself straighter, smiling more widely, giving off an aura that is causing the other men to turn and look at her in admiration.

Because tonight, thanks to this younger man who is paying her attention, Gabby feels alluring. Despite her incredulity that he may be flirting, deep down she is aware of a connection between them. She has no plans to do anything about it – Gabby would never be unfaithful – but it has been years since she felt desirable, years since she felt sexy, beautiful. It is a powerful, heady feeling, and once tonight is over it will be gone. When tonight is over she will once again be a middle-aged suburban housewife, caught up in the pots and pans of life.

What's the harm in dragging it out just a little bit longer? She isn't going to do anything.

Absolutely not.

'Everything okay?' Matt flicks his eyes to her phone.

'Just my husband. Checking in.' Now she has said it again. She has a husband. 'He's with our girls, camping in Vermont.' She breathes a sigh of relief, knowing she is safe now the information is out there. There is no pretence at being available any more, and what man would not respect the presence of another?

'What's your husband like?'

This is unexpected. 'You'd love him,' she says. 'Seriously. The two of you would get on like a house on fire.'

'I'm sure we would. He's a man of excellent taste.' Matt grins.

Gabby giggles and teasingly smacks him on the arm. 'Flatterer.'

'Truth-teller,' he counters. 'So what *is* he like?'

How does she describe Elliott? From the moment she met him, both of them sitting at the same table, at the same time, at a coffee shop in New York, she knew he was exactly the kind of man she had been waiting for. She was twenty-three, working at a bookstore in the city; he was five years older, a doctor, doing his internship at Columbia-Presbyterian.

He had asked if he could share her table, even though there were several empty ones, then he spent the next two hours distracting Gabby from her work, and making her laugh with his impromptu stories about the people waiting in line, so that eventually she shoved her sketchbook and pencil into her bag and gave up any attempt at drawing.

The next day she met him at Central Park for a walk. He showed up with a hamper that had belonged to his grandmother, stuffed full of badly made sandwiches and packets of crisps in every flavour because, he explained, he didn't know which flavour she'd like and didn't want her to be disappointed.

'I am married to the most wonderful man in the world.'

Matt smiles. 'What makes him wonderful?'

'He's brilliant,' she starts. 'And kind. He's curious about everyone and everything, and is the kind of man that everyone feels instantly relaxed with. He's warm, and caring. And a great father. We have two girls, and they're the apple of his eye. He's a great husband. I'm lucky . . .' She tails off, aware she is doing a hard sell, but unsure suddenly of who she is doing the hard sell for.

'He really does sound wonderful,' Matt agrees.

'He is.'

'What does he do?'

'He's a doctor. Gastroenterologist. So, obviously, the good bedside manner helps.'

I am a doctor's wife, she thinks. Which is exactly what it sounds like. Stable. Safe. And just a tiny bit dull.

Briefly, she indulges in a fantasy. What if she were a

dot-com billionaire's wife? What then? She sees herself padding around a glass house in Malibu, in one of Matt's shirts, her legs having suddenly become miraculously tanned and toned, her hair a good six inches longer than it could ever be, given that she has been trying to grow it for many years and it still doesn't reach much further than her shoulders.

Imagine the parties they would go to! She and Matt laughing together as they lean on a deck overlooking the ocean, the wind blowing her very long hair around; no sign of cellulite, children, or ex-husband; no sign of anything from her former life.

She shakes her head. What are you doing, Gabby? Are you completely mad?

'Another Martini?' Matt is about to gesture the bartender over.

'God, no!' she says. 'A Martini is like –'

'A woman's breasts,' he finishes. 'I know.'

'I should probably think about leaving,' she says regretfully, not wanting to leave but feeling as if they have reached the end. What is the point in staying, after all? There is a ripple of danger just below the surface of her consciousness, and she knows she has to go.

'How are you getting home?' There is disappointment in his eyes. 'You can't drive.'

Gabby laughs. 'Trust me, I know that. One of the girls is driving,' she says, and looks over to where her friends are, were, but there is no sign of them. 'Oh shit,' she mutters. 'Where are they?'

Matt is amused. 'They deserted you? What kind of friends are they?'

'Crap ones,' Gabby says, annoyed, as she gets out her phone to text them. Matt laughs.

> We didn't want to disturb you ;)
> tell us everything tomorrow!

'They've gone?' Matt doesn't see the text, but sees the look on Gabby's face.

'I can't believe they left without me. That's just awful.'

'Tell you what,' Matt says. 'Why don't you come to the hotel? We can have some coffee and they'll call you a cab.'

Gabby studies his face. There is no ulterior motive. It is just a coffee, and she could do with a coffee right now.

He pulls notes out of a wallet and lays them on the bar, refusing to let Gabby contribute. Then he stands up and Gabby does the same. He is tall, much taller than she is, and her heart does a small flip as she sizes him up.

Despite being twelve, he is unutterably gorgeous. Oh if only this was several lifetimes ago, she thinks, looking up at him, at the thick brown hair, the strength and breadth of his shoulders.

Matt checks in at the hotel while Gabby curls up on a sofa in the lobby. Suddenly she feels unsure. Why is she here? Why is she having coffee in a hotel with a stranger while her husband is away? Of course she's not going to do anything, but hasn't this gone far enough? Wouldn't it be so very much better if she went home now?

Matt turns round and smiles at her from across the room, and her heart does that thing again, that flip. Not because she's planning on doing anything, but because being with him makes her feel beautiful again. It's been so long since anyone has noticed her; so long since she has been *seen*.

She will not be unfaithful; she would never be unfaithful to Elliott, whom she loves with all her heart and soul. But for years to come her self-esteem, recently so fragile, will be able to treasure this evening, this gentle chemistry, this feeling of someone as gorgeous as Matt being interested in her.

And what would be the harm?

'I've really had fun tonight,' Gabby sighs, a couple of hours later. Coffee became Irish coffee, and she is aware that her sobriety said goodbye a very long time ago.

'For the record,' Matt says, 'I don't make a habit of sitting at bars and flirting with lovely-looking ladies. Especially when I'm travelling for work. You have made a boring business trip completely delightful.'

Gabby says nothing, too busy turning the words he just used over and over in her mind. 'Lovely-looking'! 'Flirting'! I wasn't imagining it!

'I'll have them call you a cab.' He doesn't move.

It is now the early hours of the morning. There is no

one else in the dimly lit hotel lounge. One receptionist is over at the desk.

Matt and Gabby stare at each other, and Gabby wills herself to move, to get up, to get out and go home before . . . before it's too late. But she can't move. Her heart is pounding, an unfamiliar heat is coursing through her body, and she knows she has to go, but she can't do anything other than gaze into the eyes of this man as she lets out a deep sigh.

'Why are all the women I like unavailable?' he murmurs, making Gabby's heart threaten to jump out of her body. She doesn't know what to say. She wants to leave, knows she has to leave, but oh, how she wants to stay.

'I should go.' Her voice is a whisper, and mustering all the strength she can she reluctantly climbs to her feet.

Chapter Two

Minutes stretch into hours as Gabby thinks about getting out of bed. As a student at Bristol University, hangovers were a way of life for her. Her group of friends would toss back shots on pub crawls, but they still somehow managed to crawl out of bed the next morning and make it to lectures.

Despite the hangovers, the nausea, she didn't stop drinking. It was part and parcel of university life in England, part and parcel of growing up. She hasn't been drunk in years, not since she and Elliott first started dating. Well, perhaps there have been a few times, a handful – fewer – since the girls were born.

She now knows her limits. Being drunk may be fun, but it isn't worth it. This isn't worth it. She had no idea, last night, that she had drunk enough to make her feel as bad as she does now. Martinis. Irish coffees. Mixing drinks. That's what did it. That's why she feels like living death this morning.

The bathroom used to be so close, but overnight it appears to have moved three miles away. If I can get to the shower, she thinks, I'll feel so much better. She can almost sense the cold water pouring over her head, the relief the shower will bring, but making the journey from the bed to the bathroom seems like an impossible task. She actually doesn't believe she can move. What she wants to do is think about last night, but thinking about it means thinking about the Martinis she drank, and if she thinks about those she may very well throw up. Instead she imagines jumping into a swimming pool, imagines the cool water surrounding her, bringing her back to normality. It helps.

Her head is pounding, her throat is dry. She squints at the curtains, then at the clock, knowing there is nothing to do but wait until she feels strong enough to make it to the bathroom, the shower, life.

Hours later, she stands under the shower, making the water as cold as she can bear, until she finally starts to feel human again. She scrubs her skin, then wraps herself in a terrycloth robe and goes downstairs to make some strong black coffee.

Years ago, watching *Cabaret*, she was struck by the sight of Sally Bowles swigging a prairie oyster – a raw egg swirled with Worcestershire sauce – as a hangover cure. As a teenager she would do this regularly, not because she was convinced it worked, but because she wanted to be like Sally Bowles.

As a forty-something mother, she's pretty certain a prairie oyster would make her throw up. Instead she brews coffee so strong and thick it's almost Turkish, and intersperses sips of that with sips of ginger ale.

Elliott and the girls will be back later. She has hours

for herself, but wishes she didn't feel quite so awful, wishes she could actually do something with this afternoon off, rather than slump on the sofa with coffee and the remote control.

Her phone buzzes.

'I've been trying you all morning!' Claire says. 'Where have you been?'

'I had the sound switched off and the phone was in my bag. I didn't hear it. What's going on?'

Claire barks with laughter. 'Never mind me, what's going on with you? Or should I say, what was going on with you last night? When we left you were deep in conversation with the totally hot guy at the bar. Tell me you were a good girl . . .'

There is a smile in Claire's voice, only because she *knows* Gabby was a good girl. If she suspected anything else she would never ask with this lilt in her voice, never dare tease about something so serious.

For a second Gabby is tempted to tell her how close she came, and how confusing she finds this today. She loves her husband, so how could she be attracted to someone else? And this morning she is quite clear: she was attracted to him.

A problem shared is a problem halved, and even though this isn't a problem, there is a part of her that wants to shout out that she is still desirable, that she isn't as middle-aged and dowdy as she might appear, that someone young and hot wanted her.

But she could never tell anyone what she's thinking.

Not even Claire, whom she trusts above everyone else. Except Elliott.

'Of course I was a good girl.' Gabby forces a laugh. 'But God, he was so cute! And so young! If ever I am going to be a bad girl, please let it be with someone who looks like that . . .'

'Aw,' grumbles Claire. 'We were taking bets on whether you'd be a bad girl.'

'That's terrible!' Gabby says. 'This is me you're talking about, remember? I'm the last person in the world who'd misbehave.'

'Exactly! That's what I said, but Ella insisted you were in the zone, and once you're in the zone rational thought goes out of the window. She was convinced you would have made out with him, even though I told her you'd never do that.'

'What does that mean, "in the zone"?'

'When lust takes over and you forget everything except the person sitting next to you at the bar,' Claire explains. 'I have to say that when we left you were engrossed. We were all trying to get your attention from the other side of the room but you never even looked up.'

'Of course I didn't look up,' blusters Gabby. 'How could I have done when the view was so pretty? Have you heard from the boys?' she asks, changing the subject; there is too much noise in her head and she needs quiet to process what happened, or didn't happen, last night. 'Any idea when they're getting back?'

'Tim just called. They're going to leave in a couple of hours or so after some off-roading. I'm glad the two boys did this. It's good for them to have some time together, and even better for us to have down time. Don't you love it when the house is completely silent on a weekend? This just feels like luxury. I'm exhausted. I'm still in my pyjamas, and I'm not sure I'm going to get dressed at all. I may just lie on the sofa and watch *Downton Abbey*, eating chocolates. Want to come and veg with me?'

'I think I may veg on my own sofa,' Gabby says, unsure that she can face more interrogation. 'I'm feeling a day of back-to-back *Mad Men* coming on.'

'Okay. I'm going to call Ella. She had to practically push that guy off her last night.'

'Which guy?'

'That guy Nick? Oh – you weren't with us. He's one of the dads from school, apparently, but he was there with a bunch of guys, and he totally came on to Ella. Can you believe it? I mean, I know Ella was flirting, but we all were. It was just fun. This guy thought she was up for it, and Ella knows his wife!'

'Who's his wife?' Gabby is relieved someone else is the focus of the conversation.

'Jeannie. Quiet, kind of mousy. Her kid is Phoebe.'

'I know her. And I know the husband. He's a sleaze.'

'Now we know for sure. He invited Ella outside for a cigarette, then he grabbed her and tried to stick his tongue in her mouth! Can you believe it? Isn't that the grossest thing you ever heard?'

'Oh my God!' Gabby says. 'Ella *smokes*?'

The truth is that she can believe it. She can believe all of it. When they moved to the suburbs in their late twenties, every couple with their first baby, no one would have dreamed of being unfaithful. Too busy building their families, shuffling to mommy and me groups, bleary-eyed from lack of sleep, the women she knew were all wearing maternity clothes either as they waited for babies to arrive, or because they weren't able to get their pre-pregnancy figures back.

No one had time to exercise, unless it constituted a leisurely walk along the beach with children strapped safely in buggies. They certainly didn't have the time, energy or inclination to have an affair.

Even the marriages that perhaps should never have been – the marriages kept together by the glue of their children, by the routine of making new friends, building a home in an unfamiliar town – even these trundled along with no question of either husband or wife ever being unfaithful.

The years have passed, and Gabby and her friends are no longer the newcomers to town, the young women who have just had babies and behave as though they are the only women in the world to have ever had babies, demanding that the world stops to accommodate them.

Gabby finds herself standing in line at CVS as a young mother with a baby stresses out over the lack of the right formula. Everything in her body language, her speech, announces that she is a mother! She has a baby! She is more important than everyone else! Gabby looks around and catches the eye of other middle-aged mothers, their grey roots beginning to show, puffy shadows under their eyes, fleeces and clogs their uniform because they can no longer be bothered to dress to impress, and they exchange understanding smiles at these young, entitled women.

I remember when I too thought the world revolved around me, says the smile; I remember when I too thought I knew everything, deserved everything, was entitled to everything and more.

Oh how little we knew.

Few of the mothers worked when Gabby moved to town. They were, they announced proudly, 'stay-at-home moms'. They volunteered to be room mothers, joined the PTA, accompanied the children on every field trip, showed up in the classroom having spontaneously baked two dozen nut-free, lactose-free, gluten-free cupcakes.

These same women were left stranded when their children turned eleven and moved on to middle school. The women who didn't work suddenly longed to have something to do all day, wanted to reinvent themselves, or perhaps find themselves again. They would invariably take up Zumba, yoga, meet friends for lunch every day at the Organic Market, before slowly rejoining the work force, some working part-time, others attempting to be CEO of businesses from the comfort of their kitchen table.

Gabby was lucky in that she was able to follow a different path. Using her long-suppressed creativity, she started restoring furniture. Initially it was for herself, but when the other mothers saw how she picked up cheap tables at the consignment store, or the dump, and stripped them, refinishing them to look like beautiful antiques, they wanted her to do the same for them, and soon she could fill as many hours of the day as she wanted, doing something she loved.

A few of her friends have worked all along. Trish, one of the mothers Gabby knows, was one of the first women Gabby knew to have divorced. Soon after her fourth child was born, her husband announced he was leaving her for his secretary. She started designing accessories for the home – vases, trays, boxes, cachepots – and is now stocked throughout the country. Every time a new range comes out she has a house sale in town, always hosted by a different woman. At the end of the day, the hostess and the various friends who have helped her with the sale all have a renewed sense of purpose and ideas for businesses of their own.

Gabby sees how the bodies of her friends have changed. Once soft and squishy, elastic from the stresses and strains of childbirth, those bodies have, in their forties, suddenly been honed into shape by Pilates, yoga, spinning.

After the dowdiness during the days of early parent-hood, Gabby is now surrounded by two extremes of women as she approaches her mid-forties. There are the women like her, in their shapeless, comfortable clothes, secure in their husband's love, in their place in the world. These are the ones who have not felt the need to change themselves as time slips slowly away. Then there are the glamour pusses like Trish, those who have reinvented themselves in middle age – although Trish has doubtless been perfect since the day she was born.

The other glamour pusses may be forty-something, but they are fitter, prettier, far better-dressed than they were back in their late twenties.

Partly because they have to be. In this affluent town, at this age, there is always someone around the next corner who could take their place. And it isn't just the women who need to be worried. In the last twelve months alone, four women Gabby has known for years – not friends, but women from the neighbourhood – have suddenly left their husbands.

Gabby found herself sitting in their living rooms, drinking coffee and sympathizing as these women told tales of how unhappy they had been for a long time, how terrible their husbands were. She was surprised because the husbands had always seemed delightful. Then the women suddenly lit up, swooning with delight as they described the perfection of their new man. It turned out that in every single case there was another man involved. In one, it was the husband of her best friend. In the others, it was random men picked up at the gym, at an AA meeting, the contractor.

'But nothing happened,' they all swore. 'He was just a friend until we split up.'

None of them thought of herself as the kind of person who would have an affair. Each time, they described these men as their *soulmates*. Each time, they believed they had found the one person the gods had chosen for them, the one person they were supposed to have married had circumstances not got in the way and slipped in their boring old husbands instead. Why else would they have broken up their marriages, exploded their lives, alienated or, at the very least, caused immeasurable pain to their children? Why else would they have betrayed their spouse so monumentally, so unforgivably, so heartlessly, unless they had no choice?

Of the four wives that left, three of them are no longer with their *soulmates*. One of them confessed to Gabby that she had made a terrible mistake. She would do anything to turn the clock back, but her husband had met someone else. He was not only happy, but happier than he had been with wife number one. It was too late, and now she spent her kidless weekends at bars much like the one last night, wondering how her life ended up in such a mess.

Gabby, who has always thought of infidelity as a mid-life crisis, hasn't ever really understood why these women left their stable lives, their loving husbands, their comfortable homes. Until today. Today, when she slouches back on the sofa, blankly staring at the television screen, she knows exactly how these things happen.

'You have a choice,' she was fond of saying. 'Just because you're married doesn't mean you're not attracted to anyone else. You're married, not dead. We're all going to be attracted to other people at some point, but ultimately it comes down to a choice.' So easy to say when you have never been presented with a choice. And honestly? Gabby has never felt an attraction to anyone other than Elliott since the moment they met.

Last night, Gabby had a choice; she had many choices. She could have gone home with her friends. She could have called a cab from the bar. She could have declined to go back to the hotel with him, because, however much she may try to deny it, even to herself, she knew the possibility was there.

That moment in the hotel lobby, late, quiet, when their eyes locked and held, neither of them speaking, chemistry surging in waves . . . well, she had a choice then. She could so easily have stayed, let him lean forward, kiss her gently on the lips. He didn't, but she knows he could have done. She sits, playing this moment over and over again in her mind. He didn't, but he could have done. He didn't, but he would have done.

And if he had, how would it have felt?

And if he had, how would she be feeling now?

She shudders with lust, but then guilt replaces the small smile that unbeknownst to her has been playing on her lips since she started thinking about him.

She didn't do anything. She has nothing to feel guilty about. She is married, not dead. This isn't anywhere near the big deal it could have been, and if she can't stop thinking about it, so what? This is just . . . flattery. This is just . . . pleasurable. Having the undivided attention of someone other than her husband, feeling the sparks of attraction fly between them, was . . . exhilarating.

Even now, she is torn between feeling sick with guilt at even considering the thought, and elated at still being desirable, still having a sexual power she's not sure she was ever aware of having. She and Elliott have always had a great sex life, but it is great partly because they are so comfortable with each other. Making love with Elliott is a tried and tested routine, with little variation. She has never wanted more variation, has been perfectly happy with the routine they have; she is almost always brought to orgasm and feels entirely sated afterwards.

But it doesn't light fires any more. She's not sure it ever did.

Last night was a blaze of glory

She pictures Elliott moving inside her, his eyes filled with longing and love, and feels . . . content. She pictures Matt, imagines him flipping her over, his fingers inside her, his mouth on her nipple, and she gasps, her entire body flooded with desire.

Thank God nothing happened, she thinks. For if he

33

were to phone now, and say, 'Come with me; I need you at my side,' she honestly isn't sure she'd be able to say no. But there was no talk of them staying in touch. Even though Gabby could get hold of him – his contact details flash up on the home page of his website – she knows already she will not.

He is too dangerous, she decides. She cannot be in touch with him.

So it is with a mixture of horror and delight that she suddenly remembers mentioning her own email address during a silly conversation they had at one point in the evening about vanity number plates, vanity names, vanity email addresses . . . But she convinces herself he'll never get in touch. Why would he? He must have thousands of women flocking to him, and she was just a passing fancy. Perhaps he has a penchant for older women; perhaps he is attracted to the unavailable. Either way, last night has to be written off as a fun flirtation. It needs to filed away and never thought of again.

Chapter Three

Elliott tries to move away but Gabby is holding on tight, and he laughs, stepping forward again and lifting her up.

'Wow!' he murmurs into her hair. 'You really missed me, huh? I should go away more often.'

'No!' Gabby says into his shoulder, then she pulls back to gaze at her husband, the man she loves, and wells up with shame at the thought of what she could so easily have done, of even having the temerity to day-dream about another man when Elliott is here, with all the familiarity, and comfort, and love that she needs.

How could she possibly have thought about anyone else?

'I missed you.'

'Liar,' he teases. 'I heard you last night. You were having a great time with the girls. I bet you didn't even think about me.'

'I'm just glad you're home,' she says, kissing him full on the mouth. He smiles in delight and raises an eye-brow, gesturing towards the house.

'Ewww.' Olivia brushes past them, scowling the typical scowl of a seventeen-year-old. 'Can you not do that in front of us? That's gross.'

'Kissing is entirely natural,' Elliott says. 'And we are your parents. It's not like there's anything illicit going on here.'

Gabby quickly looks away. Why did he say that? Why would he choose those words? She looks at him carefully but there is no way he knows anything, not that there's anything to know; it was merely a harmless flirtation. Thank God.

'Hi, sweetie.' Gabby puts an arm round Alanna and pulls her in to kiss the side of her head. 'Did you have fun?'

'Uh-huh,' Alanna manages, her attention focused on her phone.

Gabby suppresses a pang. Grief would be too strong a word for it, but oh how she misses the days when her girls were tiny, when they adored everything she did; when they wanted nothing other than to spend time with their mother.

Looking at them now – Alanna so petite, with her dark blonde hair streaming down her back, the image of her father, and Olivia, tall and curvy, her curly hair just like Gabby's, just beginning to find comfort in her skin – it is hard to reconcile them with the small girls they once were.

Olivia, when young, wouldn't let her mother leave the bedroom at night. Gabby would go in to snuggle, adoring how Olivia's tiny body fitted so perfectly into hers, adoring how Olivia would chatter away, doing everything she could to make her mother stay longer.

Gabby never wanted to leave, and only ever did when the clock ticked on, and she knew Olivia had to go to sleep.

Now, Gabby doesn't remember the last time she snuggled in behind Olivia and gave her a cuddle. At seventeen, Olivia barely allows Gabby into her room. Even Alanna, at eleven, so calm, so wise, is now far more interested in her friends than in her mother. Gabby knows so little about what is going on with Alanna in school that she has started doing the unthinkable and going through her texts. Still, she learns nothing.

Oh how she misses the early years, the delicious all-consuming love, the hours and hours of doing nothing other than playing with the babies, watching them with wonder and love, unable to believe she had created these two miraculous little lives.

'Tell me she didn't spend the entire camping trip on the phone,' she says, turning to Elliott.

'Not the entire time,' he says.

Alanna looks up. 'I'm not on the phone. I'm on Instagram.'

'Oh.' Gabby nods. 'Well, that's okay, then. So how many followers do you have now?'

Alanna smiles. 'Three hundred and forty-two.'

'Wow. You are popular!'

'Mom!' She rolls her eyes. 'It's not about popular.'

'So what is it about?'

Alanna shakes her head dismissively as she disappears inside. 'You wouldn't understand.'

'You wouldn't,' Elliott corroborates, pulling their bags from the car and handing some to Gabby. 'Neither would I, apparently. We're too old.'

Usually Gabby would laugh and agree, except she didn't feel old this weekend. For the first time in years she didn't feel like she was past it, and she's not ready to relinquish the feeling that life still holds possibilities, that there are still adventures to be had, even if she will never repeat the adventure of last night.

'How was Alanna? Was she sweet?'

Alanna, always known as the good one, has become more of a handful over the past few months. Middle school, not easy for anyone, has seen Alanna finally accepted by the girls she has always referred to as 'the Populars', and with that acceptance comes an attitude that Gabby and Elliott have not welcomed in the slightest.

'She was pretty crabby when we got there, but she settled down. We really did have a lovely time. Tim and I think you and Claire should come next time.'

'I thought you said you understood that sleeping bags weren't my thing any more.'

'We could get a blow-up mattress. It was amazing, being out in nature.'

'I'm totally happy being out in nature, as long as it's at a spa.' Gabby grins.

'By the way, Tim said we should go to theirs for dinner tonight. He's got a ton of burgers and dogs he needs to get rid of.'

'Perfect.' Gabby sets the bags down on the floor of the hallway. 'I'll ring Claire and see what I can bring.'

'First, I think you should come upstairs.' Elliott puts his arms round her from behind, nuzzling her neck, and Gabby, who so often pushes him away, telling him no, insisting she's too busy, or his timing is horrible, or she's not in the mood, allows herself to be led to their room.

With the door locked, Gabby sinks to her knees, unbuckling Elliott's belt while he murmurs in surprise and delight.

It is, she realizes, the least she can do.

Years ago, when they were first married, they swore they would never become the kind of couple they so often saw in town. The couple who would sit in a restaurant and gaze around the room, having nothing to say to each other. They swore they would never become like the people they knew who would laughingly relate how little sex they had: who has the energy? Who has the time?

Gabby and Elliott have never been a couple to sit in silence. In the mornings Elliott turns to Gabby and invariably starts a conversation about something he's been thinking about since he woke up. It could be politics, the solution to the town parking problem, his fears for the future of the world.

In turn, Gabby shares everything with Elliott. Unlike so many of her friends whose husbands are gone for most of the day and who turn to their girlfriends for everything in their lives, Gabby has never needed much more than Elliott. She has Claire, her closest friend, and is included in the group of girls, but she would never phone any of them for a chat, wouldn't think to turn to them if ever there was a problem in her life. The only best friend she has ever really had, has ever wanted, could ever really count on, is Elliott.

He says it's because they have been together twenty years, but there are plenty of couples Gabby sees who have been together as long – longer – and they are not friends in the way she and Elliott are.

After their chance meeting, Elliott was talking about marriage by the end of their third date. Everyone told Gabby she was crazy, and much too young, at twenty-three, to even think about settling down.

Which is why she waited to get married until she was twenty-five. And still everyone was wrong.

Although, and it is only grudgingly she will admit this, their sex life is not what it was. Gabby loves the smell of Elliott, the warmth and closeness their love-making brings, but, and she would never say this to him, if they only had sex every once in a while, it really wouldn't bother her.

It isn't that she doesn't think about sex. It isn't that she doesn't get turned on reading certain books, or watching certain films; it isn't that she doesn't mastur-bate. It's more that Elliott is her best friend, her family, and although she always enjoys their lovemaking once they start, the idea of making love with him is just one she rarely suggests.

Frankly she'd rather read a good book and have an early night.

Claire and Tim watch porn together, which Claire says has transformed their sex life. Tim has no idea that both Gabby and Elliott know this, and although Elliott persuaded her to do the same, the few times they tried it Gabby couldn't stop herself critiquing the acting, the fake boobs and the thrusting that went on for so long that she found it exhausting.

It didn't do anything for her, although Elliott was demonstrably more imaginative for a little while.

Oral sex, while an imperative part of their lovemaking during those early years, rarely happens any more, and it is unheard of for Gabby to initiate it.

Until now. Naturally Elliott doesn't think to question why. Doesn't wonder if this is the female equivalent of the guilt gift – women get jewellery when their men have strayed, or thought too seriously about straying.

And the men? They get blow jobs.

He just closes his eyes and succumbs to the waves of pleasure washing over him.

Chapter Four

Pushing open Claire's back door, a door they know almost as well as their own, Gabby, Elliott and the girls walk through the mud room, gingerly stepping over the sneakers and backpacks littering the floor, through to the kitchen, where Claire is making a salad.

'Hi, girls!' She greets Olivia and Alanna first. 'Sasha is outside on the trampoline, and I think Jolie's upstairs. Go on out. Or up. Did you have fun camping?' she calls after them as an afterthought, but they've already gone out through the back door.

Gabby puts her bowl on the table and slides out of her fleece as Elliott walks outside to find Tim. She is grateful to be here tonight, to do something as familiar and normal as a barbecue at Claire and Tim's. Each normal step she takes is a step away from the events of last night, from thinking, in what is rapidly becoming an obsessive way, about what could have happened.

'What did you make?' Claire peers over at the bowl Gabby brought.

'Asian slaw.'

'Yum! I love that slaw. Trish is coming too. She's made some kind of meringue dessert.'

'Oh God. It's going to be some kind of perfect dessert. I wish I'd known she was coming. I would have made more of an effort,' says Gabby.

Claire laughs. 'Will you stop? Why do you always have this thing about her? You think she's judging everyone else by her standards, but she really isn't. She doesn't look to see what other people bring, and, before you say anything, she doesn't care what anyone looks like either. Despite what you're always saying. You know it's your insecurity and nothing to do with her.'

'I know. She's so nice, but she's so perfect, and, really, how is it possible for one person to be amazing at *everything*?'

'I don't know, but she's bringing some guy she's dating. Ella said he's gorgeous.'

'Of course he is. As if she'd date anyone less.' Gabby peers at Claire. 'Speaking of gorgeous, you look good. Did you spend the entire day in bed? You look totally well-rested.'

Claire smiles. 'I feel good. Hang on.' She goes to the back door. 'Tim? Will you come in? You too, Elliott.'

Tim walks in and leans down to give Claire a kiss before standing next to her with his arm round her shoulders.

'O-kay,' Gabby looks at Elliott, then back at her friends, 'would someone mind telling me what's going on here?'

'We have some news.' Claire grins. 'We wanted to tell you together and we wanted you to be the first to know.'

Gabby frowns. It can't be what she thinks, because Claire is older than she is, and it wouldn't be fair, and she has never talked about it, and she knows Gabby wanted . . .

'We're pregnant!' Tim says, and Claire's eyes fill with tears.

'Can you believe it?' she says to Gabby, opening her arms to embrace Gabby in a hug.

'Oh boy!' Elliott embraces Tim, then Claire, and Gabby does the same, as a dagger of pain slices her heart in two. It's exactly what she was dreading, exactly what she has always wanted – but for her.

'That's huge!' says Elliott.

'It *is* huge!' Gabby says. Her eyes have filled with tears, but she smiles through them, leading Tim and Claire to believe she is as overwhelmed with joy as they are. 'When did you find out?' she asks.

'About an hour ago!' Claire laughs. 'I'm not telling anyone else because God only knows what'll happen. I mean, I'm forty-four! But I told Tim I had to tell one person because I just can't keep this excitement in, and you're our closest friends, so . . . We shouldn't celebrate, not yet, but I couldn't get through the evening pretending everything was normal.'

'I'm glad you told us,' Gabby says, hugging Claire again before excusing herself to go to the bathroom.

She doesn't go to the bathroom off the kitchen. She walks through the house to the formal powder room because it is quiet there, and secluded.

She doesn't want anyone to hear her cry.

*

44

Six months ago, Gabby finally did the unthinkable, sorting through her closet and boxing up all her maternity clothes. She was less tearful than numb at finally, reluctantly, acknowledging there wouldn't be another child; her baby days were done.

She pulled the baby seats and buggies and bouncing chairs out from the attic, collected up the brightly coloured toys her daughters had long outgrown, and piled them into the car, then she dropped them off at a charity shop, feeling nothing.

She had never been able to get rid of the baby things before, knowing she wasn't done with having children, no matter what Elliott thought. Her two girls were wonderful, but three was the magic number, the number she had always dreamed of. She didn't care whether the third was a boy or a girl, only that there would be a third.

After Alanna was born they decided to wait for a while before having another baby. Elliott said he needed time to feel more established in his specialty, and a doctor's salary wasn't what it used to be. He always said, 'Let's wait until we have some more money in the bank; until we can really afford it.'

The years went by, and it never seemed like the right time. Gabby wondered whether she should accidentally-on-purpose fall pregnant: say she was on the pill but forget to take it, secretly puncture a condom, tell him the timing made pregnancy impossible, say that she had finished her period that morning, when in fact she was at the height of ovulation.

But she couldn't lie, couldn't wilfully deceive the man she loves. Not then. So she waited for the right time, for Elliott to decide that they could do it. At thirty-nine she started to panic, and Elliott started to voice his second thoughts. They were already settled; they had two beautiful girls; their family was complete.

Other people fight about money, disciplining kids, in-laws. The only thing Gabby and Elliott fight about, have ever fought about, is this. Once Elliott voiced his opinion about not wanting any more children, his stance grew ever firmer. Gabby thought she could change his mind, persuade him otherwise, but he was clear: there were going to be no more children.

And even though Gabby knew she would never deliberately trick him into having a baby, she also knew she could be a little less . . . careful. She learned to be forgetful about taking the pill; she welcomed going on antibiotics, knowing it reduced the efficacy of the pill, praying each time that she would become pregnant.

In the back of her bathroom cabinet was a paper bag filled with pregnancy tests, and each time she had been 'forgetful', she would unwrap a test on the first day her period was due then hold her breath with excited antici-pation as she peed. Her whole body would be flooded with disappointment when the tests had a negative result.

Six months ago, Elliott announced he was having a vasectomy. He had been thinking about it for a long time, and there was no question in his mind that it was the most efficient form of birth control. He couldn't ask her to have her tubes tied, and, frankly, it was bad enough that she had to take the pill. She had gone through childbirth twice; now it was his turn.

It was the fair thing to do.

The operation, minor, was booked, he said. They sat down to discuss it, and Gabby expressed her upset, her reasons for not agreeing, her wish to have another child.

'How dare you make such a momentous decision unilaterally!' She had burst into tears. 'You can't do this without my agreement.'

'But you know I don't want more children.' He was confused. He had no idea how serious Gabby was about her need for another child; he had no idea she had a stash of pregnancy tests, was still hoping against hope for another baby, despite her advancing age making it unlikely. 'You knew this. You knew I wasn't going to change my mind.'

However many times they talked, and fought, there was nothing Gabby could do to change his mind. He was only able to see it from his point of view: once she got over her disappointment, he reasoned, how could she fail to see how much easier it would be – they would be able to make love spontaneously! No more pills! No more condoms! It would free them to truly enjoy the rest of their lives.

Gabby ran out of patience explaining her reasons for him not to do it, the subject eventually becoming a no-go area. Every time they tried to talk about the vasectomy, it ended up as a fight. It was easier to stop talking about it and sweep it under the carpet.

Elliott went ahead with the appointment, figuring he would ask forgiveness, not permission. This was the right thing for their family.

Gabby, silent with resentment for a week, finally boxed up her maternity clothes and gave away her baby toys.

And still she hasn't forgiven him. It is done. The deed cannot be undone, nor can any number of apologies heal the pain of knowing she will never again hold her newborn baby in her arms, smell the new-baby smell as it suckles at her breast, blow raspberries on a chubby little belly as her tiny infant waves its arms and legs in the air, giggling with delight.

Gabby loves Elliott. She will never not love him, but she is not certain she can ever forgive him for going ahead and having the vasectomy. It is akin to how he would feel had her machinations worked, had she suddenly found herself pregnant, but that is irrelevant.

It has made the past year a hard one. Gabby knows that time will heal, that as each day goes by she will feel less anger, less resentment, but standing in the kitchen, looking at Tim and Claire aglow with joy, she felt, just now, nothing other than overwhelming fury.

It should have been them.

In the bathroom Gabby weeps. She puts the lid down on the toilet and sits, her head in her hands, her entire body wracked with sobs. She is quiet, but not so quiet that she can't be heard by anyone who should happen to be standing directly outside.

'Gabby?' Elliott leans his head on the door, his face a picture of sadness.

Gabby tries to compose herself. 'I'm okay. I'll be out in a second.'

'Let me in, Gabs,' he says, and she unlocks the door, unable to look at him.

'I'm sorry,' he whispers, taking her in his arms. 'I am so sorry. I never realized how much you wanted this. I thought you'd be okay, that you'd get over it. I was wrong.' Gabby bursts into a fresh round of sobs, her head against his chest, her tears soaking his T-shirt.

That he finally admitted it should make it better, should make the pain go away.

But it doesn't.

Chapter Five

Gabby comes back to the kitchen to find that Trish, sweeping long, streaky blonde hair over a shoulder, beaming a perfect white smile, has just deposited on the table a white-china cake plate holding a meringue piled with whipped cream and strawberries, a plate of raspberry bars and a platter of chocolate-chip cookies.

'Gabby! It's so nice to see you!'

'Hi, there,' Gabby says, then she smiles as Claire reaches for a cookie and swoons in delight after she takes a bite. 'Tell me you didn't bake all these yourself.'

'I did. It was nothing. Gavin helped.' They all turn to look approvingly at Trish's date. He is standing outside with the men.

'He's that handsome and he cooks too? Are you kidding me?' Claire murmurs. 'In my next life can I come back and be you?'

'Oh silly,' trills Trish, looking over at the chopping board. 'Can I help? I can finish off the salad if you want.'

Gabby steps forward. 'Don't worry, I'm doing it.' She moves over to the board and picks up the knife, slicing the onion while Trish watches her with a frown on her face.

'Oooh. Careful of your fingers,' she warns, just as Gabby cuts herself.

'Shit!' She immediately sticks her finger in her mouth, and Claire spins to open a drawer, pulling out the Neosporin and a Band-Aid.

Trish picks up the knife and carries on, tucking her fingers into a claw and slicing the onion into perfect, paper-thin rings, at the speed of light.

'Where did you learn to do that?' Gabby asks.

'I went to cooking school.' Trish shrugs. 'It was ages ago, but I picked up some good knife skills.'

'Is there anything you can't do?' Claire says. 'There must be something you're really, really bad at.'

Trish stands still, thinking, as Gabby and Claire exchange a secret smile. That she even has to think about it is extraordinary, thinks Gabby. Eventually Trish's face lights up.

'I'm really bad at maths,' she says. 'Like, I don't get numbers at all. I can never work out tips in restaurants.'

'Thank the Lord!' whoops Claire. 'The woman isn't perfect! So,' she says, glancing out of the window at the men standing round the barbecue, 'where did you meet the gorgeous Gavin?'

'Match.com,' Trish says confidently.

'Really? Do you do a lot of dating on match.com?' Gabby is surprised she is so open about it.

'It's become one of the only places. People do occasionally set me up, but out here in the suburbs the singles scene is very small, and you have to cast your net wider. I used to struggle with people knowing, but the stigma really doesn't exist any more. Everyone who's single does it. It's either that or going to bars, which is pretty horrendous. The last thing I'd want is to meet the kind of man who's into the bar scene.'

Claire gives Gabby a knowing look. 'They're not all awful . . .' She grins as Gabby flushes.

'No?' Trish turns to Gabby, who shrugs and looks away, as if she has no idea what Claire is implying.

'Oh, come on, Gabs.' She turns to Trish to explain. 'Ella organized a girls' night out last night at the Grey Goose. We were all there, surrounded by middle-aged cheesy men, except for Gabby. She got totally hit on by this rather adorable young guy. I'm telling you, if I wasn't married I'd have snapped him up. He was delicious!'

'What?' Elliott appears in the kitchen. 'Did I hear you just say my wife got hit on by a hot young guy?' He's smiling. 'Gabs! You didn't tell me that!'

'I didn't want you to feel threatened,' she says lightly, mortified that anyone is talking about the evening, instantly feeling guilty, wishing they would just keep quiet and move on, yet thrilled, too, that they are talking about her! Thrilled that she should be the one who was noticed last night, that perhaps Elliott, perhaps all of them, would see her in a new, flattering light.

'Apparently your wife is a MILF.' Claire laughs. 'The rest of us were stuck with the lecherous old sleazeballs. You should count yourself lucky you have a wife who's still got it.'

Elliott puts his arms round Gabby as he kisses her neck. 'Oh I do,' he says. 'I absolutely do.'

Alanna appears, sidling quietly up to the counter and attempting to slide a large handful of chocolate-chip cookies into her pocket.

'Alanna!' Gabby is shocked. 'Put those back right now! Those are for after we've eaten.'

'They're not just for me,' she protests. 'I was sent inside to get them for everyone.'

Gabby shakes her head. 'And I suppose if they asked you to jump you'd say, "How high?"'

Alanna just stares at her. 'What?'

Gabby sighs. 'Never mind. Put them back. Everyone can wait.'

Alanna grumbles in a way that seems far too teen-aged for an eleven-year-old, but puts the cookies back.

Trish walks over. 'How is Alanna finding middle school?' she says. 'My girls had such a rough time, and I hear it's got worse. A very difficult transitional phase.'

Gabby would love to be able to say that everything is fine, but everything is not fine. To others, Alanna seems to be the same girl she has always been, only quieter, but Gabby knows that, having given up trying to be in with the group she called the Populars at her old school – little girls Gabby has known all their lives, who are sweet as pie with the adults, and vicious minxes as soon as they are on their own – Alanna has found a new group of friends in middle school.

A new group of friends who were clearly the

Populars in their own elementary school and who are exactly the same as the old girls Gabby never liked, only couched in different clothes, with different names.

Alanna refuses to talk about them, and when Gabby encourages her to find different friends, ones who are not obsessed with boys at the age of eleven, ones who aren't given the iPhone 5 as soon as it comes out, Alanna doesn't want to hear. She isn't interested in the girls in the softball team, or the girls from art class. She wants only to be accepted by the cool girls in school, and nothing her mother says or does will make her want anything else.

Gabby takes a deep breath. 'Alanna's a tough cookie,' she lies to Trish. 'I think she'll be fine.'

Chapter Six

The sheets are refreshingly cool as Gabby slips between them, pulling up the covers and revelling in the comfort of her bed, the comfort of her life, all of it effectively rendering more and more dreamlike the fact that she met a man to whom she was attracted last night.

In the bathroom Elliott brushes his teeth, then he turns away from the basin and leans against the door jamb, looking at her.

'I like that Trish,' he says. 'And Gavin seems like a great guy. Young, though. How old do you think he is?'

'Thirty-five?' Gabby ventures, before making a face. 'What? You didn't like him?'

She sighs. 'It's not him. It's Trish. She's always pleasant enough, so why do I feel so damned inadequate around her?' Gabby laughs, knowing how ridiculous she sounds.

'Why would you feel inadequate? I'll admit, she's great at a lot of things, but so are you.'

Gabby gives a bark of laughter. 'You are kidding, right?'

'You don't run your own business as she does, but other than that you cook pretty well, you're fantastic at

55

restoring furniture, which I bet she can't do, and you're a great mother. You . . .' He pauses.

'See! You're struggling. Me too. That's the point. Look!' She grabs a handful of her belly. 'She's perfect! She doesn't have this! Or these!' She tries to show Elliott the two prickly hairs she's recently found on her chin, but in vain: he doesn't have his glasses on and can't see them. 'I bet Trish doesn't have any chin hairs!' They both laugh. 'Seriously! She's there with her taut, yoga-honed body, and I get hives just driving past the damn place. Everything about her is perfect. There isn't a wrinkle on her face or a grey hair on her head, and look –' Gabby bends her head down – 'look!' She sounds like she is joking, but there is a touch of hysteria in her voice as she points out her grey hairs.

'I can't see anything,' Elliott says gently.

Gabby lifts her head up. 'Oh, that's right. I just dyed them. Still, they're there. And I'm never going to get into my size six clothes again. I'm not even going to manage size eight. I can just about squeeze into size ten, but only when they're stretchy. Oh God. When did I turn into such a fat, frumpy mess?'

'First of all, you're not a fat, frumpy mess, and second of all, even if you were, you're my fat, frumpy mess, and I love you exactly as you are.'

'No, you don't,' grumbles Gabby, as Elliott sits down on her side of the bed. 'When I was thin you always used to say how sexy I was.'

'You're even sexier now,' he says with a smile, pulling

the covers down and reaching a hand to cup one of her full breasts. 'You never had these when you were thin, and I don't want to have to say goodbye to these.' Gabby rolls her eyes. 'And apparently I'm not the only one who thinks you're pretty damn hot,' Elliott reminds her, astonished to see her blush.

'What's that supposed to mean?' she says, embarrassment rising, because she knows exactly what he's talking about.

'Whoa Relax. I just meant that you were a hit last night, right? Some young guy? Whatever insecurities you may have, and however much you refuse to believe me, you're still beautiful. Even Claire said it. How did she describe you?' He laughs. 'A MILF! See? You've still got it.'

'Maybe,' Gabby concedes. 'But only for about five more minutes.'

'That's okay. I'm not going anywhere – not when my wife is so gorgeous.' And he unbuttons her nightie then tips his head to kiss her right breast.

'DAD!' The door handle is rattled. 'Open the door! Why is the door locked? Mom?'

'Jesus,' Elliott hisses through his teeth, rolling off Gabby, who pulls the covers back up. 'In a minute. Go back to your room. I'll be there in a minute.'

'Why is the door locked?' Alanna persists, rattling the door back and forth. 'Mom? Will you come and say goodnight? Let me in!'

'She'll be in in a minute,' Elliott says. 'Go, Alanna.'

'But just op–'

'NOW!' Elliott barks, and they both listen to Alanna's footsteps stomping down the corridor. 'Whose idea was it to have children?' He turns to Gabby, reaching for his shorts as Gabby smiles and pulls on her robe.

Elliott pauses by the bedroom door. 'We've lost the moment, haven't we?

'What do you mean?'

'I mean, you're not going to want to finish what we started. I know you. You'll get back into bed and grab your Kindle, and there'll be no more passion tonight.'

Gabby grins. 'You're the one who always refers to the children as passion-killers.'

'With good reason.'

'Actually, I think tonight you may get lucky.'

'Really?'

Gabby moves towards him and pulls him down to kiss him deeply. 'Meet you back here in ten minutes.'

She can't say no to Alanna's request to have her mother tuck her in, not when Alanna wants so little to do with her these days.

'Is everything okay?' Gabby asks, sitting on the bed as Alanna climbs in. 'Want me to snuggle?' This was never their thing, always hers and Olivia's, but, to her surprise, Alanna nods.

Gabby lies down and draws her daughter close, burying her nose in Alanna's hair, feeling the small body solid against her own as she wraps her arm around her and holds her.

'Is there anything you want to talk about?' she whispers, sensing there is something going on for Alanna to be so affectionate, but Alanna simply shakes her head wordlessly, shuffling back to fit perfectly into the safety of her mother's body.

Gabby knows there is something wrong. She suspects Alanna is struggling with middle school, but she also knows there is nothing she can do unless and until Alanna chooses to share it with her. As hard as everyone warned her it would be, Olivia had sailed through middle school, despite being their more challenging child. So there was no question in Gabby's mind that Alanna, easy since the day she was born, would also by-pass the social pressures and bitchy cliques that Olivia had avoided.

But Alanna, at eleven, is not the sunny, quiet child she used to be. She is suddenly determined to be in with the right crowd, seeing middle school as the opportunity to reinvent herself. Abandoning her old friends, she has been excitedly making new ones since she started middle school in September. Gabby misses Alanna's old friends, who have been deemed 'uncool' by Alanna and her new friends, and these new friends make Gabby nervous. They seem too sure of themselves, too advanced, all of them flicking straightened hair over their shoulders, posting provocative poses online, chewing gum as they check their iPhones for texts.

Gabby tucks Alanna in, and heads back to their bedroom. She wants to talk to Elliott about her fears, but Olivia has now talked him out of bed and back downstairs to watch an episode of *The Voice*, and Elliott, who can resist anything except his daughters, is now sitting on the sofa discussing the pros and cons of a one-hit wonder, who came on the show desperate to prove he was more than that but has chosen to sing his one-hit-wonder song.

Alone, Gabby reaches for the iPad rather than the Kindle, idly flicking through her Facebook newsfeed, before going to Trish's page. She has a personal page, and a business one with eighty-four thousand likes. Which upsets Gabby.

She and Trish have always been friendly without being friends, but there is a chasm between them now that can't be bridged. Gabby knows exactly when the crevice appeared.

It happened a couple of years ago, when Alanna was nine. Trish had phoned Gabby to organize a playdate, asking what her diary looked like in three weeks' time. Gabby had resisted the urge to laugh. She barely knew what day of the week it was, let alone what the girls were doing in three weeks' time. The playdates she organized tended to be last-minute, with neighbourhood kids, and more often than not the girls arranged it all themselves with little or no input from the mothers, other than the picking up or dropping off at the end of the playdate.

She dutifully looked in the diary and came up with a day. Trish explained she would be dropping Alanna back at five p.m. as she had to take her son to basketball at five thirty, on the other side of town.

'Are you sure I can't pick her up?' Gabby offered, knowing it would have been impossible, for Olivia had a dance class in Fairfield, twenty minutes away, which ended at five.

'It's no problem,' Trish said.

'Fine. My sitter will be home,' Gabby said confidently. Gabby didn't actually have a sitter, but made a mental note to make sure to find one for the day.

A week before the playdate Trish phoned again to check if Alanna had any food allergies. 'Don't worry about snacks,' Trish had reassured Gabby. 'We're a gluten-free, sugar-free household so it's only healthy snacks!' Gabby eyed her own snack drawer, stuffed with Pirate's Booty, Fruit Roll-Ups, crisps and individual packets of chocolate-chip cookies.

She forced a smile. 'Great!'

It was too late to cancel the playdate – Alanna was so excited – but Gabby already suspected these preliminary check-up calls didn't bode well.

Trish's daughter, Skylar, had always seemed lovely, but Gabby had learned not to organize playdates with kids whose parents didn't share the same sensibilities. Many of the parents at Alanna's elementary school were helicopter parents, desperately seeking opportunities, any opportunities, to muscle their way into their kids' classroom. They would always be volunteering to help in some way, to make costumes for shows, to bake class treats. Trish was one of those parents; Gabby was not. She was happy searching the local area for pieces of old furniture to restore at home. She went to a knitting class at the local yarn shop. She volunteered at the town farm. She cooked from scratch every day, proper family suppers, so they could all eat together as a family. Her days were busy; she figured the kids were perfectly fine without her pitching up at school all the time.

Her friends tended to be other mothers who were equally laid back. They let their kids ride around the neighbourhood on bikes; they pushed the children out through the back door telling them to play, not worrying about them, nor giving them a second thought, until they came home because they were hungry.

Sure enough, on the day of the playdate Alanna went home on the bus with Skylar, and Gabby took Olivia to dance, only remembering that she had meant to find a sitter when her mobile phone rang, at 5.02 p.m., her own home number flashing on the screen. Her heart plummeted to her stomach.

She'd forgotten to book a sitter.

'Mom? Where are you? Skylar's mom just dropped me home and there's no one here.'

'Oh, honey. I'm sorry. The sitter must have forgotten. I'll be home in five minutes. I know Skylar's mom has to be somewhere so tell her to leave you. It's only five minutes.'

Gabby listened while Alanna relayed this to Trish, who then came on the phone.

'Gabby? Hi. There's no sitter here.'

Was it Gabby's imagination or was there judgement in her voice? A wave of defensive panic washed over her.

'I don't know what happened. But I'm literally five minutes away,' she lied, knowing she was twenty-five minutes away. 'Just leave her. She'll be fine for five minutes. I know you have to go.'

'I'm not leaving her by herself,' Trish said. 'I'll just wait for you.'

'No, really. I'm so close and I know you have to take your son to basketball. Alanna's fine.'

'I'm not leaving a child on her own,' Trish said. 'We'll wait.' She didn't sound happy.

'I'm so sorry,' Gabby said again, now feeling sick, knowing she'd be caught out. There was no way in hell she'd be home in five minutes, or anything close.

In the end, she phoned her neighbour and begged her to run over so Trish could leave. She did, but Gabby knew Trish knew she'd lied, and there was no more talk of another playdate, nor did Gabby reciprocate.

It was, as she said to Claire at the time, too much pressure.

She is happy to be friendly at social events, but they will never be friends; of that, she is certain.

63

Scrolling through Facebook keeps her distracted until Elliott comes back up to bed. On a normal night, she might well curl up in bed and read a couple of pages on the Kindle before going to sleep, leaving Elliott's bedside lamp on for when he comes up. But tonight she needs to make love with him, needs to erase, finally, the evidence of her mental infidelity – and thank God it was merely in her head – and the only way to do that is to feel him inside her.

'You're still awake?' He crawls onto the bed, pleasantly surprised.

'I told you we had unfinished business,' she replies, and smiles, pulling him to her and kissing him deeply. Her concerns for Alanna can wait.

Their lovemaking has become a well-worn routine. Tonight Gabby pulls out all the stops. She pushes him back on the bed and climbs on top of him, feeling a passion for her husband she hasn't felt in years.

She closes her eyes and moves on top of Elliott, sighing as she gives into the temptation of fantasizing that it isn't her familiar husband underneath her, but the smooth, strong body of a thirty-something; it isn't her husband moaning as she kisses his neck, but Matt.

Chapter Seven

This house was not a house they were ever supposed to have looked at when they were wanting to upgrade to something bigger. They had a long list of houses to visit, mostly fifties and sixties ranches and splits – all that was affordable given Elliott's new residency at Norwalk Hospital.

Their realtor, flapping and stressed, announced they would have to make a quick pit stop at a house where she needed to check the back-door key.

Elliott was in the front of the car, Gabby in the rear, as their realtor turned onto a pretty street close to town, with picture-book cottages lining each side.

The house, a grey shingle, was set back from the road with a beautiful dogwood tree in the front garden. There was a natural-wood barn in the backyard, a large copper star hanging on the side of it. Once upon a time it had been a horse barn, but it was now used for storage. The house was a small Cape style; too small for Gabby and Elliott and their two young girls, the realtor pointed out, seeing how excited they were.

The downstairs had been added on to extensively and now had two newer, light-filled rooms: a sunroom and a playroom; but the upstairs had just two bedrooms and one bathroom, all of them tiny.

'Couldn't we add on above the sunroom?' Elliott peered out of the window, pointing out the flat roof.

'You could,' she said doubtfully. 'But I just don't know how much you want to put into this house.'

'Surely adding a bedroom and bathroom would be an investment?'

'Yes, but only if you got it at the right price. They're asking about thirty thousand too much, and so far they've refused to move.'

Elliott turned to Gabby, whose face had lit up. 'I love it,' she said.

'Me too.'

They made their offer, and raised it twice, only to have it rejected. Losing heart, they settled on a sixties ranch on the other side of town; it had a huge back-yard, and no charm whatsoever.

The day they were going to sign the contract their realtor phoned. The owners of the cottage had rethought. They would now accept the third and final offer if Elliott and Gabby still wanted the house.

'We do,' Elliott said, 'but I have to offer lower because of the money we've spent since then.' He named his price, shockingly low, even to the realtor, while deciding not to tell Gabby unless and until the offer was accepted.

Three months later, they moved in.

Empty, the house needed more work than they had

imagined. Paintings that had been removed left huge rectangular stains on the walls; wooden floors were stained and thirsty as they emerged after hiding underneath rugs for more than twenty years.

They worked evenings and weekends to restore the house, while the builders worked during the day to build Olivia's bedroom, and reconfigure and enlarge the rooms that were there. The job became larger, the contractor pointing out how easy it would be to cut off a chunk of the now-oversized master suite to create a walk-in closet and a spare bedroom. How could they not?

The walls were covered with fresh paint, the floors stripped and sanded before being stained a dark brown then oiled with Tung Oil for a glossy, rich finish. Gabby ran up simple curtain panels in a pale mushroom linen, the same panels in a fuchsia pink for the girls' rooms.

They had little money back then. Their furniture was a mix of consignment store and hand-me-downs. If ever anyone said they were getting rid of anything, Gabby and Elliott took it, regardless of what it was, what it looked like, or whether they had room.

What they couldn't use was stored at one end of the barn. The other was turned into a workroom where Gabby would restore furniture for their home. A huge old dresser they found at the dump one day, covered in a vile shade of green paint, was transformed into a beautiful bleached-pine period piece. Lined with linen it was perfect for their Crate & Barrel plates and bowls.

Gabby became an expert at stripping furniture and

repurposing it. Where others would see a heavy, dark, utilitarian chest of drawers, she would see an object of beauty, and once stripped and painted a soft ivory, the intricate and ugly brass pulls replaced with pretty, antique, crystal knobs, these pieces of furniture were invariably more stunning than even she expected.

Elliott made the outdoor table, and the pergola under which it sits. Gabby collected old mason jars of all shapes and sizes, filled them with votive candles and hung them at varying heights underneath the pergola.

It has become a house others describe as magical. Tiny lights twinkle from the dogwood tree in the front garden and the two apple trees in the back. It is a house that feels happy, feels like it is home to a happy family, and everyone who comes over immediately feels comfortable.

This has always felt like Gabby's haven, a place where she is safe from the world. It is the quietest, most peaceful house she can imagine, a world away from the house in which she spent her childhood.

Gabby grew up in England. She moved to the States after university, at the age of twenty-one, initially coming just for the summer, to work as a counsellor at a girls' camp in Maine. But life seemed so filled with possibility here that she never went home. First, she applied for a student visa, working as a nanny and studying in the evenings, then she met and married Elliott.

The London house in which she grew up was always filled with people. Her mother, once well-known as a stage actress, had, in later years, retrained as a therapist. Never a woman who fully understood boundaries, Natasha de Roth (no one is sure where the 'de' came from – Gabby's father went only by the surname of Roth) offered up their home as a sanctuary to waifs and strays, anyone who had nowhere else to go, including an assortment of rather scruffy dogs and unhappy cats.

Living in the large and once rather grand Roth/de Roth house at the top of Belsize Park Gardens always felt a bit like a game of Russian Roulette to Gabby – opening the front door after school you never knew what you were going to get.

There might be a woman standing shouting in the kitchen, being coached through a bipolar rage by her mother, who would smile cheerily and wave Gabby along as if this was perfectly normal and she should come back later.

Impromptu group-therapy sessions were normal round the kitchen table. Gabby would walk home, longing for a quiet hot chocolate and some digestive biscuits, only to find the larder empty, the biscuits having been eagerly consumed by the seven people currently weeping as they slumped on chairs pulled up to the old scrubbed pine table next to the Aga.

Gabby learned to stop at the newsagent's in Belsize Village on her way home from school to buy some crisps, or cookies, then go straight up to her bedroom to avoid the mayhem.

She'd sit cross-legged on the floor, leaning back on

her beanbag, plugged into her Sony Walkman and surrounded by posters of The Police, Madness, The Specials. She'd eat two or three Jaffa Cakes then put the rest away for another time.

It was peaceful in her large, sun-filled bedroom at the back of the house, with views over the tree tops. Occasionally she'd hear a door slam downstairs, or the bark of laughter, but mostly, when plugged in, she was able to lose herself in daydreams.

She dreamed, even then, of a peaceful life. She dreamed of a life when she wouldn't be surrounded by drama and chaos, by a mother who needed so desperately to be needed herself that she couldn't possibly be there for the one person who truly did need her: her daughter.

Her father, a quiet scholarly man, who made his living as an editor on one of the broadsheets, had little to do with either of them. His way of dealing with the chaos was to remove himself, if not entirely physically, then certainly emotionally. He worked late hours at the newspaper, and would, when home, drift through the house or spend hours sitting in a cracked leather wing chair by the bay window in the living room, methodically working his way through a large pile of newspapers on the floor next to him, cigarette always in hand, bottle of Scotch resting on the table.

Gabby adored him, even though she had little to do with him. He would always light up in delight when he saw her, and might, if in the mood, briefly engage her in a discussion about politics, or Ethiopia, or what her thoughts might be about the situation in Northern Ireland.

But soon he would be back with his papers, and Gabby would disappear off to her room, grateful to have had any kind of attention at all.

America. The very word seemed to be lit up, heralded by angels singing. Everything about America seemed larger than life, exotic, magical. Her favourite films were American; her favourite film stars were American. She watched *Happy Days* and was nostalgic for a life she had never known; it was a life she was certain existed across the pond and longed to share. She was sure everyone in America was always happy; they had perfect, big white teeth; they had mothers and housekeepers who were always smiling, who paid them attention, thought everything they did was wonderful, baked them fresh cakes every day for when they got off the bus, the yellow school bus – oh how she wanted to travel on a yellow school bus! – after school.

They had one family vacation when Gabby was twelve. They went to New York, which was the most vibrant, exciting city she had ever been to, and Shelter Island, to stay with friends of her mother's.

That was when Gabby fell in love. She started plotting then and there to make her way back. After university she knew she couldn't live under her mother's roof, and being a camp counsellor was a perfect stepping stone until she figured out what to do next, and how to stay in the States.

71

When she moved to New York, there were a few dates with dull men. Somewhere in her consciousness Gabby knew she had agreed to go out with them only to prove her mother wrong. 'You re-create what you know,' her mother had once said, gesturing around what even she had begun to call 'the Madhouse'. 'Or,' she'd added, shrugging sceptically, 'you go the other way entirely, but often that happens only after an intervention, years of therapy usually. I wonder,' she'd said, fixing her gaze on Gabby, 'which way will you go?'

'Duh!' Gabby had rolled her eyes. 'I'm up in my bedroom desperately trying to find peace and quiet. I hardly think there's any question about which way I'm going.'

'You say that now –' her mother had smiled knowingly – 'but you're a teenager. Wait until you're out in the world. You're going to be attracted to men who are reminiscent of your parents, whether you like it or not.'

God, no! I love my father, Gabby had thought, but I'd hate to be married to a man so distant. And as for marrying a man anything like my mother . . . She'd shuddered in horror.

The dull men proved her mother wrong. They were more present than her father, and more interested in her. But they were just . . . rather boring. Gabby would be happy to be with them for all of about five minutes, before realizing she could never spend her time with people so unconcerned about any of the things that mattered to her.

'What are you looking for?' other people would ask, curious about this bright-eyed English girl with the curly hair and large smile.

'I'm looking for peace,' she'd always say.

'No!' They'd shake their heads. 'That's not what I meant. I mean, do you want someone tall? Short? How old? Funny? What? What are you looking for?'

'Peace,' she'd say again. 'Someone who makes me feel peaceful.'

Few knew what to say after that.

Elliott was what she was looking for. From the minute he started talking to her, he made her feel peaceful. It was as if she recognized him. There were no violins or halos, no bursting stars or bolts of lightning. It was simply a quiet recognition.

You, she thought. I *know* you.

And it is peace that has been the defining quality of their relationship. Unlike her childhood, when she never felt particularly wanted, or noticed, or happy, or safe, she feels all of these things with Elliott.

They have built a beautiful life together, with beautiful children, a beautiful home.

Why on earth, Gabby thinks, as she closes the front door after the girls have gone to school, would I do anything to screw this up?

What the hell am I thinking, even fantasizing about another man? Even in my head, this isn't okay. Even in my head, this has to stop.

Chapter Eight

But she can't stop thinking about it. In the car, driving to Claire's, she has an imaginary conversation, out loud, in which her fantasy of sleeping with another man has actually become reality, and she is explaining herself to Claire, having confessed to what she has done.

'I wasn't thinking.' Gabby's voice is quiet but clear. 'I didn't think about my husband. I didn't think about anything other than how good it felt to be wanted, how alive I felt knowing that someone, and someone like him, even noticed someone like me.

'Why didn't you stop before you went too far?

'I tried. There was a part of me that kept saying, "Just ten more minutes, just a few more. I'll go home soon." But it was . . . I don't know. Heady. It was like taking drugs. I was high, and I just wanted the high to keep going.

'And if Elliott ever finds out?

'He can't ever find out. It would kill him. It would kill us. This is a secret I'm taking to my grave.'

Gabby exhales loudly, sighing as she climbs out of the car and pushes open the gate to Claire's house. Thank God I didn't do anything, she thinks. Now I just have to get the whole bloody thing out of my head.

'Are you ready?' she calls through the front door, not bothering to knock. 'I'm waiting in the car.'

Claire bounds out seconds later, giving Gabby a quick hug. 'Was it my imagination or were you just sitting in the car outside my house talking to yourself?'

Gabby flushes. 'Oh God. I can't believe you saw that.'

'You were! Gabs! That's hilarious. So, what were you talking about? Anything good? You looked pretty intense.'

Gabby sinks her head into her hands in shame. 'I can't believe I got caught,' she mumbles, before looking at Claire. 'It's just something I do sometimes to clear my thoughts. I treat myself as my own therapist.'

'O-kay.' Claire laughs. 'So how's that working out for you?'

'Surprisingly well.' Gabby turns the engine on, and laughs too.

'I do have an amazing therapist if you need one. I've told you this a million times, but if you ever do need someone to talk to I could totally get you in, and you'd love her.'

'And I've told you a million times: no therapists.' Gabby shudders. 'Only the one in my head. I've still got all this mother stuff to get over. The poor woman put me off for life.'

'Yes, well, not all of them are crazy.'

'I know that. But my mother is. And I just can't go there. I love that you keep offering, though. I just hope that things are never desperate enough for me to want to take you up on it. What are you having done at the doctor today? You're not having a scan yet, are you? Isn't it too early?'

'Just a check-up. They'll do a blood test to confirm everything. Thank you so much for driving, Gabs. I feel kind of jittery, what with my age. I know it's too soon to get excited, and the risks are huge, but it's all I'm thinking about. I couldn't sleep last night so I went online and started reading up about pregnancies in women our age. It's pretty scary, but I have this really strong belief that everything's going to be okay. Is that weird? Or wrong? I'm just so sure that this is supposed to be, and that I won't have anything to worry about. Do you think everyone feels this way, even when it doesn't turn out to be the case?'

'I don't know,' Gabby says. 'But I absolutely believe positive thinking can change the world. And the IVF wouldn't have worked if you weren't supposed to have this child – that much I'm sure of.'

'I know,' Claire says. 'I'm one of the lucky ones. It was such hell when we were going through it, and we so nearly gave up. This was our last shot and it worked. Can you believe it?'

No, thinks Gabby sadly. She can't.

Claire turns her head slightly to watch the streets flash by outside the car window, before speaking, as if reading Gabby's mind. 'You always said you wanted another child. You're younger than me; you could still do it. Imagine if you and I were pregnant together! It would be so much easier if I had someone my age going through it.'

'I can't,' Gabby says quietly. 'I wish I could. I wanted it so badly, but it just isn't meant to be.'

'Who knows?' Claire turns back to her with a smile. 'Accidents can happen. And there's always IVF.'

'Not when your husband's had a vasectomy.'

Claire's eyes open wide. 'Elliott had a vasectomy? Oh God. I had no idea. And you were okay with that?'

Gabby pauses before answering. She wasn't okay with it then, and she isn't okay with it now. But there is nothing she can do about it, and the best she can hope for is to learn to accept it.

'It is what it is,' she says lightly, ignoring the pain that wraps itself around her heart.

In the waiting room, Gabby flicks through *Parenting* magazine, not taking any of it in – she has moved so far away from babies, and toddlers, and micro-managing her children's lives in a bid to be the best mother, produce the best children.

How different she would be now, she thinks sadly. How much better, in so many respects.

Her phone buzzes. A text from Elliott:

> Just telling my wife
> how much I love her . . .

She smiles and texts back:

Love you more

xxx

Instead of putting her phone away in her bag again she decides to play a game of Words with Friends, and just as she does so a black strip appears at the top of her screen announcing she has received an email.

From: Matt@fourforesight.com

Her heart jumps with excitement as she scans the message and she is unaware of the delighted smile now stretching from ear to ear.

To: Gabby
Subject: To be continued . . .

Gabby – what an unexpected and truly great surprise it was to meet you the other day. You turned a boring business trip into what felt like a much-needed, fun-filled break. Every time I think of your sparkling green eyes I start to smile – we could all do with more friends who make us feel like that. I hope your husband made it home safely and had fun with your girls.

Life here in Malibu is as dull as ever – sand, sun, surf. It's good to be home, although I always find myself yearning for the changing seasons when I've been to New England. I should have brought back a bag of white and pink blossom to put in a bowl on the table – it might have done the trick.

As it stands, I have to come back in a couple of weeks,
and was hoping we could grab another drink.

Take care.
M x

Gabby's face lights up as she reads, rereads, rereads
again. Is he flirting? What does this mean? No. Impossible. He says quite specifically he could do with more
friends . . . but . . . 'sparkling green eyes'? Who says
that if they're not interested? Gabby! She sits up
straight, shaking her head. What are you doing? You're
married. There's nothing inappropriate in this email,
yet it feels . . . inviting. Exciting.

She reads it again, not noticing Claire until she is
standing right in front of her.

'What on earth are you reading?' says Claire. 'You
look like you're about to explode with joy.'

'Oh. Nothing,' Gabby says. 'Just an email from a
friend.'

'Really? Because you look like you've won the
lottery.'

'I'm fine.' Gabby puts her phone away. 'So tell me,
how was it? What did the doctor say?'

It is hard to concentrate on the way home. Gabby finds
her thoughts drifting back to the email as Claire talks;
she desperately wants to reach into her bag and read it
again.

She drops Claire off, declining to come in for coffee, before driving straight home, where she can read the email in solitude.

Dear Matt,

She stops typing then goes back to delete it. Not dear. He isn't dear. *She* wasn't dear.

Matt – what a lovely surprise to receive your email. I'm glad you got home safely and I know what you mean about the seasons here. California is a place I sometimes dream about, but I couldn't live without the spring and the fall.

Of all the seasons, fall is my favourite. I'm picturing it now: the leaves turning all those vibrant colours, the trees with their red and orange blankets spread on the grass beneath them. And after the hot summer days I always look forward to feeling a chill in the air, because nothing's better than lighting fires. I'm always up early, and usually downstairs with a fire lit by seven. Sometimes six. We go through wood.

No. She deletes it.

I go through wood like crazy from October onwards. I also turn into something of a sloth – I could curl up on the sofa with books for the rest of my life.

But having said all that, spring is wonderful too. There's a freshness after the winter months and with all the new growth everything is bright and colourful. I'm looking out of the window now at a huge old dogwood tree whose canopy spreads over the entire front yard, and it is a rich mass of deep-pink blossom. It is really quite beautiful. If I knew your address, I'd send you some . . .

How exciting that you're coming back, and the blossom will still be glorious in two weeks.

She pauses. She should invite him over for dinner, have him meet Elliott? Isn't that the way to have a proper friendship?

Does she, in fact, want a friendship? Isn't she the one who always said that once you are married you do not get to make new friends of the opposite sex? Ever. You are allowed to befriend other couples, and if you get on particularly well with the husband that is allowed, but single members of the opposite sex?

No. It's just not done.

But why not? Why should she not have a new friend? He's by far the most interesting and glamorous person she's met in ages. Elliott would be fascinated by him, even though she doesn't yet want them to meet. Matt met her on her own, and this friendship has to develop on that basis before she is ready to reveal her true self.

She doesn't want him to see her as a wife, a mother, a middle-aged housewife. For just a little while longer she wants to keep the illusion going that she is, as he thinks, clever and strong, with sparkling green eyes.

My schedule's so crazy, I don't know if I'll be able to get away for a drink, but if I can I definitely will. It would be fun.

She takes a deep breath.

> Just as long as you promise not to get me drunk and take
> advantage of me . . . :)
>
> Gabby x

One kiss. That's enough. That wasn't flirtatious, was it? Maybe just the tiniest bit, but, well, Gabby's only having fun. It isn't as if she's going to actually *do* anything – she isn't the slightest bit interested in actually doing anything – but what fun to play at being the sort of woman that men, other than their husband, want. What would be the harm?

Two emails arrive, back to back, three minutes later. The first:

> 33624 Malibu Cove Colony Drive, Malibu, CA. 90265. xxx

The second:

> I can't promise anything of the sort . . . ;)

With a spring in her step, Gabby grabs a Ziploc bag and runs out to the front garden, grinning as she stuffs the bag full with the most perfect dogwood blooms. Sealing it up, she slips the Ziploc into an envelope, scribbles Matt's address on the front, then jumps in the car to drive over to the post office, feeling younger than she has in years.

After handing in the envelope at the counter, Gabby walks out, checking her email, hoping there might be an additional response. She holds the phone in her hand for the rest of the day, glancing at it every few minutes, wanting to feel the exhilaration she felt earlier, when she first saw his lovely, and unexpected, email.

By nine fifteen, sitting on the sofa with her family to watch television, present in body but a million miles away in her head, she starts to feel depressed, berating herself for being so ridiculous, for acting like a lovelorn teenager when she is a forty-three-year-old married mother of two.

'Mom? Mom? Mom!' She breaks out of her reverie to see three sets of eyes staring at her.

'Hmm?' She is still worlds away.

'What's the matter with you?' Olivia's voice is filled with teenage disdain. As she tilts her head, her dark hair tumbling over her shoulder, her full lips in a pout, Gabby sees, suddenly, the beauty she is becoming.

'Nothing.' She smiles. 'Sorry. Just thinking about everything I have to do.'

'Can you take me to Benefit tomorrow? I need some make-up,' Olivia says.

'Benefit?' Gabby blurts out. 'What's wrong with CVS?'

Olivia gives her a withering look. 'At seventeen? I need the good stuff for my skin now.'

'I go to CVS!' pipes up Alanna.

'For make-up?' Gabby looks at her eleven-year-old in horror.

Alanna shrugs. 'Just mascara. And maybe lip gloss.'

'First of all, no,' Gabby says to Alanna. 'You shouldn't be wearing any make-up at this age, and Olivia, I don't know about Benefit. That stuff's expensive. Can't we please just go to CVS?'

'No!' Olivia says. 'Everyone goes to Benefit, and I can't wear the stuff from CVS any more. It gives me allergies.'

Gabby looks at her sceptically. 'Since when?'

Olivia doesn't break eye contact. 'Since it started giving me allergies.'

'Well, what do you need? Maybe we can go to Benefit, but it depends how much you need. I don't mind buying one or two things.'

'Thank you, Mom!' Olivia leans over and plants a kiss on Gabby's cheek. They both know they will be walking out of the store with a bag filled with make-up. Olivia is delighted she will get her way; Gabby is happy not to have a fight on her hands and can go back to thinking about Matt.

The more she thinks, the more humiliated she becomes. She wishes she hadn't sent the blossom, wishes she wasn't sitting here feeling stupid for having done so, wishes she hadn't responded to anything, and certainly not with the overt flirtation she now deeply regrets.

'I'm going to bed.' Gabby leans over to kiss Elliott, then the girls, all transfixed by *The Voice*.

'Stay!' Elliott says. 'You always watch this with us.'

She stands up. 'Not tonight. I'm tired. I'm going up to read.'

Her book manages to take her mind off the lack of response, although she allows herself another read of his emails before she switches off the light. Perhaps it is her turn to write back, she thinks suddenly, making sense of his silence throughout the afternoon. Perhaps that's what he's waiting for?

But no. She can't. Stop this, she tells herself. You are a grown-up getting yourself worked into a state over a man you don't care about. If you're getting attached to some outcome here, it's you that's doing it, not him. This is ridiculous, and I'm not going to respond any more.

Feeling much better, she switches off the light, curls up and goes to sleep.

At 2.34 a.m., Gabby wakes up. Next to her, Elliott lies on his back, snoring loudly.

'Ssssh,' she says loudly, close to his ear. He doesn't move. 'Elliott, you're snoring,' she says, pushing him so that he rolls over gently, still fast asleep.

Gabby slides her iPhone off the nightstand and scrolls through her emails. Junk, mostly. And one from Matt.

Her heart pounds as she creeps out of bed and into the bathroom, refusing to read the email until she is alone and safe; it is a treat she wants to savour.

Ms Sloth – I love the picture of you curling up on the sofa in the fall. And your description of spring makes me long to be there – I'm going to have to start marking off the days.
I went surfing today, which is the greatest advantage of living here. I'm attaching a picture taken with a group of my surf friends. Surfing, to me, is the greatest feeling in the world. You can probably tell by my smile that the waves were awesome today. So however much I miss the changing seasons, take me away from the water for any length of time and I suspect I'd die.

An ex-girlfriend of mine was just like you. She loved winter, and warmth, and just didn't understand surfing. No surprise why that relationship didn't work out – although had she had sparkling green eyes, things might have ended differently . . . who knows :)

I must stop flirting with you! I'm sorry, I know it's inappropriate. You just make me smile.

M x

Matt, or as I now think of you, Surf Dude – um . . . your friends look great but . . . wow. It was hard to focus on them when . . . I mean . . . good LORD! Well, thank you for sending me a half-naked picture of you with a surfboard and a tan – I'll say this for you: you definitely know how to brighten up the day of a middle-aged housewife. I'm tempted to print it out and put it on the fridge – you'd be next to the calendar of the local firefighters, and you'd definitely give them a run for their money – but then I might have some explaining to do . . .

I have no idea why I'm awake in the middle of the night. It seems to be the curse of middle age (I know, I know, I'll shut up about it in a minute), but no one I know sleeps any more. Oh, all the men do – they're sleeping like babies, but all us women are up at 2.46 writing emails and reading the *Huffington Post*.

I should really get up – there's so much I could get done, but bed is so warm and cosy that I'm quite happy lying there, just letting my mind play havoc and losing myself in fantasies . . .

Oh no. I think I'm giving away all my innermost secrets. I'm supposed to let you think I'm super-fit and healthy, and interested in all sports, especially surfing, and instead I'm revealing that I'm happiest curled up either on the sofa or in my bed. It's pathetic. I don't know what's happened to me. I used to be filled with energy. When I was even younger than you (I know how patronizing that sounds and I'm sorry, but bear with me) I wasn't surfing, but I was skiing, and ice-skating, and in summer I'd go hiking all the time. I got completely addicted to spinning, for about five minutes, but it was a pretty intense and happy five minutes.

The last couple of years have been . . . harder. It used to be that my husband was paid a decent salary and was able to be home tons, but now his salary has been cut, and, in order to make anything like he used to, he has to work every hour that God sends.

Gabby presses delete and erases that last paragraph in its entirety.

I keep thinking that one day I'll wake up and feel alive again, instead of sleepwalking through my life, but I'm still waiting . . . Maybe I should take up surfing?

Sorry to be on a downer. Clearly I need more sleep . . . Am off to try to trick my brain into thinking it's tired.

Big hug,
Ms Sloth xo

P. S. I didn't even realize you were flirting! Keep calm and carry on . . .

Oh Ms Sloth – you sent me a package of spring! Thank you for the blossom that arrived today. Now I can't wait until I'm back on the east coast.

I wish I was there now and could give you a big hug and make you feel better. The only thing I know for certain is that everything passes. The good times, the bad times . . . not that these are bad times, but if you're feeling down it will pass.

Did I ever tell you, by the way, how much I love your accent? I've always wanted to go to London but the timing's never been right. I think you said that's where you're from. Do you miss it?

If I plan a trip, you'll have to tell me all the places to see and things to do. One of the things I hate is seeing anywhere as a tourist – I always try to go with contacts ready so I can see the real city, rather than the tourist version.

I want to know what the locals do, where they eat, what bars they go to. Even writing this now is getting me excited – I'm thinking London needs to be next on my list.

And now I have to be serious with you. Listen very carefully. YOU ARE NOT A MIDDLE-AGED HOUSEWIFE. God, woman. Will you listen to yourself? You're gorgeous! I don't want to hear those words from you ever again. Seriously. You're doing yourself a massive disservice every time you think those words, and I can tell you think them all the time, which is nuts.

So, I am sending you a sandy hug from Malibu – I hope the blues go flying out through the window . . .

SD x

SD – the blues did indeed fly out through the window and I have started sleeping extremely well. You obviously have the magic touch. And I have to say I've been feeling better the last few days than I have done in years. I'm also mortified about revealing quite so much to a relative stranger on email. I'm truly sorry, and I promise to keep things light from here on.

You asked if I miss London. I never miss it when I'm here. My life is here, my friends, my family, although, obviously, my parents are still in London, but I have always felt as at home here as I felt over there. Often more so. But I have to be honest: whenever we visit, and as soon as I touch down at Heathrow, I start to feel desperately homesick. That's when I realize I've missed the cabbies that start chatting to you about politics the moment you get in the cab; I've missed the café culture – sitting around for hours drinking cappuccinos and putting the world to rights. I've missed Europe – hopping over to France or Italy for the weekend, mixing with other cosmopolitan people who have travelled, seen the world, are interested in everything around them.

But there are pros and cons to everything. It's shockingly expensive, and I suspect I couldn't raise my kids there even if I wanted to. The British love children as long as they're basically seen and not heard, and I can't imagine my very American children going down too well – they're much too loud and opinionated.

Actually, that's not strictly true. Olivia, the elder, has always been loud and opinionated, and as stubborn as an elephant. Alanna was always my baby, and so easy, but she's at that awkward age when the social pressures of school are starting to get to her, and she's becoming more and more moody by the day.

Despite all that, and particularly despite missing the days when they were tiny – how easy it was and how lovely they were – I wouldn't change a thing.

One of the things I have always adored about this country is how easy it is to live here, especially with children. You can park everywhere, take them anywhere. So many places to go, things to do. We live an hour outside of New York City in a town that has fantastic beaches and a municipal country club! What's not to love?

I guess, if I had to pick one thing I miss, it's the sophistica-tion of Europe. I miss the culture. It's so easy to get lazy living in a small suburban town, and I worry I've become very lazy. Why go anywhere else when you have everything you need on your doorstep, and that doorstep is so pretty?

So . . . changing tack entirely. You mentioned an ex-girlfriend. I imagine you're extremely busy playing the field – a different girl in every port, and probably more than one, you charmer, you!

Miss Sloth xo

My dearest Ms Sloth – apologies for not replying sooner, but work was just crazy for a while.

Anyway, to pick up the thread, how very wrong you are about a different girl in every port. I will admit that I'm not exactly a hermit, and yes, I certainly do manage to go out and party quite a bit, and yes, I'll also admit that I like women. A lot. But as much as I like having fun, there's a part of me that would love to settle down.

In many ways, dating was much easier before we set up the company and it grew into the business it is now. When I was just 'Matt', I never had to question people's motives in wanting to befriend me, or flirt with me. The hardest thing about having any kind of public profile is that suddenly everyone knows who you are. You find yourself surrounded by people, and yes, by people I mean women, and they're fun, and gorgeous, and all over you, but there's this part of your brain that's always asking: are they with me for 'me', or because of who I am, because they think I have power, or money, or whatever?

During the last year there were times when I started to think very seriously about settling down. I come from a big family – I have four brothers and sisters, and I'm the only one not married. My mom keeps hinting that she'd love grandchildren, and I have to say that when I'm around friends with kids, I start wondering if I might be getting closer . . .

What are your girls like? How old are they? I bet you're an amazing mother. I see you as being really fun, but probably quite strict. I have a great friend here, Eleanor, who's English, and she's really stern with her kids, but they all adore her. They also all have the greatest manners of any kids I know. They actually shake hands and look you in the eye, and always say please and thank you. I've asked Eleanor if she might consider having my kids, because when I have them I want them to be exactly like hers, but she said her husband wouldn't be too happy.

You apologized for revealing so much to a relative stranger. The weird thing is, you don't feel like a stranger. I know we hardly know each other, but you feel like a really close friend. In fact, I don't think I've revealed this much of myself to anyone before. I have no idea why that is – you're just really easy to 'talk' to. When I read your emails I can picture you talking, and it makes me happy. I like having a new best friend on email. I like even more that I get to see you in just a few days . . .

SD x

SD – isn't it amazing how quickly the time is flying by? But, rest assured, I have no ulterior motive. Well, I may insist the Martinis are on you, but that's as far as it goes. Luckily for all of us, I'm married, so you're safe from my evil advances and plans to kill you off and steal all your money.

I do understand how hard it must be. A boy I knew from schooldays has become a world-famous actor. I haven't seen him for years, but we have a really good mutual friend, and apparently he only fraternizes with people he's known for ever, or with other famous people who understand what it's like. And he also says he resents how distrustful he's become, but he's been burned too many times. Years ago some young tart he had a thing with sold her story to the Sunday papers, and he just retreated after that.

I like what you said about children. It seems I misjudged you, my Surf Dude friend, and thank you for saying such nice things about what you think I must be like as a mother. My children would disagree entirely! In truth, I do adore being a mother, but it isn't, as it seems to be for so many of the women around here, the be-all and end-all. I love my children, but I don't need, nor do I want, to be involved in every aspect of their lives. There's a woman in town, Trish, who has a hugely successful business and yet she manages to be at the school pretty much every day. I have no idea what she's doing there, but she volunteers for everything, and if there's nothing on offer she'll just show up with a tray of cupcakes and a large smile.

It makes me furious! Bitch that I am! I am firmly of the belief that what your children do at school is in the hands of the school. There are so many women here who are defined solely by their children; they're women who don't even exist in their own right any more because they see themselves only as X's mom. I've always done stuff outside of motherhood, even though I haven't had a 'job' for years. Amongst other things, I restore furniture, and paint, and can make pretty much anything if you give me a workbench and a jigsaw.

Oh, the things you're learning about me! Nothing quite as sexy as a woman with a hammer. Kidding! But I am reaching the point where I've actually started to want to do something. For years I've talked about not being defined by my kids, by motherhood, but now I'm feeling that I need a job. And it's more than want . . . it is NEED. The truth is, I always thought I was going to have another child. I just never felt done, and even though the window of opportunity was narrowing, I kept thinking it would happen. But what's become very clear over the last six months is that there will be no more babies in my future, and that dream has left me with an emptiness inside that needs to be filled somehow.

I need something to fill my mind, something to keep me busy. I've thought about turning my hobby into a bigger project, a business – I have sold restored pieces to friends over the years, and Claire, who's my closest friend, has always said I should open some kind of a store. We have a barn on our property and I turned half of it into a workshop, so that's where I work, and she thinks I should open it as a store. I love the idea, but get a little overwhelmed when I think of all I'd have to do.

94

But I do know I need to fill the void.

Counting the days until I see you!

Ms Sloth xo

Ms Sloth – it isn't lucky you're married. I'd say it's hugely unlucky. For me. ;)

Also, I beg to differ about a woman with a hammer . . .

And finally, I know you have no ulterior motive. That's why I like you. I'm leaving now for the airport. I wish I didn't have so many meetings before I see you, but I'll email when I land!

M x

Chapter Nine

Gabby is not a woman who particularly enjoys shopping. Most of her clothes are bought online; when forced to buy in person she is most likely to run to Main Street for stretch trousers and some long-sleeved T-shirts from Gap, rarely anything more sophisticated. Dressing up has never been very interesting to her.

When she was young and growing up in London, she would watch movies about American teenagers and long to wear the clothes they wore. She wanted faded jeans and Converse trainers, baseball shirts and topsiders.

She was something of a tomboy back then, and even now, if she isn't in clogs or Merrells, she is most likely to be in her Converse trainers, although she will team them with yoga pants and a cute hoodie.

She pulls her curls back into a ponytail and jumps in the car, actually looking forward to shopping, hoping she will find the outfit she's looking for, because she has one in mind. She knows exactly what she wants to project: rumpled, sexy, confident − a woman who is fully aware of the power she holds.

Leggings and boots made of the softest leather, ones that reach up to her knees, maybe over. The long, sky-blue, sheer alpaca sweater she noticed in the window of Great Stuff, with the great charm necklace they paired with it, and the fine cashmere scarf in the same colour, twisted loosely round the neck.

That's what she wants to wear when she meets Matt for a drink this week. Nothing suggestive. She certainly doesn't want to be provocative – but how lovely it is to be noticed, to be flirted with. This is an outfit that Gabby has carefully put together in her mind, hoping it will be beautiful and sexy, without shouting anything, without sending any messages to Matt that she is interested in anything other than a friendship.

Not that she hasn't imagined something happening, but she has thought it only a handful of times, and is trying very hard to stop. She knows this is an indulgence, a fantasy. This isn't what their correspondence is about, and even if there may be chemistry between them, that doesn't mean anything.

Gabby thinks of all the times she and her friends have discussed people who have been caught having affairs. None of them have ever understood it. Just because you're married doesn't mean you'll never be attracted to anyone else, Gabby has always said. But the point is that you have a choice, and you should choose to do the right thing; you shouldn't act on your attraction.

She still believes those words to be true, but when she was discussing this with her friends she hadn't ever been attracted to anyone else. It is very easy to say things like that when temptation has never crossed your path.

Temptation is crossing her path now. She absolutely wants to believe she won't do anything; she is telling herself over and over that they are just friends. But if he were to lean over and kiss her, she honestly doesn't know if she would have the strength to resist.

In her mind, she pushes him away. But not before she feels his lips, his tongue, holds his top lip between her own. She will push him back gently while shaking her head. 'No,' she will say, regret and desire etched on her face. 'We can't. I'm married. I love my husband.'

He will understand, and let her go, knowing that he may have lost the one woman who could make him happy. They will resolve not to stay in touch, and Gabby will be weighed down with sadness for a few days; but then she will be buoyed by the rightness of her decision and fall in love with Elliott all over again.

Where is Elliott in all this? He doesn't feature much. Her thoughts have been wholly and all-consumingly filled with Matt. She wakes up in the night with his name on her lips, and carries her mobile phone with her all day, glancing at the screen every few minutes to see if there is a new message.

Elliott is accusing her of daydreaming all the time. And it is true – she may be going through the motions but she is not present in her life. Half the time she has a dreamy smile on her lips which, when asked, she will put down to thinking about a funny TV show, or something that the girls said (and she is getting used to having stories ready); the rest of the time she is trying not to feel blue that six hours, twelve, eighteen, have gone by and still Matt hasn't responded. She will feel embarrassed, and angry, will vow not to respond to his next email, but then it will arrive, and it will be so lovely that she will stop whatever she is doing to find a quiet corner so that she can send him back her innermost thoughts.

Gabby pulls into a spot behind Main Street, then cuts through Gap, not glancing around today, but going straight to the shoe store. The boots have no heel, but are beautifully cut, narrow, made of Italian leather. She pulls them on then tucks her yoga pants into them as she studies herself in the mirror, a smile on her face.

This morning she told Elliott she was thinking of going shopping. Because she is so bad at it, because she dislikes it so much, on those rare occasions she announces she is going to spend some money Elliott always encourages her.

'What are you looking for?' Elliott asked, watching her as she pulled off her robe to get dressed.

Gabby shrugged. 'I just feel like all I wear is jeans or leggings. I have no idea why I grew up to be a teenage boy, but I feel like I need some more feminine clothes. I saw a sweater on Main Street that I'm slightly obsessing about, and I thought I might get some new knee-high boots.'

Elliott's face lit up. 'Mmm, sexy!' He pulled Gabby over, murmuring in pleasure as he held her naked body close.

'Oh stop.' Gabby stepped back, laughing.

'Why stop?' Elliott said, moving back in, but Gabby's smile disappeared.

'I'm serious, Ell. I have a ton to do. I need to get dressed.'

Elliott put up his hands. 'Okay, okay. Sorry. Forgive me.'

Gabby got dressed quickly and silently, not looking at Elliott again. There were times of late when he had been getting on her nerves, and she found herself snapping at him far more than she would like.

She knows her hormones are raging, and does plan to see a doctor, an endocrinologist, someone to help, but life is always so busy, and tomorrow never comes. And so she is left to take it out on her husband. She is filled with remorse afterwards and tries to make it up to him, only to find she is still irritated.

Gabby is not stupid. She knows this is her resentment at his decision to have the vasectomy, a resentment that is choosing to come out now because she is projecting perfection onto an alternative man. Which doesn't mean it isn't real. This is the resentment she has been trying to push down so hard for so many months; but it is refusing to disappear and is instead growing stronger.

In the store she tries on the sweater. It is even better than she had imagined. The girls in the store crowd round to compliment her, layering on jewellery, scarves, a shearling vest, then running to the other side of the store and coming back with trousers and another wonderful sweater that would look perfect on her.

She leaves with three large bags, and walks straight into Claire on the street outside.

'What are you doing here?' Claire looks at her bags, aghast. 'Am I sleepwalking? I'm looking at three bags of clothes from my favourite store, and you hate shopping. Actually, you hate clothes.'

'I know! Can you believe it?' Gabby laughs. 'Elliott gave me permission to feminize my wardrobe, so what's a girl to do? I had to take him up on it.'

'Great. You finally decide you want to be a girl, and I can't even enjoy it with you.' She proffers her own bag. 'A Pea in the Pod. That's all I've got to look forward to.'

Gabby grins. 'Want to grab a coffee?'

'Only if it's decaf. So what's up with you recently? You look all glowing. If I didn't know better I'd say you were pregnant.'

'Sadly not. Must be the menopause,' Gabby says. 'Haven't you ever heard of the menopausal glow? No? Me neither. I think it's just that life is going well. I feel . . . happy. You know how you always said you loved being in your forties because you felt truly comfortable in your skin, that you didn't need to prove yourself to anyone any more? Well, I get that. I do. I've just suddenly found myself feeling really good.'

'That's great. I remember a couple of months ago you were saying you felt really middle-aged. It's great you're feeling better. Is this what the whole makeover's about?'

'Makeover?'

'Your grey hair has disappeared, and you're spending fortunes. If I didn't know better,' Claire peers at her as they stand in line in Starbucks, 'I'd think you were having an affair.'

'Oh ha ha.' Gabby rolls her eyes. 'Yes. I am having an affair, for I am exactly the type. In fact, I'm having three affairs, all at the same time. Why do you think I had to cover the grey hair? It was the only way I could attract all three gorgeous lovers.'

Gabby may not be having an affair, but she is planning to have a drink with a man who isn't her husband. She has no idea what to say, how to explain it to Elliott. It occurred to her that she could orchestrate another girls' night out, and – coincidence! – the same man would be at the bar and the two of them could, as they had before, spend the evening talking together.

This time her friends would grow suspicious. Who even knows if Gabby and Matt would be left alone? She doesn't want to lie to Elliott. A lie, however small, feels like the beginning of a slippery slope, but how can she possibly explain it? Should she tell the truth, couched in a white lie, so she will still be able to live with herself?

'Are you sure you don't mind?' Gabby now feels guilty at buying so much, even though Elliott is delighted with her new wardrobe.

'Are you kidding? Gabby, you look amazing! I feel

like I have a new wife! I had no idea you were this sexy, honey!'

'Great,' she grumbles. 'Thanks a lot.'

'Gabs, you know what I mean. Everything you bought looks incredible on you. Usually you wear such shapeless clothes no one can even see your figure – you know that. But everything you bought just shows it off. You are seriously hot.'

'I've lost a few pounds.' Gabby turns to look at her side view in the closet mirror. 'I kind of needed these trousers because the ones I have are swimming on me.'

'I can see,' Elliott says approvingly. 'Not that you needed to lose anything, but it suits you. How much have you lost?'

'About six pounds,' Gabby says. 'I wasn't even trying. I just haven't been hungry.'

Elliott looks down at his own stomach; he is more cuddly than ever before. 'I wish I knew what that felt like,' he says. 'Oh well. At least there's more of me to love.'

Gabby, looking at him, feels a surge of love. 'The more of you to love, the better.' She leans down and kisses him before sitting on his lap and sliding her arms up round his neck. 'Anyway, you're still as gorgeous as the day we met.'

He laughs. 'Liar.'

'Oh! Guess what!' She stands up and starts to undress, carefully folding the scarf. 'You know that Fourforesight website I joined?'

'No.'

'It's another social media thing.'

'I know that, but I didn't know you joined it.' Elliott shakes his head. 'Isn't that like a Facebook for hipsters? You and the girls with all this stuff – I don't know how you find the time. What was your last obsession? Pinterest?'

'Yes. Over it. This one's the new one, and they contacted me and asked if I wanted to take part in a study, a focus group. Isn't that exciting! The guy who started it is flying around meeting people and talking to them about the website and what changes they'd like to see!'

'Okay,' Elliott says, and shrugs. 'If you say it's exciting then I'm excited for you.'

'Well, I am excited. I feel like I could be part of a huge change. So it's Wednesday night. I have to go to some hotel in Stamford.'

'Sounds great. Just make sure you wear some of these new clothes – you want them to think you're a hot mommy, right?'

'You'd better believe it.' Gabby's smile is large as she turns to slide the scarf onto a shelf.

Chapter Ten

As Gabby walks through the lobby of the hotel she is conscious that each of the three men sitting or standing around by the front door is following her with his eyes. She isn't so much walking, as sailing, an assured smile on her face as she takes long strides, her new boots click-clacking on the marble floor, her hips swaying, her hair, styled into soft sexy waves instead of the more usual unruly curls, bouncing gently on her shoulders.

She has a quality tonight that is more than mere beauty. It is clear to anyone watching that this is a woman well aware of how powerful, sexy, gorgeous she is, who exudes confidence from every pore, and it is this that makes her so compelling.

Gabby walks through to the bar, and stands for a few seconds in the doorway, squinting slightly as she looks around for Matt. She has made sure to be fifteen minutes late, so she won't be the first one here.

And there he is. At one end of the bar. Her heart jumps into her mouth at the exact moment he turns and sees her. As his face lights up, Gabby falters suddenly.

Oh *God*, she thinks. Look how . . . *gorgeous* he is. What

am I *doing* here? What the *hell* am I doing here? I need to leave.

But she doesn't. She walks towards him, the smile on her face matching the smile on his, and they stand for a second or two, grinning at each other, before he extends his arms and wraps them round Gabby, who closes her eyes as he holds her tightly.

This is fine, she thinks. I can do this. We are friends. I'm just going to be chatty and friendly while still retaining my distance. I'm the one in control here and I will not let this stray into territory that might be dangerous.

They sit down at the bar, Matt swivelling his stool so he is facing her, and they look at each other and both start to laugh, Gabby shaking her head and looking away.

'I don't know why I'm laughing,' Matt splutters.

'I don't know either,' Gabby manages to say. 'But I'd love a drink.'

'Coming right up.' He orders before sitting back to gaze at her.

'What?' Gabby is self-conscious. 'Do I have something in my teeth?'

'No. You look great.' She notices his eyes darken as he says this and she knows it means he's aroused. She feels waves of embarrassment, of pleasure, before remembering her manners. 'Thank you. How were your meetings?'

'All good. How's the piece you're working on. Didn't you say it was a desk?'

Gabby smiles. He remembered. She had found a dark wooden desk at the consignment store and had stripped it with the intention of painting it a soft dove grey, replacing the handles with small, black, iron knobs, and thereby reinventing it as a Gustavian-style desk, perfect for the study. 'It's going well,' she says, getting out her phone and scrolling through for pictures.

As she scrolls, she realizes Matt is looking at the screen, at all the evidence of her life, her real life, which she doesn't want him to see. She doesn't want him to see her husband, her children, the signs of a middle-aged housewife – which is what she is, however much he may want to think otherwise. She tilts her screen slightly to prevent him seeing, but it isn't enough.

'Wait! Is that your husband?'

They haven't talked very much about Elliott. Gabby isn't even sure Matt knows his name. It wouldn't feel right to discuss him, nor does she want Matt to see him. 'No,' she lies. 'Just some friends back home.'

'Oh come on, let me see,' he insists.

'No.' She is firm as she lets the phone fall back into her bag. 'Can't find the desk, sorry. Take my word for it, though, that I'm doing an amazing job.'

'I don't doubt it.' Matt raises his glass, dropping the subject. 'Cheers!' he says as Gabby raises hers. 'To us.'

Gabby says nothing as she drinks. Us? To *us*? What us? There is no 'us'. And yet she can't deny a thrill at hearing him say the word, and she can't deny a thrill as her eyes unconsciously move across his body, remembering the picture of him surfing. She can't deny a thrill as he watches her looking at him then gives her a slow, sexy smile that makes her tingle down to her toes.

What am I *doing*? She thinks: I need to leave.

She doesn't. Of course she doesn't. She has another drink.

Their smiles do not fade, each of them is high on the other's company, and it is only as Gabby sips her third drink that she realizes Matt is talking, has been talking for quite some time, and she has no idea what he is saying.

'I'm drunk,' she says suddenly, staring at the glass as she tries to focus, pushing it away and shaking her head as if to clear her thoughts.

Matt raises his eyebrows. 'You haven't had that much.'

'I know. I'm a total lightweight,' she says. 'Drinking on an empty stomach has never been good for me.'

'Or perhaps it's very good for you. Depends which way you look at it.'

Gabby snorts with laughter then looks up at him through her mascaraed eyelashes.

'What? Why are you looking at me like that?'

'Because you,' she says, wagging a finger at him, knowing she has had too much to drink and it is making her bold, knowing she would never dare say this when sober, 'are dangerous.'

Matt sits back, feigning dismay. 'Me? *Me*? *Dangerous*?

I'm not the dangerous one.' Once again, a slow smile spreads across his face. '*You're* the dangerous one.'

'I'm an old married woman,' Gabby protests, able to say these words only because she doesn't feel like an old married woman at all, knows she doesn't look like an old married woman. 'You're the sexy younger man flirting with a woman he can't have.'

'Oh?' Matt sits forward, leaning very close, and as his lips brush her ear a shiver runs through her entire body. 'Are you absolutely sure I'm flirting with a woman I can't have?' His voice is a whisper of desire and Gabby closes her eyes, her whole body on fire, knowing this is too much, this is more than she can handle. His hand is on her knee, and it is as if it is burning through her skin. She can feel him in every bone, every fibre, every tendon of her body, and it is so delicious, so intoxicating, she wants to just sit like this for ever, with his breath brushing her ear, his hand on her leg.

But she is married. To a wonderful man. The thought of Elliott, of his face if he could see them, of his devastation if she was unfaithful, if he ever found out, is sobering.

She opens her eyes to see Matt, his face inches from hers. A few seconds go by as they stare at each other, before Gabby shakes her head.

'Matt, I . . . I can't do this. I'm not the sort of woman . . .' She stops. She doesn't know how to say this. 'I'm married. This feels like too much. I'm sorry.'

'It's fine.' He jumps back, his face filled with apology.

'I didn't want to make you uncomfortable. I'm sorry. It's my fault.'

'Oh, Matt. If I was ten years younger, and single . . .' Her voice tails off.

'You're perfect exactly as you are,' he says. 'You are. Truly.' He gives a wry smile. 'It's my bad luck that when I've found the perfect woman, she's unavailable.'

'We can still be friends,' Gabby says.

'Absolutely,' Matt says. 'Friends.'

He calls Gabby a cab while she mentally kicks herself. She did the right thing, of course she did the right thing, but he is slightly distant now. The playful flirtatiousness, the dangerous edge of earlier has gone, and Gabby would do anything, *anything*, to get it back.

When the cab arrives and Matt has put his arms round her in a perfunctory hug, Gabby steps back, then moves forward again, taking his face gently in her hands. She opens her lips as she kisses him slowly, softly, moving back when she feels his tongue. No tongues. Just . . . teasing. She needs to keep him wanting her. She needs to continue feeling as beautiful as he has made her feel, and if that requires a tiny bit of teasing, so be it.

This time she pulls back to see a smile of delight on his face.

'Friends?' he whispers.

'Friends,' she nods, climbing into the cab, her heart threatening to pound right out of her chest.

*

The girls are fast asleep when she walks in. Olivia sleeps in the dark, her face as soft and peaceful as when she was a baby. Gabby brushes her hair off her face and kisses her on the forehead, then the cheek, then the cheek again. When the girls are asleep, at their most vulnerable, not fighting, not looking at her with disdain, not being the vocal, confident children they are, she is reminded of their innocence and she feels herself falling in love with them all over again, every night.

Alanna's light is on, her iTouch still clutched in her hand. Gabby hesitates, then prises it out and clicks the screen on. Sometime in the last six weeks Alanna set up an Instagram account, and Gabby, not allowed to look under normal circumstances, could perhaps find out more about what's going on.

But the iTouch is now password-protected, and nothing Gabby can think of will work. With a sigh, and after several kisses on the forehead and cheek of her younger daughter, she turns off the light and moves quietly down the hallway to her own bedroom.

The television is on when she walks in, Elliott illuminated by the bluish light of *Homeland*. His mouth is open as he snores gently, the covers mussed up around his legs, his T-shirt ridden up to expose the rounded belly she has always loved so much.

And suddenly Gabby feels like crying. The familiarity, the comfort in seeing Elliott, the relief at having come so close to doing something so terrible – and she did come close, as close as she has ever come – all makes her eyes prick with tears.

Kicking off her boots she snuggles into Elliott's side, wanting to smell him, feel him, wanting the safety of her husband to somehow negate the danger of the evening. She nuzzles into his neck just as he stirs.

'Oh – hey! What time is it?'

'Eleven-ish. I just got back.'

'It must have been fun.' Elliott pushes himself up on the pillows and smiles at his wife. 'Did they think you were a total hot mommy?'

'You know what?' She is coquettish. 'I think he did. This kid, Matt, who started the website, definitely seemed to think I was a MILF.'

'He's clearly a man of excellent taste.' Elliott grins, tracing a hand lazily along the neck of her sweater then moving down to the waistband of her trousers, before pulling her towards him.

As they kiss Gabby helps him ease off her sweater and trousers, and draws his T-shirt over his head.

'Did you lock the door?' he whispers, reaching for the remote and turning off the television.

'No. Hang on.' She jumps off the bed and comes back seconds later, rolling on top of him. His fingers are between her legs, her own stroking him to hardness as she closes her eyes, and once again – please let this be the last time – imagines that it is not her familiar, loved, teddy bear of a husband beneath her, but a hard-bodied, virile, unbelievably sexy thirty-something.

It is Matt's fingers she feels inside her, Matt's body she moves her lips down until she takes him in her mouth, and she is more active, more energetic, more turned-on than she has been in years.

Afterwards, Elliott cradles her in his arms and laughs. 'What got into you tonight? You were amazing.'

'Isn't that how MILFs are supposed to show their husbands the love?'

'I don't know, but I sure as hell hope so,' he says, and laughs again, turning the television back on. Within five minutes, he is gently snoring, leaving Gabby to replay every single thing that happened tonight, or, rather, every single thing that happened before she came home.

Chapter Eleven

Gabby doesn't realize how obsessed she has become until the emails stop coming.

She waits, all morning, for Matt to send one of his customary emails, determining he should be the one to make the first move, not her; but by lunchtime she is worried. Everything changed when she said no. Why did she say no? Why did she not keep it going for just a while longer?

At two o'clock she can't take it any more. She can't focus on anything, and with a shaking hand she sends him a text, attempting to keep it light, fun; attempting to stay in the spirit of their correspondence before last night.

But she is careful not to assume that the intimacy that existed between them is still there, not until she is reassured that he feels the same way. No 'Surf Dude' today, no easy jokes. She needs to wait to see where she stands.

> Matt, just wanted to
> thank you for a wonderful evening.
> Hope your meetings go well.
> Speak soon . . .

Delete.

Much too formal.

> Dear Matt,
> great evening! Thank you!
> Let's do it again!

Delete.

> M – A delicious, dangerous
> night. Thank you. xx

Send.

'Hi, Liv.' Gabby comes into the kitchen just after Olivia, who caught the bus home, has walked through the back door. 'How was school?'

She doesn't know why she asks this question. Every day, when the girls get home, Gabby has a need to ask them how school was. Perhaps, she reasons, this is because she was never asked. Somehow this has become cemented in her head as being symbolic of what kind of a mother you are: a good mother, an interested mother, always asks how your day was.

Alanna usually says fine, even when Gabby can see the day hasn't been fine. She is quiet these days, frequently going straight upstairs to do her homework, rather than sit at the kitchen table, as she has always done.

Even when her teen and tween both grunt in response, Gabby has to ask the question. There are other things she tries to do in order to be a good mother: freshly baked cakes sit on the cake stand for when her children get home, although Olivia announced lately that she is on a diet and will not eat anything with sugar or flour in it. Still, there is something about a kitchen that smells of cinnamon and sugar and caramelizing butter that is homely, that makes their house what Gabby thinks a home should be like.

Olivia duly grunts in answer to Gabby's question before dumping her backpack in the middle of the floor and opening the fridge, peering in at the shelves.

'There's nothing for me to eat,' she says belligerently, and Gabby slides her out of the way to point out the cheese, the yoghurts, the fruit.

'I don't want fruit.'

'So have a yoghurt.'

'I don't eat yoghurt. I'm vegan.'

'What?' Gabby shuts the fridge and turns to stare at her. 'Since when?'

Olivia shrugs. 'I've been avoiding meat for a while. I just decided today to go completely vegan.'

'Great,' Gabby says, not unsarcastically. 'What am I supposed to feed you?'

'Vegetables. Salads. Bread. Pasta. Quinoa.'

'Eggs?'

'No. Nothing from an animal.'

'Cheese?'

'No. Dairy products are the worst.'

Gabby sighs dramatically. 'What am I supposed to do with the macaroni cheese I made for dinner tonight?' She suppresses a smile as Olivia pauses, her mother's home-made macaroni cheese being her most favourite food in the world.

'Are you just saying that?'

'No!' Gabby opens the fridge again and pulls the foil off an oval dish to show her.

'I guess I could eat it tonight. I'll start again tomorrow.'

'Absolutely.' Gabby turns away, knowing full well that this, as with all of Olivia's fads, will last approximately two weeks, at most.

'The garden guy wants to see you. He's outside,' Olivia offers nonchalantly as an afterthought.

Gabby grabs her chequebook from the desk drawer and runs outside, writing a cheque for fifty dollars made payable to cash for the mow, blow and go guy in the driveway, then she goes straight back inside to check her phone, except it isn't where she left it – on the desk above the chequebook drawer. Damn. Where the hell is it? She turns and casts her eyes over the counter, until Olivia's voice, filled with suspicion, pipes up from the family room.

'Mom? Who's Matt?'

Her heart thumps in her chest. 'What do you mean?'

Olivia stands up from where she has been hidden, slumped down in an armchair facing the fireplace, and turns to face her mother, her expression a mixture of distrust and confusion, anger and also a need to be reassured.

'"ur wicked sexy when drunk . . . wink Matt kiss kiss

hug kiss."' Olivia, her hand on her hip, her eyebrows raised as she reads, stares at her mother accusingly.

Gabby is aware that the colour has drained from her face. How should she play it? What should she say? What the fuck was she thinking, leaving her phone around unlocked? But, wait ... she didn't leave it unlocked.

'How did you unlock my phone?'

'Alanna and I have both known your code for ages. Which doesn't explain why you're getting these texts from someone other than Dad.'

'It's not what you think,' Gabby says quickly. 'Dad knows about it. It's the guy who interviewed me and we were joking that he fancied me. Let me see.' She holds out her hand for the phone and reads the text. 'Wow, it sounds like he really did fancy me.' She feigns surprise. Badly.

'What about your text to him before that? I'm not stupid, Mom.' Olivia grabs the phone from Gabby. '"A delicious and dangerous night"? What the fuck does that mean?'

'Excuse me?' Gabby's voice rises in shock and guilt. 'Don't you dare speak to your mother like that.'

Olivia's voice also rises. 'Don't you dare send texts like that to someone who isn't Dad!'

'I'm not doing anything,' Gabby says weakly, deflated, overwhelmed with shame.

'Tell that to Dad,' Olivia spits.

'You know what, Olivia? I plan to. This isn't what

you think.' Gabby snatches the phone back and deletes the texts, before turning abruptly, going upstairs to her bedroom and shutting the door.

First she emails Elliott.

> Our daughter seems to think I am having an affair with the child I met with last night, and is now being a teenage bitch from hell. Incidentally, though, he did send me a text saying I'm sexy! You were right – the hot-mommy clothes worked! Meanwhile, I'm flying high that I've still got it (you lucky man, you). Will you talk to Olivia? She seems to think I encouraged him, which is laughable. What time are you home tonight?
>
> Love you,
> G xxx

And next, Matt.

> My dangerous friend – it might be wiser not to text. My fault entirely, as I texted first, but it seems my daughters are adept at breaking codes to unlock my phone. I truly did love seeing you last night. I don't remember the last time I had so much fun. You are utterly delicious, which you know, and you have brought sunshine into my life all day today.
>
> Thank you.
> G xoxox

From then on Gabby keeps her phone tucked into the rear pocket of her jeans, going to the bathroom occasionally to pull it out and check for a response, but none comes. The high from the night before starts to wane. By the time Elliott comes home she is feeling a mixture of depression and anger.

Why hasn't he responded? What's wrong with her? Why did she have to send that email to him? Why does she now feel so humiliated? The sight of Elliott walking in just before seven raises in her both relief and guilt.

'Where are the girls?'

'Alanna's watching TV, and Olivia's in her room, still not speaking to me. She thinks I wrote something provocative to that guy, Matt.'

Elliott cocks his head to one side. 'Did you?'

'No!' Gabby looks away, shaking her head dismissively. 'I wrote it was delightful, but also dangerous because I had to reveal stuff about myself in the questionnaire. I think she thought it meant something else.'

'Ohhh.' His voice is drawn out as he laughs. 'Okay. She phoned me, upset, and did tell me you had written a text saying something about dangerous.'

'See? I think she thinks I'm having an affair.'

'Yup. That's exactly what she thinks. And she thinks I'm an idiot for not seeing it.'

'Well, she's right, because I am exactly the kind of woman to have an affair. After all, I'm married to a terrible man, and, really, my life is utterly awful so why not blow it up? Just for fun?'

Elliott shrugs his shoulders and sighs. 'Teenagers. Their frontal lobe isn't fully connected. As we well know, it leads to all kinds of disasters. I'll go and talk to her now, because she was really upset. You should talk to her afterwards. Don't be hard on her; just reassure her.'

'Okay,' Gabby says, although at this moment in time she'd be just as happy not having to look her daughter in the eye.

Twenty minutes later Elliott comes downstairs with Olivia, who is looking both grumpy and sheepish.

'Anything you'd like to say to your mother?'

'Sorry,' she mumbles.

'And Gabby? Anything you'd like to say to Olivia?'

Gabby frowns at Elliott; she has no idea what he means. 'Sorry?' she attempts.

'Right,' he replies. 'And we both want Olivia to know that you are not having an affair, nor would you have an affair.'

'Exactly,' Gabby says, wishing she could be as certain, although there is still no response from Matt and anger is starting to set in.

'Come on, cheer up.' Elliott gives his elder daughter a kiss. 'Go get Alanna and let's have dinner.'

Their evening is uneventful, but Gabby is acutely aware that she has had something of a lucky escape. She has to stop. She wants to stop. But all she can think about, all she has been thinking about for weeks, is Matt.

She is finishing off stacking the dishwasher when Elliott walks up behind her.

'By the way, Gabs, I have to be at a GI conference on the twenty-third. Harvey was going but it turns out it's his anniversary and one of us needs to be there. You don't mind if I go, do you?'

'Of course not. Isn't that the weekend the girls are going to see Jill?'

'We're going to Aunt Jill's?' Alanna's face lights up. 'You didn't tell me.'

'I forgot,' Elliott says. 'Sorry. Your cousins are desperate to see you so we were going to drop you off and have a romantic weekend.' He turns back to Gabby. 'I'm really sorry, sweetie. The conference is in New Mexico, at a big hotel. Maybe you could come and have spa treatments. We could turn it into a romantic weekend there.'

'Right,' Gabby says wryly, shaking her head. 'A romantic weekend during which time I wouldn't actually see you.'

'Probably not, but you could have massages and spa treatments, and I think the weather's great.'

'It sounds glorious, but not nearly as glorious as being in my own house, all by myself, for a whole weekend!' She shudders with pleasure. 'Now that's a treat that never happens. I get to sleep in our great big bed with no one stealing the covers. I can eat sandwiches from Trader Joe's for two whole days if I feel like it. I can work in the barn without worrying about having to come in and cook for anyone, or clean, or do laundry. Bliss!'

'Great, Mom,' Alanna says. 'Why don't you just say you hate being a mother?'

'Okay,' Gabby says, and she shrugs cheerfully. 'I hate being a mother.'

'Mom!' Both girls look at her, horrified.

She smiles. 'I am so kidding. I love being a mother. You know I love being your mother more than anything. I've always loved it. Especially when you were little. How did the two of you get so big? When did you stop needing me so much?'

'Uh-oh!' Alanna flashes a look at Olivia. 'Mom's getting sentimental.'

'I'm sorry,' Gabby says, blinking, aware her eyes are glistening. 'I just miss those days so much. Meanwhile, I love the two of you more than anything, but so rarely have time that's just for me. And count yourself lucky, girls. I had a mother who really did hate being a mother.'

'No!' Olivia, who adores her grandmother, protests. 'Grasha says she was just busy.'

'That's the point,' Gabby says. 'Grasha was far more interested in everyone else than she was in me. But,' she concedes, 'she is a much better grandmother than she ever was a mother, it's true.'

'When are we going to see her?' Alanna says. 'Can we go to London again by ourselves?'

'I think maybe Grasha should come here next time.' She and Elliott exchange a look. They had sent the girls over to London last year as unaccompanied minors.

All had gone extremely well until the girls actually reached the Roth/de Roth house, at which point it became clear that Grasha was a far better grandmother than mother only when not on her own turf.

On her own turf, she hadn't changed at all. The girls came home excitedly reporting the streams of freaks sitting around Grasha's kitchen table. Because their grandmother was 'so busy' they were left to explore London by themselves, which they adored, although Gabby had blanched at the thought of a ten-year-old and a sixteen-year-old making their way around London alone.

'Darling, *you* did it,' her mother said innocently, when pressed. But, as Gabby pointed out, she had been *raised* in London; she wasn't a naive child from the suburbs of Connecticut.

To their credit, and making Gabby enormously proud of them, the girls had not spent all their time in Topshop and Primark, but they had been to Tate Modern, ridden the London Eye, visited various markets, and even – and of this Gabby was most proud – watched *A Midsummer Night's Dream* in Regent's Park. All by themselves!

Going to stay with Jill, Elliott's sister in Manhattan, is a far safer proposition.

Being on her own, given Gabby's recent obsession, may, on the other hand, turn out to be the most dangerous proposition of all.

*

There is no response from Matt by bedtime, leaving Gabby in a haze of anger and insecurity. She is tempted to email, asking if she did something wrong, but manages to resist, telling herself not to act like a crazy woman, telling herself she is married and has to let this obsession go, telling herself to grow up and move on.

'Are you okay?' Elliott has been standing in the doorway, watching her.

'Fine. Why?'

'You keep putting the Kindle down and frowning. It looks like you're either very worried or very angry about something.'

Gabby puts the Kindle down and holds her arms out for Elliott. 'I'm sorry, sweetie. I guess I was just thinking about Olivia, and the teenage stuff. I've always felt that we've managed pretty well, but I really didn't like the way she spoke to me tonight. I've noticed this a few times recently. I was thinking about whether we're in for a rocky ride.'

Gabby hugs Elliott, knowing how he loves being in her arms. She is aware she hasn't been as affectionate of late, has been distracted, and she can feel him relax, happy to have her back.

'She just misinterpreted and she was angry,' he says. 'I understand. Perhaps she was rude, but she was scared. All in all, Olivia's a great kid, and I think we've got off pretty unscathed. If she has a few moments of rudeness we're still doing pretty damn well. Compare her to Jolie, Gabs. Look at what we could be dealing with.'

Claire's daughter, Jolie, once one of Olivia's best friends, has gravitated towards the fast crowd in school. Once one of the brightest, she is now far more interested in drinking and partying. Her clothes have gone from classic cute prepster – J.Crew, Sperry's and cashmere cardigans, to juvenile hooker – micro skirts, five-inch platform heels and tight shirts to show off the cleavage pushed up by her Victoria's Secret leopard-print bra.

Over the last two years Jolie has become surly and truculent, screaming at her parents for no apparent reason. Claire, often despairing, has confessed she hopes to God this baby she's carrying is a boy because she never wants another one like Jolie.

Gabby sighs. 'You're right, you're right. I know you're right. It just . . . worries me when she acts like that.'

'Don't worry.' Elliott smiles at his wife and traces the frown lines on her forehead. 'It ages you and I can't have my hot wife looking old.'

'There's always Botox,' Gabby says, half joking. For years she has denigrated the many women she knows who suddenly appear looking, not younger, exactly, but . . . smoother. There is something almost indefinably different about them, and it took her and Claire a while before they figured it out. Botox smoothes the women's foreheads, in many cases unnaturally arching their eyebrows and giving them a look of permanent surprise; cheekbones miraculously grow into Marlene

Dietrich-style high apples; their skin is strangely taut and shiny, thanks to chemical peels.

Claire is desperate for Botox, but has a fear of needles and will never do it, and Gabby has never wanted any of it, until very recently, when she started to think it might be rather wonderful if she was able to look younger. Why not erase the frown lines, eradicate the crow's feet? Would her lips not look better if slightly plumped? Wouldn't her face look more radiant if some filler were added to raise her cheekbones to where they would have been had the good Lord been generous enough to actually grace her with high ones in the first place?

But Elliott will not allow it. The very idea of injecting anything unnatural for the sake of vanity is anathema to him. The side effects are unknown, he said. Wait ten years and we will find out terrible things, he warned.

The lure is getting stronger. Gabby stands in the bathroom sometimes, staring at her face in the mirror, her fingers pulling her skin ever so slightly tighter, pouting to see what her lips would look like bigger.

'You're not having Botox,' Elliott says, moving to his side of the bed and reaching for the remote control to turn on the television.

At 4.23 a.m. Gabby is wide awake, and has been for two hours. As soon as she woke up, and as she so often does these days, she grabbed her iPhone, now kept charging next to the bed, to see if Matt had responded. Her heart leaped with exhilaration when she saw he had.

> Do you know the song about a girl called Gabrielle, a girl who is very dangerous . . . ? Shades Apart? You ought to listen to it . . . I'm sorry I've been out of touch – things have been a little crazy again over here. I had a wonderful time with you the other night. You are just as beautiful, bright, clever and special as I remember. Actually, more so. And that 'friendly' kiss goodbye? What can I say? WOW. Your husband is a lucky guy and I'm jealous as hell. I'm flying off to Cincinnati this week and have a ton of meetings so I may not have the chance to email. What do you have going on this week? I'm hoping to be back in about a month – cannot wait to see you again. xxxx

Gabby takes her iPhone into the bathroom, shuts the door and rereads the email. What does it mean? He can't wait to see her again, and yet the earlier part, the mention of her husband, seems so light, as if he doesn't really care, as if he's already written her off, already realized she is truly out of bounds.

But she is, as she keeps reminding herself, out of bounds. She is happily married, with no idea why she has this desperate need to keep this young man interested, other than to inflate her ego, which is both sad and shameful.

Aware of all of this, Gabby still can't help the soaring of her heart when his emails come in, nor the ensuing obsessive picking apart of every paragraph, every word as she looks for meaning between the lines.

Going straight to iTunes she downloads the Shades Apart song, playing it over and over in her bathroom, searching the lyrics for hidden messages, hoping Matt has deliberately picked this song because it will tell her how he truly feels about her. She listens, and she smiles.

Finally she knows she'll sleep well, but first she'll reply.

My friend – Cincinnati sounds . . . Midwestern. I've never
been. That's how you can tell how very English I am. I've lived
in Connecticut for years, but other than California, New York,
Massachusetts, New Hampshire and Maine I'm a disaster –
couldn't tell you anything about the rest of the country. Oh.
Missed Arizona. We once had a wedding in Tucson. My
husband's off to New Mexico for a conference the weekend
of the twenty-third. I was thinking of going too, but the girls
are away that weekend, and the prospect of a weekend
alone, in my own house, is just too tempting. Wouldn't it be
fun if your schedule coincided with that weekend – think of
the Martinis we could drink! The fun we would have! Hope
you travel safely, and don't worry about being out of
touch – I have a busy week too. xxx

It is a test. Of course it is a test. She hits send with a smile on her face, a clutch of anticipation around her heart. Will he rise to meet the challenge, and, if so, what does that mean?

Gabby glides back to bed, plugs her iPhone into the charger again, then lies down, eyes closed, thinking about the weekend she'll be alone, fantasizing about Matt coming here.

Would she have him over to the house? No. That would be far too inappropriate. Would she sleep with him? No! Absolutely not. She just wants the flirtation to continue a little longer, wants to continue to feel the high she gets from being appreciated, desired, by someone other than her husband.

On the night she sees Matt she'd wear something devastatingly fabulous, and she would undoubtedly have lost ten pounds by the twenty-third.

Maybe she'd even get Botox. She'd never tell Elliott, but she would explain to him that her visit to the dermatologist is because she's having moles removed.

If Matt comes on the weekend she's on her own, Botox it is.

Chapter Twelve

'I can't believe you're actually doing this,' Claire says, turning to study Gabby's face as she drives. 'And behind Elliott's back! How are you going to explain it?'

'Moles and skin tags removed.'

'No! I mean, how are you going to explain your sudden lack of lines?' Claire bursts out laughing.

Gabby looks at Claire in disbelief. 'Do you know my husband? Hello? He's a man. They never notice things like that.'

'True,' Claire says. 'Trish said the first time she got Botox her husband — she was still married at the time — just kept saying how beautiful she was. He had no idea. He thought she'd simply woken up one day looking years younger.'

'She *would* have Botox,' mutters Gabby. 'I knew she wasn't that beautiful naturally.'

'Stop being jealous. She is that beautiful naturally. Botox just erases the lines; it doesn't change your features. God, I'm jealous, though. I can't even dye my hair while I'm pregnant. Will you look at this?' She dips her head down to show the grey.

'I can't see,' Gabby says. 'I'm driving.'

'You know I won't be able to come in and actually

watch while they put the needles in, right? Even the thought of it makes me feel woozy and nauseous. But I cannot wait to see. You know it doesn't have an immediate effect, don't you? It takes a few days.'

'I know. But you have to swear not to tell anyone, ever, that I did this.'

'I swear. I only told Trish . . .'

'What!'

'Kidding. This stays between you and me. It's only Botox. It's not like you're getting a facelift, although I suppose these days Botox is the equivalent of a facial. Really, it's no big deal. If I didn't have my needle phobia I'd be on that Botox wagon quicker than you could say "frown".'

The dermatologist, her long blonde hair pulled back in a ponytail to frame her exquisite face, steps back to gaze at Gabby. 'Have you ever thought about a little filler?'

'Not really,' Gabby says dumbly.

'You could have Restylane or Perlane. Just here in the cheekbones. Look –' she hands Gabby a small mirror, gesturing for Gabby to look at her face – 'you see these lines from your nose to your lips? As we age our faces drop, but if we added just a tiny bit of filler here,' she touches Gabby's cheekbones, 'it would not only add back the volume you've lost, but it would pull your face up and erase those lines. See?'

Gabby's eyes widen with pleasure as her face is pulled up and the lines disappear.

'I wouldn't do too much,' the clinician reassures her.

'You mustn't do too much,' Gabby says. 'I can't stand seeing those women with apple-like cheekbones.'

'Absolutely. You just need a touch to restore volume. I do it on myself and do my cheekbones look bad?' She turns her head slowly from side to side, knowing how beautiful she is, how perfect her cheekbones are. 'I'm forty-seven but these treatments have helped me stay young.'

Gabby gasps in awe. 'Forty-seven! No! What else do you do?' she asks, wanting to look exactly like her.

'Sculptra,' the clinician says matter-of-factly. 'You'd be wonderful for Sculptra, and you'd love it. Everyone I do it for loves it. You do it twice, all over the face, and it stimulates your body to start producing collagen again, so you immediately start looking younger. Even better, the effects are cumulative and last a couple of years. The more time that passes, the better you look. You'd look fantastic with Sculptra. It's the best thing I've ever done.'

'I want it,' Gabby bursts out, feeling entirely unlike herself. 'When could you do it?'

The dermatologist laughs. 'We'll do it all right now. And the Perlane too?'

'Yes!' Gabby finds herself saying. 'All of it!'

*

'What took you so long?' Claire grumbles, throwing down a three-month-old copy of *Better Homes and Gardens*, as Gabby finally appears in the waiting room, a series of small red bumps on her forehead.

'Ouch!' Claire winces. 'Did it hurt? Was it awful?' She squints. 'You did something to your cheekbones! Oh my God! What's the matter with your mouth?'

'It's numb. I had some other stuff and they gave me a local anaesthetic. Do I look freaky?'

'What other stuff? Yes, you look freaky. What did you do?'

'Let's get out of here. I've just handed over a shocking amount of money. I need to recover and figure out a new story. There's no way in hell Elliott's going to believe I had a few moles removed for that price. It's at least a leg. Maybe both. Jesus, Claire. What the hell was I thinking?'

'I don't know. What were you thinking?'

'I wasn't. I just got completely carried away when I saw the dermatologist. Have you seen her? She's forty-seven! The woman looks thirty. I asked her for everything she has.'

They are in the car park when Claire starts laughing uncontrollably, crossing her legs as she holds onto the boot of a car for support. 'Oh no,' she weeps. 'Don't make me laugh. I'll have an accident.'

'I wasn't making you laugh. I'm telling you what happened.'

'I know.' Claire calms down enough to stand up

straight, wiping her eyes. 'I think you're having a mid-life crisis.'

Gabby doesn't say anything until they are in the car and driving, but Claire's words keep reverberating through her head. Is that really what is happening? There is no question that she feels as if her days as an attractive woman are numbered, but does that explain all that she has been going through? Is it really something as predictable as that?

'Do you think women *have* mid-life crises?' she asks, as they approach traffic lights. 'And does this mean I'll be going out and buying a red sports car and chatting up twenty-year-old hunks?' She tries to sound flippant, but thoughts of Matt fill her head – his impending trip back to Connecticut, the way he smiles at her, the way his eyes darken when he looks at her – making her heart, even now, skip a beat.

Claire raises an eyebrow. 'You were chatting up a rather gorgeous young man at the bar that time we went out,' she says.

'I wasn't chatting him up.' Gabby is indignant. 'He was chatting *me* up.'

'Are you still emailing him?'

Gabby, unable to keep it to herself, desperate to talk about him to someone, if only to say that he is a new friend, had confided in Claire a few days after Matt sent the first email.

'Sporadically,' she lies. 'I actually saw him last week. He was in town and we had a drink.'

'No!' Claire's eyes are wide. 'Gabby! You're so bad!' She peers at her friend. 'Just a drink, right? Tell me nothing happened.' Her face becomes stern.

'God, no!' Gabby says. 'Just a drink. He was flirting, though.'

'And how about you? Were you flirting back?'

'Maybe just a tiny bit. But I wouldn't do anything. I'm married, and I love Elliott. There's absolutely no way in hell I would ever have an affair, nor do anything to jeopardize my marriage.'

'Did you tell Elliott you were having a drink with a guy you met in a bar?'

Gabby shifts uncomfortably in her seat. 'Sort of. I told him I was meeting a guy. I didn't tell him how we met initially.'

Claire shakes her head. 'Oh, Gabby. You know this is how these things always start, right?'

'What do you mean?'

'No one thinks they're going to have an affair. Everyone starts by thinking it's just a fun flirtation, or a new friendship, that they'll never let anything happen. So they pretend to be friends, even though the only thing these two people have in common is a mutual lust, which eventually has to ignite. It's one of the laws of the universe. They have an affair, and mitigate it by deciding that it isn't just an affair, that this is their soulmate. They aren't supposed to be married to the lovely, stable lawyer in boring old Connecticut; instead they are meant to be living with the dangerous, unstable, inappropriately young surfer in

136

San Diego, or wherever it is the interloper happens to be from. They blow up their marriages, leaving devastation in their wake, to run off with said surfer, only for them both to discover, several weeks, months, but no more than a year down the line, that in fact they have nothing in common other than that lust, which has now, shock horror, completely disappeared.'

'Claire, I –'

'Then they realize what a terrible mistake they've made, which is when they go back to their husband, tail between their legs, begging to be allowed to come back, telling them how sorry they are, what a terrible error of judgement they made. The husbands have invariably moved on, and these women spend the rest of their lives beating off sad, middle-aged, professional singles at the handful of bars around town. It happened to Alison and Denise. Oh, and Cathy. Same story. There. That's my cautionary tale for you. I shall say no more about it.'

'You're so convinced. You don't really know what happens behind closed doors.'

Claire shrugs. 'It happened to my sister. Who's now in a crappy walk-up apartment in Pelham Manor, taking any job she can find and bitterly regretting leaving her rather wonderful husband for her metal teacher. The thing with Rodrigo lasted six months. Her husband has now remarried and had a baby, and the new wife, ten years younger, is living the life my sister should be living – in the Upper East Side apartment with doorman, nanny and housekeeper. I've seen it happen time and time again.'

Gabby laughs nervously. 'That is so not going to happen to me.'

'So stop the emailing,' Claire says. 'How would you feel if Elliott was emailing a younger, gorgeous woman? If he insisted they were just good friends it wouldn't make you feel any better, would it?'

Gabby shakes her head. This has occurred to her. Particularly the last email referencing their 'friendly' kiss. It wouldn't do for Elliott to read that. Not at all. But there's no way Matt is her soulmate. So this would never follow the trajectory taken by Claire's sister. How ridiculous.

Although . . . she has indulged in the odd fantasy of what it would be like to live in Malibu, to be Matt's . . . partner. Not at the expense of leaving Elliott, though. Her fantasy is more of a daydream about a life entirely different to her current one.

Sober, reasonable Gabby knows these are only fun fantasies, that she is not seriously thinking she and Matt may be an item. Sober, reasonable Gabby recognizes she is obsessed in an unnatural and unhealthy way, and that it can't go on much longer.

Sober, reasonable Gabby is hoping that, perhaps, after the twenty-third, she'll be able to let go of it entirely.

Chapter Thirteen

'Darling? Your car's here,' Gabby calls up the stairs before opening the front door and gesturing to the driver, holding her fingers up to let him know Elliott will be down in five minutes.

'I wish you were coming,' Elliott says as he comes down the stairs, carry-on bag in hand. 'I know we wouldn't have seen each other much, but we could have had dinner together at night. Now I'll have to go out with a bunch of boring old doctors.'

'Yeah, right.' Gabby snorts. 'The last conference you went to you ended up drinking and dancing all night. If I recall correctly you came home saying something like you hadn't had so much fun in years.'

Elliott laughs, dropping his bag on the floor to encircle his wife's waist with his arms. 'Have I told you lately how beautiful you are?'

'Yes. You told me yesterday.' Gabby smiles, still delighted.

'It's true. The older you get the more beautiful you become.' Gabby declines to point out that this is, in fact, largely due to the Botox, Perlane and Sculptra; but she is grateful that it worked, and that he hasn't realized.

'Have a safe flight,' she says, then kisses him deeply. 'I love you. And behave yourself.'

'I will,' he says with a grin, picking up his bag and taking it to the car, blowing her a kiss as he is driven out of the driveway, leaving Gabby, finally, entirely alone.

I want to see where you live.

Gabby has already planned dinner when the text arrives, coming up with a small hole-in-the-wall place in Bridgeport, a place where they are unlikely to run into anyone they know. But Matt is saying he wants to see her home. Where she lives with her husband and daughters. That doesn't feel right. That feels . . . wrong, too intimate.

Why would you want to see where
I live? I've already described it
to you.

Why wouldn't you want me to see
where you live? I want to see the
books you read, the paintings on
your wall, the food in your fridge.

Gabby smiles when she reads that. She'd love to see his home, for exactly those reasons. She wants to see who he is when he isn't out in the world, composing himself, carefully contorting himself into the man he wants others to think he is.

And who is *she*? She asks herself this as she walks

around her house trying to look at it through his eyes, wondering what a newcomer might infer from what he sees.

The paintings in the house are, indeed, almost unanimously reflective of her. Elliott, never particularly interested in art, has indulged her love of drawings. Sketches of people, delicate line drawings of cities she has been to, life studies in pen and ink fill every available wall space, apart from one wall in the dining room. This is where they hung the huge oil cityscape that Elliott fell in love with. He insisted on having it, despite having to pay a small fortune, and Gabby has never grown to like it.

Books line the bookshelves, along with various *objets* they have collected over the years. Ammonite fossils, small pots, porcelain sculptures of chickens that make her laugh. A bronze hand, fingers outstretched, filled with yearning. A bottom shelf crammed with old paperbacks she used to read as light relief from the heavier, hardback literary tomes that are required reading for local dinner parties. These days her lighter reading is all done on the Kindle but she has never got round to giving these paperbacks away. She takes them now and stuffs them under the sofa. No one needs to see those – they make her look flighty and insubstantial.

Why do you even care what he thinks? You are, after all, ten years older than he is, which automatically makes you substantial. Less substantial, she smiles to herself, than she was three weeks ago. She hasn't weighed herself, but her jeans are loose, and her cheekbones more pronounced than ever; surely they would not be that pronounced from Perlane alone. Getting down on her knees, Gabby pulls the paperbacks from beneath the sofa and puts them back.

I'm not doing anything, she thinks. We'll have a quick drink here, then go out. No romantic fires, no candles. This is not a seduction. I'm not even that comfortable having him here, she realizes, as the day progresses and her butterflies start to multiply. I can't wait to see him, but in my own home? Not so much.

Gabby is ready by six forty-five. Tonight she is dressing down. Tonight she can dress down because her weight loss has given her a confidence she was missing before. In jeans and a T-shirt, she accessorizes with a long thin strand of tiny labradorite and seed pearls looped around her neck.

She looks at herself in the mirror, and even she is impressed. But the shoes have to go. Barefoot is better, at least when he gets here. That way she will look as if she's made no effort at all.

Her heart almost bursts out of her chest as she hears a taxi pull up and a door slam, then her own doorbell is ringing, and she is suddenly so nervous she feels as if she might throw up.

She doesn't. She walks downstairs, forcing herself to take deep breaths, and opens the door to find Matt grinning at her. And then she is grinning back, and she isn't scared, or nervous, just truly, deeply happy to see him, and they step towards each other and hug, and it doesn't feel inappropriate, or wrong. It feels lovely, and very, very right.

'You look amazing!' Matt steps back and looks at her. 'Did you change your hair? Something's different. You look so beautiful.'

'I lost some weight,' Gabby says. 'And a good hair day. That's it.'

'I love that I'm here! Your home! I can't wait to get the full tour.'

'Do you want some wine first?'

'Sure,' he says, following her into the kitchen, admiring the Aga stove she insisted on having to remind her of her childhood home, even though it was the most expensive thing in the kitchen.

'I'm sure I have a bottle in here,' Gabby says, rooting around in the fridge, but knowing full well there is a bottle in there, exactly where she placed it this morning. She turns and reaches for the corkscrew, stepping back as Matt steps in to take both corkscrew and bottle from her hand. He smiles down at her as he uncorks.

When she goes to get glasses from the other side of the kitchen, Gabby is aware Matt is watching her walk. It makes her feel sexy, and young, and more alive than ever before. There is a charge in the room that touches everything; a charge that has given both Gabby and Matt permanent smiles, smiles that occasionally dissolve into embarrassed laughter as they catch each other's eyes. They are both relieved, excited, drunk on the chemistry. Gabby is busy pretending to be someone she may not be, and Matt is too caught up in the thrill of the chase, the lure of the unobtainable being not quite as unobtainable as he once thought.

'Do you want nuts?' Gabby pulls out a packet, but Matt shakes his head.

'I'm good. Here,' he says, handing her a glass of wine. 'Cheers.'

'Cheers,' she replies, and holds eye contact with him as they both sip, then she is the first to look away. 'Do you want to see the house?'

'You know what I really want to see?'

Please don't say the bedroom, she thinks. That would be so predictable, and so sleazy. And I would have no idea what to say.

'What?'

'The barn. I want to see your work.'

Gabby's shoulders instantly relax.

They put down their glasses and she leads the way outside and across the garden to the barn, wrapping her arms around herself against the evening chill.

'Are you sure you're ready for this?' she teases, pausing by the door.

'This is your space, right? This is the place where I'm really going to be able to tell who you are.'

'Oh God,' she groans as she pushes the door open. 'You're going to think I'm a disorganized, crazy mess.'

She stands there, Matt next to her, as he slowly looks

around, impressed. He takes in the old beams, the workbenches, the furniture. He asks her questions about the furniture, exclaiming with delight over her work, the painting techniques; he is drawn to the notice-board on which she has pinned photos of her befores and afters.

'What's up there?' He points to the staircase.

'Bedroom and bathroom,' she says. 'Supposed to be for guests but they always end up staying in the house. It's too far away for most people. I love it, though – I sneak in a nap from time to time.'

'Let me see!' he says, heading for the stairs.

'Matt, there's nothing to see. It's very dull.'

'Come on. I want to see.' He's upstairs, and in the doorway of the bedroom before she can say anything else.

Gabby walks up and watches Matt as he stands in the doorway surveying the room with pleasure. The rest of the barn is natural wood, but in here she colour-washed the walls a pale grey, the same colour as the pretty antique iron bed. An old pine dresser sits at one end of the room, and there is also an antique wing chair, covered in a natural soft linen, and an antique Swedish Mora clock. The bed is covered with a soft matelassé bedspread and piled with plush white pillows; a sump-tuous blue and white quilt is folded at the foot. It is picture-perfect, and its simple charm gives Gabby a deep sense of calm every time she walks in here.

'See,' she says. 'Nothing to write home about.'

He walks into the tiny room. 'Not true. I bet that bed has a story.'

Gabby laughs. 'Only that I found it at a tag sale when we were first married. I fell completely in love with it and forced my husband to sleep in it, even though it was way too small. I painted the iron, and now . . . it's here.'

'And the clock?'

'That was my mother's. They decided to reorganize a few years ago and my mother did something uncharacteristically generous – she sent me a few pieces that had been my favourites when I was a child. That clock had been in my bedroom, and I always loved it.'

'Now it's in your bedroom here.'

'Indeed.'

The air is very still. Gabby knows she cannot step further into the room, knows, in fact, she should leave now and walk down the stairs, back to safety, but everything is frozen, and she isn't able to move. She can hear everything. Even, it seems, the particles of dust flying in the evening light; Matt's breathing; her own heart pounding in her ears.

It happens very slowly. Matt's head coming towards hers, bending, dropping the gentlest of kisses on her frozen lips. She stands, not moving, feeling on the edge of a terrible precipice, unable to go forward, definitely unable to go back.

And then she is kissing him back, and it is her tongue in his mouth, her groan of anticipation, of desire, of longing that comes out first.

They are tangled in each other's arms, and she is feeling his body, so young, so hard, such an unbelievable turn-on. When he pulls his T-shirt off she actually gasps, unable to believe how smooth his skin is, how taut, how firm.

Gabby is no longer a forty-three-year-old housewife, no longer a mother, no longer dull, well into middle age. She is thirty, twenty, eighteen. She is wild and ferocious. She doesn't care about stretch marks, or sags, or pouches; she cares only about pleasure, giving and receiving more pleasure than she had thought possible.

She tears off her bra, not thinking, not planning. Nothing exists beyond this room, beyond this beautiful man who is exploring her with his fingers, his mouth, who is writhing when she flips over and does the same to him.

This isn't lovemaking. This isn't the safe, familiar routine she has with Elliott. This is raw, animalistic. Gabby slides her fingers into places she would never dream to probe with her husband, laughing as he moans in surprise. And pleasure. She licks, and swallows, and engulfs, her appetite insatiable, her energy unstoppable.

Finally he is above her, his eyes locked with hers as he slips inside, moving slowly while she closes her eyes, groaning in pleasure before she opens them to lose herself in his gaze.

There is nothing in the future, nothing in the past. Just the two of them, just this moment, and let this moment, these moments, go on for ever and ever, for

she can suspend her life during this, can suspend everything as long as they are here in this room together,
releasing all the pent-up attraction, longing, the weeks
of flirtation; but after this?

After this?

Afterwards, Gabby gets up from the bed and goes
towards the bathroom. She may have lost several pounds
but, naked, she knows she cannot pull it off quite so
well. She has no butt any more, just a flat slab where
there used to be a peach; her varicose veins are clearly
visible. Undressed, she looks like the middle-aged
woman she is.

She doesn't care.

Numb, she walks into the bathroom, staring deeply
into her eyes in the mirror as she washes her hands,
unsurprised that all she sees is shame.

Chapter Fourteen

Something is different about his wife, but Elliott is too frightened to ask what it is. It started a few months ago, around the time she went to be interviewed by the man who started that website. *Man.* Hardly. Elliott Googled him extensively and is pretty confident that 'boy' is the right term for him.

It was clear to him that Gabby had developed a crush. In some ways he understood it. This young fellow had clearly flirted with her, and, almost in her mid-forties, she had been flattered and had reacted to it inappropriately. Not that he knew this for certain, but she had a lilt in her step that she hadn't had for years, and she had started taking care of herself in a way she hadn't before.

Gabby had worn make-up and fluffed her hair and done those things when they were first married, but after years of him telling her he preferred her natural, with no adornments, nothing artificial, she finally believed him. Up until a few months ago, he couldn't remember the last time she'd worn make-up.

What that man, *boy* – Matt – had obviously done was wake Gabby up, make her nostalgic for her youth. Why else would she suddenly start wearing tight jeans and high-heeled boots, putting on make-up, blowing out her hair? Why else would she stop eating carbohydrates and turn down chocolate, even her beloved Butterfingers?

Why else would she spend so much money at the dermatologist, then lie about the procedure? Elliott had phoned the office to question the bill, which seemed outrageous for a minor procedure even in this day and age, even in this town.

Botox, Perlane, Sculptra. He hasn't even heard of the last two and he's a doctor. No wonder she looked so fresh, so young. No wonder she seemed to glow. For weeks she seemed to glow, then, suddenly, she plummeted.

She stopped wearing the make-up, put all the weight back on, and more. She can barely rouse herself to get out of bed in the mornings, and it is not unusual, when he calls in the afternoons, for Gabby to be fast asleep.

He has found her, on occasion, in tears. At other times she snaps at him or the girls in anger; she apologizes swiftly, but there doesn't seem to be anything to explain these outbursts. She can be loving, affectionate, over-affectionate even, then quickly flares up into a rage over nothing.

'Have you been to see a doctor recently?' he asked gently, just the other night.

'You're a doctor,' she retorted. 'What do *you* think is wrong with me?'

'Have you had a period recently?'

'Why? What's that got to do with anything?'

'I think you're menopausal. I think you might actually be going through the menopause. When was the last period? Do you remember? I don't. Perhaps you need to get your hormones checked.'

The tears come. 'Thank you. Thank you. I thought I was going mad. You're right. I'll make an appointment tomorrow. What would I do without you?'

'Find someone else to pick on?' Elliott jokes, only he isn't joking.

'I'm sorry,' she says, laughing through her tears. 'You know I love you and only you?'

'You'd better,' he says, surprised.

Of course she loves him and only him. He can see she has had an infatuation, but it has passed. He is grateful it didn't become anything he would have to worry about.

Chapter Fifteen

Gabby is trying very hard to pretend her night with Matt never happened. Immediately afterwards, when they had consummated their lust, when the full impact of what she had done was already hitting, Gabby found it hard to even look at Matt.

All of a sudden they were moving around each other awkwardly, until Gabby dropped the pretence that they would be spending the rest of the evening together; she even invented a headache so she could drive him back to the hotel.

Matt was puzzled. Hurt. He could see that she deeply regretted what they'd done and he tried to talk to her, to reach out to her, but she'd retreated so far within herself that, in the end, he gave up trying. He understood she was doing what she had to do.

She went home and stood under scalding water in the shower for twenty-five minutes, attempting to wash away the stain of her betrayal. She put on her fluffiest, most comforting pyjamas, and curled up in bed, phoning Elliott, wanting to be enveloped in the safety of his voice.

Every morning since that night, after she awakes, the shame and guilt of her betrayal come flooding back.

Some days she feels so disgusted with herself, so filled with remorse, she can't look Elliott in the eye, and she screams at him over nothing, not because she is angry with him, but because she is so angry with herself.

Other days, overwhelmed with love, or with fear that he will leave, she is sexually voracious, pushing him onto the bed, taking him in her mouth, desperate to prove to him how much she loves him, how much she still wants him. She is terrified that this is the only way she can keep him.

Never has she wanted Elliott as much as she has since she betrayed him. Never has she been more aware of the fragility of marriage, of a relationship that once seemed so unbreakable, so strong.

And now that it is over she cannot believe she has spent months of her life obsessing over another man. The minute it was over, everything was over. She never wanted to see him again.

A week later Matt emailed her. He thanked her for a lovely time, said he hoped she was okay, that they would still be friends. There was nothing flirtatious in the email, nothing leading, but Gabby, sick with shame when she saw his name in her inbox, wrote back to say it was better if they didn't speak for a while.

She had tremendous affection for him, she said, but it should never have happened and she needed to refocus on her family. Matt didn't write again after that, and Gabby didn't expect him to.

She sensed that the email exchange – brief but

warm – was closure for both of them. There was nothing further that needed to be said, and she was able to walk away without hating him, or blaming him, or wanting anything more from him than he had already given.

He had already given too much.

Or perhaps she had taken too much. Either way, Gabby knew, even before it was over, that it would never happen again. Not just with Matt, but she never again will she jeopardize everything she cares about, never again will she be unfaithful, no matter how great the temptation.

She would do anything to go back in time and change what happened, and is hopeful that every passing day that brings normality with it will help her transgression feel more and more like a dream.

It still burns, that nugget of guilt, each time she and Elliott make love. At times it feels as if she is play-acting at being herself, at being the kind of woman who is loyal, faithful, who would never betray her husband.

She cannot change it, but she can hope to learn from it and protect those around her from being hurt by it.

She wasn't caught. No one knows. She does not have to live in fear of Elliott waking up and asking who she is typing to at three o'clock in the morning. It is something of a relief to look at her inbox now and not see an email from Matt. It is something of a relief to sleep through the night, not waking up several times in the early hours, reaching over for her iPhone to see if he has been in touch. It is something of a relief to not have to lie, or deceive, or withhold, any more.

Gabby did a terrible thing, but it was one time only. She did a terrible thing but she has to try to forgive herself and move on. The terrible thing served only to prove how much she loves her husband; how lucky she is. She will never make that mistake again.

Three months later, however, she is still feeling sick with shame, although she is convinced her hormones have something to do with her sickness, her crazy mood swings.

Finally, thank heavens, she has a doctor's appointment.

Please God, she thinks, let the doctor put me on something that will make this all better. Please let them have a pill that will make me feel normal once more.

Please let me have my life back, and I'll never do anything wrong again.

The gynaecologist comes back in the room with a large smile on his face. As he walks over and sits behind his desk he asks, 'Do you want the good news or the good news?'

Gabby stares at her OB/GYN, mystified. 'What's the good news?'

'The good news is you're not going through menopause.'

She breathes a sigh of relief. As mentally prepared as

Gabby thought she was, menopause would mean she had crossed to the other side, and she isn't old enough for that. Not yet. 'Great. So what's the good news?'

'Congratulations, Gabby! You're pregnant!'

PART TWO

Chapter Sixteen

It is three days since Gabby's visit to the doctor. Three days since everything in her life was destroyed. Three days of acting as if everything is normal, trying to put off the pain she knows is inevitable, unavoidable.

Each morning she wakes up with a sense of something not being right, then the full force of what it is shocks her into consciousness.

'Mom? What's going on?' Even Olivia, usually so wrapped up in herself, has noticed. 'You don't seem like yourself.'

Gabby forces a tight smile. 'I'm fine,' she says.

But she isn't fine. How can she be fine?

For three days Gabby has been replaying in her mind the scene in the OB/GYN office. She is aware that even as the doctor's pronouncement reverberated in her head, the horror of his words was mixed with immediate, but secret, elation at carrying a new life, at having the one thing she has always wanted. Just not in this way.

'You're pregnant . . . You're pregnant . . . You're pregnant . . .'

Gabby could only stare at her doctor as the static built in her head.

'What?' Her voice was barely a whisper.

'I know,' he said, with a laugh. 'A lot of my older mothers are surprised, particularly when they're convinced their lack of menstruation is due to menopause, but I'd say –' he looked down at his notes as she fought a wave of nausea – 'judging from the date of your last period, you're about fourteen weeks. Obviously we can be more specific when we do the scan, which we'd like to do today, plus the blood work. You can talk to Jacqui outside about making an appointment with the genetics counsellor before you go. Given how late you are, we need to get you in as soon as possible. This afternoon would be best.' He looked at Gabby kindly. 'I can see this is a shock. Do you have any questions you'd like to ask me?'

Gabby's voice was low and quiet. 'What are the chances of getting pregnant after a vasectomy?'

The doctor stared at her, the smile sliding off his face as comprehension dawned. 'Oh dear,' he said, with no idea what to say next.

She went straight in for the nuchal scan, lying on the table, still numb, still unable to believe this was happening. The baby couldn't be Elliott's, and no further lies would change that or give her an opportunity to spin it in any way other than the awful, shattering truth. She stared at the ceiling, blinking back her tears, as the sonographer put the warm gel on her belly. She didn't want to look at the screen, didn't want any of this to be real, but it was. Burying her head in the sand wasn't an option any more, but still she couldn't look at the screen; she wasn't willing to see the tangible evidence of what she had done.

Naive enough to think she had got away with it, as she lay there Gabby knew, with sudden clarity, that this was her penance. You do not get to betray a man such as Elliott and walk away scot-free. You do not get to play around with your marriage, your future, and expect to get away with it.

'There you are,' the sonographer said, and Gabby was aware of the worried glance she gave as she tried to draw Gabby's attention to the screen. Gabby supposed most new mothers, particularly the older ones, do not lie staring at the ceiling, tears streaming down their cheeks, during their first scan. 'What a perfect picture!' the sonographer continued, and Gabby slowly, reluctantly, turned her head, not wanting to look, but unable not to.

There it was. On the screen, in a hazy blur of greys, an unmistakable life: a perfect curled-up baby, thumb brought up to his mouth, tiny legs furled inwards. No amount of guilt and shame could prevent the magic of that moment stealing up and catching Gabby in its grasp.

'A good, strong, healthy heartbeat.' The sonographer stopped moving the wand for a few seconds and Gabby's eyes widened with wonder. A baby! *Her* baby. The life she had wanted for so long, a life she thought she would never be privileged enough to create. Not again, not after Olivia and Alanna.

She caught her breath, taking in every curve, wanting to stop time, wanting to lie there, on that table, and drink in the marvel of the moment for ever.

'That's my baby,' she whispered, and everything else was forgotten as her heart exploded with maternal protection and devotion.

Gabby's shock at what has happened is interspersed with utter terror when she thinks about the moment of breaking the news to Elliott. She knows she cannot put that moment off for very much longer. Gabby has never been a very good liar, and she can't keep pretending this is the menopause. She has done enough damage. The very least she can do now is step up and take responsibility for her actions.

Every time she tries to think of the words, tries to think of how to frame her announcement to cause the least impact, to somehow make it palatable, to ease the pain she knows is inescapable, her mind goes blank.

How do you tell the man you love that you have done the worst thing possible; that you have betrayed his trust; that you will have to live with the evidence for the rest of your life?

Chapter Seventeen

'I am not stupid, Gabby!' Elliott is back to shouting again, as Gabby, exhausted, sits on the small sofa by the window, her head hung low.

'I didn't say you were stupid. It's possible. It happens. There's a chance, a very slight chance . . .'

'Gabby, don't lie to me. All I'm asking for is the truth. If you're honest with me, I can deal with anything, but what I can't deal with are lies. The chances of you getting pregnant by me are, as you pointed out, infinitesimal. We are a family, and you know I don't believe families are necessarily blood, but if you lie to me and tell me that somehow, despite the vasectomy, this baby could only be mine, and I do genetics testing and discover that you are lying to me, I will never recover. Do you understand that, Gabby? I will never get over you lying to me.'

'I'm sorry. I'm so sorry. I love you so much,' Gabby blurts out, and she starts to sob. 'I know you won't forgive me. I don't know how to . . .'

Sitting down on the bed, Elliott takes a deep breath and his voice is calm. 'Just tell me.'

'It was nothing. It was just . . . once.'

Gabby watches as a muscle starts to twitch in Elliott's jaw.

'It . . . it was only one time. It didn't mean anything.'

Elliott turns to look at her, his face blank. 'What?'

'I slept with him once. It was a mistake.'

'Gabby, what are you saying? You slept with whom once?'

'The guy from the website.'

'Jesus Christ!' Elliott's voice is a roar of pain as he leaps up. 'Are you serious? You're pregnant with another man's baby?'

Elliott thought he was prepared to hear the truth, thought he would be able to handle it, already knowing, deep in his gut, that this baby could not possibly be his. But to hear the words, to hear Gabby admitting that she has betrayed him, that she has slept with another man, is more than he can bear.

Gabby has never seen her husband like this. She cowers back against the sofa as Elliott looms above her, his face, always so loving and kind, now contorted with rage. He looks as if he is about to hit her, but then he turns and whirls out of the room, storming down the stairs.

Gabby is right behind him. 'Where are you going?' she screams.

'I don't know,' he says, slamming the door and gunning the engine before screeching off down the street.

There is a gentle tapping on the door that Gabby doesn't hear for a while because her face is buried in the pillow as she sobs.

Eventually she hears the sound, lifts her head, and attempts to calm down. 'Elliott?'

The door cracks open. 'No, Mom. It's me. Alanna. What's the matter?'

Gabby tries to crack a smile. 'I'm just having a bad day. I'll be okay.'

'Mom, were you and Dad fighting?'

Oh God. Please let them not have heard what happened. 'What did you hear?'

'Nothing. I was in the sunroom but I heard raised voices. Did you have a fight?'

'Yes, but it's all going to be fine.'

'Mom, I've never heard you and Dad shout at each other before.' Her face falls. 'You're not going to get a divorce, are you?'

'Absolutely not!' she says firmly. 'Not a chance in hell.' She holds out her arms to give Alanna a reassuring hug, preventing her daughter from seeing the fresh tears rolling down her cheeks.

It is night time before Elliott returns. Gabby is freshly showered, and she has made his favourite: pork chops and mashed potatoes. The table is set for two, even though she has no appetite, and yellow chrysanthemums, cut from the pot on the front doorstep, are in a vase, bravely pretending everything is sunny and bright.

Alanna is up in her room, getting ready for bed; Olivia is out at the movies with friends. Gabby is exhausted, and terrified, feeling trapped in a bad dream, desperate to make it better. She knows that pork chops and mashed potatoes probably won't make all that much of a difference, but she doesn't know what else to do.

She has been sitting at the kitchen table for the last two hours, waiting for Elliott to come home. He has switched off his mobile phone, and there has been nothing to do but wait. She hasn't been able to read, or watch television, or focus on anything other than the return of her husband and what he might have to say.

Relief floods her body when she eventually hears the car. He opens the front door and glances through to her, in the kitchen, before sighing and taking off his jacket.

'I made you dinner,' she says. 'Pork chops and mashed potato.'

'I'm not hungry,' he says slowly, walking in.

'Can I get you a drink? Would you like a beer?'

'No.'

He pulls out a chair and sits at the table, staring straight ahead, his jaw clenched. He keeps starting to say something, but then he stops. Finally, he takes a deep breath, and bursts into loud, wracking sobs.

'Oh, Elliott.' Gabby gets up and flies to him, cradling him in her arms, resting her forehead against his. 'Baby. I'm sorry. I'm so sorry.' She is weeping too. 'I never meant this to happen. What will it take for you to forgive me? Whatever it is, I'll do it. Anything.'

There is a long silence as they both weep. Elliott makes no move to touch Gabby, but lets himself be held by her until he is calm. Gabby goes back to her chair, but reaches out for his hand, certain this is a step in the right direction, that the very fact he allowed himself to be held means there is hope.

'The thing is,' Elliott whispers, not looking at Gabby, 'I'm not sure I *can* forgive you.'

Gabby's voice catches in her throat. 'What do you mean?'

'I want to. I want to be able to put this behind us and move on, but I don't know how to do that. It would be one thing if you had just been unfaithful, but you're pregnant. With another man's child. How am I supposed to get over something like that? I thought it would be possible, but it isn't. How am I supposed to forgive a betrayal like that?' He looks up at her then.

'I don't know,' Gabby says, careful to keep the desperation out of her voice. 'Maybe the only thing we can do is try. You know how Harvey's always using that expression he learned in al-anon, the one about *acting as if*. Maybe that's what we have to do. Act as if everything's fine, and then one day we'll wake up and it will be fine.'

'But it isn't fine. And it will never be fine.' Elliott starts to weep again. 'How could you do this to me, Gabby? How could you do this to us? How could you take a marriage that was so damn good and drop a bomb on it? Was I not a good husband to you? Was I deficient? How could you sleep with another man?' His voice is rising in anger again as he speaks. 'How could you?'

'I don't know,' Gabby says. 'It wasn't about you. I think it was about me feeling middle-aged. I know how awful that sounds, but it meant nothing. I swear.'

'When did it happen?' Elliott, tortured by not knowing, will be doubly tortured by knowing, but he cannot resist asking.

'It was the weekend you were away.'

He shakes his head. 'Jesus. You planned the whole thing. You waited for me to go.'

'No. It wasn't like that. He was going to be in town,' she says. 'And it was coincidence. I was just meeting him for a drink.'

'Where did it happen?'

'Elliott. Please. Don't do this. Don't ask. You don't want to know.'

'Just tell me it wasn't in our bed. Tell me you didn't fuck another man in our bed.'

'No, I didn't fuck another man in our bed. I . . . I wouldn't do that. It happened in the barn.'

'In our barn? So he was here? He was in my home?'

'Elliott, I told you not to do this. He was barely here.'

'You mean he came in, went out to the barn, fucked my wife and left?'

'Elliott. Please. It was nothing.'

'No, Gabriella. It wasn't "nothing". It was a betrayal. And now it's a new life.'

Gabby turns pale; she can almost feel her blood freeze as he says these words. She has always been able to get through to Elliott, but, for the first time ever, she knows she has lost him. Permanently.

'I'm sorry,' Gabby weeps. 'I'm so sorry. I love you.'

'You should have thought of that before.' Elliott gets up, and wearily goes upstairs.

'What are you doing?'

Elliott is walking down the hallway with some clothes and toiletries under his arm.

'I'm going to sleep in the spare room.'

Gabby's face starts to crumple. 'Elliott, please don't leave our room. I won't touch you, I swear, but please stay in our room. I need you. Please.'

He hesitates, and Gabby thinks she has got through to him, but then he shakes his head. 'I can't. I'm sorry. It's just too painful. I need to be on my own.'

Gabby crawls into bed and sobs until the bedroom door opens and Elliott is standing there. Flooded with relief, Gabby looks up at him, her eyes puffy and red raw.

'I just have to ask,' Elliott says. 'Was he better than me?'

'What?' Gabby says in disbelief. 'What are you talking about?'

'In bed. Was he better? More creative? Was he bigger than me?'

'Oh Jesus, Elliott. I'm not doing this. Please.'

'Please? You owe me, Gabby. You fucked another man so now you have to tell me. Was he?'

'No, he was not better than you, and no, he was not bigger. I don't even know. I barely even looked. It was over so quickly.'

Elliott says nothing. Just stares at Gabby. Then he backs out of the room and closes the door.

Elliott is gone by the time Gabby wakes up the next morning.

'Mom? You look terrible.' Olivia glances up at her. 'What's the matter with your eyes?'

'I had a migraine last night,' Gabby lies. 'It's still there. It's made me puff up like a balloon.'

Alanna looks up. 'Is that why Dad slept in the spare room?'

Gabby nods.

'So it wasn't because of that fight you had?'

'What fight?' Olivia says.

'Never mind what fight,' Gabby says. 'Don't worry about it. I've been very headachy and I get up a lot, which disturbs Dad. Can you please not ask any more about it?'

'Okay, okay,' Alanna says. 'Sorry I asked.'

'I'm sorry, sweetie. I just get grouchy when I'm tired. Did you see your dad this morning?'

'Yes.'

'How did he seem?'

Alanna looks at her mother weirdly. 'Fine. Why?'

'Oh. Good. Just glad he slept well.' Gabby turns to go upstairs, trying to hide a fresh round of tears. How can her husband, the love of her life, have turned into a stranger overnight, into someone she has to ask her daughter about in order to know his state of mind?

This is the man she is supposed to know best in the world, the man she turns to when the rest of her life is falling apart; if she can't turn to him, if he can't ease her pain, what is she supposed to do?

Gabby thinks perhaps she should just end it. Terminate the pregnancy. She should have done it before she even told Elliott. Why didn't she? It's a question Gabby doesn't have an answer to.

Chapter Eighteen

Gabby and Elliott circle each other all week, as polite as strangers. Each time Gabby makes an overture, suggesting dinner, a walk, some time to talk, Elliott politely declines. He has made no move to leave the guest room, and Gabby is shrouded in sadness at the knowledge that there will be no good ending to this, and that it is entirely her fault.

She makes dinner and they sit at the table with the girls, Elliott pretending to be his normal self, making jokes and asking them about their day, while Gabby sits quietly opposite him, attempting to join in, feeling him drifting further and further away from her.

When Alanna came home yesterday she didn't run straight to her room. Instead she came to the kitchen and sat down with her mother at the table.

'I'm worried about you, Mom,' she said, her small brow furrowed with anxiety. 'And I'm worried about Dad. Something's going on and I'm scared you're going to get divorced.'

Gabby gasped. 'What?' she said, immediately welling up. 'Oh, baby. I'm so sorry. We're not getting divorced, we're just . . .' She had no idea what to say. 'Sometimes grown-ups go through some hard times. It's nothing for you to worry about, and Dad and I will figure it out.'

'So you're not going to get divorced? Promise me you won't get divorced.'

Gabby winced at the prospect, but knew she couldn't lie any more. She didn't know herself what would happen. How could she make a promise to her daughter knowing it wasn't up to her to fulfil it?

'I promise you this,' she said. 'I love your father more than any other man in the world and I do not want a divorce. I know it seems like the end of the world when your parents are having a rough time, but I do not want a divorce. We will figure this out.'

It was as close to the truth as she was able to get, and seemed to placate Alanna. For now.

Before she sits down at the dinner table these days Gabby makes mental lists of what to talk about, stories she can tell about her day, newspaper articles she can share to ensure they are not sitting in an awkward silence.

She studies Elliott across the table, astonished at how fragile her marriage is, at how quickly and easily their relationship can unravel. Of course this is her fault; she knows this is her fault. But it was one mistake, and now she will do anything, will fight with all that she has, to save her marriage.

Why doesn't Elliott feel the same way?

He has to. He must. It will just take him a little longer.

In the meantime Gabby will be the perfect wife, will cook him all the foods he loves, will tend to his every need, will show him that he cannot find better, that he must not leave.

On Thursday morning, she gets a text from Claire.

> So excited for tonight – the four of us
> haven't been out for ages! I booked at
> Finalmente at 7.30. OK?

She had forgotten. It is Tim's birthday, therefore dinner with Claire and Tim. Oh God. The prospect of even leaving her house right now is terrifying, let alone seeing other people. But Claire and Tim don't really count as other people. They are almost family. Perhaps seeing them will be a good thing, will remind Elliott of the life they have built, the friends they have; perhaps it will give him a dose of reality.

> Sounds great. See you later. G xx

'I don't think we should be seeing them,' Elliott says as they pull out of the driveway. 'We should have cancelled.'

'We can't cancel. It's Tim's birthday. We have to go.'

'I'm not ready for this. How do we tell other people what's happened?'

'Elliott! We don't tell other people what's happened. No one needs to know anything. We're just going to have a nice evening with our closest friends.'

'You don't think you need to let our closest friends

know you're pregnant – with another man's baby?' He mutters the last part of the sentence, disgust in his eyes.

'I don't think we need to tell them anything. Maybe they'll just think I've put on weight during the holidays.'

Elliott rolls his eyes.

'Elliott, please. Can you at least pretend? Can you at least be civil to me tonight? I'm not asking you to profess undying love, but can you at least try to look at me with something other than disdain?'

Elliott says nothing.

'Elliott?'

'I'll try.'

'Look at me!' Claire proudly steps back from their hug, showing off her growing bump. 'I'm in my first maternity trousers! Can you believe the size of me? I swear this is because I'm so old.'

'You look amazing,' Gabby says, wishing she could tell Claire that she too is pregnant, and feeling odd, and awkward, that she has to withhold such huge news. This pregnancy is so different from her previous pregnancies, when she was filled with excitement and joy.

All she feels with this one, from the moment she wakes up until the moment she manages to gain some respite with a few hours' sleep, is dread. This isn't even a child she wants; in some sick way she harbours a small hope that something will happen to end this pregnancy, to enable her to put this all behind her so that she can carry on with her life, with Elliott, finally removing all evidence of her transgression.

But her scan, carried out this morning, was fine. She went to the doctor's office alone, wiping a tear from her eye as she remembered going to another doctor for a scan that produced the first picture of Olivia. Elliott had been with her, perched on a stool at her head as the sonographer moved the slick gel around her belly, and they had both gasped at the sight of what was already so clearly a baby, her thumb at her mouth. He had been there for Alanna's sonogram too, but there was no question of him being there for this one.

She lay there silently, alone, while the sonographer moved that familiar wand. And as she thought about how much she had wanted one more baby she heard the words of her mother echo through her head: 'Be careful what you wish for.'

She could never have imagined that this is how her wish would be fulfilled.

Looking at the screen she didn't react as she saw the baby growing in her stomach. She watched passively as the sonographer measured the nuchal fold, the limbs, and checked to see everything was growing normally.

Gabby wasn't overwhelmed in the way she had been when Olivia and Alanna had been scanned. She felt . . . detached. In much the same way she feels with Elliott. *Detached*. As if this is all happening to someone else. That it is someone else's baby on that screen. The marriage break-up is happening to someone else. Not me. It couldn't possibly be happening to me.

Her need to share the news of her pregnancy with Claire is not to share each other's joy, even supposing Gabby will ever feel any, but to prove to herself that the bond of their friendship is as strong as she needs it to be. But Gabby is scared. What will Claire do when she finds out? How will she react? Claire will know immediately that Elliott cannot be the father because she knows about his vasectomy. Why didn't Gabby withhold that information? So now, even if she and Elliott can work through this and stay intact, Claire will know the secret truth, the truth that Gabby had an affair. Will she stand by Gabby?

She will have to. Surely. That's what best friends do.

'How do you feel?' She focuses her attention back on Claire, aware that Elliott and Tim are busy talking, which means that there may be a semblance of normality tonight if only because Elliott and Tim are always perfectly happy to talk, just the two of them, for hours.

'I feel exhausted. Terrible. I could sleep all day and all night. Honestly? I have no idea what I'm doing having a baby at my age. Tim was saying just the other night that we should be planning a retirement home, never mind saving for yet another one's college. I swear to God, we just cancelled our vacation.'

Tim breaks off his conversation with Elliott to correct her. 'We didn't cancel. We just . . . rearranged.'

'Yup. We were all going to Cancun, and now we're

driving up to Grafton to stay at a friend's house for a couple of days. Big difference.'

'At least you're going away,' says Gabby. 'We haven't had a vacation for years. Remember when we went away by ourselves?' She looks at Elliott, reminding him of the good times, the happier times. 'To Antigua?' She turns back to Claire and Tim. 'We went to Galley Bay in Antigua and it was amazing. A second honeymoon. Apart from when we got stuck on the yacht. Remember that?' She's smiling as she looks at Elliott, who shrugs.

'Vaguely,' he says, before turning to Tim. 'Are you going to coach softball again this year? I was thinking about doing it but I figured I'd check with you first.'

Gabby looks up to find Claire frowning at her.

'I have to go to the bathroom,' Claire says. 'Gabby, come with me.'

In the bathroom she turns to Gabby as soon as the door is closed. 'What the hell's going on with you two? Have you had a fight?'

And Gabby bursts into tears.

She cannot stop for a long time. Her body is heaving with sobs as a shocked Claire tries to comfort her. Eventually Gabby manages to calm down, the odd shudder running through her body every few seconds.

'Gabby, what is it?' Claire asks softly, awkwardly crouching next to her. 'What's happened?'

'I think Elliott is leaving me,' Gabby says, staring at the floor.

'Don't be ridiculous,' Claire says. 'Elliott would never leave you. You two are the strongest couple we know. Why would you say such a thing?'

Gabby looks up then, into Claire's eyes, and it is with an expression of such pleading despair that Claire feels a cold clutch of fear.

'It was the guy, wasn't it?'

Gabby nods.

'You had an affair and Elliott found out.'

'It wasn't an affair. It was one night. Not even. One incident. And Elliott can't forgive me. He won't ever be able to forgive me.'

Claire sighs. 'Look, it's terrible. We all know it's terrible, but you're human, Gabby. I don't condone it, but I understand that we all make mistakes, and no one understands that better than Elliott. He's the most compassionate man I know. I'm not saying it's going to be easy, but I truly believe that you'll be able to work through this together. Have you talked about seeing a couple counsellor? Couple therapy can completely transform a relationship, and you already know I have someone amazing. Gabby, this doesn't have to be the end of the marriage.' Claire takes her hand. 'It's going to be okay.'

'It's not,' Gabby says, looking up at Claire again as she takes a deep breath. 'I'm pregnant. And you know as well as I do that the baby can't be Elliott's.'

Claire's mouth drops open. There is confusion in her eyes, then horror as the words sink in and she remembers

Gabby telling her about the vasectomy. She actually reaches out for the sink to steady herself, her face a whiter shade of pale.

'Gabby, you . . .' She is shocked to the core, and as her eyes flick to Gabby's stomach, registering the weight gain, the small bump, her voice is no more than a whisper. 'Gabby, you can't have it. You need to end this pregnancy.'

Gabby, feeling an unexpected surge of anger at her friend, shakes her head. Who does Claire, pregnant herself, think she is telling Gabby to have an abortion?

'I know,' says Gabby coldly. 'But I don't think I can.'

'I . . . Oh God. I don't know what to say.'

'I'm not sure there *is* anything to say.' Gabby's hands reflexively go to her stomach, protecting the baby she wanted so badly, but not like this. 'It's the one thing I wanted so desperately. And it's the worst thing that's ever happened to me.'

Claire regains enough composure to reach out to Gabby and put her arms round her, but neither of them is comforted; neither of them is able to fool the other.

They leave the room a couple of minutes later, Gabby imploring Claire to act normally, to make it seem as though she doesn't know, but Claire, always a terrible liar, is still in shock, and truly doesn't know how to pretend everything's normal.

'You know,' she says, after the waiter has brought them their drinks, 'I know this is terrible, and I was so looking forward to this evening, but I'm feeling really nauseous. I think I may have to go home.'

'It's fine,' Elliott is quick to say. 'Of course.'

Claire hugs Gabby, whispering in her ear, 'I'm sorry. I love you. Let's speak tomorrow.'

And then they are gone, leaving Elliott to pick up the bill for drinks.

As they walk out of the restaurant, Gabby is embarrassed, but also grateful because she is sure it would have been impossible for Claire to keep up an act all evening once she knew the truth.

'You told her,' Elliott says as they get in the car.

Gabby is silent.

'Gabby –' Her name sounds strange coming from his lips and since her betrayal he is reluctant to say it, even to taste the shape of her name. 'I can't do this any more.'

Gabby's heart leaps into her mouth. 'What do you mean?'

'I mean I can't be with you. I wanted to try, but I can't. Every time I look at you, every time I hear your name, I just think of you with another man, and his child growing inside you, and I can't stand it.'

'Elliott,' Gabby forces her voice to be calm, 'I know how hard this is right now, but I think we should go and see a couple therapist. I know of someone who's meant to be fan—'

'No.' He stops her. 'I'm not going to see a couple

therapist. It won't help. It won't change what you did, nor how I feel about it. Gabby, I love you. I don't want to feel this way, but I do, and no amount of talking about it will make a difference to that. I'm sorry. I'm moving out.'

'Elliott?' Gabby's voice is shaking. 'If I ended this pregnancy would you still leave me?'

Elliott stares at her. 'Yes,' he says. 'Yes, I would. I would still leave.'

Chapter Nineteen

Elliott stands in Claire's kitchen, a kitchen that is starting to feel like home, as Olivia rails at him. The baby Gabby is carrying has nothing to do with Elliott, so he decided not to mention it to the girls, but, evidently, Gabby has now shared at least part of her news, and Olivia has not taken it well.

'How can you leave?' she hisses, having just been dropped off here by her mother. 'What kind of a father are you that you can leave Mom when she's having a baby? I'm just . . . disgusted. I can't believe you're doing this. I can't believe you're leaving her now.'

'Olivia,' he says calmly, 'there are things you know nothing about. You may think you know the whole story but you don't. I'm sorry, I truly am, that this has happened, and if there was any other way, if there was any way for me to make this work, don't you think that's what I would be doing? Do you think I want to leave my family? Do you really think I want to be staying in Tim and Claire's house? Much as I love them, this isn't my home, and I would never, ever leave you and Alanna. I wouldn't.'

'So why did you?' Olivia spits, welling up with tears. 'You have a choice. This is all bullshit. You didn't have to leave. You don't have to leave. I will never be able to forgive you for this, Dad.'

Elliott is pained. 'You don't understand,' he says wearily.

'No. You're right. I don't understand. So explain it to me. Help me.'

'I can't,' he says, after a pause. 'It's not something that's for me to tell.'

'Great.' The sarcasm drips from her voice. 'You're trying to blame Mom for this, but she didn't leave. Whatever fight you've had, the fact that you left, when she's pregnant with your child, is unforgivable.'

'It's not,' he says quietly, unable to help himself.

'It's not what?'

'Nothing.'

'No. It's not nothing.' Olivia's voice starts to rise. 'It's not what? What do you mean? Tell me, Dad! Tell me!' She is shouting now.

'It's not my child.'

Olivia stares at him in shock, before running out of the door. Elliott goes after her, calling her name, but she is faster than he is and she doesn't stop, and soon she is out of view entirely.

He shouldn't have said it. He knows he shouldn't have said it. But he cannot stand being blamed by his daughters when he is not the one at fault. He has tried to protect his wife, tried not to talk about it, but he will not allow his daughters to portray him as the bad guy.

He will not allow Gabby to take away what little he has left.

Olivia bursts through the door of the barn, frantically looking for her mother. She finds her on a chair in the corner, sitting staring into the space.

'Is it true?' Olivia demands, standing in front of her mother with crossed arms.

'Is what true?'

'The baby isn't Dad's.'

Gabby just gapes at her daughter, stunned. She wasn't going to tell her daughters. Certainly not yet, not while they were still struggling with the fact their father has moved out. She hasn't discussed this with Elliott, but she assumed she had a few months. She wanted time for them to get adjusted, time for them to get used to this new life before she dropped another clanger on them.

'Well?' Olivia pushes. 'Is it true?'

'What did your father tell you? Oh God. I can't believe he told you. What did he say?'

Olivia stares at her mother, incredulity and sadness in her eyes, and Gabby is filled with regret for doing this to her, doing this to all of them.

'You're pregnant with somebody else's baby? No wonder he left. How could you? How could you sleep with another man when you're married to Dad and he's so . . . he's so great? What are you thinking? What *were* you thinking?' Olivia is shaking her head in disbelief, trying to comprehend. 'How could you do this to him? To us? I have no idea who you are because my mother wouldn't do that. My mother would never do something so hurtful and wrong. You even promised me you weren't having an affair – remember?'

Gabby is not sure she has ever been in so much pain. She wants to explain to Olivia how it happened, why, and that it didn't mean anything, but Olivia is only seventeen, not old enough to understand the feelings ignited in a middle-aged woman when a young and attractive man finds her alluring.

'Who is it? Who is he? Who's the baby's father?' Olivia says, realizing her mother isn't going to say anything, can barely look her in the eye.

'No one. No one you know. It doesn't matter,' Gabby says quietly through her tears.

'Even better, Mom. You threw away your life for nothing? For no one? You ruined all of our lives for, what? For nothing.' Her voice drops then. 'How could you?' she says quietly, turning to hide the tears that are starting to fall. She doesn't see Gabby sink to the floor, distraught, because she goes up to her room to pack, to be with her father, to stay anywhere but under her mother's roof.

Gabby doesn't move, other than to curl up. Her body heaves with sobs, for she knows Olivia is absolutely right. She has thrown away her life for no one, for nothing. And no one could be more disgusted with her than she is herself.

She has lost her husband. Now, she has lost her daughter. And she is fairly certain she has lost her best friend, because although she has assumed true best friends don't have to choose sides during a marriage split, given that Claire and Tim have opened their lives to Elliott, given that Claire has not been in touch for days, she is in little doubt about what is happening.

What the hell was she thinking? What came over her? She doesn't think about Matt at all. They have had only one exchange of emails since the day they slept together. It had been so awkward afterwards, her guilt, and remorse, and shame were immediate and over-whelming, and they both recognized, without having to say anything, that that was the end.

She will never tell him about the baby. Even thinking of him makes her feel physically sick. No matter what the outcome of her life, she will do this without his help, without having anything more, ever, to do with the man who she now thinks of as ruining her life.

But it wasn't just him. If he hadn't come along per-haps there would have been someone else. Gabby still thinks of those weeks – the frantic emailing, being up all night thinking about him, messages flying back and forth, their flirtation growing stronger and stronger – as something akin to an out-of-body experience. He came along at a time when she felt invisible, when she felt that she was growing old and dull, that life would never again be exciting or glamorous.

She became obsessed with the thrill of it all, the

roller coaster of highs when he emailed, the lows when he didn't. Looking back, which she tries not to do, she can think of it only as an addiction: short-lived, intense, unmanageable. It possessed her, leaving no room for reason or rationality. She couldn't have stopped it even if she wanted to. And she did want to; she never wanted it to go as far as it did. She just wanted to feel beautiful for a bit longer; to feel alive; to feel wanted.

Now she is left with nothing, nothing but a future of swimming in the morass of remorse and shame she created all by herself.

She doesn't hear the door of the barn open. She is too busy crying. But she feels the hand on her leg, the heat of a small body curled up next to her.

'Don't cry, Mommy.' Alanna takes her hand and strokes it. 'It's going to be okay.' This only makes Gabby cry harder, but eventually she is able to smile at Alanna through her tears, noticing that Alanna's blue eyes are glistening.

'Have you seen your sister?' Gabby strokes Alanna's hair back behind her ears, tracing her fingers along her daughter's cheekbones, noticing the tiny glittering flower ear rings she is wearing, the ones Elliott bought for her the last time they went to Main Street.

Alanna nods. 'She left. She told me.'

Gabby doesn't say anything. What is left for her to say?

'I still love you,' Alanna says. 'And it's still my baby brother or sister. I'll be here to look after it even if Olivia isn't.'

'You're the best,' Gabby whispers. 'Do you have any idea how much I love you?'

Alanna nods, and the two of them sit, together, for a very long time.

Chapter Twenty

Gabby has texted Claire a few times, receiving responses that are barely responses, their abruptness and detachment supposedly mitigated by an emoticon of a smiley face or a frown.

Cant. Frantic :(

Maybe tomorrow

Am good. Talk later! :)

But they don't talk later. They don't talk at all. Gabby has left voicemail messages on Claire's mobile phone, thinking this would be a sure way to get hold of her, but they have not been returned.

There are other women Gabby could talk to, but none she trusts in the way she trusts Claire.

Never has she felt more alone than now, abandoned by her husband, daughter and best friend.

She examines her sideways reflection. She might have got away with saying she's just put on weight, but anyone who knows would see she is pregnant. It isn't just the weight, it's the shape. Her breasts are full and heavy, her stomach extended in a way that can only suggest a baby. Mid-life weight gain is often around the belly, she knows, but it is soft and fleshy, not low and firm as hers is.

Do people know? Gabby has no idea whether people are gossiping or not but she assumes they are, and at times like this she is aware of living in a very small town. All it takes is one person to tell another. Even though she trusts Claire not to speak, even now, she knows Olivia will not be able to hold it in. Olivia will have told a friend, who will have told her mother, who will have spread it around town.

Her phone has rung more of late. Not her mobile – anyone who really wants to get hold of her knows to call only her mobile phone for she never picks up the one at home – but the home phone has been ringing frequently, especially since school has begun again. She always lets it go to the machine and doesn't bother listening, but occasionally she scrolls through the display to see the numbers that have called, noting that various women she knows only vaguely are phoning her. These are women who never ring her, but they are doubtless phoning under some pretext – would she like to help with the bake sale; does she have a piece of furniture she'd like to donate to the upcoming auction – because they are, in fact, just itching to find out what's going on, to be able to go to school tomorrow and whisper excitedly that they know something no one else knows.

Gabby has to go to school today. It is the seventh-grade Poetry Café, and even though she would do almost anything to avoid being there she knows she must make the effort.

When they were tiny, in kindergarten and first grade, she made a decision, based largely on the fact she had a mother entirely uninterested in her school life, that she would go to everything.

While not very keen to be a room mother, or volunteer extensively, for years she has shown up for every reading, performance, concert.

In the early days Gabby needed to go, not just to see the girls perform, but to try to make herself part of the community. She has tried so hard to make herself fit in, and yet she still feels as though she has never quite managed it. She has copied the uniform of bootleg jeans and clogs, puffy vests, cute scarves. She has entered into conversations about babysitters and sports teams, dance classes and softball coaches – conversations she so often finds mindless – with an enthusiasm she doesn't feel. She has grown accustomed to showing up to Saturday morning games with her collapsible chair and coffee in a portable mug, setting up the chair in a huddle of other mothers. She has become used to the gossipy chat being interrupted time and time again as, one by one, each mother puts the conversation on hold and screams words of encouragement when it is her daughter's turn, paying attention to the group again only when the daughter goes back to the dugout, at which point the game is ignored again until another of the daughters is up.

Gabby has had to learn all the rules, the rules of the games as well as the social rules. From the outside, she looks and behaves like the other mothers; if you ignore her accent, still so very English, she speaks like the others, uses the same language, the same cadences, but inside she knows she doesn't belong.

Inside she knows she can dress, speak, pretend as much as she wants to, but you cannot take a girl from north-west London, drop her in suburban Connecticut and expect her to fit in.

None of which bothers her now. She is used to her life, loves her life, and only ever misses the sophistication and glamour of London when she – very occasionally – goes back there, but today she isn't sure she is up to the pretence. Today she isn't sure she can stand there and make small talk about softball, or gossip about coaches, or ask questions about how the house renovation is coming along.

Today she'd much rather stay at home and hide. If it wasn't for Alanna, forgiving, loving, lovely Alanna, that is exactly what she would do. She is wearing yoga pants that are stretched to a shine over her burgeoning bump, with a long tunic-style T-shirt and a voluminous scarf that drapes round her neck and falls in generous folds, covering her torso in swathes of linen.

If they don't know she's pregnant they might not necessarily guess today. Gabby takes a deep breath. She doesn't have to do anything other than smile and be polite. And if Claire is there, which she undoubtedly will be, maybe they can grab a coffee afterwards. Perhaps when Claire sees Gabby at the Poetry Café she will be able to forgive her; perhaps she will be able to be a true friend still.

Chapter Twenty-One

As usual, Gabby is late. She pops into the school office to sign in, then walks quickly down the hallway to the library. The homeroom teacher is talking, introducing the Language Arts project, as Gabby waves at the couple of women who look up to see who has come in.

In the front row is Claire. She does not turn round but Gabby can see her profile and would recognize her anywhere.

Next to her is Elliott.

Gabby is shaken. She takes a seat in the back row, her mind whirring. Why is Elliott here? He never comes to school events; he is always too busy with work to make it to anything. How did he even organize his schedule to be here, and why? This is her domain; it has always been her domain. She looks around the room at the handful of other fathers that are always there, fathers who work from home, who run their own hedge funds in town, who are on 'gardening leave', the ironic but oh-so-handy euphemism for being unemployed.

Elliott is not one of those fathers. Had this happened before she would have been delighted; nothing would have made her happier than Elliott turning up unexpectedly at an event at school. But now this feels like a betrayal. She cannot take her eyes off the back of his head. He is her husband, the man she loves. He shouldn't be sitting over there, so far away. If he is here, he should be by her side.

But the chasm between them is growing wider and wider, and she still struggles to understand how something so good can fall apart so quickly and so easily. It doesn't make sense to her that everything they have built up over twenty years can be ruined by one moment of madness.

Claire turns and looks straight at Gabby, who smiles awkwardly and raises her hand in an almost-wave. Claire smiles in return, then turns back. Gabby watches to see if she will tell Elliott, and sure enough, a couple of minutes later, Claire tilts her head to Elliott's and clearly tells him. Gabby knows this because his shoulders tense immediately, while hers sag in dismay.

Elliott has been avoiding her, and Olivia refuses to see her. Gabby drives Alanna back and forth to Claire's house to stay with Elliott, never getting out of the car, texting Alanna from her position of safety if she needs to let her know she is outside. She asks Alanna if Dad is coming out, but Alanna always says no, and Gabby doesn't want to put her in the middle, doesn't want to ask Alanna to tell Elliott to come outside.

Nor can she walk up the garden path and into the house in the way she has done a million times before. This house is now surrounded by an invisible barrier that keeps Gabby out. Gabby isn't the type to trample

195

on boundaries, to walk into homes where she knows she is unwanted. She has already pictured the look of shock and dismay on the faces of all of them should she have the temerity to walk into the kitchen.

No. That isn't something Gabby will be doing.

Alanna steps up to the front of the class, a piece of white paper held firmly in her hands. Poised and confident, she reads a poem she has written about fall. Gabby's heart threatens to burst with pride. Cheering and clapping, she has to physically restrain herself from jumping up and throwing her arms round her little girl.

As Alanna goes back to her seat Gabby catches Elliott staring at his daughter, and the expression on his face is exactly the same as on hers. Pride and love. An acknowledgment of the extraordinary girl they have created.

If only he would look at Gabby that way too.

Gabby is standing by the table that has been covered with paper plates of snacks: chocolate-chip cookies, cut-up chunks of cantaloupe, cheese sticks, grapes, chocolate brownies.

The children have raided the snack table, but Gabby is helping herself to the brownies. She would not normally allow herself to eat them but she is pregnant – although never, during her last two pregnancies, did she use that as an excuse to eat whatever she wanted. She remembers being terrified of becoming a whale, of never being able to get rid of the excess weight.

This time round she doesn't care. She's a pregnant single mother, or at least it looks that way. If she can't comfort herself with food, what hope is left?

She turns, chewing a mouthful of brownie, to find herself inches from Elliott, so achingly familiar and lovely it almost makes her burst into tears there and then. His twinkling blue eyes. The stubble that never goes away, even immediately after he shaves. His Barbour, the coat she bought him for his fortieth birthday, which smells of waxed cotton and of Elliott, and is so lived-in and loved it is now as soft as silk. All of him is hers. Was hers. His strong, masculine hands. His salt-and-pepper hair, as tousled as ever. She wants to reach up, as she always does, to tuck the stray bits back, but she no longer has that right.

This is her husband, her man, her best friend. The man to whom she has told everything for twenty years, yet now she finds herself looking at him with no idea what to say.

Elliott clears his throat. 'Hi.'

'Hi.'

There is an awkward silence.

'You look good.' She is lying, because in fact he looks terrible. His face is gaunt, his clothes are hanging off him.

'I look terrible,' he says.

'You're right. I'm sorry. You look terrible. Can I

just . . .' And she reaches up to tuck back his hair, except when he realizes what she's doing he turns his head sharply, so she brushes the air and has to withdraw her hand, embarrassed. 'I'm sorry,' she says again. 'Just . . . your hair.'

'Oh. Right.' He brushes it back himself. 'Alanna was good, wasn't she?'

'I was so proud.' Gabby puts her hand on her heart. 'Our little girl. Who knew she had such a talent for poetry? And performing!'

'Who knew?' echoes Elliott.

'How did you get time off work?'

'Harvey's taking my patients while I'm here. I thought it best, while we figure things out, to be there for the kids. They need both of us. Especially now.'

Gabby tries to swallow the lump in her throat. 'Elliott, can we talk? I know it's been only a few weeks, and I know you may not be ready, but there's stuff we have to figure out. I can't keep driving Alanna back and forth, and I need to see Olivia.'

'She doesn't want to see you.'

'I know. But I'm her mother. She and I have to work this out. Please, Elliott. Can we at least have coffee? Can we just sit down and talk about it?'

Elliott thinks, then nods. 'Okay. Coffee.'

'Do you want to come over after this?'

'No!' He is vehement. Nothing would cause him more pain right now than going back to the house he no longer lives in, back to the life he has been forced to leave. 'I'll meet you at Starbucks on the Post Road. In an hour?'

Gabby, seeing a glimmer of hope, agrees. 'Okay. An hour.' She walks towards the door, turning, surprised, when she feels a hand on her arm. It is Claire.

'How are you?' Claire's face is filled with sadness.

'Pretty terrible. How are you?'

'Okay. Fat. Emotional. Tired.'

'How's Elliott?'

'You were just talking to him.'

'I know, but you're with him every night, Claire. How is he?'

Claire looks at her for a few seconds before shrugging. 'He's pretty terrible too. He cries at night. A lot. Sometimes I have to take him in my arms and hold him until he stops. Tim has tried to take him out with the boys for a drink, to take his mind off it, but he doesn't want to do anything other than sit on the sofa and cry. He pretends to be okay until Olivia goes to bed, but then his pain just fills the house and –'

'Oh God, Claire. Why are you telling me this?'

'Because you asked, Gabby. I don't know what to say. I'm trying so hard to forgive you, and I love you and Elliott so much, and . . . that's why I'm struggling. I can't see him in this kind of pain and get together with you and pretend I'm okay with all of it.'

'I'm not asking you to pretend to be okay with all of

it. I don't expect you to be okay with it. God, I'm not okay with it. I'm disgusted with myself. I am ashamed, and if I could think of anything in the world I could do to change it, I would. Jesus, Claire . . .' Gabby fights to keep her voice low enough that it doesn't project to everyone in the room. 'If I could, do you not think I would turn back the clock? I'm twenty-five weeks pregnant and there is nothing I can do about it other than feel sick for ruining my life, everyone's life, with one mistake. Sick. And disgusted. And the last thing I need is for my best friend to abandon me through this. The last thing I need is to feel judged, and hated, by you.' Tears are now streaming down Gabby's cheeks.

'I could never hate you,' whispers Claire. 'I love you, but I can't be there for both of you. It's too draining. This isn't my choice. It isn't that I've chosen Elliott over you, but Elliott has chosen us, and I haven't got the strength right now for both of you. I'm sorry. I know you won't understand . . .'

'You're right,' Gabby snaps, whirling as she prepares to leave the room. 'I don't understand.'

There is a table in the corner of Starbucks, by the window, which Gabby grabs, cradling her green tea as she looks out onto the Post Road, lulled into calm by the passing cars. She still can't believe the conversation she had with Claire, can't believe that, despite the way

Claire has decided to reframe it in her mind, Claire has chosen Elliott over Gabby.

And then there were none, she thinks.

She looks up to see Elliott approaching the table.

'Hi. Sorry I'm a bit late.' He sits down as Gabby jumps up.

'Let me get you something,' she blurts, in a reversal of their roles, for Elliott would always be the one to get coffee, or food, or anything, while Gabby and the girls sat at the table.

'No, I'm fine.'

'You must have something. Tea? I'm drinking green tea. It's good. You'll like it.'

'Okay,' he acquiesces. 'Sure.'

She goes to the counter to place the order, knowing this would never happen if they were still a couple. Elliott would automatically order the tea, pulling his wallet from his pocket to pay for it. Back at the table she sets down his mug and sits.

'Thanks. I just came from the realtor's office.' Elliott takes a sip of his tea. 'That's why I was late. They're going to phone you to make an appointment to come and value the house.'

Gabby stares at him. 'What?'

'I thought it would make sense to sell the house, and even though they don't recommend putting it on the market until the spring, I'd like to have an idea of what it's worth.'

'Why would we sell the house?'

Elliott snorts. 'Gabby, if we're not together, we each need money for our separate homes, and the only place that money's going to come from is the house. This is the most practical solution.'

Gabby's heart is pounding. 'If we're not together. But what if we are? What if we are able to work through this? What if we get back together, but we've lost our home? Elliott, you and I both love the house; think of all the work we put into it. We can't sell our house.' There is an urgency to her voice.

'Gabby,' he says quietly, 'I don't think there's anything to work through.'

She makes an effort to calm her voice, even though her body is jittery with panic. 'What do you mean?'

'I mean, you're pregnant with a baby by another man. That's it. It's done.'

'You want to divorce me?' Of course deep down she knew that this was the way things were going, but they haven't mentioned the D word before and she thought, hoped, that as long as it wasn't mentioned then getting back together was always a possibility.

Elliott stares at the table, grimacing with discomfort and pain, unable to believe he is sitting inches from his wife and having this discussion with her, the woman he thought he would spend the rest of his life with, the woman he imagined growing old with, a woman so perfect for him he has never, not for a second, even thought about anyone else.

'No,' he says, looking up at her, wincing as he speaks. 'I don't want to divorce you. But you've left me no other choice.'

Gabby holds it in until she is in her car. She holds it in until she turns onto Center Street. She holds it in until she finds a quiet spot on the side of an empty street at the edge of town, where she parks, hides her head in her hands, and howls.

Putting her head back she screams at the roof of the car, pounding the steering wheel until, exhausted, she just lays her forehead on the wheel and sobs, moaning in pain.

Her mobile phone rings. Maybe it's Elliott. It must be Elliott. He must be phoning to say he made a terrible mistake; he's thought things through and he can't throw away twenty years of marriage like this. Frantically she roots through her handbag, pulling out the crap that mysteriously makes its way into all her bags – tissues, earplugs, leaflets, more leaflets, tampons with torn wrappers, hair bands – until she finds the phone.

It isn't Elliott. It's her mum.

'Darling!' Natasha trills down the phone. 'I haven't heard from you for ages. I just turned to your father earlier and said, "Have you heard from our naughty daughter recently?" And he said, "Not for months." So I decided to call! How are you? And how are my gorgeous granddaughters?'

'Hi, Mum.' Gabby's voice is reedy and thin, despite her attempt to disguise her tears. 'We're good.'

'You don't sound good, darling. You sound terrible. What's the matter? Do you have a cold?'

Gabby has never turned to her mother in her life. Her mother, who was there for everyone else, who took in strangers and helped them sort out their lives, is the very last person Gabby would ever think to turn in a crisis.

She rarely thinks to call them, and they, she assumes, are too wrapped up in their own worlds to call her. She loves her parents, naturally, but when people talk of their support systems, their families, Gabby has always known that the only support system to whom she would turn is her family of choice: Elliott, the girls, Claire.

Now that support system has broken down, and the only person that's left is the woman on the end of the phone right now.

'I don't have a cold.' Gabby can feel herself starting to break down. 'Elliott's left me.'

Natasha doesn't say a word of interruption, just lets her daughter tell her the whole story. She asks questions when necessary, prompts Gabby when needed, but there is no judgement in her voice, only kindness, compassion and love.

'What am I going to do?' Gabby says, over and over. 'What am I going to do?'

'You're going to get the local paper, you're going to go to the noticeboard in the library, and you're going to go online and Google. You're going to find yourself a divorce support group with a bloody good therapist leading the group. You're going to find other women going through the same thing, because you cannot be alone through this. You will not be alone. My God, Gabby, if I have to come out there myself and help you through it, I will. Darling girl, you aren't alone. I promise you.'

'You'd really come out?' Her mother has come to America three times in the last twenty years, the last of which was five years ago. It was much easier, she'd taken to saying, if they all came to London. Gabby would think: easier for whom? Although she never put up much of a fight as she did so love going home.

'I would. I will. You just say the word and I'll book my flight.'

Gabby lies in bed, her hands resting on her belly as she feels the baby do a lazy somersault. She moves her nightshirt aside and watches her stomach undulate, a knee or an elbow pushing out her skin, and despite all that has happened, despite wishing she could go back and do things differently, she cannot help but gasp with amazement that she is carrying another life inside her.

Today it feels as magical as it was with Olivia and Alanna – the miracle of a tiny person in her stomach – and for the first time, as the tears roll gently down her cheeks, she smiles, just a little.

This time, they are tears of wonder and joy.

Chapter Twenty-Two

Gabby has passed the big white church many times, but has never had any reason to go inside. She has always found it easier to say she is not a believer in organized religion than to offer up the truth, which is that she is slightly envious of people who have faith, religion, whatever it is you want to call it.

When she first arrived in the suburbs she looked in astonishment at the smartly dressed people teeming out of their houses on a Sunday.

'Where are they all going?' she asked Elliott.

He was amazed she genuinely didn't know. 'To church.'

No one she knew in London went to church, other than for weddings and, perhaps, christenings. She knew plenty of Jewish people who went to synagogue, but even then it was only for the major holidays, often only Yom Kippur.

When she was growing up Gabby had always wanted somewhere to go. Her parents didn't believe in organized religion; they had decided it was the root of the world's evils.

'The only religion your father follows is that of the Liberal Intelligentsia,' her mother would say with a laugh if ever Gabby tried to question him. Her mother, having renounced Catholicism, had spent most of Gabby's childhood trying Buddhism. There were various kinds. She tried the Nam Myoho Renge Kyo kind, which was said to manifest anything you should want; then she tried Zen Buddhism; then finally she tried to follow the teachings of Thich Nhat Hanh, with his suggestions of daily Mindful Meditations.

Elliott would admit to being Episcopalian only if pushed. He too had religious confusion. It was one of the things they had always shared, always laughed about.

There is a white sign pasted up on the door with an arrow pointing upstairs to the church library. Gabby hesitates in the doorway, wanting suddenly to get back in her car, anxious about what a divorce support group might entail.

Perhaps she can sit quietly in the back and listen to the others. Perhaps pearls of wisdom will fall from the lips of the therapist who leads the group – Sally, who, incidentally, seemed lovely on the phone. Gabby hopes these pearls will instantaneously give her the peace and serenity she has been looking for, enabling her to leave silently, renewed.

As she is standing there another woman walks in, hesitating when she sees Gabby.

'Are you here for the . . . support group?' she asks, nervously smoothing her blonde ponytail.

'The divorce support group?' As if there would be

more than one support group meeting at this time, in this church.

The woman nods, and, relieved to have found strength in the power of two, they both walk up the stairs to push open the library door.

A couple of women who appear to know each other stand at one end by a large table with some leaflets on it, while others are dotted sporadically around the room. One is on a soft loveseat and others are perched on folding chairs that have been placed in a circle in the centre of the room.

Opposite the loveseat is a wing chair, in which sits a woman with glasses, grey hair and a warm smile.

'Welcome,' she says, standing up and coming over to greet the women. 'I'm Sally.'

The woman Gabby came in with, with whom she feels an instant affinity, is Josephine. They move in unison towards two chairs, their heads together as they make small talk, establishing their bond. Where do they live, do they have children, is this their first group . . . ?

It is a disparate group of women, a group you would never put together. They age from early thirties to terribly sad late sixties. There is one gorgeous, glamorous, high-heeled and sexed-up girl, or woman – it is hard to tell for she is unlined and overly made-up – and the rest look much like Gabby: tired, weary, colourless.

After a few moments Sally calls the group together and suggests they make a start.

'First of all, I want to commend each and every one

of you,' she looks at each of the women as she talks, her eyes slowly scanning the room, 'for coming to this meeting. It is an incredibly brave thing to do, to bring out your pain in public, but sharing that pain with other women who are going through the same thing is ultimately the most healing thing you can do for yourself. So well done. All of you.' She claps her hands and the room slowly joins in, a round of applause for each of them, none of whom feel remotely brave.

'We're going to meet, in this room, for the next eight weeks, and we're going to get to know one another very well. I'd like each of you in this room to take what I call the privacy vow. We need this to be a safe space, a sacred space. We need to be able to trust that we can say anything we want in this room, to express our pain, our fears, our grief, and know that nothing we say will ever leave this room. I'm going to vow that I will not discuss anything in this room with anyone outside this room, ever. Nor will I discuss any of the members of this group, with any of the other members. And, finally, I will not divulge who the members of this group are. What you see here, what you hear here, when you leave here, let it stay here. Please, one by one, raise your hand after me and say, "I vow."'

Gabby turns to Josephine, wide-eyed, to see her expression reflected back at her. They give each other a small smile as Sally looks round the circle.

'I vow.'

'I vow.'

'I vow,' says Josephine.

'I vow,' says Gabby.

'Perhaps we can all go round the room telling every-one our names and a little about our divorce. I'd like to start by saying I'm Sally, and I started my first divorce support group eight years ago when I went through my own divorce. I thought I had been very happily married for twenty-three years, except my then-husband claimed I was wrong.' She smiles. 'It wasn't, as I thought, a happy marriage, but a terrible one.' There is a ripple of laughter through the room, this story clearly resonating with more than one woman there. 'It was, without question, the most painful thing I have ever been through. I could not believe that my husband, the man I had loved for most of my adult life, was one day a lov-ing husband, and the next, a stranger.' Another ripple as a wave of familiarity washes over the room. 'I tried leaning on the women I thought of as my closest friends, but it was as if a chasm had developed between us. They didn't know what to say, or how to help, or, in some cases, how to be there for me in any way, shape or form, because they'd never been divorced themselves. I tried not to blame them, but I felt abandoned, and betrayed.'

Several women are now nodding, two leaning for-ward at exactly the same time to pluck a Kleenex from the box on the coffee table, dabbing at the corners of their eyes.

'As a therapist myself, I am, of course, a huge believer

in therapy, but I had been in therapy for years, and therapy alone couldn't help my pain. I knew I needed to talk to other women who were going through what I was going through. I knew I could help them and, in doing so, I could help myself. I started this group not as a therapist but as a woman in pain, looking for help. The first group met here, in this library, on the tenth of October almost exactly eight years ago. The women who sat in a circle in this room are, today, amongst my closest friends.' She smiles again. 'And finally I have to tell you that there is life after divorce. I was married two years ago to the most wonderful man, a man who is, truly, my soulmate, my partner, in a way my prior husband never could have been. However much you feel your life is ending, I urge you to think of this as a new beginning. It won't always be easy, but there is more joy and laughter and love to come, once you have worked through your pain and are open to it. Thank you.'

There is silence as the women digest what Sally has said, then she catches the eye of the woman sitting next to her, the gorgeous, glamorous, made-up woman, and gives her a small nod, indicating she should talk next.

'Hi. I'm Michelle,' she says, stretching out her legs and showing off high platform sandals and black toenails, an ankle bracelet glinting as she moves. 'Wow. Where to begin.' She gives a nervous laugh. 'I have three beautiful children. Jason, who's nine, and Emily, who's six, and Alex, who is four. My . . . husband and

I met in high school. We've been together for ever, and he is the love of my life.' Her voice cracks. 'He has his own business, a chain of retail stores, and for the last few months they've been struggling, so he's had to work like a crazy person to get the business back up and running again. Or at least, that's what he said. While he was at work, I was doing everything. I kept a happy home for him, and raised the children. I'm a full-time, stay-at-home mom, and proud of it. I loved being a wife, and a mother, and I stepped in to pick up the slack during those months when he wasn't home. Two months ago he came home from work and I could see something was wrong. I thought he was losing the business, but he said . . .' Her voice cracks again. 'He said he was leaving me. He was in love with this woman who works for him. Gina.' She spits out her name. 'His slutty twenty-five-year-old assistant, who I had given jewellery to!'

She looks around the room at the women, their faces all aghast.

'She'd babysat our kids when we went away and I gave her jewellery to thank her! On top of money! It turns out they have been having an affair for almost a year, and he wants to reinvent himself with her. We live in a big, gorgeous house in Fairfield, which is on the market now, and the bastard is refusing to pay for anything. I'm trying to cook for people to make some extra cash but I have no idea what I'm going to do. The lawyer says he'll have to disclose all his assets, but I know my husband. If there is anything left in the business by the time we get to the divorce courts, he'll have it wrapped and hidden so well even a forensic accountant won't be able to find it. So here I am. Crying myself to sleep every night, then waking up two hours later and staying awake the rest of the night, worrying how I'm going to feed my children and where I'm going to live. The only good thing to have come of it is I've lost thirty pounds. Seriously. I've never been this size in my life.' She smiles as Gabby mentally berates herself for judging. She thought this girl was one of the wealthy, entitled housewives, the kind of girl she crossed the room to avoid, but how wrong she was.

'Thank you for sharing with us, Michelle,' Sally says, looking at the next woman.

Four women later, Gabby has heard roughly the same story four times, but with slightly different scenery in each retelling. In every story the husband has unexpectedly left the wife; in every story the wife thought she had, if not the perfect marriage, then certainly one that was good enough. The women are angry, resentful, upset. They do not understand why this has happened to them. They do not know what they did to deserve this, other than be a wonderful wife, a faithful wife, a wife who bore their husband's children and raised them well, kept beautiful homes.

And then it is Gabby's turn.

'I'm Gabby,' she says quietly. 'And, as you can hear, I'm English. As you can probably see, I'm also pregnant.

I am married to a wonderful man. Like many of you, I married the great love of my life. He is the kindest, funniest, greatest guy, and there was never any question in my mind that I would grow old and die with him. And I screwed it up. I made a mistake that threw everything I cared about into jeopardy, and I am so disgusted with myself I can barely even look at my reflection in the mirror. I wish I could sit here and say I have no idea why he left, but I know exactly why. And I don't blame him. I just wish I could turn back the clock.'

The other women wait for her to carry on; they want to hear more, wonder what mistake she is talking about.

But Gabby is done. She turns her head to Josephine with a half-smile. 'There's nothing more I can say right now. Sorry.'

'My turn?' Josephine asks and Gabby shrugs apologetically. 'Great,' she says. 'I'm Josephine and I left my husband. I married him seven years ago, thinking I was doing the right thing, even though I knew I didn't love him, not in the way you're supposed to love your husband. But I wanted kids, and love had always been so difficult for me, so when he came along and promised to take care of me, it felt like I'd been sent a knight in shining armour. I was a good girl; I was trained to say the right thing. When he asked me to marry him I thought it would be rude to say no. So we got married, and we had kids. Two boys. I adore them. My husband, who had been so incredibly charming, and wonderful, and gentle during the courtship, started to change. He became aggressive and demanding. And so controlling. He'd tell me what I could and couldn't eat, what I was and wasn't allowed to wear. He'd put me down in front of friends, and scream at me about how incompetent I was. I had been so strong before I met him, and I started off fighting back, but after a while the fight went out of me and I just . . . gave up. He never hit me, not slapping, or punching, but when his rages were out of control he was terrifying, and often he'd push me into a wall, or shove me across a room.'

She is dispassionate as she talks, the story made even more powerful by her lack of emotion.

'I used to lie in bed at night and dream about divorce, but I was too terrified to leave. I knew that if I ever said I wanted a divorce he'd fly into a rage so awful I couldn't even begin to contemplate it. I thought I was stuck. I was terrified of what he would do. I could actually see him spitting with rage, "You want to leave? You leave. I'm keeping the house. And the boys." When the boys leave for college, I thought, then I'll go. When they're protected and he has no power over me any more. But then –' a small smile crosses her lips – 'I met someone. Not an affair,' she quickly explains. 'He's a friend. We've become very close. Actually, I don't think I've ever been so close to anyone before. He knows everything about me, and I know it was this friendship that gave me the strength to leave. It made me see that marriages don't have to be filled with rage, and anger, and fear. It made me see that there are men out there that are kind. And gentle. And loving.' She sighs. 'You know, the truth is I think I am a little bit in love with my friend. And he says he's a little bit in love with me, but nothing's happened. Nothing will happen,' she says firmly. 'We've agreed we are only ever going to be friends. But it's his love that gave me the strength to leave. I started looking ahead to the future, to a future without my husband, rather than dwelling in the fear of anticipation that was based on the past. So now I'm on my own, and, remarkably, I am still in the family home, and I thought getting rid of my husband would be fantastic, and some of the time it is.'

She stops as her voice begins to break, and leans over for a tissue.

'But on the weekends,' she says, her voice quieter than before, 'when my kids are with him, and I'm in my house without them, I have no idea who I'm supposed to be. If I'm not someone's wife, someone's mother, who the hell am I? He's spreading stories about me having an affair, which isn't true, and I've been cut dead by some of the women in school, which shouldn't bother me because it's not like I liked these women anyway, but it does. And I honestly have no idea if I can make it on my own. I'm relieved, and scared, and overwhelmed, and I needed to talk to others who understand.'

'Well done,' Sally says gently. 'You sound like a woman of tremendous courage.'

The introductions and personal stories take up the entire hour. Gabby still feels, as she so often does, like a fish out of water, and rather than mill around afterwards, talking to strangers, she heads for the door, hoping to make it to the car park without getting caught.

But she is caught. By Josephine.

'Do you want to grab some tea?' she asks.

Gabby is about to decline and make her excuses, but this fresh-faced woman looks exactly like someone Gabby would be friends with, and instead she finds herself saying yes.

'The thing is . . .' Josephine stops to tear open a packet of sugar and tip it into her tea, stirring it with a plastic spoon. 'It isn't the same when you've left your husband. It just isn't the same as having them walk out on you. Those women seem . . . I don't know. I'm sure they're nice, but the only one I felt I had anything in common with is you.'

'Do you think that matters, though?' Gabby can't help but feel flattered. 'Do we have to like each other? Obviously it's nicer for everyone if we do, but I don't know that it's essential.'

'All I know is that if you hadn't been there I'm not sure I'd be coming back. It just seemed that so many of those other women were angry. I'm not angry. I'm relieved. And terrified.'

'Tell me about it,' Gabby says. 'I still wake up every morning thinking this is a bad dream.'

'So what *was* your mistake? How did you screw it up?'

'Isn't it obvious?' Gabby gestures to her stomach.

'You had an affair?'

'I'm not even sure you could call it that. An emotional affair, perhaps. I had a . . . friendship. Probably one just like yours. Lots of flirtatious emails, lots of banter. It made me feel beautiful again. And alive. We slept together once, but once is all you need, it seems. I thought I was going through the menopause and pregnancy was the last thing I'd have to worry about.'

'I know this sounds deceitful, but didn't you think about telling your husband it was his? If it was just once, couldn't you have just, I don't know, put it behind you and moved on?'

'I could have done. If my husband hadn't had a vasectomy last year.'

Josephine claps her hands over her mouth. 'Oh shit!'

'Exactly.' Even Gabby smiles at the irony. 'Oh shit indeed.'

'Okay,' Josephine says, leaning forward. 'Seeing as we're now at secret level, I will confess that my . . . friendship . . .'

'You're sleeping with him,' Gabby says matter-of-factly.

Josephine's face falls. 'How do you know?'

'I didn't know for sure, but it seemed likely. Only because you left your husband. I don't know that women ever leave their husbands unless there's someone else. Actually, I don't think you necessarily have to be sleeping with them, but you have to be emotionally attached to someone other than your husband. A close friendship with an unspoken attraction, maybe. An unfulfilled dream. Or, in my case, a flirtation with an inappropriate man and one night that screws everything up.'

'You realize you just got hugely unlucky, don't you?' Josephine says. 'If you hadn't got pregnant, you could have got away with it.'

Gabby gives a deep sigh. 'That's the thing I can't believe. It still would have been wrong, and I would have had to live with the fact that I had betrayed my husband. And honestly? I don't know that I would have been able to do it, but at least he would still be my husband. At least the man I love, the only man I have ever loved, would still be by my side.' She looks at Josephine. 'Enough about me. Did you sleep with your friend before or after leaving your husband?'

'After!' Josephine looks shocked. 'I could never sleep with another man then climb into bed with my husband! Oh Lord.' She realizes who she's talking to. 'I'm sorry. I'm not judging you. It's just a personal thing . . .'

'Oh trust me, I'm not offended. I never thought that either – I never thought *I* could sleep with another man then climb into bed with my husband. Amazing the things you end up doing during your mid-life crisis. Are you going to run off into the sunset with this other man and live happily ever after?'

Sadness crosses Josephine's face. 'That's the thing. It's complicated. He was incredible when I was sharing my unhappiness with him, and then immediately after I left, when things became physical, I presumed we'd be together. I told everyone else I was leaving Chris because I was so unhappy and because I'd had enough, and, even though that was true, I knew deep down I wouldn't be leaving if James wasn't waiting in the wings.'

'And?'

'Now James isn't sure we should get involved. Not seriously. He says he loves me but he's worried he's the rebound guy, and I need to heal before he can get involved with me.'

'What do you think?'

'I think it's bullshit. I think this is one of the things men say when they're trying to let you down gently. It's like that whole "it's not me, it's you" thing. I'm on this goddamned roller coaster where I have no idea what's going on. When he calls and says he's coming over I'm flying high as a kite, then when he doesn't respond to a text, or disappears for two days, I sink into the depths of depression and all I can do is lie in bed and cry. You probably think I'm crazy.'

Gabby smiles. 'I do. But only because I've experienced all kinds of crazy myself. That was me with the guy who got me pregnant. A roller coaster. I was obsessed with him, to the exclusion of everything that was important in my life. My husband, my kids. All I thought about was him. I had no idea how crazy, and how unhealthy, it was. Nor did I have any idea how it would screw up my life.'

'Do you think this is crazy and unhealthy?' Josephine's voice is a fearful whisper.

'What do you think?' Gabby asks gently.

'I think it's crazy and unhealthy.' She grimaces as she says the words. 'I know it is. But I can't help it. I feel like I've jumped into the ocean and he's the only lifeline I have.'

'He can't be a lifeline when he's drifting away from you,' says Gabby. 'Look. I'm not saying you were wrong to leave your husband. Clearly you were terribly unhappy, and he sounds like a dreadfully abusive and difficult man. You needed to leave, and this man – James?' Josephine nods. 'James saved your life. You should always be grateful to him for getting you out of the marriage, but the ones that get you out are never the ones you end up with.'

'You don't think so?'

'I think it can happen but it's rare. He had a specific role in your life: to get you over the fear enough for you to leave your husband. Of course it's scary. Trust me, I know how terrifying it is to face the prospect of life on your own when you've had a partner for so many years, but you have to face those fears. You can't immediately look to another man to rescue you. That will bring you nothing but pain.'

'I know you're right,' Josephine says. 'It's still pretty

shitty to hear. It's a shame you're pregnant – I could do with a glass of wine just about now.'

'It's the middle of the afternoon!' Gabby laughs. 'A bit early, isn't it?'

'Never too early for a glass of wine when you're going through a divorce!' Josephine laughs too, lifting her mug of tea. 'Cheers. I'm glad I met you, and I'm glad I came today. I didn't expect this, but I feel a little bit better already.'

Gabby opens the front door, immediately seeing Olivia's Uggs, kicked off in the hallway in just the way that always drives her nuts. Usually she would shout up the stairs, demanding Olivia come down and put her boots away in the cubby, where they belong, but the very fact that Olivia is here is so thrilling that she doesn't want to do anything to destroy whatever peace she may have brought with her.

Should she go upstairs and knock on Olivia's door? Should she bring tea? Olivia has refused to speak to Gabby for weeks, and Gabby wants to make this easy, doesn't want to do anything to further stir up the situation.

Things are not easy, apparently, at Tim and Claire's house. The house really isn't big enough for two extra bodies, and nerves are starting to fray. Elliott is on the sofa bed in the TV room, which is fine during the week, but disastrous at the weekends. Elliott likes to sleep in then, but Tim and Claire's kids like to tumble downstairs at the crack of dawn, to flop on the sofa in the TV room and watch the Disney Channel for hours, until someone remembers to scream at them to turn the damned thing off.

Olivia is sleeping on a camp bed in Jolie's room, but Jolie's room is only big enough for one bed, one camp bed, one nightstand and one dresser. This means that Olivia's stuff – and teenage girls have a tremendous amount of stuff – is spilling out over everything, which is starting to drive Jolie nuts.

This is all according to Alanna, who sleeps on a blow-up bed in the playroom. She insists on sleeping over at Tim and Claire's because she misses her father so much and wants to spend as much time with him as possible, even though the family are out of beds and the house is clearly overcrowded.

The whole thing sounds like a nightmare. Olivia, Gabby is told, desperately misses her bedroom at home, her things, but she is refusing to set foot in the house, blaming her mother for ruining her life.

Gabby tiptoes into the kitchen and makes tea. Being English, she has raised her children in the tradition of tea. Not fancy, herbal, gourmet tea, and nothing that blooms like a flower or comes in a triangular gauze tea bag, but proper builder's tea. Strong, sweet, milky. The kind of tea that can lift you out of a depression, warm you to your bones, chase the blues right out of the door.

There is nothing as comforting as a proper cup of

tea and when Olivia's favourite mug is full to the brim with it, Gabby carries it up the stairs, with a chocolate-wrapped marshmallow. She raps lightly on the door.

'Who is it?'

'It's me. Mum. Can I come in?'

There is a silence.

'I brought you tea.'

A rustling, then the door is open, and Olivia, trying so hard to retain her expression of disdain, looks at her mother before bursting into tears.

'It's okay,' croons Gabby, cradling her daughter's head as they sit on her bed. 'Ssssh. It's okay.'

'I hate it there,' Olivia cries. 'I hate not being at home, and sleeping on that shitty bed, and not having any of my stuff.'

'So come home,' Gabby says. 'Come home right now. It's easy.'

'I can't.'

'Why not?'

Olivia raises her head to look at her mother, her dark eyebrows coming together in a frown. 'Because that would be betraying Dad.'

'How would that betray Dad?'

'Because that would mean I choose you, and I can't do that to him. He's already hurting so much, and I'm the only one looking after him. I can't leave him too.' Olivia's big brown eyes are now smudged with mascara,

making them look even bigger, giving her a youthful-
ness she had almost grown out of.

'Oh, sweetie.' Gabby takes her hand, noticing the
chipped blue nail polish, resolving not to point it out.
'It's not your job to look after Dad. I know you want to,
and I know you feel responsible for him, but you're
seventeen. The only person responsible for looking
after Dad is Dad.'

'And you,' Olivia spits. 'It should have been you.'

Gabby sighs. Olivia really isn't a child any more, and
there doesn't seem any point in protecting her. Gabby
senses that if there is to be any hope at all of rebuilding
her relationship with Olivia she needs to be honest with
her. However much that might hurt, and however
wrong it may feel to tell your child the truth, a truth that
paints you in a terrible light, it has to be done.

'You're right,' she says. 'It was my job to look after
your dad, and I spent many years doing that. I would
like to be doing that still but I screwed up. I was feeling
old, and unattractive, and that my life was slipping away
from me. A man came along, someone younger, who
told me I was beautiful, who made me feel young again.
I swear to you, Olivia, I never meant for anything to
happen, but something did, just once, and as soon as it
was over I knew I'd made a terrible mistake, and that it
would never happen again. Except I'd become pregnant. And now I have ruined not only my life, but
Dad's, and yours and Alanna's. I will never be able to
apologize enough, and I will never be able to make you

understand how ashamed I am. But I will have to live with my mistake for the rest of my life. As we all will, and we have to find a way to forgive and move on, because, Olivia, you are still my daughter. My firstborn. And I love you today as much as I did the day you emerged from my body. Do you understand that, Olivia? *Can* you understand that?'

Olivia, staring silently at the floor, reluctantly nods.

Chapter Twenty-Three

Gabby had no idea how hard it is to be a single mother. She remembers looking around at women she knew, newly separated or divorced, not understanding why they kept complaining.

Now she understands. There is no Elliott to take out the trash, or deal with the bills, or phone whoever you're supposed to phone when the sump pump isn't working and the mud-room floor is now one large and growing puddle.

There is no Elliott to help the girls with school assignments, to break up a fight, to get up at the crack of dawn, leaving her to sleep in, because one of the girls has to be in New Haven by eight. There is no one for her to talk to about her growing concerns regarding Alanna's unhappiness in middle school; no partner to sit by her side as they try to figure out what is wrong with their daughter, and what to do about it.

There is no one, in short, to take the flack, to ease the burden, to give Gabby a break.

In the beginning she hated the weekends when both the girls were staying with Elliott. Gabby had no idea what to do with herself during those endless days, often staying in bed for most of the time, counting the hours until she could go to Claire and Tim's house and bring Alanna back. Once home Alanna would bring not only the house but also Gabby back to life again.

Much has changed since those early days. Both girls now live at home and the house is once more filled with their laughter and shouting and messiness and energy. And Elliott, thanks to a long-overdue pay rise, finally moved out of Claire and Tim's house and rented a small house off Greens Farms Road, a Cape style, with three bedrooms and one bathroom.

He came back to Gabby's house a couple of times to pick up his things and some furniture he needed. The bed from the guest room, the sofa from the family room, a couple of tables. It wasn't much, yet the house feels strangely empty. The only consolation is that, for the moment at least, Elliott is no longer talking about putting the house on the market, and Gabby is grateful for that. But, nevertheless, since the furniture went she has not been able to go into the family room, with its two beanbags and coffee table and the large space where the sofa once was.

The house feels emptiest, of course, when the girls are with their father. But Gabby now counts off the days until the girls go to Elliott's. No fighting. No getting up long before her body's natural wake-up time. No meals to worry about, no chauffeuring back and forth to friends' houses or sports events.

She has come to treasure the weekends she is on her own. She now welcomes the peace, the solitude, the quiet. She welcomes padding down to the kitchen in the morning, at whatever time she wakes up, making herself coffee and sitting in the easy chair by the window, with the papers, or a book.

She has started painting again. She sits on a stool because her poor legs and feet are swollen and she cannot handle standing for the long hours necessary for the work she is doing. She has no models, but has files of pictures of pregnant women, and is painting a vast canvas of burgeoning bellies, glowing faces.

The heartache and discord that marked the beginning of this pregnancy have given way to a beauteous glow, a constant marvelling at the miracle of life, an appreciation of what a blessing it is to be lucky enough to have a child at her age.

Even if it isn't Elliott's child.

Gabby feels nothing but relief to have reached this stage in her pregnancy. The minute she saw the tiny black and white body on the sonographer's screen, that very first time, her bonding began. But then for a long time afterwards, once she realized Elliott was not prepared to accept the baby, once she knew she'd destroyed their life together, she was so scared she wouldn't feel connected to this child again, so scared she wouldn't feel maternal. For many terrible weeks she felt she didn't want the child that had changed her life so irreparably.

She did all the right things: the scans, the genetic counselling, but reluctantly; she didn't want a baby this way, and wished desperately that she could turn back the clock.

But now she takes her pre-natal vitamins eagerly, turns up to her doctor's appointments, does the blood work, gives the urine samples. She smiles when strangers stop her and ask her when she's due, congratulate her, tell her, with great conviction, that they can tell it is a girl. Or a boy. *And they have never been wrong.*

When the alarm on her iPhone goes off at three p.m., Gabby is fast asleep. In fact she sleeps away most of the days of this pregnancy. But she is determined to be fully awake when Alanna comes home. She is convinced that Alanna's veering off into unknown territory is because of her own lack of presence. She is certain that part of the reason Alanna's unhappiness in middle school is continuing into her second year is that Gabby has not been there for her, being too caught up first with her infatuation with Matt and now with her separation.

Poor Alanna. Her new friends continue to come, and go; none of them lasts. Each week there is another 'new best friend', another girl with long, straightened hair – straightened! At the age of twelve! – wearing designer clothes, giving nonchalant shrugs and making no eye contact. Gabby didn't approve of the last crowd of popular girls, the ones at elementary school, but they were, at least, known to her, and she knew their mothers. When Alanna overheard one girl saying, 'You wouldn't believe the shit I had to put up with when I was best friends with Alanna,' Gabby knew she could phone the mother and that the mother would hear.

These new girls have mothers as terrifyingly blasé and disconnected as the girls themselves. Alanna needs her mother more than ever. So Gabby forces herself out of bed, blinking until she starts to swim back into consciousness, then goes downstairs to heat up scones she had made earlier. Alanna's favourite.

The back door slams, followed by the sound of foot-steps going upstairs.

'Alanna? I have scones!' Gabby shouts up the stairs, sighing at the lack of response. Then the phone starts to ring.

'This is Lisa Cooperville, Principal of Springs Middle School.'

Gabby freezes, forcing her voice to sound normal. 'Yes?' She can't hide her hesitancy, even with the polite-ness that follows. 'How are you?'

'I'm fine, and I'm sorry to call with this news, but there has been an incident at school involving your daughter Alanna, and we would like you to come in as soon as possible.'

'What kind of incident?'

'Alanna has been involved in a bullying incident. As you know, we have a zero-tolerance policy, and we need to gather all the parents involved to let you know the procedures for the next step.'

Oh God. That explains so much. Alanna has been

bullied. Sweet, loving Alanna has been a target for those vicious bitches. No wonder she has been so quiet of late; no wonder she is withdrawn.

'I had no idea,' Gabby whispers. 'My poor baby. Do you know what happened? She hasn't said anything but she's been so quiet. It never occurred to me she was being bullied.'

There is an awkward silence.

'Your daughter is the protagonist, Mrs Cartwright. She tackled Josh Gordon to the ground, with the help of three of the other girls, then Alanna cut off his hair. She is the bully. I know this may not be easy for you to hear, but there were numerous witnesses, and the boy, Josh, is extremely upset.'

Gabby gasps, but has no words. There is nothing she can say; her mind is a jumble of thoughts and feelings – denial, defensiveness, acceptance – all mixed up together.

'When shall I come in?' Her voice is a whisper.

'We would like you and your husband to come in tomorrow morning at nine o'clock. Alanna and the three other girls are on suspension until we decide how to progress, so she will be at home tomorrow. I will make sure her teachers send you the work so she doesn't miss out.'

Gabby and Elliott sit outside the principal's office, Gabby occasionally letting out a deep sigh, Elliott pretending to be engrossed in vital emails on his iPhone.

'Why do you think she did it?' Gabby asks again. 'Do you really think there hasn't been some kind of mistake?'

'She said there were witnesses.' Elliott keeps his voice low, aware of the hustle and bustle of people passing them in the corridor, all looking at them curiously, doubtless already having heard the story, wanting to see the terrible creatures that spawned the girl that committed the terrible act. 'I have no idea why she did it. She was with you last night. What did she say?'

'I already told you. She screamed at me, telling me I didn't understand anything and that she hates me. She refused to even talk about it. I still have no idea.'

The door to the principal's office opens, and Gabby and Elliott look up at the same time to see the parents of one of Alanna's new 'friends', both grave-faced. Gabby has met the mother once – she was frosty and disinclined to make small talk – and their unwanted link today brings them no closer together. The mother deliberately avoids looking at them, although Gabby knows there is also a distinct possibility that the mother, who didn't openly acknowledge her when they did meet, has no idea who she is.

The principal walks them to the end of the corridor, nodding an acknowledgement at Gabby and Elliott but not officially greeting them until the other parents have gone.

Another couple come to sit on the bench opposite Gabby and Elliott, with their son. Gabby has not met

Josh Gordon, but this must, surely, be him, with his new buzz cut. She knows of him, though, for the last time Alanna had these girls over, they spent the time prank-calling a boy called Josh, a boy she overheard them describing disdainfully as 'so gay'.

Gabby is mortified, remembering that. Would her daughter, whom she has raised to be accepting of all, truly do this to a child just because he is slight and effeminate, unlike the other boys?

She is grateful she does not know the family, that they don't know her. The principal ushers them in, without mentioning their names, and Gabby attempts to ignore the couple's searching looks as it dawns on them who they might be.

'This is enormously distressing to all concerned, as you can imagine,' Mrs Cooperville says. 'Josh has been the target of some mean behaviour already this year. He is a sensitive and sweet child, but those are not qualities that necessarily serve you well in middle school. Your daughter, and others, physically pinned him down while Alanna cut off his hair. We gather it was a dare, and I understand some of the unique pressures involved in middle school, particularly for girls who are struggling to fit in, but on no level is this behaviour acceptable. I have spoken to the Board of Education, and we believe that after a period of suspension Alanna must be transferred to one of the other middle schools, Highvale.' Her face suddenly softens. 'I know Alanna,' she says. 'And I don't believe she's a bad kid. Unfortunately she's got in with a crowd here that is . . . challenging. I don't believe she would ever have entertained doing anything like this had she not felt pressure. I understand from two of the girls involved that they threatened to turn the entire grade against her if she didn't do it.'

'So why are you punishing her?' Gabby blurts out. 'She was being bullied herself.'

'I appreciate that, but they are all culpable. Each one is being punished. You have to understand that while Alanna may have felt she had no other option when she picked up those scissors, in fact she did have a choice. And it's terrible for everyone that she made the wrong one. But she has to take the consequences for making that wrong choice.'

'But it's not right that our daughter was bullied into doing something she clearly didn't want to do, and is now being forced to change schools. What's happening to the other girls? Are they being punished in the same way?'

Gabby has never been more grateful that Elliott is by her side. She has been feeling increasingly worn down by the single-parent role but at least, for this, Elliott has been able to step up and be the co-parent with her, to ease some of the burden.

She is bordering on hysteria, but Elliott seems calm. She knows it is not the case, for his jaw is clenched, the muscle in his cheek twitching, but the way he appears in control of his feelings has always had the effect of calming her down.

The other girls are having the same punishment, they are told, and will also have to change schools, though they will not be attending the same one as Alanna. No distinction is being made. This shouldn't help, even though it does.

But what are they supposed to do with Alanna?

'How dare you!' The built-up stress flies out in a rage when they get home. Elliott stands in the doorway as Gabby screams for Alanna to come down from her room. 'What the hell were you thinking? What kind of monster did I raise for you to be able to do that? How dare you? Who do you think you are?'

'Gabby. Stop.' Elliott lays a hand on her arm, jolting her out of her fury slightly.

'You're going to apologize,' she spits. 'I'm disgusted. You're going to apologize to him, and to his parents. How could you? How could any child of mine do this?' Gabby is so appalled she is breaking into sobs as she shouts.

Alanna is already crying. 'Sophie said I could be part of the Populars if I did it,' she howls. 'If I didn't she said she'd make everyone in seventh grade hate me. I didn't want to do it. I knew it was mean, but I didn't know what else to do. I didn't want everyone else to hate me.' Her voice turns into a wail as she collapses on the stairs, and Gabby instantly switches from fury to remorse.

'Oh, darling,' she says, gathering Alanna in her arms.

'I'm sorry. I didn't mean to say all the things I said and I love you so much. I'm just so upset. And I don't understand. I don't know what we're going to do, how we're going to manage school.' She looks up then, her eyes filled with tears, knowing that Elliott will say something like, 'Don't worry, we'll get through it together,' or 'We're a family and we love each other, and we'll find a way.' But he doesn't. He merely looks at the floor.

Chapter Twenty-Four

It is early December and most of her Christmas shopping has been done, courtesy of Amazon. Giant boxes are piled in the closet in the barn, waiting to be unpacked and rewrapped in brightly coloured paper.

She isn't yet sure what they will do about Christmas. It has always been their favourite holiday. They have never been a family to vacation at Christmas, choosing instead to huddle up indoors, decorating the tree, praying for snow.

Gabby always cooks a turkey, English-style, on Christmas Eve. She lays bacon on the breast, makes a sage and chestnut stuffing, prepares Brussels sprouts and roast potatoes. They have Christmas pudding with brandy butter her mother sends over from Fortnum & Mason, and when they are all stuffed and sleepy they build a fire in the family room and decorate the tree.

The lights – miles of white lights plugged together – are wrapped round the tree, pushed carefully into the centre of the branches, as far as they can go, so the tree appears to glow from the inside. The decorations have been collected over many years, each of the family choosing a new one every year to add to others that have been in their respective families for decades.

They are carefully unwrapped and placed on the branches.

The girls decorate while Gabby and Elliott sit on the sofa, a giant bowl of popcorn and a box of cranberries between them, stringing the corn and berries onto dental floss, to make a garland for the tree.

Stockings are hung, and quietly filled in the early hours of the morning when the house is asleep, to be discovered with shrieks of joy on Christmas Day, and unpacked during a breakfast of blueberry pancakes, scrambled eggs and extra-crispy bacon.

But this Christmas? It hasn't been discussed yet.

Alanna has not been back to school, and the home-schooling is adding yet another stress to Gabby's life, but in January she will start at Highvale. Neither Elliott nor Gabby wants this; they would prefer to send her to a small private school instead but, since they cannot afford to do so, they are hopeful this new school, which has less of a reputation for trouble than the one from which she has been suspended, might be better.

Either way, Alanna has been encouraged to find friends outside of school: the lovely girl from gymnastics who lives in Fairfield; the daughter of people they know who live in Norwalk; other children not connected to her school, girls who have no knowledge of the scandal.

The scandal, as Gabby thinks of it, has changed her thoughts about Christmas. Initially she supposed that they would split it up – Christmas Eve with one parent,

Christmas Day with the other, but the very thought of having Christmas without Elliott is heartbreaking, particularly given Alanna's recent behaviour. They need to be together as one family, if only over the holiday. How could it be Christmas if they are not all together as a family, exchanging gifts over bacon and eggs?

For ages Alanna has been wanting a Parka she saw in a store in town, and Olivia is desperate for the Uggs with sweater-style cuffs and buttons.

Before the separation Gabby would have refused point-blank to buy those Uggs, for what seventeen-year-old deserves a pair of two-hundred-dollar boots? Particularly when those boots are likely to be ruined or lost within the month. The same went for the Parka Alanna had her eye on.

Now she wants the girls to be happy, wants to make up for the pain she is forcing on them. It may be materialistic, and superficial, and oh-so-very-clichéd, but if buying them nice things will make them feel better, make them love her more, help them to forgive her for what she has done, then buy them nice things is what she will do.

Gabby pulls into the parking plaza behind Main Street, frustrated at herself for leaving this until now. From Thanksgiving onwards, Main Street turns into an outdoor mall, with hundreds of people, most from out of town, descending for their holiday shopping and huddling en masse on street corners, waiting for the seasonal traffic cops to wave them across from Tiffany to Pottery Barn.

Each time she thinks she sees an empty bay, she pulls up, excitement building, only to discover a little car in the spot, its shadow hidden by the SUVs sandwiching it.

'Bloody little cars,' she mutters. 'I *hate* those little cars.' But she brightens up, seeing a Land Rover's reversing lights come on.

At this stage of her pregnancy she is grateful to have found a spot at the right end of Main Street. The two stores she wants are next to each other, and after buying most of the products in Benefit for Olivia, she moves next door for the Parka.

As she reaches for it so too does another hand, and she turns, with an apologetic smile, for she is sure she reached it first, to see Elliott.

'Oh.' She drops the Parka.

'Ah.' He drops the Parka.

They both stand there, looking at each other, until he clears his throat.

'I was Christmas shopping. For the girls.'

'Tell me you haven't just cleared the shelves at Benefit,' she says, looking down with relief to see he is carrying bags from Jack Wills and J.Crew.

'I just have Alanna's main present left,' he says. 'And I know she wanted this Parka.'

'Could that be because it's all she's been talking about for the past month?'

Elliott laughs.

'We could buy it together,' Gabby says carefully. 'It could be from both of us. Then we could each get something small to give to her individually. I have junky stuff for her stocking, but there's a craft set I know she's been looking at.'

'Stockings,' Elliott says thoughtfully, nodding his head. 'I hadn't thought about stockings. I'm going to have to get some for my house. Where do I even get stockings from?'

'I don't know,' Gabby says, because she has had their stockings for years, each of them finely needlepointed with Christmas scenes, their names embroidered at the top. She has no idea where they came from, only that they appear to have been there for ever. 'Do you think it would be weird for Santa to do two stockings each? I think it might be . . . overkill. Which raises the point, how are we going to do Christmas this year?'

Elliott shrugs sadly. 'Split up Christmas Eve and Christmas Day?'

'We could,' Gabby grudgingly admits, 'but I think the girls would hate it. And honestly? I'd hate it. I know we aren't a family any more, but don't you think, for something like this, we could come together? Not for us, Elliott, and I know the last thing you probably want to do is spend Christmas with me, but this is a holiday for the girls; this has always been a holiday about the girls, and nothing would make them happier.'

'I don't know.' Elliott frowns. 'I think it might confuse them.'

'What do you mean?'

'I don't want to give them false hope. It might make them think this means we're getting back together.'

'Oh no, no,' Gabby says quickly, pushing aside the pictures that were already invading her head: the four of them laughing over eggnog and spiced apple cider, her eyes and Elliott's meeting in a meaningfully soulful manner as they string popcorn, and Elliott realizing what a terrible mistake he had made in leaving, then starting to plot his way back into Gabby's heart. 'They wouldn't think that at all, not if we made it quite clear. We both love them, and Christmas is a time for children to be with their parents. We could say we didn't want to force them to make a choice, so we have all come together for the love of the children . . .' She tails off. 'Something like that.'

Elliott doesn't say anything for a while. Eventually he nods, with a half-smile. 'Okay,' he says, and a huge smile spreads on Gabby's face. 'Christmas Eve. Your place. The Parka?' he asks, turning back to the coat. 'Shall we do it together, then?'

'Absolutely.' Gabby is beaming. 'I'll wrap it and it will be from us both.'

Chapter Twenty-Five

'So how do you feel about all being together at Christmas?' Josephine says, leaning down to look at the handles on the chest Gabby had been restoring before leaning down became too cumbersome.

'Honestly?' Gabby squeezes herself. 'Thrilled. Excited. Nervous. I know Elliott. All he ever wanted was a family; nothing makes him happier than when we're all together. Add in all the Christmas joy and I think he'll realize how much he misses us. I think he'll see how much happier he is when we're all together, then he'll come home.'

'And you'll all live happily ever after?'

'Something like that.'

'Gabby, I hope you're right, but I'm worried you're getting your hopes up too much. What if it just means he's thinking about the children? What if it doesn't mean anything at all? Then you'll be left feeling horrible over the holidays.'

'I don't think I'm wrong,' Gabby says. 'But even if I am, so what? I have a couple of depressed days before I pull myself together and life carries on exactly as it has before. I'm a big girl, growing bigger –' she gestures unhappily to her stomach – 'and I can deal with it. It just might be an opportunity. I kind of told myself that if he said no, there'd be no hope, but if he said yes, it meant we'd get back together again.'

Josephine laughs. 'That's about as random as telling yourself if the lights stay green something will happen.'

'I do that all the time!' Gabby says. 'And they almost always do!'

'So you're convinced you and Elliott are going to get back together?'

'I wouldn't say that, but we have been getting on well recently, better than we have done for ages. It was a little awkward when I ran into him Christmas shopping, but that was only because neither of us expected to see the other. I really think he might be forgiving me, and I can't believe he has stopped loving me. I don't think you can switch off like that. I really don't.'

'Do you still love him?'

'Oh my God! Yes!' Gabby looks at her friend in horror. 'As if there could be any doubt. Anyway, enough about me. What are you doing for Christmas? Is James here?'

Josephine comes to sit next to Gabby, exhaling loudly. 'Oh I don't know. It's all up in the air again. He went AWOL last weekend and now he says he loves me but he's not ready.' She shakes her head. 'The thing is, I know he's going to be on the phone again next week saying how much he misses me and that he can't live without me. I love him, but this is exhausting. I don't know how much longer I can do this.'

'I've told you before, many, many times, you shouldn't be doing this. It's time to move on, and you need to be the one to say it because James clearly doesn't have the strength to do it himself.'

'I know, I know.' Josephine sighs. 'I wish you weren't pregnant.'

'Me too,' says Gabby, and Josephine laughs.

'No, seriously. If you weren't pregnant I could get a babysitter for the boys and we could go out and do the singles scene together. I keep hearing that if you're single and our age you need to be out at the Spotted Horse, or Grey Goose, or Artisan, but I don't have anyone to go with. Michelle from the divorce support group apparently goes all the time, but I can't go with her or no one will even look at me.'

'She is gorgeous,' murmurs Gabby.

'Exactly.'

'And I am hugely fat and swollen, so everyone would look at you.'

'Exactly,' Josephine says, in precisely the same tone, and they both laugh. 'Are you sure you won't come with me?'

'Not only will I not come with you, but I don't think you should be going. Trust me, you're not going to meet the sort of man who's going to take your mind off James in a bar of all places.'

'So where am I going to meet him?'

'Where you're least expecting it. You'll probably

meet him when you're engrossed in something with your sons, when you've forgotten all about men and you've decided to swear off relationships completely.'

'But that's never going to happen. What about you? If you and Elliott don't get back together what will you do?'

Gabby grimaces. 'God only knows. I can hardly bear to think about it. Thank heavens he hasn't started divorce proceedings yet – naturally, that gives me some hope – but if that *is* to happen . . . Lord. I'd have to get a job, I suppose. And one that pays enough to cover childcare for the baby.' She shudders in horror and shakes her head. 'This was not how my life was supposed to turn out, let me tell you.'

'Why don't you sell your furniture?' Josephine gestures at the unfinished pieces dotted around the barn. 'You could turn this into a store and sell from here. Imagine, you'd keep the overheads down, get to do something you love, and make money doing it. These pieces cost you nothing, right? Don't you find most of them in dumpsters?'

Gabby laughs. 'Not most – but it's true that I have found some of my best pieces in dumpsters or at the dump.'

'So? Isn't that the obvious thing to do?'

'Funny. My friend Claire always said the same thing. Exactly that, that I should clean this place up and give it a great name, then open it to friends. I couldn't open it to the public as we're not zoned for commercial use, but I could do open-house sales and invite everyone on the mailing list.'

'There you go! That's a great idea! And you should take advantage of the fact that everyone's probably talking about you, so if you manage to do it soon a ton of people would show up.'

Gabby's face falls. 'Do you really think everyone's talking about me?'

'I do. Sorry. It's part Schadenfreude, delighting in someone else's misfortune, and part relief that their marriage is okay. I think that's why everyone abandons you when you get divorced. Your crumbling marriage, when they thought you two were so perfect together, reminds them of the fragility of their own marriage, and each time they see you they feel a sliver of fear that this could so easily happen to them too.'

'How do you deal with it?'

'Same way as you. By becoming more of a hermit. And by keeping my cards very close to my chest. You wouldn't believe the number of people who have phoned expressing sympathy and concern because they heard Chris and I have split up, who then get angry and resentful because I don't fall apart on their shoulder, or confide my pain in them.'

'That's why you decided to make me your new best friend.' Gabby grins. 'I'm safe because I don't know anyone you know.'

'True. And because you fucked up as badly as I did.

248

Not that leaving Chris was a fuck-up, but, well, you know . . . James and all the drama around that. I know how dysfunctional this relationship is, and I'm desperate to get out, but I'm terrified of being on my own, a single parent.'

'Okay, I'll make you a promise. After the baby comes, after I get my figure back, I'll consider coming to a bar with you. Just once, just to prove that a bar is not where you will find your future love. But I will come, and we will drink Martinis, and we will have fun. How's that?'

'Good enough for now. And in return,' Josephine surveys the barn, 'I'll help you get this place together.'

Gabby's face lights up. 'Really? You'd do that for me?'

'Of course. That's what friends are for.'

Gabby endures the stores one more time before Christmas. Elliott has long been in love with watches. He has an ancient Patek Philippe that was passed down to him by his grandfather, and a couple of other watches that he loves. He always said to Gabby that if he had the money he would collect watches. One year she bought him a box in which to house his future collection: mahogany, with automatic turners so the watches never stop.

Gabby had sold a couple of pieces, back before the size of her stomach and general feeling of crappiness stopped her from further restoration, and she put the money aside. Walking into Mitchell's now, she goes straight to the display of watches, knowing exactly which one to get. It is still there, in the same spot as when she and Elliott were here ten months ago, when Elliott insisted on trying it on, gazing at it in awe, wanting so badly to buy it.

'In the future,' Gabby whispered to him, wishing their expenses weren't so great, or they lived in a part of the country where the cost of living is lower than it is here.

When the salesman takes the watch from the display, telling her of the history of the company and explaining how special this particular example is, she can no longer remember the price of the watch, only that it was beyond her wildest dreams. But she flinches as she turns the price tag over and sees it is so very much more than she thought.

So very much more than she brought.

But there are credit cards. And future earnings. Josephine has been as good as her word, and has been at the barn every morning, filling her car with useless junk and driving it to the dump, helping Gabby sweep out the dust and whitewash the walls, thereby turning the barn into a space clean and bright, a space in which you'd want to linger. Gabby wanted to call it The Dumpster Dive, but Josephine wouldn't hear of it.

'I know you find stuff in dumpsters but you don't want anyone else to know it. How do you expect people to pay eight hundred dollars for something if they know you got it for free?'

'Because I broke my back stripping, restoring and painting it?' grumbled Gabby.

'Doesn't matter. You have to have a story. Tell them you import faded antique pieces from England, restoring them in your New England barn.'

'It's not really New England,' Gabby said, impressed. 'It's Westport.'

'Still counts. From Old England to New England,' Josephine declared dramatically. 'A piece of the old country.'

'That's what we should call it! The Old Country!'

'I love it!' Josephine said. 'Perfect!'

They haven't opened yet, but they will, and Josephine, who seems to have become an official partner, is convinced they will sell everything. Living in New Canaan, she has access to a whole new crowd of girls, all of whom, she says, will love it.

'I thought no one was talking to you?'

'No. I'm not talking to them. They're all dying to find out what's going on. Trust me, they'll come.'

Gabby turns the watch over in her hands, mentally doing the calculations. If she put it on the credit card and sold five more pieces, that would cover it. And if she didn't sell the pieces? She could sell her engagement ring. She hasn't worn it for years anyway, never comfortable with the large solitaire diamond that seemed so essential at the time.

What if none of this works out? What if she and Elliott get divorced? Does she really want to be spending this kind of money? Yes, she decides. She loves him, has always loved him, and without doubt will always love him. This watch is her way of letting him know that. This gift will tell him know how sorry she is, and that, despite her transgressions and whatever mistakes she has made, she still loves him very deeply.

'I'll take it,' she says, her heart pounding. She is unable to believe she is spending quite so much money.

'An excellent choice,' he says. 'Your husband will love it. He's a lucky man.'

Gabby smiles sadly. There is nothing else to say.

Chapter Twenty-Six

Each year Gabby, Elliott and the girls go to Maple Row Farm for their Christmas tree, where they insist on traipsing through the fields in search of exactly the right uncut tree, despite the fact that there are lines of perfect trees, trees that would, indeed, suit them perfectly, cut and stacked up at the side of the car park.

It never takes less than two hours, the girls darting around calling, 'Over here! What about this one?' Elliott tramping over with saw in hand, Gabby yet again cursing the fact that she didn't bring extra gloves, because Olivia always forgets hers and ends up wearing Gabby's, while Gabby tucks her freezing hands into her armpits, convinced she will have frostbite by the end of the day.

They buy apple cider and doughnuts at the stand, and sit on low benches around the roaring fire to warm up, while Alanna usually wanders over to the two giant cows lazily munching hay in a small paddock next to the barn.

They haul the tree up to the roof rack, Gabby on one side of the car, Elliott on the other, then loop orange twine round and round, Elliott saying next year they'll get a smaller tree, and Gabby agreeing, although the tree gets bigger year by year.

There will be no Maple Row Farm this year. Not without Elliott. It wouldn't be the same, and Gabby could never manage to cut down and haul a tree by herself, and certainly not in this condition.

She drives instead to the Audubon Society, where there are pre-cut trees that are absolutely fine, and they tie it to the roof of her car for her. When she gets home she runs next door to her neighbours and the husband comes out to bring it into the house.

Gabby has become increasingly reliant on the kindness of neighbours. And strangers. She didn't realize how much she needed Elliott around, until there was no Elliott.

There was the night she heard a rustling coming from downstairs, and came down to find a frantic and terrified squirrel, which had somehow fallen down the chimney, tearing up the living room. She had always adored squirrels as a child – she would crouch down to feed them peanuts in Regent's Park – but they were, she discovered, infinitely scary when trapped inside your home.

A neighbour's husband – different neighbour – came to help, swiftly accompanied by two other husbands as word of the rampaging squirrel spread around the local area.

As a thank you, Gabby has baked mince pies and Florentine biscuits, and delivered them, beautifully wrapped in cellophane and plaid ribbon, with wishes for a wonderful holiday season.

More mince pies and Florentines, Elliott's favourite, are laid out now, on a white platter, on the dining-room table. The turkey is roasting, and Frank Sinatra has been replaced – at Olivia's insistence – with the Christmas album from *Glee*.

Swags of spruce, garlanded with burlap, drape the fireplace and banister in the front hall, where the theme is white and silver: thick white pillar candles wrapped in silver birch glisten at each end of the mantelpiece with wreaths of white feathers between them, while glittery silver deer traipse along the hearth.

On into the family room, where all is red and green and tartan. Plaid throws adorn the sofa that Gabby and the girls have brought down from her bedroom, making it cosy and warm. More spruce is draped along the mantelpiece, this time with red velvet ribbons. A fire is blazing, but the stockings hang high out of reach of the licking flames.

The tiny electric model ice rink has been dug out, with its twinkling lights and miniature skaters, who do endless magnetic figures of eight. They found this together in Boston one year. The girls were fascinated by the little skaters, and delighted that Elliott and Gabby bought it. Still, today, Alanna will sit and watch the skaters, lulled into a zombie-like state by the repetitive motion. Flicking a switch turns on tinny Christmas carols, but none of them flick the switch, preferring to watch the skaters in silence.

The gifts are piled high under the tree. Large ones

for the girls and, at the back, where no one can see it, a beautifully wrapped bronze box, with a striped gold ribbon, for Elliott.

Elliott will be here soon. And the turkey is almost ready. But there is just time for a phone call. Gabby ladles some eggnog into a cup and takes the phone into the hallway, where she sits on the stairs and dials home.

'Darling!' her mother answers. 'I was just saying to your father that I wondered where you were! Where are you? What are you doing this year for Christmas?'

'The same as always,' Gabby says. 'I invited Elliott to come and he said yes, so we're all together again. Like a proper family.'

'Oh. That sounds . . . cosy.'

'Why do you say it like that?' Gabby feels herself bristle.

'I'm sorry. I didn't mean anything. I just don't want you to get your hopes up.'

Gabby remembers how Josephine said the same thing. Her hopes are up, it is true, but why is everyone so worried about it? The worst that can happen is nothing, in which case life will carry on. Gabby is sure there really is no greater hurt that can occur, nothing more that can happen to make things worse than they already are. And would she have wanted the excitement and anticipation of the last few days to have been different? No! They have been the single bright spots in her life of late. Even if that is all there is – and those moments of joy at the prospect of what might be are followed by days, weeks of disappointment – it will, surely, have been worth it.

'What's the worst that can happen?' Gabby says lightly. 'That my hopes are dashed? So what? Mum, he's my husband. I love him. I never wanted us to be apart, and please don't say I should have thought of that before I was unfaithful, because I already know.'

'I wasn't going to say that, darling. I know you love him. We love him too. Nothing would make me happier than for the two of you to get back together, and I can't bear seeing you in pain.'

'You haven't seen me.'

'Ah. Yes. I know. But I am planning on coming when the baby's born.'

'You'd better, because the only thing I'm certain of is that I won't be able to do it all by myself.'

'Actually, I beg to differ,' her mother says. 'I will come, and I will do everything you need me to do, but, Gabby, you have always been the most independent and self-sufficient of children. I so wanted you to need me when you were little, but you never did; you were always perfectly happy off on your own.'

But that's not true, Gabby wants to say. I did need you. I just couldn't tell you because you never wanted to hear me.

She doesn't say that. It's Christmas. Why rock the boat now?

Chapter Twenty-Seven

'Elliott? Will you carve the turkey?' Gabby frowns, wishing she didn't have to call him in such a formal way to come into the kitchen to help. Yearning for the old days, when he automatically assumed certain roles, turkey carving being one of them.

'Coming!' he calls from the dining room, where he has been laughing with the girls, who are giddy with delight at their family being back together again. Elliott has been on fine form. He looks wonderful, thinks Gabby, much more . . . handsome . . . than he used to be. He has lost weight and looks younger.

He is wearing his old cords tonight, his old loafers, but the shirt is new, and it galls Gabby slightly to see him in something she doesn't know, something she has not bought him, because Gabby has always been in charge of Elliott's wardrobe, Elliott professing to hate nothing more than buying clothes.

'That's nice,' she said when he walked in and took off his Barbour. She fingered the soft sleeve of the shirt. 'It brings out the blue of your eyes.'

'Oh this?' He looked down, as if surprised to see himself wearing that particular shirt on this particular day. 'I got it a couple of days ago. Glad you like it.'

Gabby smiled, attempting to keep her voice light, wanting to know more. 'You hate shopping for clothes. Where did you get it?'

'Somewhere on Main Street,' he said nonchalantly, turning away and leaving Gabby wondering why he seemed reluctant to pursue the conversation.

'Here,' Gabby says as she pulls open a drawer and withdraws Elliott's apron. 'You don't want to stain your new shirt.'

'Oh. Thanks.' He smiles a smile of genuine gratitude as he ties the apron round himself, and the awkwardness they have both been feeling finally loses its edge as he falls into a routine unchanged for many years.

'Honey? Can you bring me the board with the ridge?' he calls after a while, and Gabby's heart skips a beat. Honey. He called her honey. This meaningless word seems loaded, has more meaning than anything else Elliott has said in months.

Seeing how friendly and warm, how relaxed he is, eases Gabby's anxiety and makes her see a burning light at the end of the tunnel.

If you were to peep through the window, and didn't know otherwise, you would look at the family eating this meal together and think them unutterably happy. No, more than that. You would think them unequivocally *right*. They all look right together. The two pretty girls, one brunette, one strawberry blonde, the proud father and the expectant mother glowing with happiness.

Gabby looks round the table not only with happiness

but with overflowing hope. Her family is back together again. When she smiles at Elliott, with love in her eyes, he smiles back, and the girls look from one to the other with delight.

As Elliott pours brandy over the Christmas pudding and sets it alight, he and Gabby cheer while the girls roll their eyes, neither of them liking Christmas pudding, but both of them loving the tradition of doing the same thing every year; doing the same thing this year.

The mince pies follow, and the chocolate log Gabby made for the girls – the chocolate log she always makes for the girls.

Then, stuffed, they retire to the family room, where Elliott builds up the fire while Gabby starts to string popcorn and cranberries onto floss. The girls excitedly unwrap the decorations, and, catching each other's eye from time to time, they make surreptitious gestures at the sofa, where their parents are sitting together, gestures that are filled with hope and optimism.

Gabby is waiting until the girls go up to bed before giving Elliott his gift. They send Olivia and Alanna upstairs, amidst much grumbling, but then Elliott stands up, announcing he'd better make a move.

Gabby's heart plummets. 'I thought you were staying.' She wishes her voice hadn't emerged in a whine.

'I can't,' he says. 'I need to go home.'

'But I bought a bed for the spare room. It's an inflatable bed but it's really comfortable. I made it up . . .' She stops, not wanting to sound desperate. 'The girls want you to stay,' she tries a new tack. 'They've been talking about waking you up in the morning. It's Christmas, Elliott. Why not stay? Think of all the drunk drivers you'll be avoiding. I promise I won't try to seduce you.' This last is an attempt at a joke, which falls flat to both their ears.

'I'm not worried about that,' Elliott says gently. 'It's just better if I go. I'll be back early and we'll make breakfast. I won't miss anything. I promise.'

'Wait.' Gabby reaches down towards the back of the tree, where she fumbles until she finds his gift. 'I got you something. I wanted to give it to you when we were alone.'

Elliott's face falls. 'Oh, Gabby. You didn't have to. I don't have anything for you.'

'That's okay,' she lies. There is nothing material Elliott could give her that she would want, other than as evidence that he had thought of her at all. Still, she reminds herself, he is a man. They don't think in the way women do.

He stands for a while tapping the box in the palm of his hand, looking as if he doesn't quite know what to do with it.

'Open it,' she encourages, no longer certain this is the right thing to have done, to have spent quite as much money as she did on a watch for her soon-to-be-ex-husband.

Reluctantly, slowly, Elliott unwraps the paper. He folds the wrapping paper into a neat parcel then insists on rolling up the ribbon, while Gabby refrains from clicking her fingers with impatience.

He stares at the box, at the watch company's lettering on the top, looking bewildered and sad.

'Open it,' Gabby says again, softly, wishing the floor could open up and swallow her shame, for it is blindingly obvious now what she was trying to do, even though she couldn't see it at the time. This is her guilt gift. Like the gifts of adulterous men, men who leave their mistresses and stop on the way home to buy glittering bracelets for their wives. A wordless apology, an expunction of guilt.

Elliott says nothing as he opens the box and gazes at the watch.

'It's the watch you loved,' whispers Gabby. 'Remember?'

He doesn't gasp with pleasure, or amazement, or joy. He doesn't take the watch out of its box and try it on as he did all those months ago in the store, when his eyes feasted on it in awe.

Elliott closes the box and looks at Gabby. 'Thank you. It's beautiful. But I'm not going to accept it.'

Gabby feels the prick of tears. 'Why not, Elliott? It's just a gift. It's a thank you for . . . I don't know. For being such a good husband. A good father. It's an apology for everything I put you through. I want you to have it . . .' She's babbling now and tails off as Elliott gently places the watch on the hall table.

'There's something I have to tell you,' he says quietly.

A million things go through her head. Cancer. He has cancer. Oh God, that's why he's got so thin. He's being transferred. He's moving to Alaska. Or Canada. Somewhere far, far away. He's – oh God, please no – he's seen a lawyer and he's started divorce proceedings.

Gabby looks up at him with fearful eyes as Elliott swallows.

'I'm seeing someone,' he says, not looking at her as he says the words.

'Seeing someone? What do you mean? *Dating*?'

He gives an embarrassed smile. 'Yes. I suppose "dating". I wanted you to hear it from me rather than from anyone else.'

'Anyone else? Why would I hear it from anyone else?' Gabby narrows her eyes as it dawns on her. 'Do I know her?'

Elliott nods. 'It's Trish.'

Gabby sucks in her breath. Trish. Perfect, blonde Trish. Trish who is doubtless a millionaire several times over. Trish who has always made Gabby feel inadequate in every way.

Afterwards, Gabby thinks back to the moment Elliott uttered the word 'Trish', and sees herself physically deflate, like a character in a cartoon. She sees her shoulders slump and her chin drop down onto her chest, her legs giving way as she wobbles to the floor.

Of course that doesn't happen. Not externally. Externally her shoulders slump just a little, her eyes widen to a startled understanding, a disappointment, but nothing gives Elliott any indication of the pain and grief she actually feels.

Gabby doesn't say much after that. She forces a smile to acknowledge his thanks for a lovely evening, and nods when he says he'll be back in the morning. Of course he has to leave. Of course he can't stay the night. He has to go and curl up with Trish. He has to make love to Trish. He has to take Trish in his arms and kiss the tip of her nose, just as he used to with her, and tell her how much he loves her.

She waits until she can no longer hear his car driving off down the road, then she slowly sinks onto the bottom step of the stairs.

Chapter Twenty-Eight

Trish is upstairs in bed as Elliott quietly lets himself into her house, still feeling a little awkward about having a key, although Trish has insisted.

He walks through the hallway admiring her Christmas decorations and how perfect everything looks, beautiful enough for a magazine – which, in fact, it is: a huge interiors magazine has just been to take photographs for next year's edition.

The house smells of pine and cinnamon and winter warmth. Nothing is out of place here. Everything is bright and shiny and new. A huge, white, porcelain Buddha casts a benevolent smile over the living room, where the sofas are white with turquoise accents, the lamps are made from gourds painted turquoise, and the Christmas decorations have been chosen to match the decor. Even the books have been covered with white parchment paper, the odd book wrapped in turquoise alligator skin.

It is the most beautiful house Elliott has ever been in. He just wishes it was a little more comfortable. The sofas are modern and hard, and he is terrified of spilling a drink, or crumbs being ground into the rug. He teases Trish that he'll move a La-Z-Boy in while she's not looking, and although he is joking he really misses his comfortable chair at home.

The place he used to call home.

Trish wears a silk nightgown. Never before has he come across anyone who wears a nightgown, unless it's a cotton one, short and printed with a whimsical design. Trish wears a nightgown every night, always ivory, silky, strappy. This is, to her, what flannel pyjamas are to Gabby. He didn't think women like Trish existed any more, and, even if they did, he definitely wouldn't have expected a woman like Trish to be interested in a man like him.

It was Tim's idea. Elliott didn't know this until afterwards. Tim and Claire invited Trish to join them for dinner one night, Trish having broken up with her boyfriend some time before.

'What was the matter with him? He seemed like a great guy,' Elliott remembers asking.

'I think he was. But he wasn't the guy for her. She needs someone older. More stable. Honestly? I think he was probably just about sex.'

'That's a problem?' Elliott asked. Tim laughed. ·

The dinner had been perfectly lovely. There certainly hadn't been any flirting as the four of them sat round the kitchen table, but there had been lots of laughing, and Trish had clearly been intrigued by Elliott, genuinely keen to hear about his work, asking him thoughtful questions. He missed being heard, being thought of as interesting, rather than being taken for granted. At the end of the night, as Trish got up to leave, Tim suggested Elliott walk her to her car.

'I really enjoyed getting to know you,' she said. 'We should do this again.'

Elliott just stared at her, having no idea what to say. He had been married for ever, had dated a hundred years ago as a very young man, had no idea how to pursue, or whether this meant something, or what he was supposed to do next.

Trish made the move for him. She leaned forward and kissed him, very softly, and not for very long, on the lips. When she stepped back she was smiling. 'You should call me,' she said before getting into her car, beaming a smile at him and reversing out of the driveway.

Elliott walked back into the house in a state of shock.

'She kissed me!' he muttered to Tim, who high-fived him. 'What do I do now?'

'Now you call her. Not now – I mean, tomorrow. Ask her for dinner. Damn. Claire was right. I can't believe she kissed you on the first date. It wasn't even a date, and she kissed you! Was it hot?'

'Claire was right about what?'

'She said she thought Trish was interested in you. Apparently she's been asking about you for a while. The only reason Claire didn't want to set up anything is because she feels she's betraying Gabby.'

'Even though they're not speaking?'

'She misses her, you know? But we made our choice.'

He gave Elliott a rueful smile, as if the choice wasn't made freely, as if their friendship had suffered from having been put in the position of making a choice.

Elliott was confused. He had gone to stay with them simply because Tim was his best friend and he couldn't think of what else to do, where else to go. He hadn't meant to force a choice on them. He never asked it of them.

There were so many things Elliott hadn't asked for, Trish being one of them.

During the first few dates, Elliott felt as if he was in some surreal version of his life. This was him. Elliott. Married with children. He didn't go to smart restaurants with glamorous women and charm them with his stories. Hell, he didn't even have any stories. Except, he found he did. He found his stories, and his humour, and his charm. He asked lots of questions, and relaxed under the gaze of a gorgeous, intelligent woman.

The first time they slept together was strange. Fantastic. Overwhelming. Terrifying. He and Gabby had a routine. It was comfortable and quick and suited them both. Here he found himself with new territory to explore. Trish didn't like being touched like that; she wanted it softer, but harder there . . .

They both moved over and under, excited by the discovery, flipping like slippery fish until they exploded, first Trish, then Elliott, in unexpected delight.

Afterwards they hadn't, as he and Gabby had done for so long, rolled onto their respective sides of the bed, picked up their books or turned on the television, and said only a handful of words to each other before one gave the other a quick peck on the lips, switched off the bedside lamp and went to sleep.

With Trish in his arms, they lay talking softly for hours, his murmurs punctuated by the tinkle of her laughter until she fell asleep, actually in his arms. It was desperately uncomfortable, but he didn't want to move and disturb the perfection of this moment. This exquisite, tiny blonde, in her rustling silk, sleeping so prettily on his dead arm. Eventually he had to move, and Trish just burrowed under the sheet without waking up. Elliott gazed at her, unable to believe they had just made love.

Trish is, he thinks, as he walks up the stairs to her room, completely selfless. She makes him feel like the most important man in the world. She creates a beautiful home, cooks like a dream, runs a hugely successful business, is a loving and present mother. She is the woman who has it all, the domestic goddess personified.

It will kill Gabby when she finds out. When he tells her he is living with Trish, not just dating her. But he knows he will have to tell her.

Why did she have to buy the watch? It was so . . . *sad*. So desperate. So heartbreaking. The hope in her eyes and the disappointment when he couldn't take it. There was no question of him taking it. He knew exactly what it was, and he knew too that he couldn't *not* tell her about Trish. Not when Gabby's need for him was so evident.

He never wanted to hurt her. However much she has hurt him – and my God, the pain these last few months has been, at times, almost unbearable – he has never wanted to cause her pain. He did, tonight, telling her about Trish; he had no choice.

Things with Trish seem to be serious. Elliott walks into the bedroom, marvelling at how beautiful she looks, lying there with her legs crossed, not a patch of stubble on them, her nail polish always perfectly, prettily pink, her hair slicked back behind her ears.

'How was it?' she asks, craning up for a kiss.

'It was good. Good for the kids. A little awkward.'

She reaches up and caresses his cheek. 'You're a good man, Elliott. You did the right thing.'

'This is what I love about you,' he says, careful not to say he loves her, because he is not there yet, even though he suspects he may be well on the way. 'You give me room to do the things I have to do.'

'I'm not the jealous type,' she says with a smile.

'I know. And it makes it possible for me to be the man I want to be. To show up for my kids. To be a father to them, and to give them a Christmas they couldn't have otherwise had. Thank you.' He lifts her hand, brings it to his lips and kisses it. 'Honestly. Thank you for never being threatened by Gabby or the relationship I have to have with her for the sake of the children.'

'I'm not threatened by Gabby.' Trish smiles again, pulling him in for a kiss. 'I'm not threatened by anyone.'

Elliott likes being married. He likes being a father. He likes familiarity, and comfort, and knowing where he stands. These past months, marked first with the awkwardness of staying with Claire and Tim, then with the loneliness of living in the little house close to the railroad tracks that never felt like home, have thrown him.

Nothing felt right. Elliott would wake up in the morning feeling out of sorts, unable to regain his equilibrium, no matter what he did. His equilibrium had always come from being married and everything that derived from that: waking up next to a woman you love; raising your children together; phoning each other a couple of times during the day just to check in, or remind the other of a dinner date they may have forgotten about. His equilibrium came from being able to go down to the boatyard at the weekends and chat with the men there about the old boats for sale, knowing his wife was at home, taking care of the kids, getting lunch ready, keeping everything balanced and even.

Until Trish, nothing had felt balanced for a while, and Elliott wasn't a man able to deal with his life being off-kilter. If it hadn't been Trish, it might have been someone else.

Yet if it hadn't been for Trish, it is entirely possible

Elliott would have found himself staying in the spare room tonight.

If it hadn't been for Trish, it is entirely possible Elliott would have lain under the blanket on the new bed in the spare room, listening to Gabby as she finished clearing up the kitchen.

It is entirely possible he would have fallen asleep thinking about the years they were married, how happy they were, how she looked when she lay underneath him, gazing into his eyes with love. He would have been woken up in the early hours of the morning by the creaking of the stairs, would have emerged from his bedroom to find Gabby creeping down to fill the stockings while the girls were fast asleep, moving as quietly as she could to avoid the danger of them waking up and seeing that there is no Santa Claus, even though they both know there is no Santa Claus.

He would have crept down alongside her, smiling in the darkness, to help with the stockings, and while they were filling them perhaps their hands would have met, in the soft illumination of the Christmas tree, and then they wouldn't have been smiling, and he would have been kissing her, melting in the familiarity of her lips, the smell of her, the feel of her hair.

If it hadn't been for Trish, perhaps he would have gone home.

But then he remembers the bump, the baby. Then he remembers the betrayal that ruined his life, that will never go away, that will be a daily reminder of how his wife screwed him – screwed someone other than him. And his heart closes down, and he is thankful, so thankful, that Trish came along when she did.

Chapter Twenty-Nine

Gabby is weighed down with dread in the morning. Elliott and Trish. Trish and Elliott. She slept terribly, waking up all night with visions of her husband and Trish playing in her mind. She hadn't prepared for this, hadn't imagined, not for a second, that Elliott would even be thinking about dating anyone else.

Don't they say that men take far longer to get over things because they can't process them emotionally in the way women can? Why isn't Elliott taking longer to get over her? How is it possible that he has moved on so quickly? Jesus. It's hardly been any time at all.

With Trish of all people. She groans out loud. 'I hate her,' she says suddenly.

Alanna overhears as she passes Gabby's bedroom, her arms filled with goodies from her stocking. 'Who do you hate?'

'What? No one,' she says quickly. 'I was just thinking of the lyrics to a song.'

'I hate her?' Alanna gives her a strange look. 'Are you sure?'

'Yes,' Gabby insists, heaving herself out of bed and stumbling to the bathroom.

'Wow, Mom! You're huge.'

'Thanks, Alanna,' Gabby snaps. 'Way to go to make your mom feel good at Christmas.'

Alanna follows her into the doorway. 'Sorry, Mom. It's just . . . you look like you're about to give birth.'

'I hope not.' Then Gabby reconsiders. 'Actually I wish. But it's still rather early. I have to tell you, I feel ready. I cannot wait to hold this new baby in my arms.' She looks up at her daughter. 'I can't believe I'm going to have another little one. Oh, Alanna, you were both so gorgeous when you were tiny. I don't mean that you aren't gorgeous now, but I still can't quite believe I'm going to have a tiny baby again.'

'Don't cry, Mom. You should be happy.'

Gabby starts to laugh. 'I am! I'm just sentimental. I'm so crazy about babies, and I never thought I'd have another one. These are tears of joy.'

'Mom? Can I ask you something? The baby's father. Are you still in touch with him?'

Gabby sighs. This is so hard. She didn't want the girls to know, but in the end she couldn't protect them. But how does she explain this, when she isn't even sure she's doing the right thing?

'I'm not, and I honestly don't know what I'm going to do. He's young, and not ready for children. I don't want to impose upon his life. I think at some point I might let him know, but I have no expectations, and I think it's better this way.'

Alanna thinks for a while. 'But don't you think the baby deserves to know who his father is?'

Yes, thinks Gabby. But she always hoped Elliott would step up to fill the role; she still hopes Elliott will step up to fill the role. 'I think,' she says, 'we'll cross that bridge when we come to it.'

Alanna says nothing, leaving the room to take her stash of goodies back downstairs.

Today, Elliott's presence is getting on Gabby's nerves. The fantasies of them all playing a happy family, the fake perfection and cosiness of last night are long gone. Gabby watches him frying bacon, pretending that everything's fine, and feels a surge of anger. His happiness has nothing to do with her, and everything to do with that bitch Trish.

How she blames Trish. It doesn't matter that it could have been anyone, that Elliott is free to date, given that they are officially separated; it doesn't matter that Gabby was unfaithful to him, is pregnant with another man's child; all that matters is that Trish is the woman who stole her husband, and Gabby will never be able to say her name without gnashing her teeth in rage.

I bet this is Claire's doing, she thinks, in a flash of fury. For years she called herself my best friend, then couldn't wait to set my husband up with Trish, the one woman guaranteed to make me nuts. Claire, who emailed her a while back out of the blue, who now sends her emails on a fairly regular basis, as if nothing is wrong between them, as if they are still great friends.

Claire, who fills those emails with funny stories about her child, the horrors of being the oldest mother in the mommy and me group, the bags under her eyes large enough to carry groceries in, thanks to the endless sleepless nights.

Initially flabbergasted to receive a chatty, warm, information-filled email from her former best friend, speaking to Gabby as if she hadn't dropped her like a dirty shirt at a time when Gabby needed her most, after a while she couldn't help but enjoy Claire's emails.

Gabby wanted to write back telling her how disgusted she was, but as she read through that first email she realized how much she missed Claire's voice, her point of view, her guidance and wisdom.

She has grown to look forward to the emails, even though she doesn't respond. She isn't ready to forgive Claire for not standing by her, not being there for her. But at the same time she can't help but laugh at the things Claire writes; can't help but miss having a friend like her.

And yet, however much she longs to have Claire back in her life she isn't able to forget Claire's betrayal. Why did Claire 'choose' Elliott, to the exclusion of her best friend? Gabby can't see that a choice even had to be made.

And Elliott? He is trying, oh how he is trying, to make things right, to recreate last night, but their easy camaraderie is gone, and Gabby looks grim as she takes the strawberries out of the fridge and pours hot chocolate for the girls.

She closes her eyes for a second as she stands by the fridge, so tired, so desperately wanting her life to be something, anything, other than the life she has.

'Mom? Are you okay?' Olivia is watching her.

'I'm fine. I'm just really tired suddenly.'

'Why don't you go upstairs and lie down?' Elliott is concerned. 'The girls will bring you breakfast in bed.'

What do you care? She wants to say it, but she doesn't. She nods and goes upstairs, relieved as soon as she lies on her bed, cradled in the heap of pillows. Elliott telling her about his girlfriend – the word is snarled nastily in her head – has thrown her. She hasn't felt right since then. Sick and tired. Ha! She is, indeed, sick and tired. And terrified, now, of what this means.

All this time, she has harboured the hope that they will get back together. More than hoped. Known. She has presumed Elliott will come home, because this is where he belongs. This is where he has always belonged. She has been able to keep away, to give him space, only because she has always known that at some point he is going to take her face in his hands and gently kiss her, telling her how sorry he is, asking her to give things another chance.

But she was wrong. Which means she is on her own. Which means that life will never be the same again. And despite what Sally at the divorce support group said, despite her assurances that there would be love, and possibility, and joy again, Gabby knows that's not true.

Not without Elliott.

After breakfast, brought up by the girls, Gabby falls asleep. When she awakes, the house is quiet. She crawls out from under the covers and takes the tray downstairs, finding Elliott asleep on the sofa in the family room, Olivia and Alanna on either side of him, both of them avidly watching some movie as a fire dies down in the fireplace.

Gabby stands watching them for a while. Alanna notices her and waves, then Olivia does the same, neither of them talking.

'What are you watching?' she asks finally.

'*Love Actually*,' mumbles Alanna. 'Ssshh.'

'Shall I make popcorn?' Gabby offers, as she feels a warm whoosh of liquid down her legs. 'Oh God,' she says, reaching out a hand to steady herself, trying to make sense of what has happened. Could she have had an accident? Has her bladder been rendered so weak by pregnancy that she could just stand and wet herself?

'What's the matter?' Both girls look alarmed. 'What is it?'

Gabby reaches down to swipe her legs and then inspects the liquid. It's clear. Has no colour, no scent.

'I think,' she moans, 'my waters just broke.'

*

Elliott keeps turning to her. 'Are you okay? Are you sure you're okay?'

Gabby clutches the armrests, furiously breathing in and out, nodding with wide, scared eyes.

'Mom?' Olivia, excited and terrified, peers over the back of Gabby's seat. 'I saw in a movie someone doing some counting. Do you want me to count?'

'I don't know,' Gabby puffs, exhaling as the contraction passes, leaning her head back on the headrest with a groan. 'Oh God. I should have gone to Lamaze classes.'

'I remember Lamaze classes,' Elliott says. 'We did them before.'

'Yes, but that was for Olivia. That was almost eighteen years ago. I don't remember anything.'

'You're doing great.' Alanna reaches forward and rubs her mother's arm, before turning to Olivia. 'I can't believe we get to watch!'

'No!' Gabby shakes her head in horror. 'You're not watching!'

'Aw, Mom!' Alanna grumbles. 'It's natural. Childbirth. What could be more beautiful?'

Olivia grimaces. 'Ewww. I do not want to watch. No, thank you. Call me in when it's all over.'

'I'll call you both in when it's all over,' says Gabby. 'Oh God, here comes another one. Elliott? Can you drive faster? Fuck!' And she's breathing hard again, trying to ease the pain, looking not unlike a terrified blowfish.

Elliott says nothing more. He doesn't want to be here. He can't believe he *is* here; it's just his bad luck that Gabby's waters broke when he happened to be in the house. And yet, there is a part of him grateful to be here, for what the hell would Gabby have done if she'd been on her own with the girls?

All he has to do is get her safely to the hospital and deliver her into the arms of a waiting doctor. Perhaps he'll go with them to the room, make sure the girls are okay, then leave just before they put the epidural in.

That would be the perfect time to leave. The one thing he's certain of is that he doesn't want to be anywhere near the place when the baby's about to be born.

Chapter Thirty

'Come on, nearly there. You can do it. Keep pushing, Gabby, one last time.'

Gabby leans her head back in exhaustion, summoning all her strength to push the baby out, certain that if it doesn't come out with this push, it's not coming out at all.

With a long grunt, Gabby pushes hard, feeling the release as the slick of life leaves her body, slithering into the waiting hands.

'Congratulations!' The doctor smiles. 'You have a beautiful baby boy.'

The baby is placed gently in Gabby's arms as tears of wonder roll down her face.

'A boy!' she whispers, her face lit with a beatific smile. 'He's perfect!' Despite the tiniest of features being scrunched up, he is still the most beautiful baby she has ever seen, more beautiful perhaps because he was so unexpected. Whatever misgivings she may have had, whatever regrets, she knows she wouldn't change this moment for anything.

The surge of love is instant and all-consuming. She will do anything for this baby; this baby will make everything okay; this baby is the only thing that matters in the world.

A nurse catches Elliott's eye. 'Congratulations, Dr Cartwright,' she says with a big smile. 'Or perhaps I should say "Dad".' Elliott smiles awkwardly, nodding in acknowledgement. How can he tell her, tell anyone here, that he is not the father? How can he admit that he is overwhelmed by the miracle of birth, by the fact of this new life now squalling in Gabby's arms, but that it has nothing to do with him?

He wasn't able to leave. He tried, many times, but on each occasion a nurse or a doctor would come in and address him as 'Dad', or give him instructions – not to let Gabby have too many ice chips – or simply speak to him as if he was supposed to be there, and he didn't know how to just walk away.

The truth is that he doesn't feel angry at Gabby any more. Not since his relationship with Trish began. He feels, mostly, sad. Sad for her, for her predicament, for what she has done to her life. He, after all, is in a relationship, and can, at times, see it becoming serious. This has less to do with Trish, and more – everything, in fact – to do with Elliott liking being married, needing the security, the routine, the comfort of having someone to come home to.

Here at the hospital, with Gabby, he feels at once connected, and curiously detached. She is the mother of his children, the woman he knows better than anyone in the world, but there is a barrier between them now that can never be removed.

In the hospital, being treated like the father of this

baby, Elliott feels like an imposter. Few of his colleagues, and certainly not the staff of different departments, know he is separated from his wife. Why would they think he is not the father?

As for who the baby looks like? Well, the baby is fair, and long and thin – so unlike the dark, chubby girls when they were born. But the baby looks like . . . a baby. Elliott has never been able to see familial likenesses in newborns. When both Olivia and Alanna were born everyone said they looked exactly like Elliott, but he could never see it. Now, when he looks at Olivia, he sees only Gabby. Alanna looks like her maternal grandmother. Clearly Gabby's genes are stronger than his.

The baby is four weeks early, but six pounds, and healthy. Back in the room he is placed in a crib next to Gabby's bed, and the girls, who had been waiting there on their own, are now crowing over their new brother.

'Look how tiny his fingers are!' Olivia grins as she places her finger against his and he wraps his minuscule fist around it, squeezing tight. 'Oh, Mom! He loves me!'

'Look at his teeny nose!' Alanna, not to be outdone by her sister, reaches down to brush his other hand, for him to wrap her finger too. 'He's perfect!' she whispers in awe. 'Can we hold him?'

Elliott is about to say they can hold him later, but it is not his place to say that. This has nothing to do with him. It is time for him to leave.

'Congratulations,' he says, and he walks to the side of the bed, leaning down to kiss Gabby's cheek. She tears her eyes away from the baby to look up at him.

'What am I supposed to do with a boy?' she says. 'I have no idea what boys are like.'

Elliott smiles. 'You'll have to fill the house with Tonka trucks and Lego. It will be a disaster area.'

'Oh God,' she groans. 'I hadn't thought of that. No more pink tutus and fairy castles.' They share a smile of remembrance.

'I have to go,' he says gently.

'Thank you for staying with me. For being here. It means the world to me.'

'You're welcome,' Elliott says automatically. 'Have you thought of a name for him?'

'Henry. Henry William Cartwright.'

Elliott starts. Hearing the baby with his last name is strange. He hadn't thought about what the baby would be called, but realizes now that he had subconsciously assumed the baby would have his father's surname. Not Elliott's.

'Isn't his last name something else?'

Gabby shakes her head. 'It's the same as mine.'

Elliott can't find the words for an argument. He suspects he is being petty, or would be accused of being churlish if he voiced his discomfort. It is true; Cartwright is Gabby's last name, but not by birth. He isn't sure she has the right to convey it to another, but doesn't know how to voice that, doesn't know if he

285

wants to be the kind of man who is so ungracious, so ungenerous.

He kisses his daughters, then leaves the room and takes the elevator downstairs. His mobile phone starts buzzing as soon as he switches it on. Texts and texts and missed calls from Trish. He should call her, but he doesn't know how to explain that he was present at the birth of his soon-to-be-ex-wife's baby.

As understanding as Trish has been, as encouraging as she has been for him to be present in his daughters' lives, as willing as she is to accept that with the daughters comes his soon-to-be-ex, this is not something he can easily explain.

Nor can he easily explain that Gabby is still his soon-to-be-ex-wife, that he hasn't yet summoned the courage to speak to a divorce lawyer. In an email Trish sent him last week, she'd attached an article she had 'stumbled upon' online, recommending the ten best divorce lawyers in Connecticut.

He thanked her, and, when pushed, agreed to start making calls, but he hasn't. He is filled with dread at the thought of the whole process, of the expense of it, of having to paint Gabby as the wicked witch – because he knows the lawyers will encourage him to think of her that way and that it behoves them to stir up the acrimony and bad feeling.

He knows he can't put it off for ever, but he hasn't been able to stomach the stress of making it official.

He sits in his car, in his reserved spot in the car park

of the hospital, and wonders what to do. Finally he calls Trish to let her know what has happened. He doesn't add that he was present at the birth, but explains that he will be taking the girls back to his house with him for the night because he doesn't want to leave them on their own.

The following morning Elliott knows he can't procrastinate any longer. He scrolls through his emails and finds the one with Trish's attachment, rereading the article carefully. He picks the lawyer referred to as 'The Divorce Lawyers' Lawyer: the lawyer the others choose to steer them safely through their own divorces.' He likes that they refer to him as clean, quick, thorough. They say he is 'no-nonsense' and gets the job done 'painlessly'.

On the phone with the receptionist he is asked for his children's names and dates of birth, then left on hold while the receptionist checks a computer. She comes back saying they are fine to set up an appointment, and he realizes only afterwards that she had gone to check if Gabby has already been to see them.

The appointment is made and he ends the call, but feels none of the relief Trish said he would feel once he had taken the first step towards the second part of his life.

How *does* he feel?

Guilty.

Chapter Thirty-One

The girls have been in a buzz of excitement for days. First, the baby has come home, and it is like having their very own breathing, crying, living doll. They fight over who gets to change him, who gets to hold him, who gets to dress him.

Gabby knows this won't continue, that they will be bored of doing everything for their brother once this becomes routine, and has wondered whether, while it lasts, she might be able to let them take over the night duty so she can catch up on sleep, but as tempting as it is in theory, she would never let the girls have that much responsibility. Apart from anything else the girls also need to have a full night's sleep now that they are back at school.

Secondly, her mother is flying in. This afternoon. Gabby has arranged a car service to pick her up from JFK, and the girls are both thrilled that Grasha will be here by the time they get home.

This may not be a good idea, but it's too late to do anything about it now. Gabby has always got into trouble when she has expected more from her parents than they have been able to give. Each time it happens she berates herself for behaving like a child, but still the disappointment comes.

Even now, knowing what she knows, she harbours a hope that her mother will actually be of help with the baby. It's not that she has to do much, but it would be wonderful if her mother helped drive Alanna to her practices, or took the baby for a couple of hours during the day so that Gabby could shower or nap.

She has been exhausted these past two weeks since the baby was born. A tiredness unlike any she experienced with the girls. A tiredness doubtless born of age, and lack of partner.

I had no idea, she thinks. But this wasn't something she wanted. Or planned. A baby on her own, at her age. Yet, clutching tiny Henry to her breast as he suckles on her nipple, she loves him. Despite the circumstances in which he came to be, she feels a fierce, binding love quite unlike the love she remembers feeling for her daughters. The girls were always shared between herself and Elliott, but this little boy is hers alone, and there is something different about having a son. She had always dismissed the old wives' tale that every father needs a daughter, every mother needs a son, but the love she feels for him is so all-consuming, she wonders if they are right.

Gabby places Henry in the bassinet at the end of her bed and tiptoes out of the room. He is fed, full, happy. Perhaps, if she is lucky, she will get a couple of hours to herself before he wakes up, shrieking in fury that he is on his own.

She dumps a pile of baby clothes and burp cloths in the washing machine before heading downstairs to make some tea, just as a town car pulls into the driveway.

Gabby watches through the window as the driver opens the rear door, and there is her mother, draped in asymmetrical oatmeal fabrics, her neck swathed in cashmere, her feet clad in beige suede slippers that will, Gabby is certain, have cost a small fortune. She is dressed as haute hippy by way of north-west London. Her hair, currently a dark shade of auburn, is clasped back in a clip. She looks chic. Comfortable. She has always seemed to Gabby to be beautiful, but now, ageing, she has an elegance that eluded her when young. The lines on her face only add to her grace, and Gabby smiles as she watches her mother extend her arms to give the driver a warm hug, knowing she will have extracted his life story during the drive here from the airport.

In the driveway, Natasha's face lights up when she sees Gabby, her arms extending yet again to hug her, before she holds her out at arm's length, inspecting her delightedly from head to toe.

'You don't look like you just had a baby. You look fabulous! How did you get your figure back so quickly?'

'Oh, Mum,' Gabby tuts, 'I'm still a stone overweight. But separating from your husband while you're pregnant does wonders for keeping the weight gain down. I highly recommend it.' She shoots her mother an ironic grin as she reaches for her suitcase. 'The girls are at school and the baby's asleep. I just put the kettle on. Do you want some tea?'

'I'll do it,' her mother says, taking the suitcase out of Gabby's hand and going inside. 'You go upstairs and have a rest. I'm here to take the strain off you, not have you running after me making me cups of tea. I'll make the tea. Milk, one sweetener, yes?'

A wave of relief washes over Gabby. 'Perfect,' she says as she goes upstairs.

'A boy!' her mother keeps whispering, looking from the bassinet to Gabby, who is lying in bed with – oh the bliss! – a stack of trashy magazines by her side. 'Look how different he is! How lean! And, my goodness, so long! Is his father tall?'

Leading up to the birth, Gabby had deliberately pushed aside all thoughts of Matt. She used to shudder with disdain when she pictured him, remembering how he had caused her life to fall apart. But he has unknowingly redeemed himself by giving her this beautiful child, so now she finds herself softening, looking at Henry's face and seeing Matt's features.

Wondering if she ought to let him know.

'His father is tall, yes,' Gabby says, hesitating for a second before reaching for her MacBook. 'Do you want to see a picture?'

'I would,' her mother says, nodding. 'Because he certainly doesn't look anything like our side of the family.'

Gabby goes to Google and types in his name, finding a picture of him at a tech conference. She turns the screen around. Her mother fishes inside the folds of her cardigan for her reading glasses before peering at the photo.

'My God, he's a hunk!' She sounds astonished, and picks up the Mac to hold it closer. 'And a child. Good Lord, darling. How old is he?'

'Older than he looks,' Gabby says. 'Thirty-three.'

'Well, that's a relief. I was worried someone might call the police on you. He's so handsome, isn't he? No wonder you weren't able to resist.'

'It wasn't really like that,' Gabby says. 'We became friends. It was all on email. I suppose I was still harbouring resentment at Elliott, because of the vasectomy. Here was this, as you see, gorgeous young man who seemed to find me irresistible. It was less about him, and more about how he made me feel.'

Her mother gives a small laugh. 'It so often is,' she says. 'Especially at your age.'

'Why my age?'

'Because you are entering the afternoon of life, and all is different. There is a wonderful quote by Jung. Let me see if I can remember it correctly.'

Her mother takes off her glasses as she thinks, then she shakes her head. 'No, I can't remember it well enough to quote it, but the gist of it is that if you think of life as a day, the morning – your youth – is full of truths and idealism. By the afternoon – your age – you assume these same truths will hold good. But Jung says you shouldn't, because by the evening – old age – you will realize that everything has been reversed. What was true in your youth turns out to be a lie, what was great has become little. Everything changes as the day goes on. You, my darling, are in the afternoon of life.'

She looks at Gabby with a loving smile. 'Marriage is hard, my dear girl. You and Elliott always had a charmed life, but even those with charmed lives hit the bumps in the road from time to time.'

'What about you and Dad? You never seemed to hit bumps in the road. You've been happy for ever. You managed to enter into the afternoon of your life pretty unscathed.'

Her mother smiles again. 'That's how it appeared, yes.'

'What does that mean?'

Another smile. 'It means that when I was forty six I fell in love.'

'With someone other than Dad, you mean?' Gabby is part-fascinated, part-horrified, not at all sure she wants to hear the story, but also knowing she cannot live without hearing it.

Natasha laughs. 'Oh yes. Someone other than Dad.'

'So? What happened? You had an affair?'

'I had . . .' She tails off, thinking. 'An awakening. An earthquake. A seismic shift in who I thought I was.'

'Mum? I have no idea what you're talking about.'

Her mother raises her eyes and looks at her. This time her smile is sad. 'Remember Joanie?'

Gabby does remember Joanie. One of the waifs and strays her mother collected, Joanie had recently divorced her husband, and was, Gabby recalls, something of an emotional wreck. She became part of their family for a while, for longer than the others. She moved in with them; she was her mother's new project, her mother's new best friend.

She recovered quickly. Those first few weeks of sobbing at the kitchen table gave way to peals of laughter. She made Gabby's mother laugh more than Gabby had ever heard. Gabby would come home from school and find them cooking together, both of them giggling at something unspoken. Joanie made her mother seem younger, happier, softer.

One morning she was gone. There was no goodbye, no warning, just a stripped bed and empty wardrobe. Natasha refused to answer any questions Gabby had, stonewalling her and asking her not to mention her name. It was clear to Gabby there had been a betrayal, but she knew not to ask.

Gabby frowns. What did Joanie have to do with anything?

'I fell in love with Joanie,' her mother says simply, and Gabby's eyes open wide in shock.

'You had an affair with *Joanie*?' But that's not what she's thinking. My mother is a *lesbian*? How is this possible? How is it possible that I do not know my mother at all?

'I did. Oh don't look so shocked. I didn't plan to have an affair with anyone, and I certainly never thought I'd fall in love with a woman, of all things, but there it is. Joanie was utterly compelling. I wasn't just in love with her, I was obsessed.'

'Mum, I'm not sure I want to know all this.'

'Oh, darling, I'm not going to give you any gory details. The point is, I fell in love with her, at an age not dissimilar to yours now, and part of it, so much of it, was me desperately trying to run away from the dreadful spectre of middle age. Joanie was much younger than me, and she made me laugh more than anyone had in years. And she made me feel young. Alive.'

This time Gabby nods silently. She knows what her mother's talking about.

'I was happily married, but this was something I couldn't resist. I told myself it didn't count, being a woman, but of course it did.'

'Did Dad know?'

'He knew I was infatuated with her, but he didn't think, of course he didn't, that it was anything more than a strong friendship. He didn't know until afterwards, when I was so floored by grief I couldn't get out of bed. Even then, I'm not sure he knew for certain.'

'And he never confronted you, or said he was leaving?'

'The thing is that I love your father. I have always loved your father. Of all the gifts he has given me, this was the greatest. I think he understood that I needed to have one final fling before settling into the afternoon of life. To be honest, I think the fact that it was a woman probably made things easier. I'm not sure he would have been so quietly circumspect had Joanie been Johnny.'

'I'm sorry, Mum. I still can't quite get over my mother revealing her secret lesbian tendencies. I'm a bit freaked-out right now.'

'Get over it,' Natasha says matter-of-factly. 'And stop thinking about the sex stuff. I fell in love with a person who happened to be a woman, end of story.'

'So, do you regret it?'

'I regret causing pain to your father. When it ended and he was so sweet and solicitous to me, as I lay there sobbing in my pillows for weeks, I felt awful. You know your father. He went very quiet. Well, he's always quiet, but for those weeks he barely said anything at all, and I regretted that. But I think he understood. We never spoke of her again.'

'Do you know what happened to her?'

'She left me for a young man she'd met at the book-store. I know they split up after a couple of years and I lost track of her after that. I get cards from her some-times, on my birthday. She never says anything other than wishing me a happy birthday, and I tend to put them in the bin. It was . . . a moment of madness. I'm lucky your father is the sort of man he is.'

'The sort of man Elliott is not.'

'I think Elliott might have handled things in much the same way had this little bundle of joy not come along. It's very difficult for men to handle betrayal when they are forced to look at the evidence every day. It is, for them, a daily reminder that they somehow fell short, they weren't able to make their wives happy, or happy enough.'

'Do you really think that's true?'

'I do. But how about the father of delicious Henry? What does he have to say about all of this?'

Gabby turns her computer around so she can see the screen: Matt in his golden loveliness, smiling into her bedroom. 'He doesn't know.'

Natasha is shocked. 'But you must tell him.'

'Mum. Please. I've made a decision. This is my baby, and I don't want him to feel obligated to be involved, or feel pressurized, or think I'm coming after him for money, or anything else. I made a decision, as soon as I found out, that he would never know.'

'But what if he wants to be involved? What if he wants a child?'

'Even worse!' sputters Gabby. 'The last thing I could handle right now is a custody battle. And he has money. Enough to pay for the best lawyers in the world. It would be a disaster. Anyway, I haven't spoken to him in . . . nine months. It was one night. Nothing. I need to move on.'

'Then what will you tell Henry about his father?'

'I'll cross that bridge when I come to it.'

'I can't tell you what to do, but I urge you to reconsider. Henry has a right to know his father, and his father has a right, certainly, to know about Henry. The biggest mistake any of us can make is to keep secrets. They always come out in the end, and it is the ones that people make most effort to hide that cause the greatest problems. I truly believe that what is called for here is absolute clarity. You need to give his father the opportunity to step up. If he doesn't, you will always know you have done the right thing.'

Gabby just stares at her mother. Everything she has told herself, every argument she has used to convince herself she is doing the best thing, now falls flat. Her mother is right.

She has to get in touch with Matt.

Gabby – I can't believe I heard from you! It's been, what? A year? Feels like for ever since you and I were in touch. After I came to visit, when everything got really awkward, I could tell you were uncomfortable so I thought it best to just keep my distance and give you some space. I figured you'd get in touch when you were ready, and this morning – there you were! Bringing a huge smile to my face. But you told me nothing – I don't know anything about your life these past few months and I'm dying to hear your news. Did you turn the barn into a store? Are you now a furniture-restoring/furniture-selling mogul? Are you happy?

Life here is as crazy busy as ever. Remarkably, I'm in a relationship! Yes, you heard me right. A real relationship.

Monroe is her name – I know, so LA :) – and she's truly a great girl. She's a model, but completely unlike so many of the airhead models I've come across out here. She has a degree in physics, and is very precise, and organized, and competent. I suppose I would describe her as a woman of substance. She reminds me of you in a lot of ways. She's warm, and fun, and wickedly clever. She's also the most secure woman I've ever met, other than you. She inhabits her skin comfortably and easily. I hope the two of you can meet – I know you'd get on.

So, what's the cryptic message about wanting to talk to me? We could chat on Skype, but I'm coming to New York next week and it would be easy to fly out to Connecticut for lunch. Are you around next week? Does that work? Tuesday?

Am sending you a big hug, and I want to hear all your news. I'm so happy you got back in touch!

Matt xoxoxoxox

As soon as Gabby reads the message all traces of the anger and resentment she'd harboured towards Matt for months disappear entirely. She reads the email over and over, a large smile on her face.

Her own, to him, was stilted and short. She never expected such warmth, and, dare she say it, even love, in his email. But there is undoubtedly affection in every line, and the prospect of seeing him, of telling him about Henry, is suddenly far less frightening.

She sends him an email in reply, managing to fill it

with fluff – books she has read that she loves, her happiness at him having found someone, her life being busier than ever.

She resists the temptation to drop even a hint into the email. Such life-changing, momentous news needs to be delivered in person, even in these digital times, and she phones Le Farm to book a quiet table so she can break the news.

Her figure is nowhere near ready for the jeans to be done up, so it is the ubiquitous yoga pants for her today, teamed with a flowing sweater and scarf, cute white sneakers.

I look like my mother, she thinks to herself with a smile as she checks her reflection before going downstairs.

'You look like me!' her mother exclaims as Gabby walks into the kitchen. She finds Henry reclining in a bouncing chair on the table, being fed, Natasha having warmed up a bottle of pre-pumped breast milk that was left in the fridge.

'Mum!' Gabby warns. 'It's not time. He's not supposed to have that for another twenty minutes.'

'But he was hungry!' complains her mother, who still does not understand Gabby's need to follow a routine, particularly since Gabby was fed on demand and slept in the family bed long before the concept of the family bed even had a name.

'Okay, okay.' Gabby can't be bothered to argue. She

has little tolerance for the screaming of a hungry new-born baby either. When Olivia and Alanna used to scream Elliott would take them in his arms and walk them endlessly up and down the stairs until they were quiet. With no Elliott, it is far easier to just feed Henry when he wants it.

Perhaps her mother is right after all.

'You look beautiful,' her mother says. 'In all serious-ness. You really ought to wear make-up more often.'

'Thank you.' Gabby leans down to give her a kiss, before planting a kiss on Henry. 'Wish me luck.'

Natasha raises her free hand to show her fingers are crossed, before blowing Gabby a kiss as she heads out of the door.

She wasn't nervous in the slightest before she pulled into the parking space outside the restaurant, but as soon as she parks she starts to feel slightly sick. How is she supposed to tell him? And when? Does she make small talk throughout lunch and drop the news like a bombshell over coffee? Would she even be able to do that? To pretend everything is fine, knowing she is about to change his life for ever?

Or does she blurt it out at the beginning, risking him storming out of the restaurant, leaving her alone and embarrassed to pay the bill? What if there's someone she knows in there? What if there are women who overhear, who then spread rumours, or pass her pitying looks as she stumbles out in a fog of humiliation?

She pushes open the door, passes the heavy curtain, and scans the tiny restaurant to see Matt already there, in the corner, his face lighting up as he sees her. There is something so familiar about him, so reassuring about seeing him, and yet all the attraction she once felt has disappeared. It is like seeing a long-lost brother, not a man with whom she was once obsessed.

'Gabby!' He holds out his arms, giving her a huge hug, and she allows herself to be held, relieved not to have seen disappointment in his eyes. She no longer wants him, not in that way, but for him to be so instantly comfortable, so warm, so clearly pleased to see her gives her confidence, sets her at ease.

'You look beautiful,' he says, and it is clear he means it. 'This has obviously been a good year for you.'

'It has been . . . a tumultuous year,' she says, seeing the opportunity, wishing it hadn't presented itself quite so early on in the lunch. 'You look handsome. And happy. I love your hair longer. It suits you.'

He blushes. 'You won't believe this but I think I've finally met the girl to . . . tame me. I've actually fallen in love, and she, Monroe, likes my hair longer.' He is bashful telling Gabby this. 'This is all her doing, I'm afraid.' He runs his fingers through his hair and grins self-consciously.

'You're in love!' Gabby teases. 'Oh, Matt. I'm so happy for you. You deserve it.'

She is astonished to find she means these words, that

there is not a hint of jealousy in her being, only pleasure that he has found happiness.

'What's she like?'

'Funny. Smart as a whip. No-nonsense. She's a little like you. And she's practical – she can make anything, and she's far better with a screwdriver than I am.'

'And beautiful, I'm sure.'

'She does some modelling.' He shrugs as if to apologize. 'But enough about me and my love. You said you've had a tumultuous year. What does that mean?'

'Oh God. It's a very long story. One that needs a drink.' She smiles. 'Will you join me?'

'Martinis at lunchtime? How decadent!' He grins. 'I'd forgotten what a good drinking partner you are.'

'No Martinis for me at the moment. But a weak white-wine spritzer would be lovely.'

They order drinks and chat about the restaurant, the menu, the deliciousness of the dishes that pass them, until there is a pause.

'You still haven't told me about the tumultuous year.'

Gabby nods slowly. 'That's because I'm not sure where to start.' She takes a deep breath. 'I separated from my husband.'

Matt's eyes fill with sympathy and he reaches across the table for her hand. 'Oh, Gabby. I'm so sorry.'

'Thank you. It's been devastating. Oh God.' She starts to laugh, raising her eyes to the ceiling, unable to believe how like a bad movie this is feeling. 'I just don't know how to say this, so I'll come out with it. I had a baby.'

'Are you serious?' Matt's smile contains astonishment and confusion. 'My God. That was quick! You look amazing.'

'Matt, my husband had a vasectomy. The baby isn't his.'

Matt just stares at her, uncomprehending, until the expression on his face conveys that he understands what she is saying, or, rather, what she is saying by saying nothing at all.

Chapter Thirty-Two

Grateful he didn't ask whether she was sure, Gabby steers the car up Post Road, checking in her rear-view mirror that Matt, in his rental car, is still behind her. She thought about offering him a ride, but she needed some time alone to think about what just happened, so, instead, she quietly suggested leading him back to her house to meet Henry.

She knows now that her mother was absolutely right in advising her to contact Matt. Gabby had been so afraid of having anything to do with him, with this man she had turned into a powerful demonic figure. In her mind he had become the wicked person solely responsible for breaking up her marriage; she was terrified that he would also destroy the new happiness she had found with the baby. She knew that she wouldn't be able to lose that, to have Henry taken from her.

As she drives she almost laughs with relief that her fears were so way out of proportion.

In all the possible scenarios, never had she imagined him to be so . . . calm. He was, he said, 'blown away', but not unhappily so. 'A son,' he kept repeating. 'A *son*!'

He was boyishly bewildered, incredulous that he had managed to create another life.

And instinctively Gabby knew he wouldn't fight her for custody, or try to steal Henry. She had the strong feeling that Matt would play a part in Henry's life, but that it wouldn't be a bad thing.

Seeing Matt behind her, concentrating on following her, she has a sudden vision of Henry as a small boy, holding Matt's hand, splashing in the water and learning to surf.

She is there, watching, as the matriarch. Perhaps his girlfriend will be there too, in the water with them, but she will not be threatened by Gabby. Gabby has no designs on Matt.

Seeing him today, without the rose-coloured glasses of obsession and intoxication she once wore whenever he was around, she is able to enjoy his youthful enthusiasm, his guileless charm.

Quite how they will figure this out, with her on the east coast, him on the west, remains to be seen, but Gabby is curiously content with his reaction, with the knowledge that he wants to be involved.

'You're back so soon!' Her mother's voice comes from the kitchen. 'Henry's upstairs sleeping. How was it? How did he –'

'Mum! We're here. He, Matt, is here.' Gabby shoots Matt an apologetic grin as she leads him through to the kitchen.

'Oh!' Natasha stands up. 'Gosh. You are tall. I'm Gabby's mother, Natasha de Roth. How do you do?' She extends a hand as Matt smiles awkwardly.

'It's nice to meet you, Mrs de Roth. Are you staying here for long?'

'Call me Natasha,' she says. 'And you don't have to make small talk with me. Questions like that always make me think of the Queen. Do you know that at her garden parties she's reported to always ask people, "Have you travelled far?" She asks the same thing over and over again. Can you imagine? I'd rather kill myself. I'd much rather ask someone what's their favourite car, or what would be their movie-star name.'

'Nineteen fifty-six Porsche Speedster. George Lazenby.'

'You can't have George Lazenby,' Natasha says, her eyes sparkling with delight. 'It's taken.'

'I know. But you have to admit it's the perfect name. Most people my age have no idea that there ever was a George Lazenby, so I could easily steal it.'

'True. And a nineteen fifty-six Porsche Speedster sounds glamorous. And expensive.'

Matt grins. 'It is. Both.'

'Okay, you two,' Gabby says. 'We're going to go upstairs. How long has Henry been asleep?'

'Almost two hours. Go on up.'

Gabby motions for Matt to lead the way through the door, but her mother grabs her arm and pulls her back to whisper furiously in her ear, 'He's adorable!'

Gabby just smiles and shakes her head, detaching herself, then she and Matt go upstairs.

'I'm so scared I'll drop him.' Matt has a look of terror on his face when Gabby offers him Henry.

'You'll be fine.' She shows him how to support the baby's head, then sits down next to him on the bed as they both gaze at their son.

'Wow!' Matt's voice is low and soft. 'I think he looks like me. Don't you think he has my eyes?' Henry is staring up at his father. 'I think he knows me. Hi, little dude. Do you know who I am? I'm your daddy.' He is filled with wonder, and Gabby has sudden memories of when Olivia was born.

Each of her children's births was awesome, but none quite so magical nor overwhelming as the first. The first time she held Olivia she couldn't tear her eyes from her, wanting to drink her in, unable to believe this mysterious, magnificent creature had grown inside her body, had been created by her.

Matt feels it too. The awe at the life he has created. When he finally turns his head to look at Gabby there are tears in his eyes, and a lump in his throat.

'He's amazing,' he whispers. 'I can't believe it.'

'I know,' she says.

Just then the front door bangs open and, with shock, she hears the girls come in from school, their footsteps thumping on the stairs as they scramble up to see their brother.

Olivia is first, and she pulls up short, the smile wiped off her face as she stares at this strange man holding her baby brother. Alanna, coming up next, still smiles but is curious as to who this man is, this man cradling Henry in her mother's bedroom.

'Hi?' Olivia's greeting is a question.

Gabby immediately thinks of her mother saying absolute clarity is called for. No more lies; no more evasion.

'Hi, girls,' she says warily. 'I'd like you to meet some-one. This is Matt.' She takes a deep breath. 'This is Henry's father.'

'Wow. Hi!' Alanna comes in and bends down to inspect her brother, completely unfazed by this infor-mation, but Olivia stays in the doorway, her eyes narrowing as she glares at Matt.

'Olivia?' Gabby prompts. 'Please come in and say hello properly.'

But Olivia says nothing. She whirls round and stalks down the hallway, and the next thing to be heard is the slamming of her bedroom door.

Gabby is mortified. 'I'm so sorry,' she says, turning to Matt. 'I don't know why she was so rude.'

'Yes, you do,' Matt says, because as lunch progressed he learned the remainder of the story about her marriage breaking up due to the pregnancy. 'It's understandable. She blames me.'

'I'll go and talk to her. Are you okay being here with the baby?'

His face lights up. 'You don't mind leaving me with him?'

'Can you handle it?'

'If you can.' He looks nervous. 'What do I do if he cries?'

'Alanna's here. She's very good with him, and I'm only two rooms away. If he cries, cuddle him. He loves being rocked and going up and down stairs.' She lays a hand on his arm just as she leaves. 'Relax,' she says. 'You're going to be great.'

There is not a peep from Henry as Gabby walks down the hallway to Olivia's room. She knocks tentatively on the door and waits, but there is no response.

'Olivia? Let me come in.'

She turns the handle and opens the door. Olivia is sitting at her desk, pretending to be immersed in work; but her back and shoulders are tense, and she won't turn round and look at her mother, won't respond.

'I talked to your grandmother last week about what to do, whether or not to tell Henry's father he has a son, because I wasn't going to. She pointed out, and I agree, that the father has a right to know Henry; that Henry has a right to know his father. He flew in from California today and I told him at lunch, and I honestly didn't know what his reaction would be, but he wants to be involved.'

'Involved how?' Olivia spits. 'Involved with you?'

'No. Not with me. There is nothing between us any

more.' Gabby doesn't know if it is her imagination but she is certain she sees a slight relaxation of Olivia's shoulders. 'Involved with Henry.'

'But he's in your bedroom. And he's the man responsible for Dad leaving. If it wasn't for him, you and Dad would still be together. We'd still be a real family.'

'Oh, Olivia. We are still a real family. If you're going to blame anyone at all for what happened, blame me. I know you *have* blamed me, but don't blame Matt. He had no idea of the circumstances of my life, and he's a nice man.'

'I just . . .' Olivia's voice chokes. 'I just wish things were how they used to be. I wish you and Dad were still together. I wish he wasn't with that horrible Trish. I wish everything was like the old days.' She dissolves in tears and Gabby rushes to comfort her.

'I know,' she croons. 'I wish that too, but we have to accept that things are different. This is our life now. We can't keep looking into the past and wishing for something that no longer exists. We have to move forward. You have to find a way to accept Henry's father because, like it or not, he's a part of this family.'

'He's not a part of *my* family.'

There is little point in saying anything else, in trying to persuade Olivia otherwise when she is in a mood like this. Gabby kisses her daughter on the top of her head and leaves her, knowing that she needs some time on her own, that she will re-emerge in an hour or so, pretending to still be grumpy, although she will, in fact, be fine.

Gabby closes Olivia's bedroom door softly then stands and thinks for a moment about what Olivia said in there, her description of 'that horrible Trish'. Thank God, she thinks, feeling ever so slightly guilty. But thank God it isn't just me.

In her bedroom Matt is now standing, walking around, gently rocking Henry and singing him nursery rhymes, while Alanna lies on stomach on the bed, heels up in the air, laughing each time Matt gets the words wrong, which he is clearly doing deliberately to make Alanna laugh.

Gabby smiles and goes downstairs to her mother, who grins broadly at her as she finishes topping a cottage pie with grated cheese.

'Well!' She turns, folding her arms and beaming. 'What a wonderful man. Boy. I'm not sure which, but he's wonderful. What does he think of his son?'

'I think he thinks he's pretty amazing.' Gabby wells up, sitting at the table and running her fingers through her hair. 'God, I feel emotionally exhausted. All the pent-up dread and anticipation, but it couldn't feel more right. I think Matt's fallen in love.'

'Who wouldn't fall in love with that delicious little baby, who is, by the way, the best baby ever? Hardly a peep out of him. Makes me wish I'd had more.'

'Except they would undoubtedly have been screamers like me,' Gabby reminds her.

'True.' Natasha pops the cottage pie into the oven

and sets the timer. 'Now, is there any laundry to be done? I'll go upstairs and check, shall I?'

'No. Mum, it's fine. Sit.' Gabby gestures to the chair, not wanting to overtire her mother, who is turning out to have surpassed all Gabby's expectations, even the deeply hidden ones she had thought were no more than wild hopes. Natasha hasn't stopped looking after all of them, making Gabby wonder if, in fact, part of the problem had been that Gabby was an only child. Natasha needs a crowd, needs to be needed by a large number of people, not one independent, self-sufficient child.

Perhaps she could see Gabby never needed her, which is why she pulled in all the waifs and strays in the first place. Now she is needed. By Gabby. By the girls. By Henry, and now, perhaps, by Matt.

Natasha is in her element, cooking, doing laundry, and Gabby wants to tell her how grateful she is, but doesn't know how to say the words. Instead she reaches out and squeezes her mother's hand, and her mother squeezes back, because she knows what Gabby would say if she was able to say the words.

They both turn as Matt comes into the room, Henry starting to fuss in his arms. Matt holds him out, panicked, and Gabby takes her son, who instantly calms down when his mother holds him.

'Would you like to stay for supper?' Natasha asks with a bright smile. 'It's cottage pie.'

'What's cottage pie?'

'Shepherd's pie,' explains Gabby. 'In England shepherd's pie is made with lamb, and cottage pie with beef, but here I know everyone just calls it shepherd's pie.'

Matt looks at Natasha, shaking his head slowly. 'I have no idea how you knew this, but that happens to be my favourite dish.'

'There are those who have called me something of a witch,' Natasha says, twinkling.

'No, I think it was a "b",' Gabby says. 'Bitch. They said you were a bitch.' Matt watches as she and her mother crack up.

'Well? Are you staying?' Natasha directs her attention back to Matt.

'Let me talk to Gabby,' he says, for which she is entirely grateful. It is so like her mother to invite all and sundry to stay, and she cannot blame her for inviting Matt, who she has clearly taken an immediate shine to.

There is Olivia to think of, and Alanna, although Alanna seems fine. And there is Gabby, who is delighted, but unprepared for Matt to suddenly be a part of this family. She thinks it is probably the right thing for the future, but needs to take it slowly.

'Do you want to go for a walk?' Matt says.

Gabby puts Henry in his bouncing chair, grabs her coat and gloves, slips her feet into snow boots, then they set off down the road.

'I feel completely overwhelmed,' Matt confesses, as they reach the corner. 'I have no idea what to feel about this. I'm thrilled, and awed. And scared. I don't know if I'm ready to be a father.'

Gabby says nothing, but gives him room to try to sort out his thoughts, imagining how hard this must be for him, dealing with such unexpected news.

'At lunch, when you told me, I was freaking out inside, but then I thought, okay, so I made you pregnant, but it didn't mean my life would have to change. I hadn't thought about kids, other than to assume I'd have them at some point, but I figured that was all down the road. I guess I came back to meet him because it felt like something I had to do, but I didn't expect to feel . . .' He shakes his head. 'I didn't expect to *love* him. *Instantly*. To feel this . . . this, bond. Like I would do anything for him, would throw myself off a bridge for him. I know it sounds dramatic, but it's just that I have never felt anything like this, and I've spent, what? An hour with him? Two?'

'He's your son,' Gabby says simply. 'You're *supposed* to feel that way. That's what parenthood is. It's utterly selfless. You put your own thoughts and feelings and desires aside, without even being aware of doing it, and you put your children first.'

'So what do we do now? How do we do this? I have to be a part of his life, but I don't want to get in the way of yours, or do anything that would make you uncomfortable.'

Gabby stops and turns to him, tears in her eyes. 'Thank you. Thank you for saying that.'

'Gabby, I didn't expect this. But now that he's here, I couldn't hope for a better mother for my son. I know you're an amazing mother, and I know how much you do for your kids. I don't want to do anything other than be there for Henry when he needs me. Listen, your mom is awesome, and I love that she invited me for dinner, but I don't know that I should stay. I was thinking that maybe, if I go back to the hotel this evening, I could change my flights and stick around for a few days. I could spend time with Henry, and you and I could perhaps figure out some kind of schedule. You know, I could fly over here a couple of times a month to see him, or something.'

'That sounds perfect,' Gabby says. And it does.

Chapter Thirty-Three

'Are you nearly ready?' Trish calls out from the bathroom, where she is finishing putting on her make-up, while Elliott sifts through the handful of clothes he now keeps in her closet.

This is all moving very fast. A little too fast, he thinks, pulling out another new shirt Trish had insisted on buying him. He looks at himself in the mirror, not quite recognizing the man who stares back at him.

It isn't that Trish is trying to change him, she teased him; she is just trying to gently propel him from eighteenth-century New England wasp to a modern man.

She has bought him Italian suede driving loafers to replace his old loafers; deck shoes from France; fine cashmere shirts; Ermenegildo Zegna jeans, which, he had to admit, did fit him beautifully.

'See how elegant you are now?' she said in the dressing room of the store, where she insisted he came out to show her every new outfit.

'But I can't let you buy this for me,' he said, fishing in his wallet for his credit card, terrified of the thousands of dollars this little spree was going to cost, but feeling like he'd travelled too far down the road to get out of it now.

'Absolutely not!' Trish insisted, before leaning forward and whispering how much net profit her company made the previous year. Elliott put his wallet back in his pocket as she instructed the sales assistant to put the bill on the house account.

Tonight they are having dinner with friends of Trish's, friends she has been anxious for him to meet. Jennifer and Colin. He is a hedge fund something, and she is an aspiring photographer and fellow yoga-addict – she and Trish do yoga together several times a week.

Elliott hardly ever went out for dinner when he was with Gabby. It was a rare treat when they did, but they were far more likely to cook dinner themselves, have people over, or go to other friends' houses.

He had no idea, prior to dating Trish, that there is a whole other world that exists in this town: a world where couples get together to 'couple date'. They dress up in their finest clothes and go to the newest restaurants, striding through with an air of authority, if only because they are the most beautiful people in the room, the people everyone else in there watches with envy.

He has had, now, a number of these evenings with Trish, as she brings him deeper into her world. They have eaten at all the trendiest restaurants in the area, which stretches over three towns. She has worn one of a never-ending selection of chiffon tops, long chunky necklaces, high platform heels that make her almost as tall as he is.

She looks gorgeous. Exquisite. Together, with his new, fashionable wardrobe, they look gorgeous. Exquisite.

Yet it all feels like so much effort for so little return.

Tonight, as he walks into the bathroom and sees Trish in yet another diaphanous top, large diamond hoops in her ears, skin-tight trousers and high silver pumps – ridiculous, given the snow outside – he is hit with a sense of dread.

He doesn't want to sip a cocktail in a trendy restaurant and think of things to say to a man with whom he has nothing in common, while the women chatter animatedly between themselves. He doesn't want to pretend to be interested in sports, which he couldn't care less about, or ask questions about derivatives, and acquisitions, and futures, none of which he understands, nor wants to understand.

He doesn't want to have yet another conversation about house values, or the new mansions going up, or how much value for money there is in town now, and how, if they had spare cash, they should really be buying up the tear-downs and rebuilding for under two hundred a square foot.

Trish is wonderful, but her lifestyle is tiring. Elliott is longing for a home-cooked meal. Trish is an amazing cook, but it is all about show; she cooks only if she entertains, or seduces. The rest of the time she expects to go out, or, perhaps, at a push, get takeout sushi.

And the house is so damned quiet. The children, Madison, Greyson, Bradley and Skylar, are usually down in their basement kingdom, playing Xbox or watching TV. He hears them laughing and shouting when they are with their friends, but around him they are the most well-mannered children Elliott has ever encountered. He misses the squabbling and fighting of his girls. He even misses their screaming and chasing each other through the house, flinging accusations of having stolen clothes, or hairbrushes, or make-up.

Trish has said he must make himself at home, but how is he supposed to make himself at home when it doesn't *feel* like home? Where are the piles of papers and magazines next to the computer in the kitchen? Where are the shoes and boots, kicked off and left strewn about the mud-room floor? Where is the clutter, the art, the knick-knacks you have collected over the years that tell the story of your life?

The objects in Trish's house have all been bought since she renovated a year ago, and chosen to match the rest of the decor. What little clutter there might be is swept away by Ester, then artfully arranged in panelled closets you would never know existed.

Elliott looks at the soap dish, thinking of the soap dish in his old bathroom, at Gabby's house. The soap was green, and there was always mushed-up green slush at the bottom of the bowl. The soap dish would never stay clean for longer than one use. Once you picked up the soap, it was all over. Here, the soap is white, and however much you use it, there is never residue left in the bowl. He walks over to the sink and picks up the soap, looking at the dry, shiny dish.

Trish finishes pushing bangles onto her wrist before swivelling and watching him finger the dish, her eyebrows raised. 'What are you doing?'

He shakes his head. 'Nothing.'

'How do I look?' she asks, knowing she looks beautiful.

'Perfect.' He sees her face fall. 'Beautiful. Stunning.'

She smiles as she approaches him for a kiss. 'You look very handsome too,' she says, admiring the shirt which she bought to turn him into the man she needs him to be in order to go out with him.

The evening is exactly as Elliott expects. Every head turns to inspect them as they walk in, and of course they should, for Trish is now, certainly amongst their age group, the most famous woman in town. Regularly profiled in magazine articles, written about in the papers, she is the woman everyone wants to be seen with.

And she wants Elliott. Which should make him the happiest man in the world. What must it say about Elliott that this beautiful, accomplished woman, this woman who could, let's face it, have pretty much any man she could want, has chosen Elliott? How lucky he must be. He can see it in the faces of the people as they walk through the restaurants, the cocktail receptions.

They scan Trish first, checking out her clothes, her

jewellery – she is famous for her sense of style – before their eyes alight on Elliott. Ah. This must be her partner. What kind of a man is it that Trish would choose?

Sometimes he wishes he could pull Trish away from all this. Away from this house, this world, these places where she feels pressure to see and be seen, to dress and act and look the part.

A cottage in the country would be perfect. Perhaps they could live somewhere remote by the ocean. A place where neither of them had to dress up, where they could wear shorts and flip-flops all summer, wrap up in fleece and down when the weather got cold.

They could cook together over a big range in the kitchen, and their children – in the fantasy all the children would be there together, both hers and his – would run through the house squabbling, as he and Trish laughed about how wonderful it was to have this chaotic blended family.

'How about we go to the country?' he says to Trish on the way home after he has lied and said how much he liked her friends. 'A friend of mine has a place in Vermont that he barely uses, and he loves friends going to stay. I thought perhaps you and I could go up there one weekend. Maybe take the kids.'

'What kind of a place?' Trish asks.

'It's wonderful.' He remembers the times he and Gabby took the kids. 'It's a big, sprawling farmhouse. Not fancy, very basic, but comfortable. There are big squishy sofas and huge fireplaces, plus board games going back centuries. It's on a large pond with a swimming deck, and it's just the most peaceful place on earth. It's really a place where you get back to your roots.'

'I'm not sure I'd ever get my kids in a swimming pond,' Trish says with a laugh. 'I'm afraid they're chlorine addicts. I took them to a hotel in Greece that had a salt-water pool and they were horrified.'

'I can understand them not liking salt water in a pool, but this is a beautiful clear-water pond. They'd love it.'

'With green slimy things underneath them?' She looks at him doubtfully. 'I'm not so sure.'

Elliott remembers going one summer when Olivia and Alanna were much younger, and they spent hours throwing themselves off the swimming deck, shrieking with laughter.

The four of them took the kayaks onto the lake, saying they were going on a bear hunt, whipping the girls into a frenzy of excitement and fear. Everything was quiet, when the air was suddenly filled with a deafening snap of branches and the girls shrieked with terror. It was probably, almost certainly, a deer, but to this day, whenever they talk about it, it was the day they got away from the bear.

They have been to the farm a few times in winter. Before the girls were born Gabby used to enjoy skiing – her enthusiasm for it had been kindled by school trips to Austria and Switzerland, when she spent much of her time either mooning over the ski instructors or desperately trying to impress them.

But at the farm Elliott would take the girls to the local ski mountain while Gabby stayed home and made huge pots of soup, stews, warming casseroles. One night she produced fondue, proudly drawing out the fondue pot she had discovered nestling in the back of the cobwebby pantry, and they sat by the fire skewering chunks of baguette and swirling them around the melted and very garlicky Gruyère and Emmental.

The house is dusty and basic, lived-in and loved. It is a house that holds nothing but happy memories for Elliott, a house in which he wants to create new memories with Trish. A house in which, surely, Trish will be able to let down her guard and be her true, natural self.

'When you say the word "basic",' Trish says slowly, 'what does that mean?'

He describes the house in more detail, trying to impart the magic of the property, the surrounding woods, the beauty.

'I don't know.' She shakes her head. 'If we're going to do Vermont, I'm thinking Twin Farms.'

'Twin Farms?'

'Oh it's *fabulous*!' she says with a smile. '*That's* what we'll do! I'll book Twin Farms for the weekend. It's the most fantastic, quiet, beautiful, luxurious place in the world. You'll go nuts! What a great idea!' She draws out her iPhone to punch in a note to herself to have her assistant book Twin Farms, while Elliott stares stonily ahead.

That is not what he had in mind at all.

*

He can't shake the feeling of things not being right. It isn't that this relationship isn't working – he is determined to make this work with Trish – but he is aware that he is being shoehorned into a life, a lifestyle, into which he doesn't quite fit, and he isn't sure what to do about it. The deeper into their relationship he goes, the stronger the feeling he has that he is trying to be something he is not.

Elliott has never been a man who has been unsure of himself. He has always known exactly who he is, where he is going, and what he has wanted. Yet here he is, nearing fifty, for the first time in his life feeling uncomfortable in his skin. It is a new feeling, and not one he enjoys.

Pulling into the driveway at Trish's, he doesn't make a move to get out of the car.

'Are you coming?' Her door already open, Trish is about to get out, pausing only when she sees Elliott is not moving.

'You know,' he says, 'I realize I have a very early start tomorrow, and I need some equipment I've left at home. I think I'm going to go home now so I won't have to stop off in the morning.' He looks at her. 'Is that okay?'

'Of course,' she replies brightly, and he thinks again how much he loves this aspect of her: that she is never jealous, nor insecure; that she never thinks his desire to go home means he doesn't want to be with her.

Even when that is the case.

He doesn't go home, though. He drives around town for a while, then down to the sea. He parks his car and sits on the low stone wall by the beach and looks out towards Long Island, where the lights from the lighthouse glitter on the black water. He wishes he smoked. Now would be a perfect time for a cigarette, but he has never indulged in that particular habit.

Back in the car, he drives aimlessly, until he finds himself drawing up outside the house that was once his. He smiles at the only light left on, in Alanna's room. She is too old to be scared of the dark, and allows her light to be turned off by her parents when they say goodnight, but always climbs out of bed when she knows they are safely in their bedroom to turn her light back on.

The privet in front is overgrown and straggly. He is tempted to creep into the garage for the clippers and prune it right now, as a surprise, for it has always been his job, and Gabby has enough to do with the new baby.

He doesn't. He sits in his car, staring at his house, thinking of his old life, trying not to compare old and new, until there is nothing else to do but drive back to his new life.

Chapter Thirty-Four

Josephine and Gabby's mother have become new best friends. Since Natasha has been here, Josephine has started coming over every day, dropping in to see how Gabby is doing, bringing something for the baby, carrying an extra pumpkin pie she made, but Gabby is convinced she's only coming to sit at the kitchen table and chat to her mother.

As a child, Gabby found her mother incomprehensible. As an adult, on Gabby's home turf, Gabby finds her magical. With no one to distract her, nothing to disturb her, no stream of people walking through the front door – and Josephine could never qualify as a stream – Natasha is warm, loving, engaged. Gabby is terrified of what she will do when her mother leaves.

The time seems to have flown by, and Gabby is grateful that her mum has been able to stay for so long, but she is talking of leaving at the end of the month, filling Gabby with dread. Being on her own and pregnant was one thing, but being on her own with a newborn baby is quite another entirely.

She comes downstairs knowing Josephine is here, having heard her car pull up earlier, and walks into the kitchen to find Josephine and Natasha sipping big mugs of tea, Natasha in peals of laughter over a story Josephine is telling her.

'Why do I always feel like the gooseberry around you two?' Gabby pulls a mug down from the cupboard, drops in a tea bag, then puts the kettle back on.

'Gooseberry?' Josephine looks at her.

'Odd man out.'

'That's because your mother and I have fallen in love.'

Gabby looks at Josephine in alarm. She is joking.

If only you knew, thinks Gabby.

'Josephine has an excellent idea. She wants you both to go on a girls' night out tonight. Her boys are with their father, and Olivia and Alanna are out with friends this evening, so you have no excuse not to go. I think it's exactly what you need.'

'It's not what I need,' Gabby says. 'It's what Josephine needs. She's been desperately trying to get me to go to some ghastly singles bar with her, and now you're press-ganging me into going too. I know I said I'd go, but not yet. I'm not ready to go out in public yet.'

'I think going out will do you good. You go nowhere,' her mother says.

'Nowhere,' echoes Josephine. 'You're turning into a dusty old maid. Let's go out and have fun! You look great, Gabby. Come on, let's flirt!'

Gabby peers at her. 'Have you seen the men in those bars? Are you seriously suggesting we put our energies into flirting with those creepy professional singles?'

'Yes!' Josephine laughs. 'Maybe tonight will be our lucky night and the two most gorgeous single men in Fairfield County will decide to be there. You're coming, whether you like it or not.' She suddenly sits up straight, turning her head to look out of the window. 'Speaking of gorgeous men, a car just pulled up and someone extremely interesting is getting out. He's coming here!' She turns back to Gabby. 'Please don't tell me that's your ex-husband or I may have to slap you.'

Gabby cranes her neck to see Matt walking up the path.

'Not ex-husband,' she explains. 'Father of my child.'

'What? And he's *here*? I thought he wasn't going to have anything to do with Henry.'

The bell rings.

'It's a long story.' Gabby gets up to open the door. 'Saved by the bell.'

Josephine does not flirt with Matt, thankfully, but she cannot take her eyes off him. When he goes upstairs to get Henry from his nap, she leans forward and hisses, 'How did I not know how adorable he is?'

Gabby laughs. 'Don't look so surprised. I'm not that awful.'

'No! That's not what I mean, but I'm wondering why I'm dragging you out to hit the singles scene when you have the perfect man right here in your house. Why aren't you up there with him? Why aren't you seducing him right now?'

'Because you and my mother are sitting round the kitchen table making my devious plan impossible?' jokes Gabby.

Josephine's face falls. 'Oh God. I'm sorry. I'll go.' She stands up before Gabby, laughing, tells her how ridiculous she is being.

'I'm not interested in Matt.'

Josephine frowns. 'But he's the father of your baby.'

'Yes. And I was interested, obviously. But . . .' She thinks. 'It's as if there was a light bulb inside me, which glowed for a while, and then, suddenly, it went out, and nothing will get the light to go back on.'

Josephine is sceptical. 'Nothing?'

'Truly. Nothing. He's adorable, and brilliant, and handsome, and funny, but he's just not for me, and, beyond that, he's a child. I don't want to be mother to anyone except to my children. We had a . . . dalliance. It was utterly all-consuming, and it changed my life. I can't say any longer that I wish it had never happened, because I have Henry, and he is amazing, but, as you know, it turned my life upside down in ways I didn't want.'

'Well,' her mother says thoughtfully, 'it may not have been what you wanted, but, as you pointed out, you have Henry, and you wouldn't change that. I always think that we are exactly where we need to be. There is a greater plan for you, and Henry is part of that plan. Perhaps Matt needed to come into your life. Perhaps, as painful as it has been, you and Elliott needed to be apart.'

Gabby says nothing. Her mother's words sound so wise, except when they refer to her.

'Meanwhile, I'm perfectly happy to babysit Henry. I imagine Matt will stay here too, to keep me company. You two go out and have fun.'

Gabby rolls her eyes. The last thing she wants to be doing tonight is hitting a bar, but she checks her watch. 'I give in.' She turns to Josephine. 'I have to drop the girls at their friends' houses. Shall I pick you up at seven?'

'Perfect,' trills Josephine. 'I'm going to run down to Main Street and get something to wear.'

'I like him,' Alanna announces, from the back seat of the car, while Olivia raises her eyebrows and glares out of the window. Gabby doesn't ask to whom she's referring.

'Good,' says Gabby. 'He's a nice man. What's not to like?'

'How about: he's young enough to be your son, and he's forcing himself into our family when he's not wanted,' mutters Olivia.

'*I* want him,' says Alanna.

'Henry wants him,' adds Gabby.

'What about you?' spits Olivia. 'You definitely want him.'

Gabby sighs. 'Only as Henry's father. I don't want him for me. Listen, Olivia. I know this is hard, to have another man around who isn't your father, but I promise you that if there was anything going on between us, or if I thought there might ever be anything going on between us, I'd tell you. I'm not going to keep any secrets from my family ever again. Whatever happened between us happened, and I can't change that, but nothing's ever going to happen between us again.' She laughs. 'Quite apart from the fact that there's no chemistry whatsoever, Matt has a girlfriend.'

'I bet she's pretty,' Alanna pipes up. 'I mean, I know Matt's old, but he's very cute.'

'I'm sure she is. She's a model. And she has the coolest name: Monroe.'

Olivia turns her head slowly towards her mother. 'He's going out with *Monroe*?'

Gabby glances at her daughter. 'Yes. Why? Do you know her?'

'Monroe the model?'

'Is there more than one?'

'No! There's only one Monroe. She's gorgeous. She's going out with him? Our brother's father?'

'Apparently so.' Gabby keeps her eyes on the road as Olivia whips out her iPhone and starts Googling.

'Oh. My. God. Mom! You didn't tell us who he is!'

'Who is he? Who is he?' Alanna bounces up and down on the back seat, stretching through the gap between the front seats to try to see Olivia's phone.

'He's, like, a *gazillionaire*. He invented Fourforesight and sold it for *bajillions*. And he dates Monroe! And he's

part of our family! Oh my *God*. I have to tell *everyone*!'
And she starts furiously texting.

'Not so bad any more, is it?' mutters Gabby, who
can't resist a small smile.

Usually the girls climb out of the car and Gabby drives
off without going into the house or seeing Elliott, or,
heaven forbid, the dreaded Trish, although according
to the girls Trish rarely comes to their dad's house – 'It's
far too small and poky for her,' Olivia said – and if they
do see her on their weekends with their dad, it's either
going to her house, where they tumble into the amazing basement to play ping-pong, air hockey, or watch
movies on the giant TV, or going out to an event.

This time they are stopping by to retrieve clothes.
The girls are running out of things to wear, and Gabby
has no idea what has happened to the rest of their
clothes. They aren't in the laundry, and unless the girls
have lent them to friends – which they swear they
haven't – they must be at their father's house.

Up until Christmas she would have just called Elli
ott, but since then things have become strained. Gabby
has found herself barely able to communicate with
him, barely able to look him in the eye, since he
embarked upon his relationship with Trish, a woman
Gabby has never liked. For a while she became obsessed
with Googling Trish. She discovered everything about
her, unable to tear her eyes away from her perfect white

smile beaming at the camera. There was even one picture that popped up on a local website of Trish and Elliott together, taken at a charity gala. Elliott looked dapper and sophisticated in a way he never had when he was married to Gabby.

Trish has always been a figure of envy and secret derision to Gabby, but in her mind Trish is now a full-blown monster. She wishes she didn't feel like this and could let her hatred go, but every time she imagines Trish with Elliott she starts gnashing her teeth together in fury.

So as they pull up outside the house and Gabby gets out of the car, she has to force a smile onto her face as if everything is fine, as if she isn't consumed by hatred of her soon-to-be-ex-husband's girlfriend, consumed by the overwhelming fear she has that she is not good enough, that Trish knows she's not good enough, that Elliott knows it now too.

The girls push open the front door. 'Dad? We're here!' Gabby is somewhat gratified to hear them say 'We're here' rather than 'We're home', but she remains on the doorstep, waiting to be invited in by Elliott. 'Dad?' They walk through the silent house. 'Dad?'

Olivia turns to Gabby. 'I don't think he's here.'

Gabby is relieved. 'Can you just run upstairs and get the clothes you think are from my house and bring them down?'

'Mom!' Olivia pouts. 'I don't know which is which. I keep telling you. You come up and take the stuff that's yours.'

334

Gabby frowns. She has never been inside this house, but, peering through the doorway, she has to admit she is curious. There is the old sofa from the family room, but she has never seen those cushions before. They're stunning. Why didn't she think of putting cushions like that on the sofa? It completely transforms it.

She steps in gingerly, her eyes scanning the rooms as she walks through. I remember that rug, she thinks. Looked better in our house. And that painting! She looks up at the huge oil cityscape. Thank God that bloody painting's finally out of my house, she thinks. I hate it even more here.

She doesn't touch anything for that would be too much of a trespass, but tiptoes up the stairs, peeking into Elliott's bedroom. The bedspread and sheets are new. Crisp white, with a matelassé cover and matching pillow cases. Two small armchairs by the fireplace, chocolate-brown velour. Gorgeous. She can't help but walk in, noticing the medical journals on Elliott's nightstand, his spare reading glasses. Her eyes flick over to the other side of the bed, *her* side of the bed, and she inhales sharply.

On the left nightstand are two glossy magazines, an eye mask, and a novel with a pink cover. The girls are wrong. Trish does sleep here after all. Gabby suddenly wants to get out as quickly as possible, her nosy exploration bringing her nothing but pain.

Chapter Thirty-Five

Her mother told her she looked beautiful. Matt told her she looked beautiful. Why is she feeling so . . . wrong?

Gabby is well aware of the uniform of the newly single, middle-aged woman. She is well aware she should have found the time, like Josephine, to run down to Main Street to buy the requisite diaphanous top, or brightly coloured little dress, the chunky jewellery, the platform heels, but she is too depressed by the memory of the nightstand on the left – it just won't leave her mind. Besides, it's not like anyone would be the slightest bit interested in a woman who has a new baby and a post-pregnancy paunch that doesn't seem to want to go away – not that she's the slightest bit interested in anyone anyway. Gabby has to admit that the last thing she wants to be doing is flirting and having fun. She'd much rather be curled up in her bathrobe, watching Apple TV, eating popcorn.

The outfit she is wearing was chosen deliberately for its lack of sex appeal. No hint of cleavage, no flash of thigh. Nothing that would make anyone think she might possibly be trying to pick up a man. She is – thank you, God – finally able to get into her 'fat' jeans. She may have a substantial roll over the top, and it is entirely possible that she will not be breathing by the end of the evening, but she got them on and got them done up, and frankly that is all that matters. The substantial roll is covered by a thin grey sweater that is simple and, to her mind, elegant. She is wearing the chunky necklace she bought, once upon a time, to impress Matt, and she is wearing the high-heeled boots she bought, once upon a time, to impress Matt, but both choices are largely to prove to Josephine that she is not the dowdy housewife she appears, and can scrub up rather well when forced.

She couldn't be bothered to blow out her hair. It feels like years since she visited the hairdresser, and her hair is now well past her shoulders. She isn't sure how appropriate it is for a forty-three-year-old mother of three – three! She still can't get over that it's now three! – to have a tumbling mane of long, curly tresses, which is why she usually clips it back, but tonight she did as she used to do when she was a teenager: scrunch mousse into the curls, tip her head upside down to dry it, then flip her head back to produce a cloud.

A touch of make-up, a clutch purse that Elliott bought her – again, once upon a time – and her look is complete. But walking through this place, with its crowds of people all busily chatting away, their eyes scouring the room to check out each new person that enters, makes her seize up with anxiety, makes her feel out of place, wrong. She resists the urge to grab Josephine and run; instead she follows Josephine to the bar, her eyes cast down to the floor, terrified to make eye contact lest anyone thinks she might be available.

They are there less than five minutes before they are surrounded – and, oh Lord, how lascivious these men seem to her, with their flashing smiles and appreciate looks. We must give off the scent of fresh meat, thinks Gabby, smiling politely but coldly, while Josephine giggles prettily and tells the men what they will be drinking.

'I haven't seen you ladies here before,' one of them says, a handsome man, but a drinker, Gabby deduces, staring at the broken veins on his nose.

'We're fresh meat,' Gabby says with a bold grin.

He raises an eyebrow. 'English fresh meat!' He seems delighted. 'Does it taste different over there?'

Gabby gives him a withering look as he laughs and throws up his hands with a boyish shrug, as if he couldn't help himself, as if he's a naughty boy. Oh *God*, she thinks. This is exactly why I didn't want to come.

She glances at Josephine, who is already in an animated discussion with one of the other men. It is hard to tell whether she is genuinely interested, or whether she is just enjoying the attention. Either way, her body language is open and flirtatious; the pair of them are both laughing. Gabby sighs, wondering if she might be able to call a cab and leave early.

The professional singles have, it seems, claimed the bar. As long as she perches on a stool by the bar she will have men like this chatting her up all night. Would it be worse, though, if men like this didn't chat her up? Would she feel inadequate? Less than? She looks around at the women, at their high, high heels, their mid-winter tans, their straightened hair and heavy make-up. It isn't about being less than, she realizes. It is about being entirely different. She isn't one of these women, nor does she want to be. She should have trusted her instincts and not agreed to come. As wise as her mother has been of late, she is not always right. This was not a good idea.

A couple gets up from a table in the bar area, and Gabby swoops in. She will sit there and lose herself in her iPhone until it is time to go, or until she feels she is able to make her escape. Her Kindle app is on the phone, and even though she doesn't find it particularly easy to read on such a small screen, it's better than being the fresh meat at the bar.

She orders a cup of tea from a passing waiter, ignoring his surprise at the unusual request in the bar that is famous for its singles night on this particular day of the week, then gets stuck into the novel she has been meaning to read for weeks.

'Is this seat taken?'

She isn't sure she heard properly as she looks up. Oh God. She should have got rid of the other chair. Why didn't she anticipate this was going to happen? She hesitates, looking at the man standing by the table, not wanting to be rude; but if she says it's taken he will soon see there is no one to join her, and if she says it's free she will have to fend off yet another awful man.

He doesn't look awful. He is wearing a Barbour, and how could she not warm to a man in the coat that always reminds her of home? He is rugged, and has kind eyes. How is she supposed to be so rude as to say it's taken?

'I'm sorry?'

'Is this seat taken? May I sit here?'

'You're English!'

He smiles. 'So are you.'

Gabby puts her phone back in her bag. 'Where are you from?'

'London.'

She looks at him. Since coming to live here she has met a lot of people who are English and say they are from London. 'Where?' she used to ask excitedly, always hoping they would be from her 'village'; hoping they might say Belsize Park, or Primrose Hill, or Camden Town.

Invariably they'd say, 'Guildford.' She has no idea why, but it seemed everyone she met who said they came from London, ended up coming from Guildford. 'Right,' she'd say, covering her disappointment. 'Surrey.'

'Where in London?' she asks dubiously, awaiting the Guildford reply.

'Maida Vale.'

'No!' She is delighted. 'I'm from Belsize Park!'

He grins from ear to ear before doing what all good Londoners do when far from home and connecting with someone from their village: declare their school. 'City of London.'

'South Hampstead!'

'Oh my God!' He laughs. 'Don't tell me – nineteen seventy-nine to eighty-six?'

'Not quite. I'd have been in the year below you.'

'I think I went out with the whole of your year.'

'Who? Who?' It is an unspoken connection, an immediate familiarity, as Gabby leans across the table towards him.

'Sarah Diamond.'

'She was in the year above me!'

'Emma Montgomery.'

'My year!'

'Daisy Luckwell.'

'My God, you were busy!'

'What can I say? I was very charming when I was at school. Didn't you know City boys?'

'Not really.' She shakes her head. 'I was too busy falling in love with the boys at UCS.'

'Oh please!' He waves a hand dismissively. 'How could you possibly have fallen in love with boys from that school? Maroon-and-black-striped blazers! What little taste you must have had. You should have looked further afield to us, where the real men were. We played rugby. And tennis. Very manly.'

'Oh yes. And cricket. *Very* manly.'

'What's the matter with cricket?' He feigns hurt. 'I'll have you know I'm an excellent bowler.'

'You're certainly bowling me over,' she says, and grins, before her hands fly up to her mouth. 'Oh my

God. I didn't mean that. I was just making a double entendre. I didn't mean that to sound like a come-on.'

He laughs. 'First of all, I'm just thrilled to hear someone pronounce "doobl ontond" correctly, and secondly I haven't had such a nice come-on in years. Even if it wasn't one. What are you drinking? Sorry, I can see you're drinking tea but that's completely ridiculous. You can't sit in a bar on this ghastly singles night and drink tea and think that's okay. You need something far stronger to give you the fortitude to get through this evening.'

Gabby cannot stop smiling at the banter. 'Why? Are you that bad?'

'Oh I'm much worse.' He grins. 'Let me guess. Cosmopolitan.'

She grimaces. 'Do I really strike you as a Cosmopolitan kind of girl?'

'Good point. Pint of Scrumpy?'

'If I knew you better I'd tell you where to go.'

'Vodka and tonic, lots of lime?'

'Perfect.' She watches him as he heads over to the bar, knowing this isn't going to be such a bad night after all.

'Excuse me?' She looks up into the face of a leering, perma-tanned man. 'Is anyone sitting here?'

'Yes,' she says, and smiles at him. 'I'm afraid there is.'

'I'm Julian.' He extends his arm over the table and they shake hands formally.

'Gabby.'

'I hate to ask the obvious question, but do you come here often? Know that if you say yes I may have to get up and leave, but no pressure.'

Gabby laughs. 'I have been here before, but for dinner. This is the first time I've been to the singles scene, and it is, as you said earlier, ghastly, as I knew it would be, and the only reason I'm here is because my girlfriend has been begging me for weeks to accompany her, and in the end I ran out of excuses. I also thought: it's one night – how bad can it be?'

'Worse,' Julian says.

'Clearly.' They chink glasses in a silent toast.

'So what brings you here, in your Barbour and brogues? Are you looking for a glamorous divorcee to tuck you up at night?'

His face grows serious as he studies his glass, before looking up at her again. 'Actually, I'm here in much the same way you are. I'm newly separated and my mates at work have been trying to get me out for a night's drinking for weeks. I kept trying to put them off, but in the end I also ran out of excuses and thought I'd just get pissed and get it over with.'

'Pissed as in English pissed?'

'Yes. Drunk. Not angry.'

'God, it's nice to meet someone who speaks the same language,' Gabby says. 'I've been here for ever – I'm an American citizen – and I love this country more than I could ever imagine, but when I'm with someone English I just feel I've come home.'

'I have that effect on all women,' Julian says. 'Ser-iously, it isn't meeting someone English, though. At least, I don't think so. It's meeting someone from your "village". We probably went to the same parties. I'm sure if we tried we'd come up with a ton of people in common. Were you hanging out at the Dome?'

'Yes!' she says in delight. 'The Mud Club?'

'Yes!'

'Hang on –' she peers at him – 'didn't I snog you on New Year's Eve in nineteen eighty-five?'

'Oh my God! That was you? I've been looking for you for ever!' They both laugh. 'So what's your story, Gabby? Husband? Kids? What brought you here . . .'

'I had a husband,' Gabby starts, leaning forward so he can hear.

'What?' The music has just been turned up and he cups his ear. 'Can you speak up?'

She leans even further forward and speaks loudly. 'Not really!'

'Have you eaten? This place is too damn noisy for me. Do you want to leave and grab something to eat?' he asks, his lips up against her ear.

She beams up at him. 'That would be lovely!'

Josephine turns to see Julian, before gaping at Gabby. 'What? How is it that you've met a cute guy already?'

'He's not a romantic prospect,' Gabby assures her. 'He's from the same place as me. We have friends in common. To be honest, it's getting a bit loud in here. Would you mind terribly if I left?'

'You're going to get in a car with him? A stranger?'

'No! We're just going across the street. I'll be back.'

'Oh. Okay.'

'You're sure? Because I won't go if you're not okay with it.'

'It's fine.' Josephine leans forward. 'This guy Rich is really nice. I'm more than fine.' And she winks.

'Be back later,' Gabby says, giving Josephine a kiss on the cheek.

She told Josephine he isn't a romantic prospect, and the truth is she is enjoying herself too much to even think about whether he is a romantic prospect or not. There is certainly banter, perhaps one might call it chemistry, but Gabby suspects it's from familiarity, rather than any sexual attraction. He feels like a brother, like someone she has known for ever, for while she does not know him, she has known a million men, boys, like him, and feels completely safe and comfortable in a way she rarely feels with people she has just met.

They walk across the street, both chattering nineteen to the dozen, and walk into the restaurant there. Julian guides her in through the door, one hand on the small of her back, then helps her off with her coat, hanging it on the rack by the door.

How lovely it is, Gabby thinks, to be with a man

who knows what to do. He pulls the chair out for her before sitting down himself, and shakes out his napkin as soon as he sits down, smiling over the table at his new friend.

Gabby sighs. 'This is so much better. Thank you for suggesting this. I felt like my ears were going to pop.'

'I haven't forgotten you were about to give me your life story,' Julian says. 'I think you were at the part where you had a husband.'

'Ah yes. I was.' Gabby is quiet for a moment, because she is not sure how to edit her story to make it palatable. He may feel like someone she has known for ever, but what will he think if she tells him the truth? Is it necessary to tell anyone the truth? Would it not be better just to say she and her husband split up and she has a baby? But she has tried that before, and everyone gasps in horror at how disgusting her husband is, that he could leave her when pregnant.

She may be furious with Elliott now, but he is not the bad guy here. He does not deserve to be castigated for something he did not do.

'I had a husband,' she starts, her eyes flicking to the door, then she stops, abruptly. 'Oh shit,' she says. 'And there he is.'

She looks at Julian like a rabbit trapped in the glare of headlights.

'Do you need to hide?' he leans forward and whispers.

'I don't want to see him,' she whispers back. 'Or his ghastly girlfriend.'

'I like it that you like the word "ghastly".' He is still whispering. 'It's my most favourite word. I've made a pact to myself to use it at least five times a day.'

'This really is ghastly,' she says. 'Seriously. I don't want to see them.'

'Stop being a baby,' he commands. 'I can't throw my Barbour over your head and pretend to be dining with the incredible shrouded woman.'

Despite herself, Gabby laughs, just as Elliott spots her, and stops in his tracks.

'Don't look now,' Julian says out of the side of his mouth, 'but the ex has seen you.'

'If you had thrown your Barbour over my head I wouldn't be able to look now,' she mutters, wishing she could stop smiling. 'I wish you had.'

'Don't be silly,' he says gently. 'If I had then we'd have to cut a hole in it so you could eat, and that wouldn't be very practical, would it?'

Gabby bursts out laughing before sinking her head in her hands. 'Oh God. This is awful. I don't mind saying hello to Elliott, but the smug ghastly girlfriend? Ghastly!'

Julian peers over. 'She does look rather smug. Very American perfect. Not my type at all.'

'Oh no? What's your type?' Gabby couldn't help the question, but Julian says nothing, merely smiles and raises an eyebrow, lifting his water glass in a silent toast.

'Watch out', he says. 'Here they come.'

'Elliott!' Gabby summons every ounce of graciousness she has ever possessed, flashing a charming smile at them both. 'Trish! What a small world!'

'Lovely to see you,' Trish replies, without stopping, continuing through the restaurant to their table, shooting a look at Elliott as if he should follow her. Which he doesn't. 'Elliott?' she says.

'Be there in a minute,' he says, turning to look at Julian. He extends a hand. 'Hi, I'm Elliott.'

'Julian. How do you do?'

'Oh. You're English. Are you a friend from home?'

'No,' Julian says pleasantly, not offering anything else. An awkward silence descends.

'How are the girls?' Elliott asks Gabby eventually.

'Fine. They're with friends this evening. Hoping to see you sometime this weekend, I think. Oh, and some of the clothes from my house are still at yours,' she adds. 'Maybe you could bring them back?'

'Do you know what they are?'

'Some leggings. Long-sleeved T-shirts. And socks. We seem to have run out of socks.'

'I'll look,' he replies, standing at their table a few moments longer but finding nothing else to say. 'Well, I'd better get going.' He looks at Julian again. 'Nice to meet you.'

'Enjoy your evening,' Gabby says, and as she watches

him walk towards Trish she is reminded so much of an unhappy little boy. She turns back to Julian, an apology already on her lips.

'Well,' he says, settling back in his chair. '*That* wasn't awkward.'

Chapter Thirty-Six

Usually Elliott is a sound sleeper. Gabby used to tease him because he could sleep anywhere, in any position, asleep almost before his head hit the pillow.

Lately, though, he has found himself waking up in the early hours of the morning, anxious, with no idea why. He has tried lying in bed counting sheep, deep breathing, meditating on ocean scenes, but nothing is able to send him back to sleep.

He turns his head and raises himself slightly, better able to see the digital clock on Trish's nightstand. She is fast asleep, her cream silk nightgown bunched up, almost to her waist. He looks at her perfectly rounded naked bottom, with no desire to touch her. He is admiring, but dispassionate; it is as if he is marvelling at the cool white perfection of a marble statue by Michelangelo.

It is 4.33 a.m. He knows he won't go back to sleep now. Occasionally, if he wakes up at two, or even, sometimes, three, he can get back to sleep, but after four he knows it's all over; there's little point even trying.

He climbs out of bed, not worrying about making a noise because Trish is dead to the world until morning. In his own house, he would lie back in his recliner and flick through the channels until he found something that caught his interest; he might catch up on his reading, or find himself playing one of the kids' mindless computer games.

Here, in Trish's house, he is a little stuck. He hovers in the doorway of the living room, negatively anticipating the feel of the hard, modern sofa. It looks beautiful, but it is not a sofa on which to lie, cushioned by down pillows, feet up on a large wide armrest as you read a book, or watch TV.

Wait, there *is* no TV in here.

The sofas in the family room are not much of an improvement, for this is not a room where anyone ever lounges, or relaxes. But there is a television; for want of something better Elliott makes himself as comfortable as he is able to and starts to flick.

He isn't looking for anything in particular. His thoughts are far away from anything on the screen, and there is little, at this point, that can bring them back.

Ever since he saw Gabby with that English man, he has felt out of sorts; wrong; ill at ease. She left him having already slept with, having been impregnated by, another man. They are getting divorced, even though he had to cancel the initial appointment with the lawyer because something came up at work – he doesn't remember what – and he is supposed to have found happiness with Trish. What right does he have to feel uncomfortable seeing his wife with another man?

He gazes blindly at the television screen and pictures Gabby with that man. Elliott was facing their table, looking directly at the pair of them, and he had to focus hard so as not to stare all evening. Even then, his eyes kept involuntarily landing on them. It wasn't so much that she was with another man – they are separated, after all, and she has the right to be with anyone – it was that she looked so happy; happier than she has looked in months.

And Julian isn't just any other man. He is English. He sounds just like her. He has that rugged English, Bear Grylls-ish quality. If you threw him in the middle of a jungle, by the end of the first day he would have built a two-storey hut out of banana leaves and twigs, caught a few fish out of the river with a stick he'd whittled into a spear, and would have a wild boar merrily roasting over a fire. He looks, Elliott realizes with shock, exactly like the sort of man Gabby should be with. They looked good together.

Better than good. *Right*.

'Hey,' he hears from behind him, turning in surprise to see a sleepy Trish padding into the room, running her fingers through her hair. She sits next to him on the sofa and kisses his cheek. 'What's up? Bad night's sleep?'

Elliott shrugs. 'You know how it is. My body's exhausted but my mind's racing.'

'Which is stress,' she says. 'What are you stressed about?'

'Who knows? Everything. Life.' His voice is light, but his expression is not.

'And Gabby,' Trish says after a pause. 'Being with another man.'

'What?' He feigns innocence, his eyes open wide. 'That? Oh no. That's no big deal.'

'Elliott.' Trish gives an ironic laugh, leaning back from him, as if her body is getting ready for the distancing that she knows is about to come. 'I'm not stupid. I was there with you all night. You couldn't take your eyes off the two of them, and you were frowning every time you looked at them. Just like you are now.'

Elliott quickly corrects his features. 'It was just a shock,' he says. 'I didn't know she was dating anyone.'

'It was more than that,' Trish says sadly. 'It was that she was dating someone appropriate. You know what I saw tonight?' Her voice is quiet. 'I saw that you still love her.'

'Of course I still love her!' Elliott says. 'I was married to her for twenty years! We have two children together. You don't just stop loving someone overnight.'

'I did,' she says.

'That's different.'

'Not much. Here's the thing. You may still love her, but what I saw tonight was that you are *in* love with her. I saw love, and loss, and all the things you're going to admit to if I push you, but I saw something else that you may not even realize. I saw *yearning*. You didn't want Gabby sitting there with some other man, and you didn't want to be sitting there with me. You wanted to be with her.'

Elliott says nothing, just looks at his hands.

'I have no idea what the future holds,' Trish says. 'I don't know if this thing she has is serious, or how she feels about you, but the one thing I'm absolutely sure about is that you're still in love with her. Which means you're not ready for a relationship with me, or anyone else.'

Still, there is nothing for Elliott to say.

'I think you're wonderful,' she says, blinking back the tears that are threatening to spring. 'I wish things were different. Who knows, maybe in a year's time you and I will circle back to each other again, when you're more ready, but I think we need to call it a day.'

She reaches out and takes his hand, squeezing it gently as Elliott just nods, ignoring the tears in his own eyes as they begin to slowly trickle down his cheeks.

Chapter Thirty-Seven

'Natasha!' Elliott stumbles on the doorstep. 'How lovely to see you.' He has always got on very well with his soon-to-be-ex-mother-in-law, and has no idea how he should greet her.

'Elliott!' With her trademark warmth, she flings her arms round him, enveloping him in gauzy scarves and a squeezing hug. Stepping back she holds him at arm's length and examines him. 'You look incredibly dapper and handsome. I hate to say it, but separation suits you.'

Elliott laughs. 'Only you could say that and not have me think you were crazy.'

'Some might say I am crazy,' she replies, and laughs too. 'Which is why I can get away with it. It is true, though. I haven't seen you look so good in years. And yet . . .' She peers at him. 'You don't look terribly happy. You look tired.'

'I didn't sleep last night. No idea what happened. Recently I've started waking up in the early hours of the morning, and once I'm up, that's it. No more sleep.'

'Sounds like you're going through the menopause,' Natasha says. 'Maybe you should go and see a doctor.'

'Ha!'

'Are you coming in?' she says after a while. 'Gabby's out but the girls are here. Are they expecting you?'

'No . . . I brought some clothes that Gabby said were missing.'

'Good. Come in.' She leads the way into the kitchen. 'Do you still take your coffee with half and half and one sugar?'

Elliott smiles in relief as he shrugs off his coat. 'Good memory.'

'It *has* been twenty years,' she says.

'True.'

He looks around at the familiar kitchen, but hesitates before sitting down at the table.

Footsteps come running down the hallway then Alanna runs into the room. '*Daddy*!' She flings herself onto his lap, giving him a reception far better than the usual grunts of hello he gets when they are dropped off at his house.

'Unexpected visits can bring unexpected pleasures.' Natasha smiles, putting a steaming coffee in front of him just as Olivia walks in, Henry leaning against her shoulder, gently burping as she pats his back.

Her face lights up as she blows her father a kiss, then she sits down, careful to sit far away from coffee or anything that could spill and hurt Henry.

'You look scarily proficient with that baby,' Elliott says, looking for Gabby in the baby's face, but not finding much. The eyebrows? Perhaps. Ears? Maybe. The baby is blond and long, as different to the girls as he could possibly be. They were dark, chubby and so obviously girl-like, with tiny delicate features.

Alanna takes Henry from Olivia and jiggles him up and down. 'Look, Dad!' she says. 'You have to see this!' She puts him in his bouncing chair in the corner of the room, then crouches in front of him.

'Atishoo!' she says, pretending to sneeze, and a huge smile comes across Henry's face.

'Atishoo! Atishoo!' Henry starts chuckling, and then, as both girls continue sneezing, his chuckling becomes full-on hysteria. Everyone is laughing. Even Elliott, for this baby, with his delighted giggling, is adorable enough to spellbind everyone who lays eyes upon him.

'Isn't he *amazing?*' Alanna looks at her dad, laughing. 'Don't you *love* him?'

'He's definitely amazing,' Elliott says, astonished that he doesn't feel more of the animosity he had anticipated. He has been dreading meeting this child properly. He has seen him bundled up in Gabby's arms, but, to her credit, she has never offered up the child for him to approve, and he has always tried not to look.

The situation is painful enough, he has always felt, without having the physical reminder being forced upon him.

But here is the physical reminder, and it isn't painful. It is adorable.

'Can I hold him?' Elliott has no idea where the words come from as he nervously looks at Natasha, knowing he has no right to this child, has nothing, in fact, to do with this child, but she just smiles approvingly as Alanna lifts him up and hands him to Elliott.

'What a good boy!' Elliott bounces him on his knee as Henry giggles, then he brings him forward and holds him, burying his nose in the baby's neck and inhaling that sweet, powdery, baby smell, which immediately sweeps him back to when the girls were little.

'Isn't he so chubby and delicious?' Olivia says. 'Don't you just want to eat him?'

'He is delicious,' Elliott croons. 'You're delicious! Yes, you are! You're delicious.'

'Wow, Dad.' Alanna watches him. 'You're really good with babies.'

Elliott fixes her with a fake hard glare. 'You would think so, given that I've had two of them myself. Hard as it is to believe the two of you were ever babies.'

'That's not what she means.' Olivia is watching. 'She means you're really good with *this* baby.'

Unseen by the girls, Natasha silently raises her eyebrows before taking a sip of tea.

'I like all babies,' Elliott says. 'When they're not screaming.'

'Henry never screams,' Alanna says. 'He's the best-behaved baby ever. He doesn't wake up at night, either. He's been sleeping right through until five o'clock. You'd love him if you lived here again.'

'Don't be stupid,' Olivia says. 'Dad's not going to live here again. Are you?' She doesn't mean for the note of hope to creep into her voice with the last two words, but, nevertheless, it is heard by everyone in the room.

Elliott doesn't know what to say. For the rest of the night he was thinking about what Trish said, and as much as it pains him to admit it, she is right. It is all true. He does still love Gabby. But things are different now; they can never go back to how it was before, and he can't see a way forward.

Gabby is dating, and she has a new baby with another man. He has to move on. It is definitely too soon for him to have another relationship, and perhaps time will heal the wound; perhaps acknowledging that he is still in love with Gabby, instead of pretending that he pities her, will allow him to move on properly, rather than attempting to project feelings he doesn't have onto the first woman who steps in his path.

But he didn't expect this: to like this baby. Any baby. He, after all, is the one who continued with the vasectomy despite knowing how much Gabby wanted a baby; he is the one who told her, in no uncertain terms, he was done. He didn't want to get up for night feeds; he didn't want to show up to pre-school events when he was old enough to be a grandfather; he didn't want to give up his life for another eighteen years when the light at the end of the tunnel was just starting to become visible.

Yet here he is, holding this chubby, chuckling boy, and all he wants to do is continue burying his nose in his neck; blowing raspberries on his tummy; bouncing him up and down to make him laugh.

And Henry isn't even his.

The front door opens and all of them start. A jingle of keys down the hallway, footsteps, and then Gabby is there in the doorway. She stops, stunned to see her baby in the arms of her husband. Soon-to-be-ex-husband.

'Elliott. What are you doing here?'

'I brought the clothes you were looking for. I couldn't find all of them but I'll check the laundry when the wash is done.'

'Oh. Great. Thanks.' She's speaking slowly, carefully, unable to believe he has Henry in his arms and is clearly comfortable. More than comfortable; he is loving it.

'Girls? Go and tidy the mud room, please,' she commands. 'Your shoes are everywhere.'

Reluctantly, for the girls can tell something interesting is going to happen and they don't want to leave, the girls sidle out of the room.

'I just made Elliott a coffee,' says her mother. 'Would you like tea? If not, I'll go upstairs and do some laundry of my own.'

'I'm fine,' Gabby says as her mother walks past her, giving her arm a discreet, supportive squeeze. She sits down at the table opposite Elliott, who is still holding Henry, and fixes a cool gaze upon him.

'I thought you didn't like babies,' she says.

'What? Of course I like babies. We had babies. I love

babies. I just didn't want one of my own at this stage in our life.' He pauses, knowing he has to tread carefully. 'I have to say, though, I'd forgotten how completely delicious they are. This little guy especially. He's so different from the girls. Remember how dark they were?'

Gabby laughs. 'Oh God. Remember Alanna? She came out with a full head of thick black hair. It was terrifying. I thought I'd given birth to a three-year-old.'

'And remember how Olivia screamed all night long? For months. That bloody colic. Alanna was the same. Oh God. I just remember that whenever the pacifier fell out there was hell to pay.'

'I remember you walking both of them up and down the stairs all night long to get them back to sleep.'

'Yes.' Elliott smiles. 'And the minute they fell back to sleep and I'd try to oh-so-gently lay them back down in their cribs, they'd start screaming again. It was hell.'

'It was,' agrees Gabby.

'I knew I couldn't go through that again.'

'Luckily,' Gabby says, holding her arms out for Henry, Elliott reluctantly giving him back, 'we don't have to with this one, do we, mister? Aren't you the best baby in the whole world? Yes, you are! You are! Because you know Mummy might run away if you weren't.'

'No up all night?'

'None. Sleeps all night.'

'No screaming for no reason?'

'None.'

'No sleepwalking through your life with exhaustion,

wondering how you're going to make it through the day, let alone the rest of your life?'

'None. He truly is the best baby I've ever known.'

There is a silence as they both watch Henry. He is grasping a rattle and waving it around, his mouth opening over it whenever he manages to bring it close enough. He looks up at each of them and breaks into a large grin.

'I'd better go.' Elliott drains his coffee cup before standing up. 'Did you have fun last night? He seems like a nice guy.'

'He is,' Gabby says simply as she shows him out of the door.

Chapter Thirty-Eight

Gabby doesn't remember laughing this much, nor feeling this comfortable, in years. She and Julian are tucked into the corner of a tiny and cosy pub, the like of which she didn't think even existed in this country, while a fire blazes and they sit and talk. They are drinking pints and half pints of lager, because Julian refuses to let her drink anything else in a pub.

For dinner they ate bangers and mash, and toad-in-the-hole, Julian expressing concern that there was no steak and kidney pie. The waitress, from Birmingham, grabbed the chef (from Guildford, naturally), who said he'll absolutely put it on the menu, and if they come back the following week, they'll have steak and kidney pie.

They order spotted dick and treacle tart for dessert, and Gabby, who is not the slightest bit interested in portraying herself as a waif-like creature who doesn't actually eat anything, is quite sure she'll have no trouble cleaning her plate.

'So,' Julian leans back against the banquette. 'Your husband. Seems like a good guy. Not wankerish in the slightest.'

'He isn't. He is a good guy. He really didn't deserve the way I treated him.'

'We all fuck up,' Julian says simply. 'Men find it harder to get over. Lack of support systems, Neanderthal mentality, blah blah blah. You've heard it all before, and it's all true. But I realize, going through it myself, that there's another factor. I think women are more detached from the ending of a marriage; they see it as the marriage having failed, whereas men see it as a personal failure.'

'You see the end of your marriage as a personal failure?'

Julian nods, sadly. 'If I had been a better husband, had been home more, been more engaged, more present, I truly don't believe this would have happened. I don't believe Stacy would have looked to someone else to provide her with what I wasn't.'

'I'm not sure that that's true,' Gabby says. 'Elliott was an amazing husband. I honestly can't say he was at fault, but when temptation presented itself, I was . . . I don't know, powerless. It was like something came over me and all reasonable and rational thought went out through the window. I threw everything away for nothing.'

'So there was absolutely no tension between you? No resentments? Nothing?'

Gabby thinks about Elliott's vasectomy, knowing that was the moment a part of her shut down, a part of her felt their relationship would never be the same again because she would never be able to forgive him for making such a momentous decision without her agreement, one that impacted her so hugely.

'There were,' she says quietly. 'I think there usually are. Ooh goody. Dessert.' She is grateful for the distraction that allows her to change the subject. The waitress puts enormous plates of treacle tart and spotted dick in front of them, with a jug of custard on the side.

'Mmmm!' Gabby moans in delight. 'You know what I've never seen anywhere since I was a child? Do you remember those huge trays of chocolate cake? The school dinner ladies would cut them into massive squares and pour over this gloopy chocolate sauce. It was disgusting, but I've never seen it since.'

'I loved that pudding! That was my favourite!' Julian says, knocking Gabby's spoon out of the way to attack her treacle tart, both of them bursting into laughter.

It has been a glorious evening. When Julian stops by his house to grab a book he wants Gabby to read about an uncomplicated divorce, she steps out of the car, curious to see how he lives, intrigued by this man who feels like someone she has known for ever.

He is handsome, and clever, and fun, and funny. He feels exactly as she imagines a brother to feel; it is like those friendships she had, lifetimes ago, with men just like him, when they were all young and single in London.

She hasn't thought of him in a romantic context, only to recognize that he has all the qualities she would be looking for, if she were looking, which she isn't.

When she feels his hands on her waist in the kitchen, she jumps in surprise, turning to tell him she doesn't think this is such a good idea, but before she has a chance to say anything he is kissing her, and it is so lovely to be held in someone's arms, so lovely to be kissed in just the way she remembers the English boys kissing – softer, more gentle, anticipation building with desire – that she relaxes, seconds later snaking her hands into his hair, gasping as an unexpected wave of desire sweeps over her.

When they finally pull away, Julian leans his forehead on hers and smiles into her eyes. 'Can we go somewhere more comfortable?'

He leads her by the hand into his bedroom, where they fall on the bed, laughing, playfully teasing each other before the kissing starts again, swiftly moving into unknown territory.

Julian's hands start to unbutton her shirt, but she stops him, suddenly horrified, because she is lactating and this wouldn't be right.

His hand moves down, stroking her urgently between her legs, through the fabric of her trousers, before moving up to undo the button, only for Gabby to move his hand gently away.

'I shouldn't be doing this,' she whispers. 'I just had a baby. I don't know that this is . . . right.'

She waits anxiously for him to ask why she came into his house with him, in that case; she knows there is nothing to say, knows he will think her ridiculous if she tells him she just wants to cuddle, wants to be held, wants to feel loved.

He isn't angry, or belligerent. He strokes her face and kisses her forehead, her nose, her cheeks, her lips. 'Will you stay?' he asks, and this time she knows it isn't because he expects them to have sex all night, but because he needs from her exactly the same thing she needs from him: affection, warmth, an embrace.

She texts home to let her mother know she will be out, and borrows a big, soft, old T-shirt and thick climbing socks from Julian. They brush their teeth, standing side by side over a tiny sink, Gabby turning to him and talking, her mouth filled with toothpaste foam that spits everywhere. His incredulous expression gives way to laughter, and soon they are having a competition to create the most toothpaste foam, both collapsing with giggles at their child-like behaviour, each egging the other on.

Gabby hasn't felt this young, this carefree, in years. In bed, Julian holds out his arms for Gabby to snuggle in, the pair of them falling asleep wrapped up together, sex the very last thing on each of their minds.

Gabby wakes up first. Disoriented for a few seconds, she lies still, letting her eyes adjust to the light, remembering why the bathroom door isn't where she expected it to be. Turning her head she sees Julian, eyes closed, mouth open, still fast asleep. She smiles to herself, fighting the urge to stroke his cheek and kiss him.

Not that she feels a burning sexual attraction for him. She doesn't fancy him, but she may love him. Not as she loved Elliott, but as a friend. She undoubtedly feels an enormous affection for him, greater now, since he didn't push for anything more than she was able to give.

Could I fall in love with him? Why *aren't* I looking at him and wanting to rip his clothes off?

Objectively, he is gorgeous. He is exactly the sort of man she should be with, and it doesn't make sense that she doesn't want more from him.

Perhaps, she thinks, this is, or could be, a different kind of love. A saner kind of love. There's no question that they fit together. She has had great love with Elliott, and she had, however misguided, great passion with Matt, even though that is increasingly hard for her to believe, now that the rose-coloured shades have fallen from her eyes.

Perhaps this third attempt could be a different kind of love. Comfort. Comfort can be love, familiarity can become love. Yes, she tells herself. Comfort is good; comfort is *comfortable*.

And who is she to expect anything more, when she has already experienced more than one woman has a right to? How lucky she is that at this stage in the game, with two children almost grown and a newborn baby, she has met a man with whom she has so much in common, a man with whom she can see herself, a man who isn't fazed by all the drama in her life.

Climbing out of bed she grabs a robe off the back of the bathroom door and goes downstairs to make breakfast. The fridge is almost empty, but there are eggs, and milk, and – oh thank you, God! – PG Tips in the drawer. In the freezer she finds pork sausages, and she is busy cooking when she hears the creak of the stairs.

She turns and grins, with no awkwardness, no morning-after-the-night-before gracelessness, for they are both adults. Would it have been different had they had sex? Gabby doubts it. She feels as if she has known him for ever.

Julian hugs her, before trying to help himself to one of the sausages, but she bats his hand out of the way.

'God, this is nice,' he says. 'I could get used to this.'

'Don't get too used to it,' Gabby replies. 'I can't actually believe I left Henry for an entire night. I know he sleeps through now, and my mother is more than capable with him, but it still feels strange. I'm going to have to run home.'

'Are you leaking?'

'No, because I carry a small pump, and he has a fridge full of pumped milk, but I miss him. I need to go straight after breakfast.'

They sit down and eat, idly chatting and flicking through the papers on the table, before Gabby gets up to leave.

'You realize my mother'll think I'm a dirty stop-out,' she says.

'You are.'

'Not that dirty.' She laughs.

'Not yet.' He takes her in his arms and kisses her. 'Thank you. This is the most fun I've had in years. I'll call you later.'

'Sounds perfect,' she says, for it does.

Chapter Thirty-Nine

Normally Elliott wouldn't just drop in to anyone's house, but given that he lived with Claire and Tim for all that time after leaving Gabby, he thinks of it as a second home, and knows they won't mind if he calls in, uninvited.

Tim's car is missing, but Claire is home. Elliott rings the back doorbell, despite knowing the door is open, and waits for Claire to come and answer.

She walks through the kitchen with Isabella on her hip, and gives Elliott a big hug.

'What a lovely surprise! I was just dying of boredom upstairs while Isabella played on her mat. God, Elliott. She's completely gorgeous and wonderful, but I'd forgotten the hours and hours of interminable tedium when you have a small baby.'

Elliott laughs. 'She's got so big!' He doesn't hold out his arms, though, just tickles her chin as she watches him carefully, her big blue eyes fixed on his. 'She's just beautiful, Claire.'

'I know. I think so too but I'm ever so slightly biased. It's just me here, I'm afraid, but will you come in?'

Elliott walks in and sits on his usual stool in his usual spot at the kitchen island, while Claire puts Isabella in a bouncing chair, where she happily gurgles, grabbing hold of the plastic toys on a rail in front of her.

'So what's up?' Claire asks, pulling up a stool. 'Actually, I know what's up. I spoke to Trish on the phone and she told me the news.'

'How did she sound?'

'I think she's fine. She's sad, but she's clear that you're not ready to be in a serious relationship, and at this stage in her life she doesn't see the point of anything unless it's a serious relationship. She also said you were clearly still in love with Gabby.'

There is a silence.

'So . . . do you want to talk about it?'

And, as before, on many occasions, Elliott finds that with Claire he can let go, he can abandon the struggle to hold it all in, to keep it together, to present a stoic face to the world. Finally Elliott crumbles.

Claire reaches forward and puts her arms round him, holding him as he cries, rubbing his back, letting go only when he has finished, when she gets up for the box of Kleenex on the other side of the kitchen.

'You're still in love with Gabby,' Claire says, a statement rather than a question. 'And you don't know what to do.'

Elliott shrugs, attempting a smile. 'I don't want to be in love with her. I've tried my damnedest to get over her, but I can't. I thought of the baby as this insurmountable wedge between us, that even if we both decided we wanted to be together, that would never happen because there is this baby in the way, this constant reminder of what happened, and I'd never be able to forgive her. I didn't think I could ever forgive her, but it seems that I have. Without wanting to, without thinking about it, I have forgiven her, and I met the baby for the first time at the weekend. Henry. I met him properly, rather than knowing Gabby was holding this bundle in her arms and doing my best not to look at him or even acknowledge his existence. I met him, and held him, and watched my daughters with him, and it broke my heart.'

Claire frowns. 'I don't understand. What do you mean, it broke your heart?'

'It broke my heart that my family are there, and I am not. And this baby is their brother, and that means he's part of the family, whether I want him or not. I didn't want him, and I didn't think I would ever want him, and I recognize he has a father and I will never have that role, but it doesn't matter any more. I want my family to be back together and I want to be with Gabby, and this baby is part of my life. Part of *my* family.'

Claire takes a deep breath. 'I know this might sound harsh, but you're sure these feelings aren't just a result of seeing her with another man? Trish told me about the night you went out for dinner. You're sure it's not just jealousy speaking?'

'I'm sure. Trish is wonderful, but she's so completely different from Gabby . . .'

Claire barks with laughter before apologizing.

'Well, yes. Exactly. But instead of appreciating Trish,

and how beautiful and perfect everything in her life is, it just made me miss Gabby. I missed the chaos, and clutter, and warmth. I found myself constantly comparing the two, and all I wanted to do was run home. Seeing Gabby the other night, with that guy, was really hard, but my feelings and thoughts didn't start after that. They started long before.'

'Do you know anything about the guy she's dating? Has it been a long time? Is it serious?'

'I have no idea. The only thing I can tell you is they looked very comfortable together. That's the other thing. When I left Gabby I knew that all I had to do, for weeks afterwards, was tell her I'd forgiven her, and my life would be put back together again. I couldn't do it then, I was so angry, but now she's moved on, and I don't have the right to say that any more.' He sighs. 'Maybe I never did.'

'What about if *I* talk to her?' Claire says slowly.

'You? But you haven't spoken to her for months. The two of you have fallen out. Why would she agree to talk to you?'

'We never fell out,' Claire says. 'I just couldn't be placed in the middle. I love both of you, but when you moved in here I couldn't be in the position of looking after you *and* looking after Gabby, so I put all my energies into you. I know Gabby didn't understand, and I know she felt betrayed by me, but I write to her.'

Elliott frowns. 'You write to her?'

'Yes. I miss her, so I email her and tell her about Isabella and attach photographs. I tell her little bits about our lives. I didn't do it until after you moved out, and I never say anything about you, but I have apologized, and I have told her that I felt I had to make a choice, and it's only now, with hindsight, I realize I didn't have to. She knows I miss her, and I love her.'

'What does she write back?'

'She doesn't. But I just have this feeling that she's softened towards me. If I asked her out for tea, maybe for the babies to meet each other, I bet she'd say yes.'

'Even if she did, what makes you think she'd listen to you?'

'Because she always listened to me,' Claire says with a laugh. 'Because I make sense. Or, in this case, you make sense. Look, none of us has any idea what the future holds, but the one thing I'm clear on is that if you don't tell her how you feel, the possibilities for you getting back together are shot. I've seen too many people regret getting divorced. They realized, as the legal proceedings were starting, that they had made a mistake; they didn't want to go through with it, but pride stopped them from telling the other how they really felt, and everyone ended up miserable. Don't let that happen to you. I tell her you're still in love with her and want to get back together, and what's the worst that can happen? That she says no, she's moved on, she's happy with someone else. You'll get over it, and at least you'll know.'

'But would it work?' Elliott shakes his head. 'I'm just not sure she'll open up to you in that way.'

'Let me at least try,' Claire says. 'What do we have to lose? I miss her, Elliott. I miss her desperately and I realize how much I screwed up by abandoning her in the way that I did. I need to see Gabby to apologize to her, if nothing else, and let me use it as an opportunity to finally do the right thing. Please. I need to do this for me.'

Chapter Forty

Josephine has become a good friend, but she doesn't have the ability to look at Gabby's life and problem-solve without getting caught up in the drama, in the way Claire was always able to. There was no one Gabby wanted more, during this past year, than Claire, and she is amazed that, without doing anything at all, her anger towards her seems to have dissipated, then disappeared.

Perhaps it was made easier by the fact that Claire never asked anything of her. She didn't ask how Gabby was. Didn't ask about Henry, or how she was getting on, or how the girls were doing through this separation. She said Henry must be getting big, and she saw the girls in school the other day and Alanna's getting so grown up, but she was careful not to ask anything lead-ing, anything that demanded a response.

Until now. When she's asking if they can get together. With the babies. To chat.

Gabby is first to show up at the Westport Library. She has dressed carefully, anxious to feel in control, confident enough to handle whatever conversation they have, whatever direction it might take. She knows

Claire, or at least she *did*. She is certain Claire wants to meet to apologize, and while she is grateful Claire has reached out, she isn't sure how she feels about their future, their friendship; whether indeed their friendship *has* a future.

Henry, in his buggy, looks adorable in tiny jeans and a cabled sweater bought on sale at Gap for ten dollars. He looks like a tiny blond banker. Matt regularly sends gifts, toys, or clothes picked out by his girlfriend, Monroe. The outfits are invariably ridiculously cool – tiny leather aviator jackets, exquisite Italian shoes, when he isn't even walking yet, T-shirts with hilarious logos that everyone comments on when he wears them in public.

Gabby's tastes run a little differently. She had no idea how she felt about boys' clothes, never having had to shop for one before. It is not nearly as much fun as shopping for the girls, and she feels guilty that many a time, when she has gone to a store for clothes for Henry, she has left with a bag full of delicious things for Alanna – she just got pulled in by the pink and couldn't get away – or for Olivia.

Claire is likely to have dressed her baby girl in something European and expensive. Her taste was always classic, from the best stores in New York. Gabby can't afford anything like that, but she has been able to put together something that may not be Ralph Lauren but is certainly Ralph Lauren-esque for a fraction of the price. She even swept Henry's hair to one side with just a touch of gel. He looks ridiculously handsome, and, as nervous as she is to see Claire, she is also proud to show off her beautiful boy.

The library has changed since she was last here, back when Alanna was still a toddler. Years and years ago she and Elliott regularly brought Olivia here for Mother Goose rhymes, sitting cross-legged on the floor with other couples, all of them still in their post-birth haze, while Miss Annie delighted the children with her renditions of 'Alligator Pie'. The parents eagerly looked around hoping to make friends just like themselves, for all of them were new to town, most having moved from New York when their children were born.

This was where she and Elliott met so many of the people who were their earliest friends here. But then different pre-schools, different grade schools, meant their lives drifted apart. The only friends that remain from that period in their lives are Claire and Tim.

Gabby's hurt and anger at being abandoned by her best friend during her pregnancy, and the subsequent craziness of looking after a newborn baby as a single mother, at her age, prevented her from thinking much about Claire and Tim and all that they had shared together over so many years. Until now, when even pulling into the car park of the library, a place that holds so many happy memories from so many years ago, is bittersweet.

There is a café in the library now, with a few people dotted around chatting, looking at laptops, reading. Gabby orders a skim cappuccino for herself, and goes to find a chair where she can sit facing the door, nervous, suddenly, at seeing a friend she hasn't seen for so long.

Until Claire enters, and a lump appears in Gabby's throat. It's Claire. Only Claire. So familiar, tears spring to her eyes. Claire stops when she sees Gabby, then Gabby sees there are tears in her eyes too, and the two of them envelop each other in a tight hug, unable to stop smiling even as they are wiping the tears from their cheeks.

'God, I've missed you,' Claire says. 'I'm desperate to see the baby. Let me see Henry.' She coos over Henry, how handsome he is, how different to the girls, remembering everything about Olivia and Alanna when they were tiny, as Gabby coos, in turn, over Isabella.

They swap babies, each bouncing and kissing the other's child, both delighted at the other's good fortune in producing such an adorable child, before putting the babies back in their buggies and settling in to catch up.

'You look amazing,' Claire says. 'How on earth did you get your figure back so quickly?'

'Are you joking?' Gabby says, looking down at her belly in horror. 'Look!' She grabs a handful to prove her point. 'I'm huge. This stomach's staying for ever. My bikini days are so long gone it's not even funny.'

'Look at mine!' Claire shows off her tiny pot belly. 'I don't even care any more. I haven't thought about Zumba in a year. I haven't thought about much other than this little munchkin. I'm totally obsessed. I think it's because I'm so much older now, and I just can't believe that at my age I was able to produce such a perfect little thing.'

Gabby grins. 'So, are you done now?'

'So done, you have no idea. I could never go through the IVF again. But we're complete. This is what I always wanted. How about you?'

'Done,' she says.

Claire peers at her. 'And are you as happy as you look?'

'I think I am. It's taken a while, but I feel very . . . peaceful. Content. I did always want another baby, but with Elliott of course, and even though that isn't how it happened, this little boy has just . . . completed my heart. I feel complete.'

Claire smiles then takes a deep breath. 'Listen. We need to talk about what happened between us. I've missed you so much, and I want you to know how sorry I am about how I screwed up.'

Gabby says nothing, just listens.

'I felt utterly torn. I love you and I love Elliott, and I had no idea what to do. I felt, at the time, that because Elliott came to us, because he was living in our house, I had to choose him, and I know, now, how massive a mistake that was. Not choosing Elliott, but making any choice at all. I was so freaked out and hormonal about being put in the middle, that I took the easiest option and cut you off, because I couldn't cut Elliott off, given he was two rooms down the hall. And I have hated myself for months because of it. It was a disgusting thing to do, and I didn't even know that you'd agree to meet me today. I thought you probably would, but I know we can't just jump into our old friendship because of how I let you down. I'm sorry. I am so, so sorry, Gabby. I would do anything to turn the clock back and change my behaviour, but I can't. All I can do is tell you how ashamed I am, and how sorry, and hope you can find a way to forgive me.'

Gabby nods, looking her friend in the eye, knowing everything she is saying is genuine, heartfelt. Gabby has always known that, as wise as Claire is and how great she is at helping other people sort out their lives, when it comes to her own she is never as clear and she often gets it wrong. But despite knowing that, at the time Claire made the decision that affected them both so disastrously, she was unable to stop herself judging her and hating her for her betrayal.

'It was a shitty thing to do,' Gabby echoes quietly. 'I'm the first to admit I fucked up. I was unfaithful to Elliott, one time, and I ended up with . . . well, I can't call Henry a mistake, because he may be the best thing that's ever happened to me, but I ended up destroying my life as a result. I was terrified, and devastated, and my best friend turning her back was one of the cruellest blows of all. I was pregnant, and a single mother, with Olivia hating me, and no one to turn to for help. Claire, I still love you, and it's amazing to see you, but

I honestly don't know how I can get over this. I want to. I'd love nothing more than for the two of us to get back to the friendship we had, but I don't know how to do that, because you aren't the person I thought you were. It isn't about forgiveness – I forgive you. It's that you're not the person I thought you were,' she repeats. 'There's a quote I once read, something about people showing you who they are not by what they say, but by what they do.' She pauses, for tears of shame are now streaming down Claire's face. 'I'm sorry. My intention is not to upset you. But if there's any chance at all of us having some kind of a friendship again, I have to say these things. I have to tell you what it was like for me. I have to be honest about how I feel.'

Claire nods.

'I don't know that I can go back to how we were, and I don't know how to go forward with you. Maybe it will get better over time, but I think, right now, I probably need to go.'

Gabby didn't expect to feel this. She thought that she would be able to move on, to listen to whatever Claire had to say, and to know that whatever happened was in the past; but she finds she has changed over the months they have not spoken, and has reprioritized the important people in her life.

People show themselves not by what they say but by what they do.

Claire said all the right things, is saying all the right

things now, but she abandoned Gabby in her hour of greatest need, and whatever the excuse, however sorry she is now, Gabby cannot feel the same way about her.

'Wait,' Claire says, wiping her tears away. 'I get it. You're right, and there's nothing I can say other than you're right, and I hope things will change over time. I really do. But there's something else. We have to talk about Elliott.'

Gabby frowns. 'What about Elliott?'

'Do you know he split up with Trish?'

'He did?' Gabby ignores the small thrill that runs through her body. 'I didn't know that. Was he not perfect enough for her?'

'I think she was a little too perfect for him. And he realized he's still in love with you.'

Gabby's heart stops still as she stares at Claire. 'What did you just say?'

'He's still in love with you.'

Gabby shakes her head. 'Claire, if you're trying to heal the rift between Elliott and me, this isn't the way to do it. We've both moved on, and as lovely as it would be to think there's still something there between us, there just isn't. And even if there is, too much has happened.' Her mind is whirling. 'Quite apart from the fact that the last thing Elliott wants at this stage of his life is a baby. I know you think you're trying to help, but you're not. It's just not feasible, even if it –'

'Gabby, stop,' Claire says urgently. 'It is true. Elliott knows I'm here. He knows I'm telling you this, and I'm telling you because he can't do it himself. You're right, he didn't want a baby, and he didn't think he could ever forgive you. Up until a week ago he wanted to pretend that Henry didn't even exist, and then something happened the other day ... you know what I'm talking about, don't you?'

The lump is back as Gabby nods, remembering how tenderly Elliott held Henry, how his eyes softened, filled with incredulous wonder at this perfect little boy. Years ago, before the girls came along, Elliott always said he wanted at least one little boy.

'He hadn't thought any of you could ever find a way back because the baby would be a permanent reminder of what happened to destroy your marriage, but something changed the other day, and he said that seeing you, seeing the girls with Henry, holding Henry, made him realize that you are a family, whether Henry has his blood or not. You're his family, Gabby. Henry too. Don't let this fall through your fingers because you don't believe me, or because you have too much pride, or because you're dating someone else – who may be cute, but he will never be a patch on Elliott, I promise you. Give him a chance, Gabby,' she whispers, laying her hand on top of Gabby's as Gabby starts to cry. 'Go to him and hear what he has to say. Leave the babies with me, and go now.'

Gabby can't make sense of what Claire has said. If Elliott does feel that, why doesn't he come to her himself?

Why use Claire, who Gabby hasn't been in touch with for so long, as the messenger?

And is this his rebound? After things didn't work out with Trish is he just thinking about her again because she is familiar, the easy option?

But she saw the look in his eyes the other day. She saw that he was over the pain of the betrayal, wasn't so consumed with hurt that he couldn't look at the baby, could barely look at Gabby.

In his eyes she saw, she realizes suddenly, something that looked suspiciously like love.

But it's been so long. So much has happened. And Julian. What about Julian? Julian is so familiar, and so much fun, and so handsome, and so . . . not her husband.

He is not her husband.

He has not known her for twenty years. He has not seen her at her worst, screaming in frustration over some little inconsequential thing, has not seen her red-faced and sweating in labour, has not seen her being selfish, or thoughtless, or unreasonable. He is not someone who has seen all that but loves her anyway, because he chose her, and he will always honour his commitment to that choice.

I didn't sleep with him, she thinks with relief. I could have, so easily, and yet it was also so easy not to. Julian is a welcome distraction but, if she is honest with herself, she knows there is little chemistry between them. He would make a wonderful best friend. Maybe he will become a wonderful best friend, but romance is truly not what she is looking for.

Not with Julian.

Elliott is her husband.

He's still in love with her.

And she is still in love with him.

Gabby pulls up outside the medical offices and takes a deep breath. She isn't sure what to say, how to say it; she isn't sure Elliott's office is the best venue in which to repair what she hopes is still reparable, but she can't wait any longer. She's waited long enough.

She walks into the office, chatting briefly with the girls on the desk, all of whom she has known for years, all of whom are as friendly as they have always been, despite knowing she and Elliott are no longer together.

'He's stepped out for lunch,' says Maria. 'He should be back in about fifteen minutes.'

'The usual place?'

Maria nods, and Gabby smiles a thank you and heads to the diner across the street. She sees him first, at the counter, hunched over a turkey and Swiss-cheese wrap, reading glasses perched on the end of his nose, paper in front of him, so familiar she actually feels an ache.

Walking over, she sits quietly on the stool next to his, saying nothing, waiting until he turns his head to look over at her, his eyes widening when he sees who it is.

So much has happened between them, there are so many things unspoken, and yet, even now, there is

387

nothing to say. Everything is in Elliott's face, as he looks into the eyes of the woman he loves; the woman he still wants to be with; the woman he wants to grow old with.

'Elliott,' Gabby whispers. It is all she needs to say.

Epilogue

'Happy birthday to you, happy birthday to you, happy birthday, dear Henry . . . happy birthday to you!'

Matt throws him up in the air, much to Henry's delight, as Alanna and Olivia start 'Are you one . . .' before the room collapses in laughter, and Matt, Gabby, Elliott and the girls all lean over the one candle to blow it out. Then Gabby takes the cake back into the kitchen to cut slices for all the guests.

'Can I help?' Monroe, all endless legs in skinny jeans, messy almond hair and almost unreal gorgeousness, comes in and swipes a big dollop of icing from the cardboard base and sucks it off her finger, Gabby looking on in approval.

'I thought you models never ate anything? How in the hell do you get to eat dollops of icing and stay the size of a stick?'

Monroe giggles. 'I'm a total sugar addict. Don't even talk to me about Reese's Pieces. I've been known to put away a whole bag in a day. But I'm pretty disciplined when I'm working. I'll juice for days to lose weight for a shoot, then celebrate with a chocolate binge. I know, disgusting. I really shouldn't admit to it.'

'You really shouldn't. I'm so jealous I could kill you.'

'What are you jealous of?' Olivia, who has been following Monroe like a lovesick puppy, appears in the kitchen, pretending to be cool, but Gabby knows she's desperate to become friends with the older girl.

'Your mom thinks I can eat whatever I want and stay thin, so I was just telling her I have to juice to get into shape for shoots. You have an amazing figure, Olivia, so you don't have to worry about it.'

Olivia blushes. 'You think so?'

'Look at you! You have natural beauty, and –'

'Ladies? As wonderful as this love fest is, I need help. Here –' Gabby hands each of them two plates with giant slices of cake – 'hand these out then come back for more.'

She continues cutting as Josephine comes in to put the kettle on for more tea.

'This is such a lovely party,' Josephine says. 'It's hard to believe Henry is one already.'

'I know. Luckily he's still too young to notice that we're celebrating a week late rather than on his real birthday – but I didn't think we could ask people to come over on Christmas Day.'

'I still can't get over everything that's happened in your life and that everyone's here together. And my God! That Monroe! I can't stand being in the same room as her, but she's so adorable you can't find it in your heart to hate her.'

Gabby laughs. 'She does seem like a lovely girl. She and Matt look perfect together.'

Josephine peers at her. 'Doesn't it feel just a little bit weird? That the father of your child is here with his girlfriend, and your husband?'

Gabby pauses in her cutting of the cake to think about it. It should feel weird. It should, by rights, be awkward, uncomfortable; but, somehow, aided by the fact that everyone in this family has been open to change, willing to work with circumstances that are unusual, it doesn't feel wrong.

It feels absolutely right.

As a young girl, with a mother who surrounded herself with people, Gabby shut herself away, feeling as if she didn't have a family of her own, or at least a family who noticed her.

Here she is, as an adult, not only with a family of her own, but with the type of family that surrounded her as a child, the type of family she never knew she wanted, but the type of family she has spent her life looking for.

They are family through choice, hard work, acceptance and love. They are family because they have found each other, often in the unlikeliest of circumstances, and have chosen to stay together, even when it would have been so much easier to walk the other way.

Matt didn't think he wanted children until he was much older and had settled down. He and Gabby were a moment in time, a brief obsession that was never destined to be anything more than it was, and shouldn't, in fact, have even been what it was. When Gabby became pregnant, by rights Elliott was supposed to have left her, and Matt was supposed to want nothing to do with the baby.

Gabby was supposed to be a single mother, struggling to raise her children on her own, working all the hours God sends to provide for them all.

Instead, here she is, slicing up a Carvel ice-cream cake, listening to shouts of laughter from the living room, knowing that in her house, right now, are all the people she loves most in the world.

Elliott comes into the kitchen to grab another bottle of Scotch. He kisses his wife as he passes, tenderly rubbing her back, as if no explosions had happened to blow apart their happiness, as if, in fact, they are newly-weds, which is how he so often feels, now that he, *they*, have been given a second chance.

Olivia, who at eighteen has come through the teenage years and is a young woman, beautiful, naturally beautiful, in a way Gabby never was, is getting ready to go off to college.

She will go to college provided, Gabby thinks wryly, she isn't derailed by a potential modelling career. Oh God, please let that not happen. Gabby has had to handle too much in the past two years but *that* might actually derail her. She smiles.

Matt appears, holding Henry up for Gabby to plant a kiss on his cheek. How could she ever have contemplated a life without Henry? No matter how her life is going to turn out, Henry will never have been a mistake. She fell in love with her daughters the moment they were born, but the love she has for Henry, a mother's love for a son, is unlike anything she has ever known. She can't bear to think she might have missed out on this.

Claire and Tim are in the other room. It is a slow journey back for Gabby. Things are not the same with her and Claire, and may never be exactly the same, but they are trying. The four of them have had dinner together once or twice, and those evenings go a long way to healing the rift. More than anything, Gabby has perhaps learned not to rely on friends in the way she once did, and that saddens her. When she had problems in the old days she would turn to Claire. Nowadays, she turns to her mother.

Her mother, who was always so busy sorting out the problems of the world that she never had time for her own daughter, is now the one person Gabby trusts to advise her, listen to her problems, offer a shoulder to cry on if need be.

Gabby carries the last of her plates herself, one for her mother, one for herself. She sits on the sofa next to Natasha and leans her head briefly on her mother's shoulder as her mother smiles and strokes her hair.

It feels natural now to allow herself to be held in her mother's arms, to have her hair stroked, to be kissed. She wonders if her mother has changed, has softened in her old age, but suspects that it is she herself who has changed. The fiery resistance Gabby used as her armour when she was young has vanished. Life is too hard to get through alone, and it was her mother who stepped up when everyone else had gone.

Alanna squeezes up on her other side, the three of them looking around: at Elliott pouring out the Scotch for a toast, at Olivia and Monroe chatting, at Matt sitting cross-legged on the floor while Henry zips around him in circles, huge smiles on both their faces.

Natasha turned out to be a good mother, after all. Gabby watches her son and her elder daughter, as her younger daughter entwines her fingers with her own. I hope, she thinks, watching all the hope and possibility in Henry's smile, I hope I turn out to be a good mother for my children. I hope I can give them everything they need. I hope I can raise them to make good choices, to be good people, to go into the world treating others with kindness and respect.

I hope our year of insanity – for this is how she and Elliott have come to refer to their separation, in terms thinly veiled with humour – I hope our year of insanity hasn't damaged them, or destroyed their belief in the power of a strong relationship.

She looks up then, aware that she is being stared at, and Elliott, standing by the fireplace, gazes at her, his eyes filled with love. He just smiles, and she knows it's all going to be fine.

Somehow, what they least expected – what they least *wanted* – has brought them full circle. A little family. *Her* little family.

Acknowledgements

As always, my extraordinary publishing team and home at St Martin's Press, and my family at Penguin in the UK. Louise Moore for so much love and support over all these years together, and Jen Enderlin, who has swept into my life and dusted out all the corners, with so much wisdom, brilliance and talent.

My agents – Anthony Goff, who has blessed me with sage advice and true friendship for such a very long time, and the incomparable Jennifer Rudolph Walsh, for whom I am truly grateful.

My friends – you know who you are.

Michael Palmer, who so graciously and kindly offered up his wonderful old farm in New Hampshire for me to use as a writing retreat. Without Michael, this book would not have been written, and that's no exaggeration.

The friends who helped enormously in coming up with the story, and those that supported me throughout.

Glenn Ferrari, Alberto Hamonet, Dusty Thomason, Randy Zuckerman.

To the many people who were open and honest

enough to share their heartbreak and their stories with me.

Finally, my husband, Ian. Who is truly the only man I want to walk with, side by side, as we continue the journey.

CREATE PERFECT PROJECTS FOR YOU AND YOUR HOME!

As well as receiving every issue overflowing with the best hints, tips, advice, projects and features for the home with beautiful photography, you will:

- Get free delivery straight to your door before it hits the shops
- Save £££s off the cover price

- Avoid any price increases on 13 issues
- Enjoy a risk-free trial offer
- Guarantee you never miss an issue!

SIMPLY SUBSCRIBE TODAY!
WWW.HOMEMAKERMAGAZINE.CO.UK/HMAJG

📞 0844 815 5870 QUOTE: HMAJG

Make a matching pyjama case! Find the details at www.homemaker magazine.co.uk

The blue and pink floral fabric brings a fresh country look up to date

BRIGHT IDEA

Join us in the Homemaker sewing room and make a bedside lamp with vintage-inspired style

It's said that we will spend a third of our life in our bedrooms. In this sense, it should provide you with a space to relax, unwind and rest. So, give your bedroom the spring-clean makeover it deserves with this delightful lampshade that can be easily sewn at home. It has been covered in a medium-weight linen and cotton mix fabric, which makes it a little easier to finish, and is topped off with a simple-to-make, but very professional looking, ruffle detail around the top edge.

lampshade

YOU'LL NEED:
Small, plain bedside lamp:
12cm high x 18cm diameter
Floral spot medium weight
cotton/linen mix fabric in
pink and blue
Plain paper
Acid-free glue
PVA glue
Clothes pegs
Iron

{1} Lay a large piece of plain paper on a table. Position the plain lampshade at the bottom left-hand corner of the paper and starting from its seam, slowly rotate the lampshade to the right marking the top edge and bottom edge with a pencil line as you go. Stop rotating when you reach the seam again and mark with a pencil. Set the plain lampshade aside.

{2} Before you cut out the paper pattern you need to add 1.5cm allowance to each end and the same at the top edge and bottom edge. Cut out the paper pattern. Lay the pattern onto your chosen fabric and cut it out. Pick out some of the floral details using either hand or machine embroidery in a slightly darker coloured thread to make the flowers and leaves really stand out. Iron on the reverse.

{3} Lay the finished piece of fabric onto the lampshade to ensure it is lined up correctly, then starting at the seam, apply the acid-free glue stick to the lampshade, 5cm at a time, and gently smooth the fabric onto it, ensuring there are no creases and that you don't stretch it. Work your way all around, ending by overlapping the seam by 1.5cm.

{4} Coat the last edge with the glue stick before you lay it flat as this

will prevent it from fraying. Once dry, use small amounts of PVA glue to secure the raw top and bottom edges over onto the inside of the shade, use pegs to hold it in place while it dries. Set aside.

{5} From the same blue fabric cut a strip 3cm x 100cm. Turn each long raw edge over by 0.5cm, stitch down and press with an iron. Now place one end of this centrally under the sewing machine foot right-side up and as you sew, fold an extra 0.5cm under every 2cm to form even pleats. To finish, and starting at the back seam, use small amounts of PVA glue in the middle of the ruffle and at the top edge of each pleat to secure it to the lampshade. Use pegs to hold it in place until it dries, and remember to secure the raw end well.

Go to www.homemaker magazine.co.uk to find the pattern you need!

OUR MAKER...
CAROLYN LETTEN

Straight Talking

Jemima J.

This could be about your best friend. Or your girlfriend. Or it might be about you.

Are you Tasha – single and still searching? Are you one of her three best friends? Andy, hooked on passion; Mel, stuck in a steady relationship with a bastard; or Emma, endlessly waiting for her other half to propose? Do you know an Andrew – suave, goodlooking and head over heels in love . . . with himself? Or a Simon – allergic to commitment and dangerously treacherous? Or an Adam – handsome, kind, humorous, but too nice to be sexy?

Follow them all in their journey to find fulfilment and love.

Jemima Jones is overweight.

About seven stone overweight.

Treated like a slave by her thin and bitchy flatmates, lorded over at the *Kilburn Herald* by the beautiful Geraldine (less talented, but better paid), her only consolation is food. What with that and her passion for her charming, sexy colleague Ben, she knows her life needs changing.

But can Jemima reinvent herself? And should she?

A brilliantly funny, honest novel about ugly ducklings and swans, attraction, addiction and the meaning of true love.

'Funny, honest, superb'
Company

'The kind of novel you'll gobble down in one sitting'
Cosmopolitan

Mr Maybe

Bookends

At twenty-seven, Libby thinks there's a lot to be said for a rich husband. So when Nick comes along – lovely, funny, handsome Nick, who has no money whatsoever, lives in a grotty bedsit and thinks the perfect night out consists of the pub and his mates – she decides he's only good for a fling. No strings attached.

Investment banker Ed, on the other hand, could possibly be the answer. His house in Regent's Park makes up for his hideous moustache and she can probably overlook his irritating habits, and anyway, he's crazy about her. But does Libby really know what she needs? Is she just in love with being loved? Or is she loving the lifestyle, rather than the man?

'You'll want to gulp it down'
Essentials

Cath and Si are best friends. Total opposites, always together, and both unlucky in love. Cath is scatty, messy and emotionally closed. Si is impossibly tidy, bitchy and desperate for a man of his own. They live near each other in West Hampstead, close to their other best friends Josh and Lucy – who are married, with a devil-spawn child called Max and a terrifying Swedish nanny, Ingrid.

When Portia steps back into their lives – beautiful Portia, the undisputed queen of their group at university, who broke their collective hearts one night and from whom they have all gradually, silently, grown apart – her reappearance sets off a chain of events that tests them to the limit. Does Portia have a hidden agenda, or is she just looking for happy endings all round? Whatever the answers, none of them could ever predict the outcome . . .

'Green is the queen of the chick literati – her books are just so damn readable'
Glamour

Babyville

Julia and Mark are stuck in a loveless relationship. Julia thinks a baby will help, but perhaps that isn't the answer to her problems.

Maeve is totally allergic to commitment – she breaks out in a rash whenever she passes a buggy. Then a one-night-stand results in an unwanted pregnancy. But just how unwanted is it?

Samantha is besotted with her newborn baby. But how is husband Chris coping with his suddenly unavailable wife, and is Samantha's obsession as healthy as it seems?

'This eventful and emotional comedy will have you hooked'
OK!

Spellbound

Alice knows she should be happy.

After all she has a handsome husband, a beautiful house and membership to all the most exclusive clubs in London. So what if the rumours about her husband's skirt-chasing are becoming harder to ignore?

When Joe's indiscretions force a transfer to New York, Alice hopes it might be a fresh start. And when they find a beautiful old house in Connecticut Alice is overjoyed. For a while she and Joe seem as happy as newlyweds.

But then the late nights and unexplained absences start again. What should Alice do? Stay and fight for him? Or leave with her head held high?

'Simply the highest quality a chick can get . . . *Spellbound* will have you hungrily turning page after page . . . So delicious you'll want to wolf it down in one go'
Heat

The Other Woman

Ellie and Dan are living proof that opposites attract. He always follows instructions and she throws the manual away. He loves sports whereas Ellie's allergic to any form of exercise. Ellie doesn't have a mother. And Dan does – a mother who wants to take over . . . EVERYTHING.

At first Ellie is thrilled to have Linda as her 'adopted' mother, but when she and Dan decide to get married and wedding plans progress, she starts to wonder: is it normal for Linda and Dan to speak on the phone twice a day? How on earth do they come to be having a reception with Chilean bloody seabass and humongous bloody white ribbons tied everywhere, when all she wanted was a quiet registry office?

In fact, is she marrying Dan . . . OR HIS MOTHER?

'A compelling page-turner
from start to finish'
Daily Express

Life Swap

From the outside Vicky Townsley would appear to have it all. Features Director of the hugely successful *Poise!* magazine, she lives alone in London, is single and seriously successful. But she'd give it all up in a heartbeat for marriage, children, and a house in the country. Amber Winslow on the other hand, has exactly what Vicky Townsley wants: a huge stone mansion in Connecticut, children and a busy charitable commitment for the local Women's League.

But Amber isn't happy either. She hasn't found quite the fulfilment she had expected from being a full-time wife and mother, so when she spots a double-page spread in *Poise!* magazine asking married readers to life swap with a glamorous, single journalist in London, she sits down and writes a letter. But she never expects to be picked . . .

'Brilliant concept, fantastic novel.
Buy it – now'
Closer

Second Chance

The Beach House

Holly Macintosh is sitting round her kitchen table with her oldest friends – friends she hasn't seen since school – now reunited by an unexpected tragedy and catching up on the past twenty years.

On the surface, they are all successful and happy. But scratch a little deeper after that extra glass of wine and it's not quite so straightforward: Paul and Anna are struggling to have a baby, Saffron the actress is still waiting for that really big break that – at thirty-nine – is looking less and less likely, and Olivia, always the wallflower of the group, is newly single and mourning her lost love.

And what about Holly Mac? Can she and her husband Marcus get their marriage back on track for the sake of the children? Or has someone just come back into her life who will change everything for ever?

One summer a group of strangers – each with their own reason for wanting to step out of their busy life – meet at a rented beach house in sunny Nantucket. There's Daniel, who's causing heartbreak for his wife Bee; recently divorced Daff, who feels she's lost touch with her daughter Jess; and Michael – son of the house's mischievous, free-spirited owner Nan, who is having an ill-advised fling with his boss.

With so many lost souls gathered under one roof, very soon there are tears and laughter, friendship and – for some – even love. Each one of them is hoping for a new beginning. But will any of them find it?

'She is Amazing, with a capital A'
Heat

'A corker of a story, sharply
and elegantly told'
Heat

Girl Friday

The Love Verb

When Kit and Adam separated after almost fifteen years of marriage, Kit felt like she had lost her lover, her best friend and her identity all in one fell swoop. But now, a year on from the divorce, Kit has found herself again and she loves her life in the idyllic Connecticut town of Highfield. She has the perfect job, two wonderful children, a good relationship with her ex-husband and time to enjoy yoga with her friends. Then Tracy, Kit's yoga instructor and close friend, introduces her to Steve – attentive, charming, the perfect gentleman – and, for the first time in years, Kit thinks she may have found the right one. But is Steve really as perfect as he seems? And why does it bother Kit when Tracy starts dating Kit's reclusive boss, Robert?

Girl Friday is a captivating tale of friendship, family and marriage and of how sometimes the people you thought you had lost make their way back into your life again . . .

'Compulsively readable'
Sunday Times

When photographer Callie has life-changing news, she – and her whole family – learn that love is not just about words. It is about deeds. After all, love means being there, through everything.

'Everyone in Callie's family is busy; her sister is a free-spirited Manhattan chef, her best friend Lila is coping with the vitriol of her new man's ex-wife, and her parents, Walter and Honor, have rich though separate lives. But when Callie discovers the breast cancer she thought she'd beaten has returned, they all find that their lives shift to focus on caring for Callie. A beautifully written and intensely sad lesson in what it really means to love someone you know you're going to lose'
Daily Telegraph

The Patchwork Marriage

The Accidental Husband

When he asked her to be his wife, he also wanted a mother for his children . . .

When Andi marries Ethan she gets a ready-made family in the shape of his daughters Emily and Sophia. Unable to have a child of her own, she has a chance to make the perfect family. But teenager Emily's hostility leaves Andi feeling hated in her own home.

And worse, Ethan, blinded by love for his daughter, cannot see that her behaviour is driving a wedge through their marriage. So when Andi and Ethan's world is rocked by an act of recklessness, Andi knows that their whole future is in doubt.

Can Andi and Ethan heal the rift in their relationship? Can each of them find enough love to go around? And how strong can a patchwork marriage ever be?

Maggie and Sylvie are perfect strangers: two very different women, living very different lives on opposite coasts. But they share more in common than they could ever imagine.

Both women have beautiful children on the verge of flying the nest, the home they worked hard to build and always longed for, and a handsome and devoted husband they can't believe belongs to them. Both women think their lives are seamlessly secure, but they couldn't be more wrong . . .

For each is about to discover a secret that will shake their world to the very core, throwing into doubt everything they ever thought they knew, and bringing Maggie and Sylvie together in the most unexpected way.

'A heartbreaking tale of love and family, truly compelling'
Closer

'Compulsively readable. I raced through it'
Daily Mail

Psst

want the latest gossip on all your favourite writers?

Then come and join us in ...

THE BOOK BOUTIQUE

... the **exclusive club** for anyone who loves to curl up with the latest reads in women's fiction.

- All the latest news on the best authors.
- Early copies of the latest reads months before they're out.
- Chat with like-minded readers as well as bestselling writers.
- Excellent recommendations for new books to read.
- Exclusive competitions to get your hands on stylish prizes.

SIGN UP for our regular newsletter by emailing
thebookboutique@uk.penguingroup.com
or if you really can't wait, get over to
www.facebook.com/TheBookBoutique

He just wanted a decent book to read ...

Not too much to ask, is it? It was in 1935 when Allen Lane, Managing Director of Bodley Head Publishers, stood on a platform at Exeter railway station looking for something good to read on his journey back to London. His choice was limited to popular magazines and poor-quality paperbacks – the same choice faced every day by the vast majority of readers, few of whom could afford hardbacks. Lane's disappointment and subsequent anger at the range of books generally available led him to found a company – and change the world.

'We believed in the existence in this country of a vast reading public for intelligent books at a low price, and staked everything on it'
Sir Allen Lane, 1902–1970, founder of Penguin Books

The quality paperback had arrived – and not just in bookshops. Lane was adamant that his Penguins should appear in chain stores and tobacconists, and should cost no more than a packet of cigarettes.

Reading habits (and cigarette prices) have changed since 1935, but Penguin still believes in publishing the best books for everybody to enjoy. We still believe that good design costs no more than bad design, and we still believe that quality books published passionately and responsibly make the world a better place.

So wherever you see the little bird – whether it's on a piece of prize-winning literary fiction or a celebrity autobiography, political tour de force or historical masterpiece, a serial-killer thriller, reference book, world classic or a piece of pure escapism – you can bet that it represents the very best that the genre has to offer.

Whatever you like to read – trust Penguin.